"Have you never wanted something you shouldn't, Bailey?"

His breathing was fast and shallow, the look in his eyes pure torment.

"Only you," she whispered.

Tasmin pulled her against him. Bay sighed as she parted her lips, melting into the kiss. She felt his need for her reverberate all the way down to her toes. She slid her arms up to twine around his neck while he drew her closer, deepening the kiss until nothing existed but the two of them, his mouth on hers. She wanted to be somewhere dark and quiet with him, skin to skin. Somewhere she could finally just give in and explore everything Tasmin had to offer. Her hands dropped to his hips, and she hissed out a breath when she realized just how hard he was for her. Last night he'd been half wild. Tonight there was a restraint that she didn't understand.

She wanted more than sweet. She wanted the lion back.

Tasmin pulled his lips from hers with a shudder and pressed his forehead against hers. "I can hear your thoughts, Bailey," he said, the harshness of his voice betraying his desire. "You have no idea what they do to me."

"Then show me."

Praise for **KENDRA LEIGH CASTLE'S DARK DYNASTIES NOVELS**

Shadow Rising

"4½ stars! Castle rejuvenates the paranormal genre with her singular take on the vampire mythos. She skillfully combines multilayered characters with a plot that's part thriller, part paranormal fantasy and all exciting fiction. And the hot and sensual love scenes don't hurt, either! Even though this is book three in the Dark Dynasties series, new readers will be enthralled." —*RT Book Reviews*

"With exceptional worldbuilding and fascinating characters, Kendra Leigh Castle has a true gift of imbuing her characters with tightly leashed passion, making this book an easy one to devour. There's no question that *Shadow Rising* is a top-notch read!" —FreshFiction.com

"A super star-crossed thriller...The action-packed storyline grips the reader from the moment a determined Ariane disobeys her leader (not an easy act) and never slows down." —Alternative-Worlds.com

"5 stars! I truly love this series...[It's] like a puzzle with a gazillion pieces that we slowly put together piece by piece with each new book...a lot of action, secrets, and twists and turns." —SeducedByABook.com

"I love the world-building, the romance...the sex...I did not want to put this book down...Castle has created such a rich canvas with her supernatural world and continues to build on it with each book...The story is loaded with great secondary characters who are practically screaming to get a book of their own one day. I can't wait to see what happens next." —RedHotBooks.com

IMMORTAL
CRAVING

Also by Kendra Leigh Castle

Dark Awakening

Midnight Reckoning

Shadow Rising

IMMORTAL CRAVING

A Tale of the Dark Dynasties

KENDRA LEIGH CASTLE

FOREVER

NEW YORK   BOSTON

Dynasty illustrations by Franklin Daley III

Forever
Hachette Book Group
237 Park Avenue
New York, NY 10017

www.HachetteBookGroup.com

Printed in the United States of America

First Edition: January 2013
10 9 8 7 6 5 4 3 2 1

OPM

Forever is an imprint of Grand Central Publishing.
The Forever name and logo are trademarks of Hachette Book Group, Inc.

The Hachette Speakers Bureau provides a wide range of authors for speaking events. To find out more, go to www.hachettespeakersbureau .com or call (866) 376-6591.

The publisher is not responsible for websites (or their content) that are not owned by the publisher.

ATTENTION CORPORATIONS AND ORGANIZATIONS:
Most HACHETTE BOOK GROUP books are available at quantity discounts with bulk purchase for educational, business, or sales promotional use. For information, please call or write:

Special Markets Department, Hachette Book Group
237 Park Avenue, New York, NY 10017
Telephone: 1-800-222-6747 Fax: 1-800-477-5925

For my father
You gave me my love of words
So these words are for you
Love you, Dad

THE DARK DYNASTIES
Known Bloodlines of the United States

THE PTOLEMY

LEADER: Queen Arsinöe

ORIGIN: Ancient Egypt and the goddess Sekhmet

STRONGHOLDS: Cities of the Eastern US, concentrated in the Mid-Atlantic

ABILITIES: Lightning speed

THE CAIT SITH

LEADER: Lily Quinn MacGillivray

ORIGIN: A Celtic line originating with the Fae

STRONGHOLDS: United with the reborn Lilim in the Northern United States

ABILITIES: Can take the form of a cat

THE DRACUL

LEADER: Vlad Dracul

ORIGIN: The goddess Nyx

STRONGHOLDS: Cities of the Northern US and Chicago (shared with the Empusae)

ABILITIES: Can take the form of a bat

THE GRIGORI

LEADER: Sammael; assumed leadership upon defeat of Sariel

ORIGIN: Fallen angels

STRONGHOLDS: The deserts of the West

ABILITIES: Winged flight

THE EMPUSAE

LEADER: Mormo, the Empusa

ORIGIN: The goddess Hecate

STRONGHOLDS: Southern United States; Chicago (shared with the Dracul)

ABILITIES: Can take the form of smoke

THE REBORN LILIM

LEADER: Lily Quinn MacGillivray

ORIGIN: Lilith, the first vampire, now merged with the blood of the Cait Sith

STRONGHOLDS: Northern United States

ABILITIES: Lethal bursts of psychic energy; can take the form of a cat

THE RAKSHASA

LEADER: None. Before their near extinction there were many prides, each self-governing. Now only Tasmin Singh remains.

ORIGIN: Unknown, but often attributed to the god Brahma

STRONGHOLDS: India

ABILITIES: Illusion; can take the form of a lion

IMMORTAL
CRAVING

Prologue

He awakened to darkness.

When sensation began to return to him, he hardly understood what it was. The weight of his body settled on him like an ill-fitting cloak at first, uncomfortable, unfamiliar. The muscles in his face contracted. A frown. Why was he cold? Why was he ... anything?

Scattered bits of memory swam tantalizingly close to the surface, shadows in the murk. But when he reached for them, they vanished. Frustrated, he inhaled, then stopped, startled, as air rushed into lungs that had long been still. Tasmin's eyes fluttered open.

Arre, kyaa?

He felt the cool damp on his skin, saw rough stone above him in the dark. He could feel the same stone beneath him, though smoother. His chest was bare, as were his feet. Words tangled together in his mind, some in a language he had never heard...and yet somehow, he understood how to use them.

Where...am I?

Tentatively, he moved fingers, toes. Another indrawn breath, such an odd sensation. The air was damp, yet strangely sweet. It tasted of life. And with that simple taste came the hunger, and he remembered what he was.

Warrior. Magic weaver. Vampire.

Rakshasa.

Tasmin heard the word from somewhere deep inside himself, whispered in a voice not his own. With that, the fog that covered his mind began to clear, and images from his past began to emerge from shadow. So many faces he had known, their voices rising and falling in the music of their native tongues.

Now...silence.

He sat up slowly, instinctively testing his movement, his muscles, and looked around. Though the darkness was absolute, he could see that he was in a small cave, only barely high enough for a man to stand upright. There was nothing inside. Nothing but him.

He was alone.

And yet he felt something, some energy that lingered in the space like a dark and malignant visitor. Perhaps someone had been here to check on him. Perhaps it was the lingering feel of whoever had put him here. Again, Tasmin wondered what had happened that he should have been torn from his brothers and placed in a hand-hewn cave alone. Had he died?

We have slept, whispered that odd voice inside of him once again. *Long enough to have the world change many times over. But we breathe again, and all the rest have gone.*

He gave his head a hard, decisive shake to silence the odd voice. These thoughts, bubbling up from the depths of his mind, did not feel like his own. Echoes, he hoped, only echoes of whatever had been done to him here. He would find his brothers, and all would be well. How long had he slept? Months? A year?

It took him a moment to get his balance, with his feet now unused to supporting him. But when he did, his movement was as fluid and natural as it ever had been. There was only one direction to go in. This cave seemed shallow, only really large enough to hold himself. Like a hiding place.

Or a grave.

Unnerved by the thought, Tasmin moved away from the back wall. He wore only his dhoti, a length of cloth wrapped and tucked around his waist and legs, then knotted at the waist. The soft fabric brushed against his legs as he moved. The stone was rough, but not uncomfortable beneath his feet, nor his hand as he trailed it along the wall. His senses were keen with newly awakened hunger. He felt wonderfully, deliciously alive as his heart resumed its slow and steady rhythm in his chest.

Tonight, he would celebrate. He and his brothers would hunt, and feast. He would drink until he was gorged with life-giving blood. And after, they would hunt down those who had done this to him. An image flickered through his mind of a brutal queen whose hatred of his kind was only surpassed by her love for herself. It was almost certain that the Ptolemy had bound him in that dark sleep, perhaps aided by some of the darkest of his bloodline, those who hid in shadow alone. He would avenge himself … soon.

The mouth of the cave was small, the ceiling grown so

low at that point that Tasmin had to go to his knees to push at the thick vegetation covering the entrance. Light, soft and faded as it always was at the end of day, began to filter through as the layers of vine parted. He heard the song of a bird, the whisper of the forest that had been his home for many years. Familiar sounds of the Gir, comforting.

When the first rays of dim light touched his skin, Tasmin drew his hand back with a startled hiss. Bright pain sent a shock up his arm, and he clutched his hand to his chest, confused.

He had built up his tolerance well over the century he had lived, able to withstand even the brightest rays of the sun for extended periods of time if he wished. It was a gift of his line, one of many. He hadn't been burned since he was a fledgling, young and untried. Even if he had slept for a year, it should not feel like this.

Suspicion, rife with horror, bloomed slowly as he held his hand before him in the darkness, saw skin so ashen it was as though he had been drained of blood and covered in dust. A corpse. Smoke coiled lazily from the place where the light had touched.

And he knew. To sleep so long, to become this dead and wraithlike thing...

It had not been a year.

It had been centuries.

Tasmin began to shake with rage and fear and hunger, lost in this strange place, lost in whatever it was he had become. He opened his mouth, pulling back his parched lips to reveal long and gleaming fangs.

And in the voice of a lion, he roared.

chapter ONE

Six months later
Tipton, Massachusetts

Don't look at me that way, Grimm. We're getting there."

The big black Newfoundland gave her another lingering, mournful look before heaving a long-suffering sigh and facing forward again. Bay Harper smirked as she continued trimming his forelegs. Grimm might be put out now, but once they were back home, the big baby would be looking for cookies and affection in short order.

Thankfully, he was not a grudge holder. She had a few clients that were . . . but she didn't have to live with them.

Bay worked, humming along with the music she played in the shop, glad she'd cleared her schedule for the afternoon so she could take it easy and work on her own dog. She hadn't realized quite how much she'd needed a break, however small. To say her life was full these days didn't even begin to cover it.

She guessed that was what happened when your best friend turned into a super-powerful vampire and needed you for moral support. Not that she had anyone with similar experiences to compare with.

"Crap," Bay murmured as her last conversation with Lily flitted through her mind. "I need to vacuum again. Lily's coming over for a movie night tomorrow."

Grimm gave a slight wag of his bushy tail at the mention of Lily's name, despite the indignities he was currently suffering, and Bay smiled. The Newf might not be sure about everyone—and everything—currently residing at the Bonner mansion, but the owner was one of his favorite people.

That made two of them. And since this was the first time in weeks Lily hadn't found a reason to cancel on her, she'd be damned if the night would be anything less than perfect. Just like old times.

Bay's smile faltered as her thoughts drifted to what was becoming well-worn territory, despite all her best efforts.

So things are different. So what? Everything changes. Change isn't always bad, Bay chided herself. And there was no question that Lily MacGillivray, once Lily Quinn, had changed since discovering she was the sole heiress of an ancient vampire bloodline.

Bay had managed to get used to the basics quickly enough. She'd ogled enough fake vampires in movies that Lily's fangs and inability to sunbathe were expected, even if they'd been slightly weird at first. But...the physical stuff was where the similarities between what she'd expected and what she'd gotten ended. Her friend, the shy professor, had stepped into a world full of cold, often cruel beings who seemed to enjoy shedding one another's blood almost as much as that of humans. They were beautiful, all of them, Bay thought. And clannish. And arrogant. And some of them had lived so long as to be downright terrifying.

Lily seemed to like them, Bay reminded herself, so the cat-shifting vampires of the Lilim had to have some redeeming qualities. Lily's husband, Ty, for instance. He was undeniably gorgeous. He'd also made a concerted effort to be friendly, which was definitely something he didn't do for everyone. The man was three hundred years old, and Bay had gotten enough of his story to know that most of those years had been rough. She just wished she could forget that he'd also been a killer, and that even now, he would never look at snuffing out a life with the same horror she did. He wasn't... well, *human*. None of the preternaturally beautiful men now prowling the streets of Tipton after dark were. And lucky her, a lot of them seemed interested in the pretty little blonde who hung out with their queen.

She had tried, very hard, to come off as intimidating. So far, she'd failed miserably. It didn't surprise her. Not when she'd been told for years that she looked like Tinker Bell.

Lily had teased her once or twice about the prospect of expanding her dating pool. Maybe she'd expected that Bay, with her love of ghost hunting and fondness for creepy movies, would jump at the chance to date an honest-to-God vampire. But the reality was so much darker than fantasy. Besides, Bay had noticed that a lot of the vamps she'd met were the usual bad ideas, just with sharper teeth and more baggage. She tried to like them, for Lily's sake. She even managed it sometimes.

But actively seeking an eternity in some kind of blood-soaked darkness? No.

"Enough," Bay muttered to herself. Lily was still Lily, and that was all that mattered. Her best friend was kind, loyal, funny, gifted with a spine of steel. And she still loved a good action-adventure flick featuring superheroes in spandex, which was exactly what Bay had planned. Not *everything* had changed.

Bay brushed absently at a big glob of black fur that had attached itself to the front of her Scooby-Doo scrubs and blew a curly lock of blond hair that had escaped her ponytail out of her face. She worked quickly, focused as she drew sections of fur through her fingers and snipped with the shears. Grimm was, for the moment, incredibly soft, smelling faintly of the sugar cookie–scented conditioner she'd used.

"Good boy," she praised him quietly. She hadn't bothered to tether him, knowing that he'd soon flop down on the table with a sigh and nap while she finished him up. For a dog that had been largely neglected for his first year before he'd come into rescue, Grimm had given her his trust quickly and completely. She figured spoiling the crap out of him probably had something to do with it. He made Bay wonder why she'd waited so long to get a dog of her own. He was a hell of a lot more rewarding than any of her boyfriends had been.

In the front of the shop, the bell above the front door jingled merrily as someone wandered in. Bay barely registered the sound, knowing it was either someone stopping by to make an appointment or to pick up something from the small selection of grooming supplies she carried. Shelby, the college student she had working the front desk part-time, could handle it.

Grimm turned his head again, but this time his deep-set eyes were focused on the doorway. An odd sound blended with the music, making Bay pause and tilt her head. It took her a minute to figure out what it was... and when she did, it surprised her.

She'd never heard Grimm growl before, not once in the six months she'd had him.

But he was sure doing it now.

"It's okay, big guy," she said, stroking a soothing hand down his side. His eyes never left the empty doorway. It was as though she wasn't even there.

There was a crash, a high-pitched yelp from the front. Bay's heart leaped into her throat as she clenched her fist around the grooming shears, a million terrible images flickering through her mind at once.

It's the middle of the damned day nobody robs a store in the middle of the day it has to be a psycho oh God what if he has a gun oh God oh God oh God...

Grimm threw back his head and bayed, then launched himself off of the table.

"Grimm, no!" she shouted, but he'd hit the ground running, vanishing quickly out the door. Bay chased after him, the only terrified thought in her head that if someone had come in armed, they would absolutely shoot a dog that plenty of casual observers likened to a bear. If she just got robbed, Bay didn't care... She would rather lose the money than lose the dog.

Bay sprinted out the doorway and around the corner, then skidded to a halt in the small waiting area. Grimm had stopped barking, but moved quickly to place himself between her and the man on the floor, using his big, warm body as a barricade.

"Bay," Shelby breathed as she hurried around the counter to join her, the pink streaks in her dark hair matching the shade staining her cheeks. "He just stumbled in here and passed out! Do you think he's a druggie or something?"

Bay was silent for a moment, staring at the figure of a man spread-eagled in a wild scatter of shampoo bottles in the middle of the room. He'd taken out her new display in his fall. Even the quickest glance told her he was likely way too young for a heart attack, but then again, weirder things had happened.

The thought of him dying on her floor while she gawked lit a fire under her.

"We may need to call nine-one-one," Bay said. She pushed around Grimm with effort, rushing to the man's side and crouching down. He was on his stomach, and only his profile was visible. She knew instantly she'd never seen him before.

Grimm joined her, pressing against her shoulder as he leaned down to give the man a wary sniff. His tail, always an indicator of his mood, was a stiff flag behind him. The dog gave a low, unhappy moan.

Bay leaned closer, inhaling. No booze—all she caught was an intriguing hint of spice that was very...male. Good cologne, she guessed, then pushed the thought away. Seeing a hint of movement, the unmistakable rhythm of breathing, sent relief coursing through her along with a whole lot of adrenaline. He wasn't dead. A junkie, maybe, though he didn't have that look about him.

Or maybe he's just sick.

Her eyes flickered over his face again, just quickly enough for her to register that he was far from sickly looking. Actually, he was gorgeous.

"Sir?" she asked loudly, shaking him by the shoulders. "Sir, can you hear me?"

A soft groan indicated he was coming to... she hoped.

"Sir, if you can hear me, I'm calling an ambulance right now. We'll get you some help."

Bay gestured to Shelby, who headed back for the counter, and the phone. Bay had only begun to turn her head back toward the man when he shot to his feet in a scatter of shampoo bottles, moving so quickly she barely knew what was happening. There was a whisper of air against her cheek, and then he was on his feet, backing away from where she crouched. His hand was at his temple, and he winced as though his head hurt.

Bay rose quickly to her feet, a protective hand on her dog as he once again put himself between her and the stranger with a volley of deep, threatening barks.

The man's eyes moved quickly from the dog to the mess, and then to the two women staring at him wide-eyed. He spat a word in a language Bay didn't understand, then held out one hand as the other fell away from his temple.

"Please... a moment. I'm not going to hurt you."

His voice was silken, a warm tenor no less commanding for its softness. His accent was a blend, faintly British but with an exotic lilt.

"You need to leave," Shelby said, her voice shaking.

"Shelby," Bay said softly, a gentle reproach. Whatever was wrong here, freaking out on their part was not going to help it. When she turned her head to look at her friend, however, she could see something was very wrong. Shelby had gone sheet-white, her dark eyes huge as she stared at the man's face.

"*Shelby*," she said more sharply, hoping to draw her attention away. The look on her friend's face wasn't one she'd ever seen before...or ever wanted to see again.

"His...*eyes*...," Shelby whispered.

Bay turned her head sharply to look at him, and when his eyes locked with hers, she finally understood.

The guy who'd just wrecked her shampoo display wasn't human. Not even close.

His eyes were a bright, burning gold, more akin to molten metal than the more muted shades she'd seen among the werewolves who stayed with Lily's dynasty. They were intense, mesmerizing. He stared at her for an instant that felt much longer than it truly was, and in her head she heard his voice as clearly as if he'd been speaking in her ear. It was far too intimate, and still it made her shiver.

Be still. I would speak with you.

His gaze returned to Shelby, who was fumbling now with the phone. Bay heard Shelby's terrified, sobbing breaths even out instantly, heard the phone being clicked off, and then the gentle creak of the stool behind the counter as the girl settled herself on it. She said nothing.

"So you're a vampire," Bay said quietly, adrenaline still pumping hard and fast through her veins. Only Grimm's reassuring presence kept her from running out the door, the urge to flee an instinct that her rational mind knew would make no difference. If he wanted to catch her, he would. She should have known what he was as soon as he'd gotten up—no human could move so fast.

"I don't know how you're out in the middle of the afternoon, but whatever you came in here for, I can't help you."

Bay was glad her voice sounded so steady, considering her legs felt like Jell-O.

The man said nothing, his expression guarded. And despite herself, despite knowing she was in the presence of a creature who had just thralled her employee into a happy stupor, a creature who was out during the day when there was no earthly way he should be, Bay felt the vampire's physical appeal slam into her like a fist.

They're all beautiful. You're used to it, she told herself, furious at the way her heartbeat quickened. And a treacherous little voice in the back of her mind responded, *They may all be beautiful...but not like this.*

Those remarkable eyes, deep set and almond shaped, watched her steadily from beneath a pair of dark, slashing brows. His nose was strong, his lips tantalizingly full, and his square jaw was covered in a light growth of stubble. The vampire's hair, wavy and black as sin, was cut short enough not to fall into his eyes but long enough to tousle, and Bay had to tear her eyes away when her fingers curled reflexively into her palm, itching to run her fingers through it, over every inch of this stranger's tanned and gold-dusted skin.

It was Grimm's soft growl that finally sliced through her haze. She blinked rapidly and shook her head, making sure not to meet the vampire's eyes again. Lily had been very clear about how to protect herself from the less well-behaved members of the species, and Bay was glad for it. Poor Shelby was going to be in her own little world until this guy left, and then, Bay knew, the girl wouldn't remember any of this. A heavy thrall could really do a number on a person.

She didn't want her own brain messed with to boot.

Finally, he spoke.

"You're close friends with the ruler of the Lilim, aren't you?" he asked. "Lily MacGillivray. And you're Bailey Harper. This is the information I was given."

"Given by who?" Bay asked, fighting back the fresh sliver of fear working its way down her spine. He'd said he had no intention of hurting them, but still...vampires didn't come looking for her. Especially not day-walking vampires with wild eyes and problems staying conscious.

He moved to pick up a pair of sunglasses on the floor, and she was struck again by his natural grace. It shouldn't have surprised her. The majority of the vampires now in Tipton had started as Cait Sith, cat-shifters, before joining Lily's dynasty. The lot of them had grace and beauty in spades. But there was something different here, something more. And she hated herself a little as her eyes crawled over the lithe, muscular frame that even his light jacket and loose jeans couldn't disguise.

Bay gritted her teeth and inhaled, trying to center herself. The vampire slid his sunglasses on. It was a small relief, but she'd take it, even though knowing he was watching her from behind them was still unnerving. He regarded her silently for a moment, studying her so intently that Bay felt a hot flush creeping into her cheeks. Finally, he spoke, and managed to surprise her.

"I...apologize," he said, his brows drawing together slightly as he looked down at the mess he'd made by falling. "We'll start over. My name is Tasmin Singh. I can walk in the light because it is a gift of my line. And I'm looking for your friend because..." He trailed off for a moment, then looked away.

"It is a long story."

"Something to do with you passing out in the middle

of my store?" Bay asked. His features tightened for an instant before his expression cleared again.

"Perhaps. I slept far longer than is natural, and I still seem to be...adjusting. That should pass in time. I came here because I seek answers. The queen of the Lilim will know those who can find them. Of this I am certain."

Bay's eyebrows rose at the cryptic response. There was something *off* about him, something she couldn't even put her finger on that went beyond the obvious weirdness. Sadly, it didn't make him any less fascinating to her.

"Okay," she said, drawing the word out. "Well, Tasmin, you, um, would have done better just waiting until nightfall and knocking on Lily's door. Whoever told you where to find me could have told you where to find her." She tilted her head at him. "Why *didn't* you just go there? You can see I'm no vamp. I'm just a dog groomer."

She thought she caught the faintest hint of a smile, if only for a moment. It turned his lips soft, sultry, and she felt a knot of pleasure coil deep in her belly.

No. No no no. She liked things that were quirky, odd, and even weird. Things. Not guys. Because every time she was drawn to one of those qualities in a guy, it ended up biting her in the ass. And this particular guy looked about as safe as a wounded tiger.

"I see. You've attracted quite a noble beast as a guardian."

She stroked her hand over Grimm's back, unsure of whether Tasmin was giving her a compliment or just being sarcastic. Grimm leaned into her harder and growled at the vampire again. The sound was soft, but it was a clear warning.

"He is noble," Bay said flatly. "More than most people manage to be. And he's an excellent judge of character."

Tasmin inclined his head slightly, any trace of a smile gone. "Of that I have no doubt. Beasts often are. That he has chosen you speaks well of you."

She blinked. "Oh. I...thanks." She tried to shrug off the pleasure she felt at the simple praise. It didn't matter what this strange, gorgeous vampire thought of her.

"That still doesn't explain why you came in here."

"The sun is still high. I had some time. And I wondered what sort of mortal would be considered such a friend to a powerful queen. I'm still not sure whether your relationship means I should expect to find her wise, or a reckless fool." He considered her. "In any case, you're not what I expected."

Bay's eyes narrowed. She knew she was considered a curiosity among the vampires here, a mortal with no apparent interest in anything Lily could offer her except friendship. But she didn't appreciate being gawked at like a sideshow freak by some outsider.

"Well," she said stiffly, "what you see is what you get. I'm not that interesting. Now if you don't mind, I've got some things to do before I close up for the day, and I need my help back."

She turned her head to look at Shelby, who was thumbing idly through a magazine, a dreamy expression on her face. Seeing how deep the thrall still was unsettled her.

"Shouldn't that have worn off by now?" Bay asked.

"It will wear off when I decide it does."

Bay looked sharply at him. "That's not how it works."

"It is how *I* work."

The matter-of-fact arrogance in his statement finally sparked her temper. She pushed aside any lingering fear and walked quickly around Grimm, striding right up to Tasmin. Despite the sunglasses, she saw his surprise, and had to fight back a thin smile. No doubt he'd expected the puny mortal to cower and grovel. But that wasn't how *she* worked.

Bay came to a stop only a foot away from him and glared up into his impassive face. Being so close, and this time with him aware and looking down at her, left her momentarily off-balance. He was just the right height—maybe five feet ten—to fit herself against, tall enough to wind herself around, short enough to reach if she rose up on her toes to press her mouth to his...

The scent of him was stronger now, intoxicating. And fending off another hot punch of desire only made her angrier. She never let men make her uncomfortable...It was a point of pride with her. So why couldn't she find her footing with this one?

"Listen," she snapped. "I don't know what you are or what's wrong with you, but if you want to find out what the Lilim are like, I suggest you head in that direction. I'm sure you'll get an answer to your questions one way or another...if you can make it through the werewolves to ask. Now if you'll excuse me, I've got better things to do than satisfy your curiosity."

She started to turn and felt his hand clamp on her wrist, not hard, but with a controlled strength that she knew could shatter bones if he wanted. Her fury was a dull roar in her ears as she whipped her head around.

"What—"

But the words died in her throat at his expression, the lips pulled back to reveal gleaming fangs. It was the snarl of a creature not remotely human, a killer. And the voice that came from his throat was nothing like the sensual purr of before.

In an instant, he'd become everything she was afraid of.

"You dare chastise me, human?" The words sounded like they'd been dragged through gravel and oil, oozing up from deep in his chest.

Then he cried out, his head snapping back, his body arching as though an electric current had just passed through his body. The sunglasses clattered to the floor again, and Grimm barked just behind her, though it sounded oddly far off. Tasmin's eyes met hers again, and the amount of pain and fear she saw in that instant left her reeling. His hand tightened on her wrist before going lax.

"Help me," he breathed.

She just managed to get her arms around him to break his fall, sinking slowly to the floor with Tasmin in her arms. Whatever this man needed, she knew, it was more than just answers.

But right this second he needed help. He needed *her*.

Even though she cursed herself for it, even though she'd declared vampire problems off limits to herself, Bay knew she was in big trouble. Her compassion had always been as much her strength as it had been her Achilles' heel.

And this time, whichever it turned out to be, she wasn't going to be able to just walk away.

chapter TWO

He DIDN'T AWAKEN FULLY until the sun went down.

Tasmin inhaled deeply as consciousness returned, grateful to be surfacing from the dreams that had plagued him ever since he'd emerged from the cave. He felt warmth, softness, a strange sense of comfort...and relief as he emerged fully from the smoke-filled visions he could only ever half remember. His sleep, once restful, now left him with an aching hunger nothing seemed to be able to fill, his head pounding with an anger that seemed to come from nowhere, directed at nothing and yet as deep and endless as the ocean.

And yet right this moment, he felt...good.

Maybe someone had finally put him out of his misery. Then again, he'd never had that kind of luck.

Tasmin kept his eyes closed, rummaging around in his murky memories for where he might have ended up this time. For a moment, he felt a cold twist of fear when he couldn't come up with anything. The blank spaces in the days that had passed since he'd left the forest yawned like bottomless chasms . . . some rimmed with blood. He'd grown to dread those empty patches in his memory more than anything else. But then images drifted up from the depths, and he remembered. Pieces, anyway.

Shampoo bottles. A woman's gentle hands. Barking.

Tasmin opened his eyes and found himself staring into a furry black face only inches from his own.

He hissed in a breath and sat upright, startled. The big black dog rose to its feet from where it had been sitting and watching him, and gave a soft *wuff.*

"Easy," Tasmin said softly, a command that did nothing to diminish the wariness he saw in the creature's deep-set eyes. It was hard to blame him.

Tasmin looked around, keeping half an eye on the animal while he got his bearings. He had been lying on a large, overstuffed couch, where someone—no, he corrected himself, *Bailey*—had covered him with a soft knit blanket. The simple gesture surprised him. But then, all of this surprised him. That he was even in her home meant she had shown him more kindness than anyone, mortal or otherwise, had since he'd awakened. He had a vague recollection of being led to her car, of staggering in the door and being eased onto the couch, which was as far as he'd been able to make it without passing out again.

He heard the soft sound of footfalls on wood, and had only a moment to take in the warmth of his surroundings: the rich burgundies and browns of the furniture, the bright glow of the fire in the fireplace, the rich and somehow sensual palette of the rugs, the art on the walls.

Then she was there, and he was aware of nothing but her scent, the quickened beat of her heart, her every breath as she entered the room. The dog immediately went to her side.

The woman, he noted, looked every bit as wary as the beast that guarded her.

"You're awake," she said, and not even her obvious nerves could mar the melody of her voice. Her hands fluttered together as she watched him, then pulled apart, quickly flexing into fists before relaxing again.

Tasmin was silent as he watched her struggle with how to deal with him, as struck by her beauty as he had been earlier. Bailey Harper looked nothing like the women who had once occupied so many of his thoughts, and yet he found himself unwillingly fascinated by every small detail. Her features were delicate, set in an oval face dominated by eyes as blue as the sky at daybreak, and the face itself was expressive, open. He had plenty of experience with deception—it was his kind's stock in trade, after all—and he sensed, with bone-deep certainty, that whatever else Bailey might be, she was not a liar.

Small consolation for this disaster of a day, but a real one. He had never much cared for picking through mortal thoughts for answers when they refused to give them, though he was more than capable. There had just been too many times when he'd infiltrated someone's mind and been utterly repulsed by what he'd found.

But then, those who had sought his kind had rarely been scrupulous.

"You brought me to your home," Tasmin said, his voice as rough as it always was after his control had slipped and his...other side...had taken over, however briefly. His throat felt as though he'd been swallowing hot coals.

"I did. Do you remember any of that?" Bailey asked. "You were pretty out of it."

He shook his head. *No.* The silence drew out between them while they studied one another, and Tasmin felt his unusually strong awareness of her intensify. She seemed uncomfortable in the quiet, so different from him. He'd never been one to fill up the empty places with meaningless words just to hear the sounds they made. And still, she fascinated him. Bailey Harper was as foreign a creature to him as the tongue she spoke had once been—a tongue he had awakened understanding, though he knew for certain he had never learned it before.

One more mystery, perhaps better left unanswered.

The firelight played over skin like rich cream as Bailey shifted, lifting a hand to tuck an escaped tendril of golden hair behind her ear. She'd twisted her hair up into a pile of curls that looked to be only moments away from tumbling down. Tasmin allowed himself, for just a moment, to imagine what she might look like with her curls loose around bare shoulders. An instant later he had to push the image away, suffused with heat that had nothing to do with the fire.

Perhaps silence wasn't the best thing right now after all.

"Why?" he asked. "Why would you bring me here?"

She frowned. "Well…the hospital seemed like kind of a bad idea. So did dumping you out on the sidewalk." A crease appeared between her brows as the frown deepened. "It's kind of interesting that you'd want me to rethink that decision, but I suppose I can throw you out now if you'd like."

Tasmin shook his head, frustrated with himself. Clarity was always a struggle for him right after awakening, especially these days. And even now, the English thoughts often jumbled with the Hindi, making it more difficult to express himself properly.

"No. I mean, why would you put yourself at risk this way? You know what I am."

A corner of her mouth curved upward, though the smile didn't quite reach her eyes. "You really think a pair of fangs would send me running? Even if I wasn't close to Lily, Tipton has become vamp central these days." She shrugged. "If you need the Lilim that badly, you won't make the mistake of hurting me. Besides . . . you asked for help."

She looked away, uncomfortable again as she wrapped her arms around herself. Tasmin watched her big black dog nudge her elbow with his nose. She immediately dropped a hand down to stroke the dog's head. Tasmin watched the interplay of the beast soothing his mistress, feeling an unfamiliar sensation curling unpleasantly in the pit of his stomach.

He had never been jealous of a dog before. It wasn't an experience he cared for.

"I don't remember asking for help," Tasmin grumbled, disconcerted by his reaction to the scene in front of him.

"Well, you did," Bailey replied, her eyes narrowing. "And I don't make a habit of walking away from *defense-less* creatures."

Tasmin snorted. "I'm hardly defenseless."

She didn't look impressed. "Yeah? Well, you weren't looking so hot back at the shop."

He pressed his lips together, torn between affront and amusement. He was used to humans fearing him. He wasn't sure what to do with one who treated him as an equal, much less a slightly annoying one.

Finally, he relented. A little. And only because he had to admit that she did have a small point.

"I . . . that much is true. I suppose I should thank you for your help," he managed, trying not to hunch his shoulders at the admission. It was humiliating, that he should have *needed* her help, but she had given it nonetheless. And he was being supremely ungrateful about it.

"Yes, you should thank me, but I can see that's about as good as I'm going to get." She sighed. "Look, I've already left a message for Lily. You want her, you got her. I'm sure she'll be here shortly." She looked away and muttered, "I'm probably going to get a lecture about having you here too."

Tasmin frowned. "I would prefer to greet her in her own court. It will offend her, being summoned to see me when it should be the other way around. She'll consider it an insult."

The last thing he needed was to get off on the wrong foot with the queen, considering his very limited options. But for reasons he couldn't even fathom, Bailey laughed. The musical sound of it rippled through him, awakening parts of himself that were better left dormant.

"You mock me?" he asked, amazed that she would even dare.

Bailey angled her head at him, widening her eyes. She still looked amused. "Seriously?" she asked.

He leveled a cool stare at her. "I suppose I shouldn't expect you to understand how things are done among my kind, despite the company you keep. You're just a mortal."

Bailey's smile faded a little, but didn't entirely disappear. She watched him closely as though he was a puzzle she was trying to figure out. Tasmin had to fight the urge to look away, to hide whatever answers she might find on his face. What did it matter, what she saw? There was nothing to see. Just the shell of who he had once been.

And still, this woman's gaze unnerved him in a way other mortals' did not.

Finally, she spoke.

"Look, I'm not *mocking* you, so calm down. I don't know what it's like where you came from, but Lily doesn't stand on ceremony. She won't mind coming here, especially because she's here a lot anyway." Her mouth tightened, just for an instant, but the emotion behind it had vanished before he could even try to read it. "Well, she was. Regardless, this isn't something that would bother her, and I wasn't sure you were going to be in any shape to go anywhere. You seemed pretty messed up."

Though he knew her words weren't a conscious dig at his ability to handle himself, Tasmin pushed aside the blanket and got quickly to his feet, his pride stinging. He was no sickly thing, damn it! He was a hunter, a creature to be reckoned with. The difficulties he'd been having changed none of that.

His speed finally made Bailey look nervous, and the dog gave a warning bark.

"I am not *ill*," Tasmin growled. "Spare me your pity."

"But then why—"

"It's not a sickness!" he interrupted her, his voice rising. "I've been asleep for over four hundred years! We were never meant to sleep so long!"

Tasmin watched her take a quick step back. He felt a nasty surge of pleasure that turned quickly to guilt. For reasons he couldn't fathom, Bailey had taken a chance and brought him into her home. Yet here he was, snapping at her like a wounded lion, taking out his fury at his weakened state on the only person who'd seemed genuinely interested in helping him in all these months.

Such a pretty thing…maybe we should have a taste…

Tasmin shook his head at the ugly impulse that drifted up from the murky depths of his mind.

No.

He slid his hands into his hair as his temples began to throb, a dull ache he was now well acquainted with. A warning. Bailey's scent, sweet as spun sugar at first blush but with something much more complex and decadent beneath, wound itself around him until all he was breathing was her. Tasmin pressed his fingers into his skull, wincing as the hunger slammed into him. She smelled so good. She would taste a thousand times better.

I'm in control. I can stop this. I CAN.

"Hey, are you all right?" Bailey asked, her voice echoing in his head.

"Don't," he murmured, so soft only he could hear it. Then she was coming to him, the foolish woman's instincts the exact opposite of what they ought to be where he was concerned. Tasmin tried to take a step back to get away from her and landed right back on the couch. The surprise of the fall cleared his head, at least for a moment. Bailey stopped short only a couple feet away. Tasmin looked up at her from where he was sprawled, astounded that he appeared to be the only one in the room with any sense of self-preservation.

"Aren't you afraid of me at all?"

"Yes. And no." She sounded as confused by the answer as he was.

"It's a wonder you haven't gotten yourself killed."

"You know, it's awfully hard to be nice to you when

you're being such an asshole," she said, whatever fear she claimed to feel overridden by a sudden burst of temper. A loose curl tumbled over one eye, but she seemed to be too busy glaring at him to notice. "Do you have any other nasty comments to make about mortals in general or me specifically?"

He could only stare for a moment. Mortals didn't challenge his kind. Ever. This one acted like she found him about as intimidating as a pet kitten. Finally, he mustered a response.

"You have a foul mouth, woman."

Bay looked irritably back at him. "*Now* are you finished?"

"I-I...yes." She didn't react like a normal human. Tasmin didn't have a clue what else to say.

Bailey stared at him, took a deep breath, and tried to brush the errant curl back into her hair.

"Okay then. Tasmin," she finally said, the sound of his name on her lips sending an unexpected shiver of pleasure skimming down his spine. "What I was going to say before you went all *'Beware, foolish mortal!'* on me was that I really think you should see a doctor or a healer or something. You might think you're all right, but you *really* don't seem like you are."

Once he was fairly certain Bailey wasn't going to try to come to his aid, Tasmin stood again, this time slowly, carefully. "I don't need a healer," he said. "I need to see the queen of the Lilim. I need to find out what happened to my people."

He saw a softening in her expression, an innate compassion that was so misplaced when it came to a creature like him. Guilt pricked at him. She might be an inconsequential human, but abusing a woman's good nature was beneath him.

"Your people," Bailey murmured. "You said you're a..."

"Rakshasa," Tasmin said. He lifted his hand to pull aside the neck of his T-shirt, baring the mark of his line: the lion's paw, created of flame. Bailey's eyes dropped to it, and he swore he could feel his skin warm where her gaze touched. Quickly, he covered his mark again. When her eyes met his again, he wasn't surprised to see her confusion. Saddened, but not surprised.

"Is that a dynasty?" she asked. "I haven't heard anyone mention it, but Lily said there are a number of bloodlines that don't come here."

His mouth curved into a small smile at the innocent questions, though it was borne of bitterness, not amusement. Once, the name of his kind had been whispered in reverence, in fear. Now, it was so much dust in the wind.

"It was," he said softly. "Many prides, one mark. Now, there is only me."

"I'm sorry," she said, and he was surprised to see her sympathy was genuine. Sympathy was something he had never seen much of, not even before he had fallen prey to whatever had left him in that cave. Few shed a tear when a Rakshasa died, no matter how sought after they were in life. It hadn't helped that the prides were so isolated from one another... The cruelest elements of his kind tainted the legacy of them all.

Bailey's sentiment was so odd to him, especially from a mortal, that he didn't quite know how to respond to it. Suspicion, as it usually did, won out first.

"I don't want your pity," he said.

"It isn't pity," she said, looking flustered. "Why wouldn't I be sorry for you, if you're the only one left?"

Now that he knew he had his footing and didn't feel a trace of the dizziness that preceded one of his blackouts, Tasmin took a step toward Bailey, then another. He knew he shouldn't get so close. Not when the scent of her was so compelling. But he couldn't stop himself. Her casual disregard of what he was left him both infuriated and fascinated. She needed to understand he was no domesticated pet to be coddled and soothed. And he...he needed to feel the warmth that seemed to pour from her, to bask in it, if only for a moment.

Tasmin didn't stop until he was only a breath away from her, looking down into her upturned face. She stood her ground, defiant. Their bodies were so close to touching that he could feel the energy crackling between them, daring him to pull her against him. It was raw attraction, Tasmin told himself, nothing more, even if it was stronger than anything he could rightly remember having experienced.

The urge to stroke his hands over her slim curves, to taste her, was almost overwhelming. Instead, he spoke, forcing out words as her breath feathered his face.

"So many questions. But the answers are not for you."

Her frown was faint, her eyes hazy. Seeing the delicate pink tip of her tongue flicker out to wet her lips before she spoke was enough to have him hard as a rock... another first since his awakening. Tasmin bit back a groan. This was *not* a good time to rediscover that part of his nature.

It might have helped if he hadn't caught the sweet, unmistakable musk of Bailey's own arousal right then.

Tasmin's nostrils flared. Only the incredible control he'd had to learn in the past few months kept him from pushing her up against the wall and having her.

Bailey seemed to sense the change in him, but instead of shrinking away she stayed put. Her pupils dilated, and her voice was breathless when she spoke. "I saved you," she said. "I think I deserve a *few* answers."

A sharp pain twisted deep in his chest. "No one can save me." Gods, she was warm, so tempting. If he was the man he had once been...but he had not come out of that cave the same. Not at all.

Her lashes lowered, her gaze dropping to his mouth. His resolve wavered, then crumbled as he fastened his hands on her hips and stepped into her. It was a wonderful shock to feel her hands fist in his shirt. She turned her face up to his, lips parted, inviting. He lowered his head...

The sound of the front door opening had Bailey leaping backward as though someone had struck her. She nearly toppled over in her haste to get away from him. Tasmin was frozen in place, afraid that if he tried to move he would quickly find Bailey back in his arms. That would be a terrible idea for both of them.

But it didn't stop him from wanting it with every wretched fiber of his being.

"Bay?"

A woman's voice, compelling and rife with concern, echoed from the front of the house.

"Right here!" Bailey called back, though her eyes never left Tasmin's. She stared at him with wide eyes. Her breathing was as uneven as his was, ragged in the sudden silence. After a moment, she shook her head.

"Yeah," she said quietly. "That was…I think…yeah. Lily's here."

She turned on her heel and left the room, vanishing almost as quickly as a vampire might.

Once Bailey's swaying hips were out of sight, Tasmin realized two things: One—she had removed his shoes while he'd slept. Two—he seemed to be standing in a puddle.

Tasmin looked down, only to meet a pair of soulful dark brown eyes watching him with a great deal of concern. The dog was sitting at—and drooling all over—his feet. It seemed the heated exchange with his mistress had not been much to the creature's liking. Tasmin could feel the dog's nerves without even touching him.

What surprised him was the cautious interest that had replaced the dog's hostility. The furry beast scooted closer when Tasmin took a step back, licking its chops and beginning to wag its tail.

"Oh, *now* you want to make friends?"

A long, luxuriant ribbon of drool separated from the dog's flews and landed directly on Tasmin's foot, starting a brand-new puddle.

Resigned, and mildly disgusted, Tasmin lifted his hand to give him a tentative pat on the head. Tasmin huffed out a surprised laugh as the dog—Grimm, Bailey had called him—snuffled at the hand and then gave it a rather sloppy lick. Tasmin ruffled the soft fur on Grimm's head and finally felt some small amount of relief from his ragged nerves. Another surprise, but it shouldn't have been. People, mortal or no, were complicated things. Beasts were more direct, easier. They either liked you or they did not.

This one seemed to have decided to like him, for whatever reason. Tasmin took some solace in that.

In this unfamiliar world, there were now two beings that seemed to care whether he lived or died.

Perhaps there was something salvageable left in him after all.

chapter THREE

W<small>HEN</small> B<small>AY</small> <small>GOT</small> to the front entryway, she saw immediately that Lily had brought reinforcements. Well, one
reinforcement. But he was the equivalent of a one-man
army when he needed to be.

Shit. He looks like he wants to kill someone. Me, probably.

"Hey, guys. I thought I might get both of you tonight,"
Bay said, keeping her tone casual. Inside, she was still
reeling. Had she seriously just been ready to drag Tasmin
to the floor and—

Her cheeks flushed. Yep. She definitely had been.

"When you start taking in stray vampires, you get
more than just me," Lily said with a smile that held a fair
amount of concern. "You lucked out, though. Ty wanted
to bring half a dozen wolves too. I said no."

The slim, auburn-haired queen of the Lilim shrugged
out of her wool coat and tossed it on the hallway bench.
Lily's husband Ty, a tall, dark-haired vamp with beautiful
silver eyes, unwound his scarf from his neck.

"You didn't *really* bring any wolves, did you?" Bay asked, her nerves prickling as she eyed the front door. She actually liked the werewolves Lily had taken on as guards a little better than the vamps. Maybe, not being immortal, they just seemed more human to her. But for all that they were warm-blooded and actually seemed to enjoy one another, it was hard not to notice that the wolves were a little less civilized than the average vampire. And a lot less predictable.

Not to mention that they *loved* hunting.

When Ty was silent, her stomach sank.

"I don't need wolves, right?" Bay rushed out. "It's only one vampire. You two could take him if you needed to. Not that you'll need to. Everything is fine."

Ty finally relented, his exasperated affection obvious in his deep, musical brogue.

"Don't worry, Bay. There's no one hiding in your bushes. No one I brought anyway."

The relief nearly had her melting into the floor, but Bay steeled herself, determined not to show it. She *had* to get over it and get used to these . . . people. Cat vamps, wolves, all of them. Lily's worried expression had Bay baring her teeth in what she hoped was a reasonable approximation of an easy smile.

I can handle this. I'll show her I can handle it.

"Great," Bay said. "Like I said, everything's fine. He just woke—"

"Fine? Are you serious?" Ty's smile vanished as quickly as it had appeared, his words cutting her off with razor-sharp precision. "This isn't some harmless charity case, Bay. You've got no idea who or what you've let in here. This isn't one of ours. Sick or not, he could have ripped your throat out."

Bay bit back an angry reply, knowing it wouldn't help anything. Did he really think she didn't know how dangerous they all were? She wasn't *stupid*. But trying to explain the absolute certainty she'd felt that Tasmin wouldn't hurt her was going to make her sound that way, and considering what had almost happened a few minutes ago, she was feeling stupid enough. She'd had to work harder at forgetting what Lily's new friends could do to her than Ty and Lily would ever know. Even if she might have forgotten a little too well this time, she didn't appreciate the scolding.

"My throat's fine," she said stiffly.

Lily sighed. She sounded so weary that for just a moment, Bay could look at her and see the old Lily. It made her realize just how long it had been since she had. The thought provoked a dull ache in her chest that she didn't know what to do with.

Lily, thankfully, seemed oblivious. Even with the ability to do so, she wasn't one to pry into Bay's thoughts.

"I'm glad you're fine, believe me," Lily said. "I'm just worried that some day-walking vampire sought you out and then"—she gestured helplessly with her hands—"all of this. You shouldn't have to deal with this stuff. Not to mention that you're very generous, and a lot of vamps just aren't that trustworthy. I don't want you to get hurt."

"I won't."

Lily's smile was only a faint shadow. "You wouldn't be so confident about that if you'd seen what the Grigori had in their basement, Bay. I'm worried. You're a lot easier to hurt than we are."

It was an argument they'd had with increasing frequency since the end of the summer, when Lily had narrowly escaped being destroyed by a soul-eating demon that was kin to the leaders of the Grigori dynasty. The demon, Chaos, had escaped by taking out most of the Grigori ancients, leaving only two. Ever since, the rest of the dynasty leaders had been on eggshells, waiting for Chaos to gather an army of his dark brethren and begin to move against the vampires as he'd promised. But there had been only silence...and Bay's growing sense that Lily was considering protective moves that would put even more distance between the two of them. Maybe permanently.

The thought of that was incredibly painful no matter how Bay tried to look at it. It wasn't her battle and she knew it...The thought of fighting the way these creatures did made her nauseous anyway. But she hated feeling like she was on the outside looking in, unneeded.

Her expression must have given her away, since Ty was as disinclined to try to pry into her thoughts as Lily was. Ty poked her in the shoulder, the brotherly gesture settling her the way little else could have.

She *did* like Ty. She needed to remember that.

"Hey. There's nothing wrong with being a sweetheart, Bay," he said. "Just...next time, if there is a next time, call Eric. His claws and fangs are good insurance, just in case. All right?"

Bay gave Ty a long-suffering look, but it was impossible not to relent. Ever since she'd met him, Ty had been inclined to play the three-hundred-year-old big brother with her. Her own big brother, Steve, hadn't been much interested in the job since he'd moved away, so she guessed the position was open. At least being treated like a little sister was familiar, if not always thrilling. And it was way better than being treated like a potential meal.

So she sucked it up, dug around for her sense of humor, and did the only thing that made any sense—she let it go.

"You know, I do have other canine options. Grimm has claws and fangs. And better people skills," Bay pointed out.

That had both of her friends chuckling.

"I have great confidence in Eric's poor people skills," Ty replied.

Bay forced a smile, wishing she could agree. Eric Black was a big, taciturn werewolf with amazing hunting ability who had barely said ten words to Bay in the four months he'd been in Tipton. He was captain of the guard in all but name already. And she shuddered to think of how he would have handled Tasmin today. He probably would have cuffed him, locked him in a closet, and waited for Lily to wake up. Considering how most vampires felt about werewolves, and vice versa, it might have turned even uglier if Tasmin had put up a fight.

No, she'd done the right thing with Tasmin, Bay decided. Even if no one else agreed, her gut told her he'd needed to come here, that he wouldn't hurt her. Weird, but her instincts had never failed her that way. Still...she'd just keep that opinion to herself.

Ty lifted his head and sniffed the air, his nose wrinkling slightly. A strange look settled on his face. "Did he mention what he was?"

Bay nodded. She'd been too frazzled to remember when she'd made the call earlier, but it was fresh in her mind now.

"He said Rakshasa."

Lily's surprise was obvious, and she and Ty shared a look Bay couldn't decipher.

"What?" Bay asked.

"I'll be damned," Ty murmured. "Part of me said it had to be, but...they've been gone for a very long time."

Bay slid a look down the hall, toward the back of the house where Tasmin was waiting for them. Her voice dropped. "Do you know what happened to them? He thinks he's the only one left."

"As far as I know, he's right," Lily said, then looked at Ty. "Anura will want to know."

Bay looked between them, confused about what the pretty Empusa from Chicago had to do with any of this. Ty's grim look, though, made even less sense.

"Maybe. You don't know much about the Rakshasa, Lily—you haven't needed to—but they weren't all like Anura's mate. Not even close." His eyes shifted to Bay. "Has anything odd happened since he got here? He's only slept, you're sure?"

She nodded, unable to keep from sounding defensive. "I'm sure. Ty, he's not scary or anything. He just wants help."

"If that's true," Ty said, "then you're luckier than you know, Bay. With the Rakshasa, you can never quite trust what you see. Remember that."

"Well," Lily said, sounding just as troubled as Bay now felt, "let's go find out what he needs."

Everyone was glaring at one another.

Well, the men, at least. Lily was just more reserved than usual. Bay couldn't blame her. Tasmin uptight was a lot more unsettling than Tasmin insulting and then trying to kiss her. Before, he'd seemed dangerous but approachable. In mixed company, the "approachable" part of the equation had been removed.

And yet, for some odd reason, Grimm had decided to flop next to him, his big head pressed up against the man's feet. Odder still was the fact that Tasmin didn't seem to mind.

"So," Lily said, "from what I understand about the Rakshasa, you must have come quite a long way to find me."

There was the briefest flicker of hope across Tasmin's face. "You have heard of my kind, then. Perhaps you know of others, scattered about this country?"

"No," Lily replied slowly. "I'm sorry."

The regret in her voice was genuine, Bay was certain. Still, Tasmin's expression was stony again in an instant. What emotions that grim mask concealed, Bay had no idea.

"Oh," was all he said.

"The prides are long gone," Ty said. "Exterminated one by one. Most of the good went first. The worst lingered...but the Ptolemy got them all, in the end. One way or another."

"I see," Tasmin said. He sounded calm, but when his eyes met Bay's for an instant, they were gold fire. She couldn't imagine what he had been through, waking up after hundreds of years to discover he'd lost everything. The fury she saw in his gaze seemed fathomless.

She only hoped he pointed it in the right direction.

Ty sighed, running a hand through his shaggy crop of dark brown hair.

"I don't feel like I should be the one telling you this. Most of your kind were gone by the time I was sired."

"Most?"

"Yeah. I saw the end of it," Ty replied. "It wasn't pretty. It never is with Arsinöe...You must remember that."

Tasmin looked as though he was fighting to keep his lip from curling.

"Yes. I remember. Emperor Akbar was infatuated with her, and she used him well to begin culling us in my time. Most of us sensed it would escalate. Arsinöe has always hated what she could not control, and our bloodline had far too much power with too little oversight for her to be comfortable with our existence. And of course... we were beasts to her."

Ty simply nodded, looking lost in thought. Bay watched him, her heart aching a little for him as it always did when his many years as a Ptolemy slave came up. Arsinöe had a legendary disdain for any creature with an animal side, and couldn't stand it when vampire animal shifters held positions of power. She'd kept the Cait Sith, Ty's bloodline, as slaves, and she'd been determined to start a war with the bat-shifting Dracul. It didn't surprise Bay to hear that the woman had been responsible for the genocide of Tasmin's kind. Especially not considering the mark she'd seen on him—a large and feline paw.

"Akbar had a few willing prides who were paid handsomely to act as his weapons," Tasmin continued. "But he never trusted them. Not really. The people said we were Brahma's dark children. Some revered us. Most were terrified of us." He shrugged. "It came to the same, in the end, I suppose."

"You didn't exactly help your cause," Ty said. "Even when there were few of you left, in my time, the Rakshasa were famous for dirty tricks. Switching sides in the middle of battle, causing havoc just for the hell of it. Bunch of bloody anarchists. And once your kind started to push into Europe, all you had to do was look for the most destructive forces at work and you'd find Rakshasa helping them along."

Bay looked sharply at Ty, surprised by the ice in his voice. Tasmin was glaring at him.

"So, *billī*, you were happy to see us go, yes? Maybe you even hunted some of us yourself."

Ty's fangs flashed. "I may be just a *cat* to you, Tasmin, but my kind has more honor than yours ever gave us credit for. The Rakshasa didn't deserve to be exterminated any more than the Cait Sith deserved to be enslaved. I knew good men who were killed just for bearing the Rakshasa mark. But I also saw some of my blood brothers and sisters, slaves with no choice of refusing to fight, who were driven mad, played with, tortured cruelly by Rakshasa before the end." He shook his head. "I didn't wish your people dead. But only a fool would forget what your bloodline was capable of."

Bay's stomach sank. Now she understood the look on Ty's face when he realized she'd taken in a Rakshasa. There was history there. And like so much of vampire history, it was ugly.

Tasmin's eyes narrowed. "Perhaps you mistake self-defense for torture."

"No. There is self-defense. And then there is sadism." Ty leaned forward. "Many of your kind crossed that line."

"And many did not. Did you live among us? Do you know anything about the world in which I lived?" Tasmin didn't bother to wait for Ty's answer, slicing a hand through the air in curt dismissal. "No, you don't. We were always scattered, always at cross-purposes. It was not in the nature of the prides to band together. The cruelty you speak of is no different than what any dynasty of highbloods has done since the bloodlines began. The worst elements are always the most visible. The difference," Tasmin said, his voice going deadly soft, "was the nature of our power. It made us a target. And now there is only me."

"Yes. Only you, but with all the gifts of your line," Ty agreed. "The prides may have been as different from one another as you claim...but I know what I saw. And I'll withhold judgment until I get a better idea of who and what you were...and are."

Tasmin winced as though his head ached, just as he'd done earlier, and Bay stood before she could think better of it. He glared up at her from where he sat pressing the fingers of one hand into his temple. She heard his voice loud and clear in her head.

Don't. Say. Anything.

She stopped, feeling incredibly awkward as both Ty and Lily stared at her curiously. She scrambled for a way to save face.

"Um," she said. "I'll be right back. Anyone need anything while I'm up?"

Ty ignored her in favor of his staring contest with Tasmin, but Lily shook her head. She looked like she wanted to be anywhere but here. Bay understood, even if it stung. This wasn't how their first get-together in weeks was supposed to go. And she wasn't used to Ty, normally one of the least judgmental vampires she knew, coming down so hard on someone because of his mark. Obviously, he'd seen things that had caused that reaction...but that didn't make it any more pleasant.

And Tasmin still didn't look well.

Bay slipped quickly away to the hall bathroom. She

went to the sink, splashed cool water on her face. After drying her hands, she headed quickly back into the family room, hoping nothing irreparable had happened in the few minutes she'd been gone. Like, say, decapitation.

Fortunately, everyone had their heads attached when she stepped back into the room. Bay took up the same perch on the arm of her couch, unnerved by the thick silence. It seemed further words had been exchanged, since Lily gave her a pleading look. Bay got it. She was usually the go-to girl for chatter, the one who set everyone else at ease. She searched desperately for something to say that wouldn't trigger a war.

"So you said prides," Bay began. "As in, lions?"

It was a relief to see Tasmin's eyes light with something other than anger.

"Lions," he agreed. "And more. We were illusionists, able to spin dreams out of shadow, to bewitch minds with fantasy. A wonderful, terrible power."

His voice was seduction itself, and Bay focused on him, managing to forget everyone else in the room.

"That sounds like magic," she said.

"We all have magic, of a sort," Tasmin replied. "It is no more and no less than what the Lilim have, or the Empusae, or the Grigori."

"It is, though," Lily said quietly. Bay turned her head to look at her, startled. Her friend looked pensive. Not entirely unhappy, but not happy either.

"What do you mean?" Tasmin asked.

"Mind control. Hallucination. I think that's a much more potent weapon than being able to throw bolts of energy at people. I have a weapon I can fight with. Your weapon can make people forget the fight exists."

Lily shook her head. "It's a wonder you didn't take over everything."

"Some vampires are more susceptible to their tricks than others," Ty interjected. "And some Rakshasa had stronger gifts than others. It's true, though. If your kind had been set up differently, with a central power instead of scattered into prides that wanted little to do with one another, it might have turned out quite differently for you. For us all."

Tasmin shrugged. "*If* does nothing for me. We were what we were. That's gone." His voice took on an edge. "I am hardly a threat to the dynasties on my own, whatever you think I am."

"How long did you sleep, Tasmin?" Lily asked.

His answer was immediate, and without reservation. "More than four hundred years."

Ty cursed softly. "Gods above and below, how is that even possible?"

"That's what I want to know. How, and why," Tasmin replied. "Just as I want to know what happened to my pride."

"But you *do* know that," Lily said, not unkindly. "I don't see how the specifics matter. One way or another, it's almost certain the Ptolemy killed them. It isn't likely you'll find anyone who knows more, except for the ones who did it. And I doubt they'd be very forthcoming if you or I asked."

Tasmin gave a harsh sigh, slouching a little as though the topic had already exhausted him. "I just can't help thinking we might all have been hidden away. It isn't an impossibility."

"It's...unlikely. There were some who searched for survivors for years afterward," Ty said. "Different reasons, but always the same result. Arsinöe was thorough. She seemed to have left no survivors. Until you."

Tasmin looked up, and Bay was startled by the weariness etched onto his face. It occurred to her that this might be the first time he'd spoken much about all of this since he'd awakened. Not for the first time today, she wondered exactly where he'd been, what he'd been doing since he'd awakened.

"I wish it were different," Tasmin said. "Still, no one found me all this time. There may be more."

"Maybe," Lily agreed. "And that brings us back to what you came here for. You need a place to stay, I assume." He bristled, but he didn't have a very convincing denial.

"I have managed well enough on my own."

"Well, if you'd like to be comfortable instead of just managing, I can offer you a place for the time being. What Lilim there are have mostly gotten their own places around town. And outside of it. And... well, that doesn't matter right now," she said with a dismissive wave of her hand. Bay watched her, suddenly curious. Lily had mentioned that her dynasty was having growing pains more than once lately. Had she meant that literally? There did seem to be an awful lot of new faces around these days. Maybe the new vampires were hard to handle.

She wouldn't know. The thought arrived on a surprising wave of sadness. Part of her hadn't wanted to know too much about the Lilim's inner workings. And part of her wished that Lily would need her enough to insist upon telling her these things anyway.

"A room," Tasmin repeated, tilting his head slightly like a watchful cat. "And your help discovering what was done to me and my pride?"

Lily frowned. "I have to ask, why me? My dynasty is young, Tasmin. I never knew your kind. We're still in a very precarious position, since Arsinöe hates us. I don't have a lot to offer."

Lily's question seemed to surprise Tasmin. He leaned forward, eyes intense. "You have everything to offer, even if you don't see it. I knew when I heard your dynasty had awakened that I had to come to you. Lilith was the mother. Your line was always the convergence point for all the bloodlines, and it's becoming so again. I know you've allied with these Dracul I keep hearing about, and the Grigori, and the werewolves. It's why Arsinöe hates you. This is the *only* place I could come and expect to find what I need."

Lily considered him for a long moment. Finally, she spoke.

"I'll do what I can to help you," Lily said. "So long as you respect the fact that as long as you're in the area you're a guest of my dynasty, and myself. We've had enough trouble lately, and more always seems to be headed our way. Create trouble, and my hospitality will end." She arched an eyebrow. "Badly."

Ty seemed to want to argue, but to his credit, he held his tongue. Bay guessed, though, that the two of them would be having a heated discussion about Tasmin staying with them once they were alone. He didn't try to run the dynasty, but he was no pushover, and Bay knew he had to have good reasons for his reservations.

For the first time since Lily and Ty's arrival, Tasmin showed an emotion besides anger: relief. Bay could see it in the subtle relaxing of his shoulders, the release of tension in his jaw. He was wound so tightly, she thought,

wishing there were something more she could do to help
with whatever burdens he carried. But as with most things
anymore, her mortality made that impossible.

Tasmin needed the help of other vampires, not her.

"Thank you," Tasmin said. "I have little to offer in
return, but you will have my loyalty. If the Ptolemy hate
you, then we should be allies for that simple fact alone."

"Oh, they hate us a lot, believe me," Lily replied, getting to her feet. The men rose quickly as well. Tasmin's
foot jostled Grimm's head and elicited an irritated sigh
from the vicinity of the floor.

Bay stayed perched where she was, feeling as awkward as she always did when she ended up in the middle
of vampire formalities. Lily always looked so *regal* in
these situations—chin up, shoulders back, wearing her
position like an invisible cloak. Bay knew that Tasmin
had been right—whatever she wanted to be called, Lily
was indeed a queen. When they were alone together, it
was different...Lily was still her *Ghost Hunters* viewing
partner, her movie buddy and confidante. Her best friend.

At least no one cared about protocol where Bay was
concerned. It made it a little easier to try and make her
world fit together with Lily's these days. Even if sometimes it felt like trying to smash the wrong puzzle piece
into a too-small, misshapen space in the larger picture.

Bay buried the thought, annoyed with herself. She'd
never been one to sit around and mope. Lily bringing Ty
here, the situation with Tasmin, *everything* had really gotten under her skin today. Once everyone had cleared out,
curling up with her dog, a blanket, and a good movie was
definitely in order. The thought brought Bay a measure
of peace. She'd shrug this weird funk off, along with her

equally weird fixation on Tasmin the bad news vampire. Tomorrow would be back to normal.

Even if she couldn't stop herself from letting her eyes wander over Tasmin, wondering whether he was as cold as the rest of his kind...or as warm as he looked.

Lily was watching him too, but more speculatively.

"One more thing," she said. "Bay told me what happened when she met you, and why she brought you here. There's a wonderful healer who's joined us recently. I understand that some of what you're experiencing may just be aftereffects from whatever was done to make you sleep so long, but—"

Bay could see Tasmin's entire body go rigid again as she spoke, his fingers flexing just once in a way she found unnerving.

"I mean no disrespect, my lady, but I am recovering," Tasmin interjected smoothly. "It's just been slow. I saw a healer back in India not long after I awakened, and he saw nothing that time wouldn't fix. I doubt your healer will find much of interest either."

Lily looked skeptical, but whatever her thoughts were on his refusal, she seemed to accept it for now.

"Well, if you change your mind, or if things get worse, let me know. Now if you're ready, you can come with us back to the mansion, and we can all get out of Bay's hair," Lily said. "Do you need a ride? We can stop and pick up your things. If you have things."

Bay felt a strange sinking sensation. He was leaving. Chances were she wouldn't be getting him to herself again. It was unlikely she would even see him again, unless she started skulking around Lily's mansion more often, a thing she tried to do as little as possible since it had turned into vampire central. She should be glad he was taking off. She knew this. But none of her reactions where Tasmin was concerned had made any sense so far... Why should that stop now?

God, I hope a good night's sleep takes care of this. She looked at Grimm, sprawled placidly by Tasmin's legs. The Newfoundland's deep-set eyes met hers, and she decided he looked as skeptical as she felt. It was a sad thing when even your dog looked as though he pitied you.

"I can find my way to your court," Tasmin said. "I need to pick up my motorcycle from where I parked it earlier, and I have a few things at the little motel on the south side of town. Those I can get myself. I won't be far behind you."

"Do you want directions?" Lily asked.

"No," Tasmin replied. "I've heard you keep wolves. I can follow the st—smell."

Lily's eyebrows lifted. "I don't *keep* wolves. The pack of the Thorn are valuable allies, and they also act as my guard. I know how most vampires feel about werewolves, and vice versa, but that doesn't fly here."

"Of course," Tasmin replied, inclining his head. "It is simply... different than what I am used to. I will adjust."

"They'll make sure you do, whether you like it or not," Ty said. Bay found herself biting back an unexpected smile at the wry humor in Ty's voice. The whole "dogs and cats living together" thing at the mansion was a subject Lily *did* talk about on a regular basis. The unusual living situation worked. Usually. But there was still adjusting going on, on both sides.

"That's fine. Just come to the gate, then, and I'll leave word you're to be let in. Then we can talk about where to start, all right?" Lily said.

Again, Tasmin inclined his head. His expression clouded as she smiled and turned away. It was, Bay thought, like watching the sun go behind a cloud. There was something so ancient in him, she thought. So very cold.

She shivered at the odd thought and then pushed it from her mind. Her life was weird enough without inventing extra things to be freaked out by.

"I will find a way to repay this kindness."

There was something strange in his voice then, some odd undercurrent that had gooseflesh rising on Bay's arms. She was sure he'd meant the words as nothing more than a courtesy. And yet somehow, the words had sounded like a threat.

Lily paused and turned back to look at Tasmin, a faint, puzzled smile on her lips. Bay wondered if her friend had heard that odd note in his voice too.

"I'm sure you will," Lily said. "And you're welcome. I'm not big on the whole 'blood is destiny' thing, to be honest. I don't care what you are. Just be willing to pitch in if it's needed, keep the bloodshed to a minimum, and we'll be fine." Then she grinned and the smile lit her up in a way that could put the most ferocious creature on earth at ease, Bay thought. Despite everything that had happened, it was a very open, very human smile.

"After you," Lily said, indicating the doorway. "I know Bay. She's already thinking about a cup of tea and her pajamas."

Bay smirked, amused even though she knew what was really going on. Lily had no intention of leaving her here alone with Tasmin again. Maybe that was best, even though she'd have preferred to make that decision for herself.

"Go ahead," Tasmin said. "I would like to Bailey privately before I leave."

Bay wasn't sure what she was more shocked by—the fact that Tasmin was openly defying Lily, or that he had something to say to her that merited being alone. Her cheeks flushed with pleasure despite the fact that the emotion went against every ounce of common sense she had. She watched Lily slide an uneasy look at Ty.

"I'm afraid I can't allow that," Lily finally said, and Bay heard the steel in her friend's tone. "Bay is under my protection."

Tasmin looked unimpressed, arching one raven brow. "If I had wanted to hurt her, it would already have been done."

"Still, you're an unknown quantity right now. I'm not leaving you here."

"I don't think that's your choice." Tasmin's voice was deceptively soft, his eyes beginning to glow. Bay looked between him and Lily, whose own eyes had narrowed, and knew she was going to have to step in. When she did, her words surprised her...though not as much as they appeared to surprise everyone else.

"He's a guest in my home, Lily," Bay said. "If he wants a minute, he can have it."

Lily blinked, and she and Ty spoke in unison to protest. "Bay—"

"It's fine," Bay interrupted, cutting them off neatly. "I'm not worried about it." Which wasn't exactly true, but close enough. Besides, it was past time she took a stand on this sort of thing. Lily had formed plenty of boundaries in her new life. Bay was entitled to have a few as well. She wouldn't be ordered around in her own home.

Lily drew herself up and looked like she wanted to argue further, while Ty simply glared at Tasmin. Bay ended the standoff neatly, and with the only words that needed to be said...no matter how they hurt her to say them.

"Lily," Bay said quietly. "I'm not one of your subjects. I'm your friend. This is my house, my choice. Respect that."

Lily's blue eyes reflected so much hurt back at Bay that for a moment she nearly took it back, tried to smooth it over. But she didn't. Couldn't. And slowly, Lily nodded.

"Okay," was all she said. Then she looked at Ty, and Bay saw some silent communication pass between them. It was hard to miss the reproach in Ty's voice when he spoke to Bay.

"We'll leave you to it, then. Enjoy your night."

The two of them left without another word, and Bay watched them go with a heavy heart. No matter what she did anymore, she felt like Lily was slipping away from her. Neither of them had asked for what had happened... and neither of them seemed to be able to find a way to bridge the gulf that had formed the instant Ty had turned Lily. She was a night creature now.

And Bay didn't think she'd ever be able to turn her face from the sunlight.

There was the sound of the front door shutting, and then the house was silent again, pulling Bay's focus to the issue at hand. She'd gotten exactly what she'd insisted on.

They were alone.

Bay's nerves returned immediately. It should have felt emptier in here once Lily and Ty had left. Instead, Tasmin's presence seemed to have expanded to fill every nook and cranny. Small wonder, she supposed, from a guy who professed to be able to bend people's brains and make them hallucinate.

"Most vampires would have killed you for that," Tasmin said, sounding genuinely awed.

"For what?"

"Disobedience. You just threw a queen out of your house."

"I didn't throw her out," Bay said, frowning. "She was leaving anyway. And she wouldn't kill me because she's my best friend, which I'm pretty sure you already knew."

Tasmin shrugged, a small, impossibly graceful movement. "It can't last. But that is something *you* already know."

It rankled, having this beautiful, strange vampire standing here lecturing on interspecies friendship when he'd been alone and mostly dead for hundreds of years.

"It *will* last. It's also none of your business," Bay said flatly, shifting her stance so that she faced him, arms folded across her chest.

He lifted his shoulders again, a casual gesture at odds with the intensity with which he watched her. Bay suddenly felt too warm.

"As you wish," Tasmin said.

They stood staring at one another. As the silence spun out, Bay fumbled for something to say. She had some vague memory of Tasmin saying he wanted to speak to her alone. She wasn't sure. Simply standing here looking at him was incapacitating functional brain cells at an alarming rate.

Grimm gave a loud yawn, breaking the silence, and got slowly to his feet in front of the chair where Tasmin had been sitting. It was a welcome break in the tension.

"Well," Bay finally said, cringing a little inside at the overly perky sound of her voice. "I hope everything works out for you."

"I doubt it will, but I appreciate the sentiment."

For whatever reason, his pessimism irritated her. "If you want it to work out, you have to push for it. And probably have a better attitude about it. You came all this way; you made a good enough impression on Lily that she's going to help you out. How is this not a good start?" Bay asked.

His lashes lowered, and she noticed they were beautifully long and black. Bay had a bad feeling she could spend hours finding things about Tasmin's looks to admire.

"Perhaps you are right," he finally allowed. "I will… try to keep that in mind." His lips quirked into a half smile. "You are a surprise, encouraging a creature like me. Driving off your friend to defend me. I am no loyal beast like your Grimm."

At the sound of his name, the dog lumbered over to Tasmin's side and looked hopefully up at him, wagging his immense brush of a tail. Bay chuckled despite herself. Especially because Tasmin's expression was so bewildered when he looked from Grimm to her.

"He likes you," Bay said with a shrug. "Don't ask me why. He makes up his own mind, and that's it."

"He is as strange as you are," Tasmin replied, shaking his head and rubbing one of Grimm's ears.

"Pretty much," Bay agreed, and he surprised her with a soft, melodious laugh that shivered pleasantly over her skin. Where had *this* guy been when Ty and Lily were here?

He's relaxed with you because you don't matter, she told herself. The idea of it, true or not, made her feel bad enough to clear her head. He was beautiful, yeah. And fun to flirt with. And off-limits. If she kept all that in mind, she'd be fine.

"I'm beginning to understand why Lily has kept you close," Tasmin said. She tilted her head at him, bemused.

"Because I'm strange?"

"Because those who have only the night treasure the sunlight where they can find it."

The room was suddenly very, very warm, and Bay couldn't quite seem to get enough air. Or formulate a coherent sentence, for that matter.

"Oh...I, I—thank you," she managed, knowing her cheeks were flame red. Her voice had begun to sound strained, and her heart pounded in her ears. "So...what did you need to tell me? Alone, I mean?"

His lips curved into a soft smile that made her forget what he was, what he could do. He was nothing more or less than the most compelling man she'd ever met.

"I wanted to thank you for your help, Bailey," Tasmin said. "You did what most would never dare in bringing me here. I won't forget."

"You can call me Bay, you know," she said, the words falling from her lips without a thought. "Everyone else does. Even my parents." It was a silly thing to say, just one more attempt at holding him here for another few seconds.

"I like Bailey better," he said, and she knew instantly that he was never going to call her by her nickname. She couldn't decide whether that was endearing or irritating. Probably both. Like him.

For a split second, she thought Tasmin might try to kiss her again. When he turned and walked away from her, she realized she'd been hoping he would try again. He paused just before turning the corner and looked back to where she stood, speechless, staring after him.

"*Phir milenge* ... Bailey," he said, and gave her a dazzling, mischievous smile that utterly transformed him. "We will meet again."

"See you," she said softly. But she was speaking to an empty room.

He was gone.

chapter FOUR

Tasmin sat at the edge of the big, four-poster bed, perfectly still.

His fingers were laced together, his breathing slow and even, his eyes closed. Outwardly, he knew he looked like he was meditating. That was by design, but also partially true. These struggles had become a form of meditation, in their way. When meditating, one had to be quiet, still, and focused on the inner self.

All of which he was. Except his inner self seemed to have split in two. It took more and more effort for the one half to tamp down the other . . . and he was no longer sure which was winning.

All he knew was that he was hungry again.

Somewhere downstairs, a clock tolled the hour. It was midnight, and though the inhabitants of this house were all awake and going about their business, no one bothered him. That was just as well, Tasmin thought, gritting his teeth as he remembered how he had been greeted last night. The Cait Sith—no, he reminded himself, the Lilim—in attendance had shied from him, preferring to gawk. Some remembered his kind. Those warned the others. And then there were the wolves . . .

With a low, soft growl, Tasmin opened his eyes.

"This isn't working," he muttered. He couldn't relax. All around him he smelled wolf and cat, strangers to him. More, there was a casual opulence to this place that left him ill at ease. He had lived in the forests most of his life, and when he'd been offered lodging, it had rarely been more than a hovel. He preferred open air, stars.

But it was so damned cold here. He wanted warmth. He wanted—

Tasmin got to his feet and began to pace the room. It didn't matter what he wanted. In fact, he had begun to think it was a very bad idea to get everything he wanted. He should never have gone to see Bailey in her shop, not with how out of sorts he'd felt that day. Of course, he'd had no idea of the effect she would have on him. What were the chances, when he hadn't given any woman so much as a second glance since he'd awakened?

This one was different. She had haunted his sleep. Even here in the mansion there were traces of her scent, taunting him. *Phir milenge,* he had told her. *We will meet again.* He knew it was a bad idea. He was not to be trusted.

But that didn't stop the desire.

From the black hole now swirling at the center of his being, the hated voice burbled up, whispering its poison.

Go to her. She'll taste so sweet. We can drain her dry, savor every drop. Go to her . . .

This time, his growl was the lion's.

"No," Tasmin said, his voice guttural. He no longer

knew what he was arguing with when he fought the voice, whether it was some broken piece of himself or something more frightening, something *other* that his long-ago captors had afflicted him with. All he knew was that he had to keep fighting it. When he had been weaker, especially in the beginning when his body's need for blood had constantly threatened to override all common sense, he had barely kept himself from toppling into the abyss.

Sometimes he thought that the only reason he was still managing to cling to the edge was that, on the days and nights when he awakened alone, covered in blood, he had no memory of what he had done.

He didn't want to know. What he had been told was bad enough...and Shakti, the healer, had warned him of what he might become. Of course, there was an obvious remedy, one that Shakti had suggested, that had sent Tasmin into a blind rage that was half himself, half...*other*.

Tasmin closed his eyes, the pain that now defined his existence filling his chest until he thought he might burst with it. He wanted so badly to live. And no matter how much of a coward it made him, he would not take his own life.

Besides, he was no longer certain that his own death would take care of the problem.

A soft knock at the door stopped him dead in his tracks, scattering his thoughts for a brief, blessed reprieve. Tasmin turned toward the sound, scenting both cat and wolf on the other side of the door. He knew exactly who the scents belonged to, and his stomach sank. There could be only one reason for this visit. He'd worried ever since awakening among all the deer...

"Tasmin?"

Ty's voice. Tasmin drew in a deep breath, trying to prepare, trying to remember *anything* from the hours he'd lost the other night.

What had he done?

Another knock.

"Tasmin? Can we talk?"

"Come in," Tasmin said, glad to hear that his voice, at least, sounded normal. He felt the dark places inside of him shift at the sound of Ty's voice, stirring in anger, in pure, blackened hate. He smothered it as best he could, straightening, making his expression blank. Hiding his weakness.

The bedroom door opened, and there was Ty, along with the big, quiet wolf who seemed to run the Lilim's guard. Neither looked happy to see him.

Seemed to be a trend these days.

Ty stepped in first, looking around the room with mild curiosity. "Everything all right? You've been shut up in here all night."

Tasmin simply looked at him. The cat didn't seem a bad sort, all things considered. But there was no doubt that the man was conflicted about Tasmin's presence here. That made two of them. He knew he should want this, be pleased with this. He was closer than he had ever been to answers.

Instead, he spent his waking moments torn between wanting to run back into the night and...other, darker things. Feeding. At the barest thought of sinking his fangs into a tender throat, Tasmin's heart quickened. He felt his fangs elongate in his mouth.

No, please, not now.

"I prefer the quiet. Did you come with news?" He

didn't mean to sound brusque when he spoke, but his words came out harsh.

"That depends on what sort of news you're asking for."

Tasmin's eyes shifted to Eric Black, whose entire being seemed to vibrate with predatory instinct despite his stillness. The man's voice was deceptively mild. Tasmin knew this type. He was the sort to die for loyalty, for what he believed in.

A dangerous sort of fool.

"You want me to guess?" Tasmin asked softly. He looked back at Ty. "Am I in trouble for something already?"

Ty sighed softly, shoving a hand through his hair. "Not *in* trouble, no. Not exactly. But you've made some trouble for us." His silver eyes were bright, direct. "You didn't tell us you ran into a group of Ptolemy on your way into town."

Tasmin's mouth went dry. He searched desperately for any shred of memory, but there was nothing. Only darkness. Whatever his body had done, his mind hadn't been present.

"I don't remember meeting anyone on the way into town," Tasmin said slowly. It was the truth, even though he saw immediately it was the wrong answer. Obviously, whatever he had done, it hadn't been very discreet.

The wolf gave him a small, incredulous smile without a hint of warmth. Tasmin felt himself bristling. Bad enough to be interrogated, but by a *wolf* . . .

"You don't remember tearing a group of about six Ptolemy limb from limb and leaving the carcasses scattered in the woods? I find that hard to believe."

Tasmin lifted his brows even as something deep inside

went dead cold. "Someone kills Ptolemy on the border of your land and you're upset about this?"

Eric's eyes narrowed. "Not someone. You."

"And you know that how?" Tasmin asked, crossing his arms over his chest. He didn't care for being cornered. He knew it was likely he had done it. Still, he felt some small relief that the victims had been interloping Ptolemy. He wouldn't be condemned for fighting a common enemy, even if it was a stretch to call it fighting. From what little he had been able to piece together about his episodes, they often had little to do with feeding. Something in him thrived on the violence. Craved it.

"Unless a lion escaped from a nearby zoo, the paw prints could only belong to you," Ty said. "Eric and a few of the other wolves headed out earlier to check the spot, make sure that this wasn't some setup."

"The trees were sprayed with Ptolemy blood," Eric said, his nose wrinkling in disgust. "The entire area smells like death." He paused. "It also smells like you."

Tasmin's jaw tightened, fury rolling through him in a wave. Some of it was visceral. A lot of it, however, was helpless fury at what was happening to him. Why couldn't he *remember*?

In the uncomfortable silence, Ty looked more closely at Tasmin's face, a crease appearing between his brows. Tasmin struggled to hold his gaze. The few Cait Sith he'd ever met had been strange cats, eerily perceptive. This one seemed no different... and that could only be a bad thing.

"You're telling me you don't remember ripping up a bunch of Ptolemy?" Ty asked.

"Of course I would remember," Tasmin snapped. "And

I don't remember any Ptolemy. I may have passed through there beforehand, taken down a deer—"

"You've been living off of deer?" Eric interrupted, beginning to look as puzzled as Ty. "Isn't that close to vampire vegetarianism? I didn't even know you guys *did* that."

"Only if there's nothing else available," Ty replied, his eyes never leaving Tasmin's face. Tasmin was glad he didn't elaborate on the fact that for a vampire, feeding on wild animals was always a sign of one of two things: either he was desperate for food, or he didn't trust his control with humans and still had enough of a soul left not to want to cause a massacre. Or both. Which it was for Tasmin most of the time now. He hadn't attempted to drink from a human in months.

At least...he hadn't been aware of doing it. Which he knew wasn't at all the same thing anymore.

"You don't remember killing the Ptolemy," Ty said again, and this time it was a statement, not a question.

"I'm not saying it again," Tasmin replied, feeling his incisors lengthening. His instincts were those of a trapped animal, and panic had begun to work its way down his spine like ice water. He darted a look at the two windows, at the hallway behind Eric and Ty. He was sure they could smell his fear, but there was nothing he could do about it. It welled in his throat, lodging there painfully.

"Tasmin," Ty said, his voice calm and even. "Calm down. We just want to know what happened."

"Why? They're your enemies. My enemies. It shouldn't matter." His voice sounded harsh and strange, and he could feel the blackness welling up, wanting to drag him down into it. If that happened, both of the men in front of him would meet the same fate as these Ptolemy he must have encountered.

"It matters because you didn't get all of them. One must have been elsewhere, and when she came back, she found... what you left," Ty said. "She ran back to her queen, who started the night here with a screaming phone call to my wife. We've picked one another off one by one with these little games at our borders, Tasmin, but that's as close as we've gotten to what you could call an uneasy peace. Between this and the business with the Grigori a few months ago, though, we run the risk of things escalating again. And we're not ready."

"Grigori?" Tasmin asked, keenly interested. He'd only heard rumors, whispers. Something had happened in the desert. He'd only barely stopped himself from traveling there first once he'd reached the States. It would make no sense... but he still struggled with the compulsion just the same.

"Nothing you need to know," Ty said sharply, "other than that we have enough problems without you stirring things up further."

"If they truly want to destroy you," Tasmin said, "it won't matter what you do or don't do. You'll be forced to fight when they wish it."

"Maybe so," Ty replied. "But we're still steering clear of deliberate provocation."

The two sets of eyes on him, one feline, one lupine, were suddenly far too weighty. They had no idea what he'd gone through to get even this far... what he grappled with even now. Who were they to judge him? Anger mingled with the fear, and he welcomed it. Anger was far easier for him to deal with. Anger he could *use*.

"I don't know how many ways I can say this to you," Tasmin growled. "I don't remember any Ptolemy. I don't remember killing anyone, only some deer I fed from. Whatever you think you found, it can't be right. Believe me or not, *I was not there.*"

He hated the defensive note in his voice. More, he hated that he sounded like he was trying to convince himself he hadn't done this. Still, it was the truth. The part of him that mattered hadn't been present. He only wished that could make him feel less responsible, but it never did.

"Wait a second," Eric said softly. "You said you've been feeding off of deer?" His eyes changed, growing piercing, more wolflike. "We passed a whole herd lying dead near where the Ptolemy were killed. I didn't take a close look. Was that... was that you?"

"No, I—"

"You don't remember that either?" Ty asked, with what might have been concern. But Tasmin heard the voices begin to echo, twisting the words in his head until they were accusatory, threatening. He felt the darkness rising within himself, the senseless drive to maim and feed and kill. It took everything he had to push it back, and even then, the room seemed to shift beneath his feet. Ty and Eric seemed to loom over him, their eyes glowing menacingly.

"I—I don't—"

"I think you need to see that healer, Tasmin," Ty said. "Just calm down. We'll take care of this."

Tasmin stumbled backward, and Ty stepped forward, arms out... perhaps to help, perhaps to grab at him, trap him. Tasmin no longer knew. Ty's words echoed in his head.

Calm down…calm down…calm down…

"Don't touch me!" Tasmin roared, his voice utterly inhuman. Everything was too much, the light, the sound, the mere presence of other people. The desire to rip into them, to see their blood spray across the walls and floor while he sank his teeth into them, was so strong he was almost choking on it. He needed space, needed to be able to breathe, to make this go away.

Ty put up his hands, but he didn't back off. The look he shared with Eric said it all. They thought he was insane, dangerous.

Tasmin had a horrible feeling they were right.

He had to get out of here.

Eric watched him steadily with his wolf's eyes. "Take it easy. You're safe."

But he wasn't, and he knew it. He was never safe, not when he carried these awful impulses within himself. There was only one way he might find some relief. He needed the night air. He needed to shed this skin and run.

For all these months, letting the lion emerge had been his last refuge, the only way to keep from losing himself.

"You want me gone? *Fine*. With pleasure."

"Tasmin, wait," Ty began. But it was too late for that. Tasmin shoved through Eric and Ty, feeling a brief, welcome instant of relief that they let him go without a fight. He had the vaguest impression of Eric stepping after him, of Ty holding Eric back, but then there was only the blessed release of his body's shifting form, lengthening, stretching. The lion roared through him like fire as he picked up speed, springing into a run. He hit the top of the stairs on foot.

He hit the bottom on four massive paws.

Tasmin's perception changed, became simpler. His senses sharpened, and all of his pain and fury and fear receded just enough to focus on the single most important task at hand.

Getting out.

There was a startled yelp from someone who had spotted him. He ignored it, all his attention on the front door. It slammed open as though there was a strong wind, and Tasmin bounded through it, paws hitting the cold, hard ground outside. He rushed into the dark, into the cold night air that was far less brutal now that he wore his fur, hot breath rising as steam in the dark. All he wanted was to run until he dropped...until he could finally escape the one who had become his biggest enemy.

Himself.

Ty and Eric appeared in the open doorway, watching him vanish.

"I've got a bad feeling about this," Eric said.

Ty tracked the last, faint flash of golden fur before Tasmin rounded the corner, then shook his head. A lion's roar, one of the most anguished sounds Ty thought he had ever heard, echoed to the cold stars above.

"You're telling me."

chapter FIVE

Bay stood at the window, watching the snow begin to drift down from the sky in fat, lazy flakes, illuminated by the soft glow of the streetlights. She smiled and took a sip from the warm mug she held in both hands, savoring the taste of chocolate and cream as it hit her tongue. Hot cocoa had definitely been the right choice for tonight. In a couple of months, once the holidays had passed, she knew she'd groan at the sight of a single snowflake. But tonight, this first snowfall was magical.

Grimm sat beside her, gazing regally out onto his domain. Bay reached a hand down and stroked his head. There was nothing better than watching the snow inside a warm house with cocoa and a dog. She already had the fire going. Maybe she'd put on something classic, like Sinatra, and curl up on the couch. It should have been movie night, but Lily, not surprisingly, had canceled.

Bay tried not to hold it against her. Lily's new duties took a lot out of her, and last night had been...tough.

Their brief conversation earlier had been way too polite, doing a lousy job of covering up hurt feelings on both sides. It was so frustrating. Why couldn't they just *talk* anymore without all of this crazy vampire stuff getting in the way? Of course, it wasn't like Lily needed to lean on Bay as much, now that she had such a well-matched partner in Ty.

Bay frowned and took another sip of her cocoa. Yeah, she was a little jealous. She could admit it. Who wouldn't be? She kept waiting for a mortal version of Ty or Jaden or hell, even that mouthy assassin Damien to show up and do the whole "you complete me" routine. Instead, even the guys who should be a natural match for her, like the cute ghost hunter she'd gone out with a few times last year, turned out to be duds in some way.

He hadn't been living in his mom's basement, at least. But he hadn't made her heart race either.

A pair of big, intense golden eyes flickered through her thoughts, and she sighed, trying to think of some-thing else even as her treacherous heart skipped a beat. Wanting a knock-you-on-your-ass love affair was one thing. Willfully chasing after a leave-you-a-shattered-wreck-of-a-human affair was a path she didn't want to go down.

But he was at the mansion, getting his answers. Soon enough he'd blow town. Life would go on. Things would get back to normal, she told herself. Eventually.

Bay's mind drifted as she sipped the cocoa, and it took her a moment before realizing that Grimm had stiffened beside her, his ears perking. He gave a low, barely audible growl. Curious, Bay looked out onto the silent street. It was so late that she felt like she had the night to herself.

Nothing moved but the snow, drifting gently in a light breeze. She blinked. And then he was just...there.

Bay froze, and nearly dropped her mug.

Tasmin stood in her yard, shoulders hunched against the cold. And no wonder—he wore no jacket, no shoes. Just a T-shirt and jeans. He stared at her, the gold of his eyes so much brighter than the streetlights, and the look on his face was utterly lost.

She felt herself responding to it, opening to him, and gave a soft groan. She remembered every word Ty and Lily had said to her in private about the other day and how badly it could have ended. They were right. She knew it.

So why couldn't she just leave well enough alone?

Grimm whined beside her, getting to his feet and looking from the window to her. His tail thumped against the glass. It finally got her moving.

"Yeah, I'm going to go see what he wants," she said, barely managing to pull her eyes from Tasmin. It was only a few steps to the door, but part of her was certain that when she opened it he'd be gone, a hallucination... and she'd be better off for it. She had no business letting him back in. Not alone, at any rate.

And yet here they were again. With a resigned sigh, Bay turned the knob and opened the door.

The breeze was light, but bitter cold, and scented with snow. It rippled over the bare skin of her arms, right through her thin cami and flannel pants, making her shiver. She took a couple steps out onto the porch, wrapping her arms around herself, and looked to her right.

She let out a shaking breath, the steam from its warmth rising in front of her face when all she saw was the empty street, an empty yard. Maybe she really *had* imagined him. Maybe—

"Bailey."

She yelped and jumped at the soft caress of his voice, then spun. He was on the porch. *Behind* her. Looking every inch as miserable as he had through the window, which was the only thing that kept her from shouting at him. Instead, she pressed her hand to her chest, feeling her heart pounding beneath.

"Damn it, Tasmin, you scared me!"

To his credit, he actually managed to look sorry, dropping his head a little. His voice was perfectly clear in the biting air. "I didn't think you'd be awake."

She raised her eyebrows and wrapped her arms around herself, rubbing the bare skin to try and warm herself.

"If you thought I'd be sleeping, then why did you come?" Bay asked. She looked at him more closely then, and even in the dark she noted a couple of disturbing things: he looked very cold, and he was beginning to shiver. Small wonder, she guessed, considering how he was dressed. But she didn't think weather really affected vampires *this* much.

Apparently she'd been wrong.

For a moment he looked as though he might answer, but finally, he simply shrugged and said, "I was in the area."

Bay wasn't sure whether to laugh or beat her head against the wall. He knew why he was here. She suspected it was because he couldn't think of anyplace else he might be welcome. Not the most flattering reason for her, but it could have been worse. And he'd thought of her, which was sweet. And—

They stared at one another, and Bay felt her skin prickle with an awareness that had nothing to do with the cold. She felt pulled toward him in a way that was completely unfamiliar to her. She loved men and the sometimes dizzying attraction that went along with them. It was fun...and it never meant anything.

Everything about Tasmin felt deadly serious. Even the heat between them.

"You should come inside," Bay said. "It's cold out here."

Tasmin's surprise was obvious. It made her wonder even more why he'd come here, if he thought she'd just make him stand out here. Was he that used to rejection?

It bothered her to think that he might be.

"It probably isn't a good idea," he said.

"Yes, well, we established that last night," Bay replied. "Lucky for you, I don't listen very well. Just looking at you is going to make me freeze to death." She sighed, utterly flustered. "Just...come in."

He hesitated, then, to her shock, shivered so hard it nearly took him down. He was colder than she'd realized. Irritation at his stubbornness overrode any remaining doubt. She planted one hand on her hip and pointed at the door.

"Get. Inside. Now."

He snorted, his breath rising between them.

"You are a very bossy woman. I don't take orders."

"Then *decide* to move your feet in the direction of my door. Your free will at work. Problem solved. It's freezing."

He shivered again while he considered this, looking at her door like it was simultaneously the most wonderful and the most horrifying thing he'd ever seen. Bay began to seriously consider smacking him and then shoving him inside.

She stepped closer, hoping she was at least a tiny bit intimidating. Instead, Bay found her mouth dropping open when she got a better look at him. Tasmin's cinnamon skin, close up, was ashen, his lips faintly blue.

"How long have you been out here like this?"

He might be part lion, but his look was mulish. "A while."

She grabbed the bare skin of Tasmin's forearm, quietly alarmed at how icy it was, and pulled him inside. To his credit, he seemed to know it was time to relent. His shoulders slumped, and he couldn't suppress his groan of pleasure when the warm air enveloped him.

Bay shut the door, flipped the dead bolt, and turned around to see Grimm doing his I'm-so-happy-to-see-you dance, totally oblivious to the fact that the object of his affection was more than halfway to being a vampire Popsicle. She heard Tasmin's teeth begin to chatter as Grimm circled him, happily wrapping his big, bulky body around the man's legs and panting excitedly.

"Grimm, no," Bay said, stepping forward to try and deter him. "Come on, scoot. Let him be. He's not interested right now."

Grimm, true to form, completely ignored her.

"At least he's warm," Tasmin shivered out.

"You won't like it so much if he decides to lie on you," Bay said, pushing the dog out of the way with her hip and taking one of Tasmin's icy hands in hers. He didn't seem to be warming up at all.

"Did something—no, you know what, never mind. You need heat," Bay said, setting aside her interest in what had possessed him to be out in the cold like this tonight. That could wait.

"The fireplace is on," she said. "You remember the way."

It was a mark of how depleted he was that he didn't even bother to argue as she led him into the family room, tugging on his hand.

His bare feet were silent on the wood floors as she led him down the hall. She was very aware of his hand in hers, and of the fact that he made no attempt to pull away. The skin warmed against her own, but slowly. When they rounded the corner to her big, comfy furniture and the glowing fire, she let him go, though reluctantly.

"You know the drill," she said. "Get comfortable. I'll be right back."

"Where are you going?" he asked, and she couldn't decide whether the tone in his voice was suspicion or worry.

"Blankets," she explained. "You could use one or… five. I'll only be a minute. They're upstairs."

Relief, clear as day, softened the harsh set of his features. He nodded. "Then I will sit." From the way he crumpled onto the couch, Bay didn't think he'd really had much choice.

She left the room and hurried up the stairs. Grimm didn't follow, apparently more interested in showering their guest with affection. Typical. She felt a little bad about leaving Tasmin to deal with the slobber king, but he was right—at least the dog was warm.

She opened the linen closet at the end of the hall, pulled out a couple of thick, fleecy blankets she sometimes liked to curl up in, and then as an afterthought made a quick dash into her bedroom to grab something out of a drawer before heading back downstairs. When she reached the family room, Bay stopped short, eyes widening. It took her a few seconds to process what she was seeing.

Grimm, not content with whatever level of acknowledgement Tasmin had given him thus far, had piled onto the couch beside the shivering vampire and draped himself across Tasmin's lap. That, in and of itself, wasn't all that surprising. When Grimm decided he liked someone, he went all out. What had Bay's feet frozen to the floor was Tasmin's reaction. He had his arms wrapped around Grimm's massive bulk, and his face was half-buried in the thick fur of the dog's neck. Most of Tasmin's face was concealed, but she could see his eyes were closed, his full mouth softened from the tense way he usually held it.

He looked weary, vulnerable, and heart-wrenchingly gorgeous as he clung to the dog as though it was the only thing anchoring him here.

Bay drew in a soft, shaky breath, trying to get her bearings. Something about Tasmin seemed to hit every single one of her hot buttons. Seeing him hug her dog didn't just hit those buttons, it slammed a fist down on them.

Tasmin's eye opened to fix on her, and he sat up, looking embarrassed while he tried to disentangle himself. Grimm panted happily, keeping his one hundred and thirty pounds right where they were.

"He, ah, did this himself. I did tell him no," Tasmin said.

"He has selective hearing. It's okay," Bay replied, forcing her feet to move forward. She looked at Grimm. "Off."

The dog waited a moment to see whether she was serious. When she narrowed her eyes and pointed at the floor,

Grimm managed to get himself down, going only a couple of feet before letting his paws slide out from under him and flopping to the floor with a sigh. Tasmin watched the interplay, looking fascinated.

"That wasn't the reaction I got when *I* told him 'off.' "

"Because I meant it. You didn't. Besides, I'm scary," Bay said, shaking open the blankets. "Looking nonthreatening is part of what makes me dangerous. Here. You need these."

"I'll do it." Tasmin snatched the first blanket away in the blink of an eye and wrapped it around his shoulders, pulling it tight and huddling into the soft fleece.

"Better," he said, though his voice was muffled from being pressed against the edge of the blanket. Bay bit back an amused smile and draped the second blanket over his lap before he could snatch that one too. At that point, he finally saw what she held in her hand.

"Is that...socks?"

"You should have something on your feet," Bay explained. He was looking at her like she had grown an extra head. She looked down at the pair she'd grabbed and realized she'd pulled out a pair covered in a garish candy cane pattern.

"Oh." She pursed her lips, quietly exasperated that she hadn't looked at what she'd grabbed, and then shrugged.

"Tasmin, it's almost one in the morning. Your feet are probably colder than your hands. No one is going to see that you're wearing my socks."

"What is *on* them?" he asked.

"They're supposed to be festive," she started to explain, and then gave up immediately when she saw his face. "Look, I have an extensive collection of fuzzy

socks because my feet are always cold. They'll work."
She tossed them into his lap, cheeks flushing at the barest
thought of kneeling down in front of him to put the socks
on for him. That was a little much, despite the situation.

"Just put them on. You can thank me later."

He gave a soft snort, but surprised her by doing what
she asked. Still, he hid them almost immediately back
under the blanket draped across his lap, so she got only a
quick glimpse of his candy cane–clad feet.

"Better?" she asked.

He made a sound that could loosely be interpreted as
affirmative, which she guessed would have to do.

There was no sound but the soft rushing of the blower
from the fireplace, filling the room with warm air. Bay
looked between the big chair and the empty space on the
couch next to Tasmin, momentarily torn.

Oh, hell with it. It's my house.

She rounded the coffee table and settled herself on
the couch beside Tasmin, pulling her knees into her chest
and folding her hands on her knees, turning herself to
face him. He seemed to be very pointedly not looking at her.

"Well?"

A quick flicker of a glance. "Well what?"

She arched an eyebrow. "Warming up?"

"Yes." A pause. "Thank you."

After another minute passed in silence, Bay gave a
soft, exasperated sigh. "So would you like to tell me what
you were doing in my yard after midnight? Or should I
guess?"

This time when he looked at her, he held her gaze.
"That depends. What sort of thing would you guess?"

Bay considered, since he looked genuinely curious.

"I'd guess things aren't going well at Lily's?" Bay asked gently. She couldn't imagine what might have sent him running—Lily was hospitable to just about everyone. And Ty, for all his wariness, would never be tough on someone unfairly.

The reply was quick, curt. "It's none of your concern."

"Oh yes it is," she shot back at him, just as curt. "Those are my friends you've asked for help. They're the ones putting you up. I know Lily better than anyone, except maybe her husband. If there's something bothering you, I can probably give you some insight. And if someone got on your case, I can probably figure out what's behind it. For some stupid reason I want to help you out, Tasmin, but you don't make it easy."

Her words seemed to take him aback. It occurred to her that after all this time, he was probably unused to dealing with people. She knew so little about him...maybe he'd never been good at it. But he didn't need coddling from her. He needed help, and he needed honesty.

They *both* needed honesty.

Tasmin was looking at the floor, frowning. When he lifted his eyes to meet hers, Bay was surprised by the earnestness in his expression.

"I know," he said softly. "It's...difficult for me. I'm not sure how to act in this place. I'm sorry if I've offended you, Bailey. Tonight, or before. That wasn't my intent."

She felt her cheeks flush, and was suddenly glad the room was dark apart from the fireplace and one small lamp. Just when she thought she'd found her footing with Tasmin, he set her off balance again. When he wasn't grumbling like a wounded bear, he swung between rather sweet politeness and off-putting arrogance.

And she still didn't know what to do with him, though it wasn't a question she felt she should let herself ponder for extended periods of time for fear of what she might come up with.

She'd gotten thinking about it earlier today and only narrowly missed giving a poor Shih Tzu a bald spot.

"You haven't offended me," she finally said. "I'm just curious about you."

That bit of honesty had him tilting his head at her. The intense scrutiny only made her cheeks hotter.

"Why?"

"Well, because you're...different...than the other vamps running around here, I suppose." She shrugged. "And none of them have passed out in my shop."

His lips quirked. "They obviously don't know that they must let you rescue them to gain your interest, then."

Her laugh fluttered as nervously as her stomach. "Yeah, they'd definitely be all over that if they knew. Shampoo bottles everywhere. I'd be ruined."

Tasmin's smile was warm, and he shifted as he adjusted the blanket around his shoulders. This was what she'd sensed about him that Lily and Ty had refused to see. Beneath the intimidating veneer, Tasmin was still a man. And that man was wary, lost, and in need of a friend who saw more than his fangs and his mark.

Weird that it would be her.

"Feeling better yet?" Bay asked.

"I am," Tasmin replied, and a closer look revealed skin that had gone back to its normal color, and shivering that had almost completely subsided. She didn't think he was going to offer any further information—actually, she was getting used to it—so when Tasmin started speaking again it took Bay a moment to process what he was saying.

"I'm weaker than I should be in some ways," Tasmin said quietly, staring into the fire. "I'm not accustomed to the cold here, but still, it shouldn't do what it did. And I was in my animal skin for most of the time I was out. My fur should have protected me."

Bay's eyes widened. "You were running around Tipton as a lion?"

"It's late," Tasmin said, sounding a little defensive. "I needed to get out. Becoming a lion is usually the easiest way."

"I bet. As long as no one sees you." She tried to picture a full-grown lion running around Tipton in the middle of the night. It was an interesting image. She knew Rick Barrie, the Animal Control officer. Seeing something like that might have given him a heart attack.

"Tell me something, Bailey."

"Hmm?"

"Why are you so interested in my problems?"

It was a question she wasn't expecting, and definitely didn't know how to answer. He watched her steadily, his eyes far more catlike than usual. Strangely, that had stopped making her quite so nervous. Maybe it was the late hour. Maybe it was the socks. Either way, it was welcome.

"I don't know," Bay admitted. "You seem pretty alone. Someone ought to be interested in your problems."

"But *you* are not alone."

She laughed at the thought, shaking her head. "No. No, I basically have people up in my business whether I want them there or not." That was her life, dependable Bay, always around for fun and chatter. Part of her loved that. And part of her chafed at the monotony of it. Something was missing…something had always been missing. She just didn't know what.

Though up until now, she'd been pretty certain that more vampires weren't the answer to that question.

Tasmin smiled, a slow, sensual curving of his lips that further stoked what was already a slow burning desire for him.

"You ought to be afraid of me. But I admit, it's refreshing that you aren't."

She shrugged. "I haven't seen anything to be afraid of."

Tasmin's smile faded, worry returning to his features. "You probably will. I think…sometimes…I'm losing my mind."

The words chilled her to the bone. Bay tried not to show it, keeping her tone casual.

"You don't seem crazy."

"It isn't that. It's my memory. I left tonight because I was accused of doing something I don't remember doing. But…I think I might have done it."

His voice was hollow, and so devoid of any sort of hope that Bay was hard-pressed to feel anything but sympathy for him. Still, she didn't know what he'd done, or thought he might have done. She wondered if she would still want him on her couch once she found out. And from the look on his face, so did he.

"They think I killed a band of Ptolemy," he said.

"Oh," Bay said slowly. Whatever she'd been expecting to hear, that wasn't it. "Near here, I guess?" He nodded. Bay blew out a breath and tipped her head back to look at the ceiling. She didn't really know what to say about it. She hated the way things were.

"You don't look surprised," Tasmin said, sounding awfully surprised himself.

"I'm not," Bay said. "They wait out there and pick off any Lilim or Cait Sith they can get their hands on. The Ptolemy hate us. I mean, them. The Lilim," Bay said, flushing a little at her slipup. She wasn't a vampire, and she never would be. "Arsinöe is so powerful that she never gets more than a slap on the wrist for it. The Council here in the States is small, and she was pretty much running it before Lily showed up. Now it's barely functioning...at least, that's how Lily and Ty feel about it."

"That explains why they weren't angrier about the deaths," Tasmin said. "They were more concerned about Arsinöe using it as an excuse to do more in retaliation." He gave a soft, feline growl and shook his head. "I don't understand any of this. The Lilim were a great power, Lilith the mother of the dynasties. I expected to find an empire in the making, not...this."

Bay bristled on her friend's behalf. "Give her time. She's only been a vampire for a little over a year. They've come a long way."

His sigh was gusty. "I suppose. Nothing is as it was. The great powers are all here: Lilim, Ptolemy, Empusae, Grigori...and these Dracul of whom I have no memory. And yet all I heard whispers of on my way here was disarray. That the Empusa herself barely lives, that the Grigori unleashed a monster that nearly unmade them. Rumors. I found no truth. I hoped to find it here."

Bay shifted uncomfortably. "You're going to want to ask Lily about all of that." She didn't know all of it. Not even close. But she knew enough to recognize that there was probably a lot more truth in the rumors Tasmin had heard than he would have liked.

"So did they throw you out, or did you leave?" Bay asked, trying to turn the topic back to something she was more comfortable discussing. "The Lilim tangle with the Ptolemy on a pretty regular basis."

"I left," Tasmin admitted. "They don't want me there any more than I really want to be there anyway."

"That's not true." The words were automatic, and she realized immediately that she was the one who sounded deluded. Lily hadn't been excited about the added burden, Ty had been unhappy...and Tasmin wanted to be anywhere but here. He was right.

He looked at her the way he might a foolish child. "You know better, I think. But nothing changes the fact that they're my only choice if I want answers." He inhaled deeply, looking resigned. "I should go."

"Back to the mansion?"

"No. Not tonight. I don't want any more questions tonight. Tomorrow is soon enough."

Bay waited for clarification, but of course, none was forthcoming. "Where do you plan on staying, since you were half-frozen not too long ago? It isn't getting any warmer out there."

His shoulders slumped as he gave the matter actual thought. "Oh," he said. Then, more vehemently, "I hate your weather."

"Just be glad it's November and not January." Bay sighed softly, seeing that Tasmin had arrived at the same conclusion she had. It was the mansion or here. And he really didn't seem keen on the mansion.

"You've done enough," Tasmin said. And just like that, he was back to grumbling. At least *that* was familiar.

Bay stood, fatigue settling on her quickly and easily like a well-worn coat. It was late. She was sleepy. And so, from the looks of him, was the vampire on her couch. That was about enough for her for the night. She needed to hide in sleep for a while before whatever craziness awaited her tomorrow.

She didn't even want to speculate.

"Just flip the switch to turn off the fireplace when you're warm enough," she said, pressing her hands against the small of her back and arching a little. She didn't think about what the position did to display her ample cleavage until she saw Tasmin's eyes drift, somewhat dreamily, in that direction. Bay straightened immediately, her cheeks burning.

"Stay as long as you like," Bay said. "I don't work in the morning, so if you're here then, you're welcome to breakfast or...whatever. Lily left a plastic drink container full of I don't want to know what in the freezer last time she was here." She shrugged. "Up to you. Get some sleep, huh? You look like you need it."

Tasmin looked uncomfortable, but he didn't argue. He knew when he was out of feasible options.

"Again, I find myself in your debt," he said, looking distinctly unhappy about it.

"Well, I'm mortal, so the debt isn't forever," Bay said with a smile. "That should be comforting, right? Good night, Tasmin."

He watched her with his strange, burning eyes. "Good night, Bailey."

Bay turned and left the room, Grimm moving as fast as

he ever did to get to his feet and accompany her upstairs. The family room was quiet as she headed up, and she wondered whether he would sleep, even though he looked like he needed to.

A lonely, misunderstood vampire who slept at night and walked in the sun. He was, without a doubt, the strangest man she'd ever met... and at this point, that was saying something.

chapter SIX

WHILE TASMIN SLEPT, another wakened.

The beast wakened in the darkest hours of night, surfacing when this body's owner was slumbering and least able to resist. It stretched languorously, enjoying the feel of taut flesh and muscle at its command. It liked the wearing of solid flesh, so well it was surprising. It had been ages since it had manifested as anything like a human. One would think it would be distasteful. And yet...no. This one was strong.

Most would have died long before now. Its host had been chosen well.

The beast got to its feet, looking around. When Tasmin was alert, it was harder to see, a struggle to stay aware of what was going on around him. Only occasionally, when something piqued its interest, did it bother with the effort to shove Tasmin's wakened soul aside and take over.

Meeting the mortal woman had been such an occasion. For them both, it seemed, since Tasmin had never put up such a fight to stay in control. The mind had simply shut down in self-defense for a time. Then they had come here, to the woman's home...and it seemed Tasmin had returned.

It smiled, and he felt the corners of Tasmin's mouth turn up. Yes, it liked this body, if it had to have one. It made pleasure so much more...tangible.

Silently, it padded through the house, examining the trappings of the woman's life. *Bailey.* He drank the word from the slumbering consciousness at the center of this body. Yes, that was her name. This place smelled of her, a warm, *alive* smell, with hints of cinnamon and vanilla. So fitting, for such a delectable treat. She fascinated it. Tasmin wanted her sexually, a waste. The beast wanted to make far better use of her. Bailey would be its pet, its pupil in the art of pain. It imagined taking her blood in teasing little sips, making her watch while it sated its hunger for blood and destruction with others. Her screams, her fear would be divine. Was that the attraction? That she didn't fear it? Yes, the beast thought it was. So it would teach her what fear was. Tenderly. Thoroughly.

But not yet. Not quite yet. Tonight, only a taste.

The beast ran Tasmin's hands over fabric, enjoying the different textures beneath his fingers. It looked at pictures under glass, picked up and put down trinkets, interested in these scattered trappings of mortal life. Not for long, though. The thirst that drove it pulsed through Tasmin's veins in time with his heart, never quite sated, always searching for more.

But then, hunger was its purpose, and it hungered for many things.

It ran Tasmin's tongue over his teeth, feeling the fangs

so suited to ripping and tearing. Need warred with reason. It didn't want to hunt more of what it had been forced to subsist on: deer and raccoon, rabbit and fox, with nary a mortal to break the tedium. The Ptolemy had been an amusing diversion, meeting its need for bloodshed, but to drink from them would have robbed this body of its singularity. It did not need Ptolemy blood in these veins.

Rakshasa blood was stronger, so that is what it would stay. For now. Until it could be free once again. One day soon, it would find the woman who had done this to it, binding it to this flesh creature, body and soul. It would get Arsinöe alone, and it would make her pay. But first, she would unbind it. It would make sure of that. Did she truly think it powerless just because she had linked its survival to this vampire's beating heart? It had ways to make her pay, make her scream until she set it free. Could another do it? Unlikely, but...perhaps. And yet it had to be Arsinöe. She would never dare try to destroy it in the vulnerable seconds as it finally emerged. It knew the rite she would use, had seen it done. If only it could manage the ritual itself...but this body did not hold the knowledge of the darkest magics. No, it needed *her*, by design. And she wanted...something.

Why had she done this, dragging it out of the blissful darkness and entombing it within a living body? It had its suspicions. And if they were correct, the Ptolemy queen's punishment would be all the more brutal...and all the sweeter.

She had no idea what she was dealing with.

All Hunger needed was a little more time. A little more control over this strong, stubborn Rakshasa. Sometimes it wished killing Tasmin outright was an option. Operating a corpse would have been less trouble. But then, there were upsides to being forced to share space.

Such keen senses to enjoy. Such power.

So many ways to kill.

The runner on the stairs was soft beneath Tasmin's feet, a fascinating change from the cool hardwood floor. Hunger took the steps one at a time, making no sound. It had grown expert at operating this body to its fullest potential when it had control. It passed dark and silent rooms, heading for the door that was cracked open at the end of the hall.

Another scent stopped it. It curled Tasmin's lip.

Dog.

Something would need to be done about that.

It closed Tasmin's eyes, pulling the needed magic from the recesses of memory. Tasmin's body reacted without any instruction, so ingrained was this ability. Power rippled down his arms, through his torso, all to pool as a ball of pale golden light in his cupped hands. It opened Tasmin's eyes to study it, still thrilling at having such a power to use whenever it wished. Then, with a simple push of the mind, the ball of light shot from Tasmin's hands and into the sliver of darkness that was the room beyond. There was a flash of light, and then . . . nothing.

Both dog and woman should now be caught deep in dreams, thralled in sleep and unable to waken until it was ready to allow it.

Unconcerned now, it padded the rest of the way down the hall and opened the door.

Even in darkness, Tasmin's eyesight was crystal clear. At the foot of a massive bed sprawled the dog, a big black thing that foolishly thought it could guard its mistress.

Hunger spared the dog only a passing glance, uninterested in its dreams of vapid dog things. No, the true interest lay curled in a tangle of blankets and sheets, breathing softly.

It moved silently to the edge of the bed and looked down.

Her head was the only part of her body that was visible, the rest concealed by a mound of covers. A swift wave of the hand, and the coverings departed to reveal the slim, curvaceous form that so preoccupied Tasmin's waking thoughts. She was curled into herself, knees up, hands tucked against her chest. Her breaths were slow and even, lips slightly parted.

Lovely.

Tasmin's tongue flickered out to lick his lips. Hunger already imagined how she would taste, sweet and rich as cream. How much to take tonight? How weak would it leave her? It reached out one of Tasmin's hands, trailed a finger down the warm, silken skin of her arm. To its surprise, she stirred with a soft little moan.

Curious, it sank down to sit on the bed beside her. Even in the deep, unnatural sleep, she sensed him. It. *Them.* But how?

Again, it pulled from Tasmin's reserves of strength and power, then reached out and dipped into Bailey's thoughts. A different sort of tasting, but satisfying in its own way. Mortals were foolish, dreaming of things they could not have and would never do. Such fruitless longing had a flavor all its own.

It lifted Tasmin's hand again, stroked the back of it down Bailey's cheek as images began to swim in its head. It closed its eyes, and for a brief moment was lost in the sensation of what she was experiencing. There was a warm night breeze, redolent with earth and life. Soft grass. Bodies entangled, so soft, so hot...

When it was yanked out of the fantasy with a painful jerk, it gave a rough cry. The body was thrown backward by some unseen force, and Tasmin ended up sprawled on the floor beside the bed.

"Get...out...of my...*head*!"

Tasmin's voice, under Tasmin's control. The Rakshasa was awake and furious at once, forcing Hunger back into the dark nest it had made deep in Tasmin's chest. Caught badly off guard, Hunger barely put up a fight. *Impossible!* The word was a silent scream as it was pushed back. Whenever Tasmin began to struggle for awareness, it was never like this, never all at once. *How?* It would have to consider this while it lay curled up to wait again, unsatisfied. *Hungry.*

And then there was only Tasmin, shaking on the floor of Bailey's bedroom, clutching his head, barely able to draw in a full breath. His eyes darted around the room as panic threatened to overwhelm him. His vision blurred and doubled, and exhaustion swamped him almost as suddenly as he'd regained awareness. He felt foul, violated, as though someone or something had been using him carelessly without his knowledge or permission.

Just as Shakti had warned him. The healer had been so sure about the demon.

And Tasmin had been so determined not to believe him.

He couldn't fight the truth any longer. He'd heard the demon screaming as he'd overtaken it, shoving it back into whatever dark recess it had carved out for itself inside of him. But...how had he done that? Before, it had always been like waking up from a long sleep, groggy and confused.

This time, his awareness had returned almost violently, and all at once. The demon hadn't been expecting it, he felt that strongly. It had been engrossed in . . . in such sweet dreams.

All at once, it registered where he was.

The demon had brought him to Bailey's bedroom. Somehow, spying on her dreams had triggered what had happened. He didn't understand. Not anything, right now. All Tasmin knew was that he had never felt so fiercely protective in his life.

Or so afraid.

Tasmin tried to rise to his feet and could not. His legs simply wouldn't hold him. Bailey and Grimm were silent and still—too much so. The demon again, but his own power. Tasmin cringed. This *thing* had made a mockery of the code he had always tried to hold himself to.

He managed to grip the edge of the bed and pull himself up to look at her.

Please be all right, Bailey. Please.

Relief flooded him as soon as he could see her face, and his legs threatened to go out from under him again. He hadn't touched her, hadn't hurt her. Her slow, even breaths sounded like music, and beneath them, Tasmin savored the lower register of Grimm's gentle snores.

He had made it stop. Somehow, this one time, he had made it stop. But his victory had come at a price. The body he'd just won back seemed to be reacting poorly to the quick change.

Maybe he would die this time, Tasmin thought. Maybe he would close his eyes and it would end. The room began to fade, his vision swimming. He wanted only one thing in that moment: comfort.

He had taken so much already. Could it hurt that badly to take just a bit more if it caused no harm?

Before he could think better of it and just collapse on the floor, Tasmin managed to haul himself onto the bed, dragging himself to lay alongside Bailey's warmth. He didn't touch her, only basked in her nearness as he sank into the softness of the mattress. He was so wretchedly tired. Tasmin fixed his hazy vision on the golden tumble of her curls spread over the pillow and wished this were a different time, a different place—that he were the sort of man who would have been invited into this bed.

Then his thoughts scattered as his body gave up for the night, drained by something he could neither see nor control. Tasmin's body relaxed, giving itself over to the dark bliss of unconsciousness.

And beside him, Bailey dreamed on.

chapter SEVEN

THE POUNDING ON THE DOOR woke her up.

Bay surfaced slowly from sleep to a strange thudding sound coming from downstairs. Her eyes took a few seconds to open. They felt glued shut, and she was as groggy as she might have been if she'd been up all night. The muffled voice was what finally got her moving.

"Bay? You in there?"

It was Shelby's voice, and the fear in it was unmistakable. As quickly as she could, Bay threw off the covers and swung her legs off the side of the bed, stumbling a little as she got to her feet. Her body felt lethargic, almost *too* well rested. Still, she managed to propel herself forward, shoving her hair out of her face as she passed a yawning Grimm.

What the hell time was it anyway?

A glance over her shoulder at the little alarm clock on her nightstand displayed a time that woke her as effectively as a cold glass of water over the head. Two in the afternoon?

Seriously?

"Bay? If you don't open up, I'm calling the cops, I mean it!"

Shelby didn't just sound scared, she sounded terrified. And Bay couldn't blame her, considering Lily's "abduction" had been big news last fall.

"Coming," Bay called, trying to sound reassuring. Instead, she sounded like her voice had been dragged through mud and gravel. She cleared her throat and tried it again, more successfully this time. That finally made the door pounding stop.

Bay got down the stairs quickly enough and cast a suspicious glance toward the family room. There was no sound, not a hint of movement. It only took her a second to figure out Tasmin was gone.

And after that, it took her no time at all to figure out why she and Grimm had slept all day.

"Bastard," she muttered. He'd seemed so sweet and lost last night. It was probably a good thing he'd now reminded her of one of the prime reasons she had a hard time trusting vampires. No matter how good they might appear, none of them seemed to be able to help messing with people's heads, and it sounded like that was his *special* area.

She flipped the dead bolt and opened the door partway, knowing she must look like a *Walking Dead* extra. Shelby's horrified expression only confirmed that.

"Bay. Oh my God, are you okay?"

"Um. Yes?" Bay shoved her curls out of her face again and tried to determine whether she was, in fact, okay. Her brain simply refused to kick in enough for her to figure it out. The only thing she was sure of was that she was going to kick Tasmin's ass if she ever saw him again.

"Whassamatter?" Bay asked, and then licked her lips, trying again *without* the mush mouth. "What's the matter, Shelby?"

"You were supposed to be in at noon. You're never late. And you never just don't show up, so we thought... well..." Shelby shuffled her feet nervously. "I called a bunch of times. Didn't you hear the phone?"

Phone. How the hell had she missed that? And her appointments. Yes, she did have a job. She smushed her hand into her face and groaned.

Bay could no longer see Shelby, or much of anything as long as she was rubbing her face, but the girl still sounded like she thought there might be a serial killer somewhere in the house.

"Are you sure you're okay? You look kind of, um..."

"I know I look like roadkill. You can say it."

Shelby laughed nervously. "Okay. A little."

Bay sighed and let her hand drop, looking into Shelby's concerned brown eyes. "Anna's there, right?"

Anna LaBounty was the other groomer she'd hired about six months ago, and she usually took Saturday mornings. Which would have been fine up until about two hours ago.

Shelby nodded.

"How backed up is it?" Then Bay shook her head. "No, don't tell me. This sucks. And I'm sure Anna is trying to do everything herself. I'll be there in ten minutes. Ten. I swear."

"Are you sure? Are you getting sick? Because we can always—"

"I'm not sick," Bay said, and a little too sharply if Shelby's flinch was any indication. Feeling like a jerk, Bay softened her tone immediately.

"I'm not sick," she repeated gently. "I overslept. I don't know how. Maybe it's a thyroid thing or something. I'll get it checked out, okay? But I'm fine, and I'll be there shortly. Tell Anna to put away the hatchet. I'll stay late."

"There's no hatchet," Shelby said, then cracked a lopsided smile. "At least, there wasn't when she thought you were dead. I'll tell her." The smile faded quickly. "You probably should see a doctor, though. You really look rough."

Bay wrinkled her nose. "Thanks," she said, knowing Shelby's heart was in the right place even if her mouth often had a tough time conveying that. "I'll set something up, okay? Now go. You're all kinds of awesome for making sure I'm alive, and I owe you for waking me up... though I don't even want to think about who's answering the phone while you're gone."

Shelby's sheepish grin did nothing for Bay's confidence, but she waved as the girl scampered off her porch. The second Shelby was out of sight, Bay shut the door and dashed upstairs, passing Grimm, who was plodding down at his usual slow pace and no doubt expecting breakfast.

"Sorry boy," Bay told him as she passed. "You're eating at the shop today. Our day is officially shot. Prepare yourself."

She sprinted into her room to throw on some clothes and twist her hair up, silently cursing Tasmin the entire time. She took him in—twice—and what she got for her trouble was some kind of knockout magic so he could sneak out of the house without having to talk to her. Nice.

She brushed her teeth, splashed water on her face, and ran back downstairs. Grimm waited for her at the bottom, giving her some serious stink eye. He wasn't stupid. He knew he wasn't getting his scrambled egg on top of his breakfast today, and she had no doubt he'd make her pay at some point. He might move slowly, but the bulk hid a devious mind.

Bay grabbed her purse, got Grimm onto his leash, and headed toward the kitchen to go out through the garage. She stopped, though, when she saw the place where Tasmin had spent at least part of the night. Slowly, she walked over to the couch, where her eyes settled on the neatly folded stack of blankets. And no socks. He'd stolen her damned socks.

She started to reach for the top blanket, stopped, and then glared down at Grimm. He looked back up at her, with a look that plainly said he thought she'd lost her mind.

"Oh, give me a break," she muttered, snatching up the blanket anyway. "It's not like I'd do this to *him*." That was a lie, but no one needed to know that except her and her dog, who was likely to forget all about this once she dumped some kibble in his bowl at work. Comforted, she stuffed her face into the soft fleece and breathed in. Immediately, she was awash in the warm scents of sandalwood and spice.

Bay rubbed her cheeks against the fabric like a cat until she realized what she was doing. Then, embarrassed at herself, she cleared her throat and fixed the blanket before depositing it back on top of the other one. A quick look around revealed no other signs that Tasmin had ever been here.

Just as well, she told herself.

"Come on, boy," Bay said quietly, eyes lingering on the spot where Tasmin had lain, allowing herself to imagine, just for a moment, him curled there asleep. It wasn't any worse than what she knew she'd spent a lot of her night doing, which was imagining him spooning her, curved against the back of her with one hand draped over her hip, his breath feathering the back of her neck.

She shook her head to clear it, then headed for the door, an irritated Grimm sauntering along beside her. Living some kind of dark fairy tale wasn't in the cards for her, and that was fine.

It was time to start her day.

Tasmin was waiting in Lily's office when the sun went down.

He heard the house begin to waken, the voices as the few Lilim staying here began the night. Tasmin stayed silent, still puzzling at the way Lily ran her court. It wasn't actually much of a court. No pomp, no pretension, no obnoxious hangers-on. Just Lily and Ty, Lilim who seemed to lead their own lives and were in and out, and the wolves who acted as guard.

In some ways, they were like his kind, or at least, the better prides among his kind. That had been their strength, and their weakness, in the end.

It worried him.

About a half hour after dusk, Lily glided into the room, all beauty and competence. There was a brief metallic tang in his mouth when he saw her, like biting on a knife's blade, but it vanished almost as quickly as it had come. It seemed to take her aback when she noticed him sitting in one of the comfortable leather chairs facing her desk.

To her credit, she collected herself quickly.

"Tasmin," she said. "No one let me know you'd come back."

"I let myself in," he said, seeing no reason to elaborate. Werewolves' minds were easy to distract, especially in animal form when their instincts were strong. He'd sent a number of them off to chase irresistible, imaginary rabbits. The illusion was far simpler than an explanation, and he had no interest in dealing with the suspicious Eric Black again.

He had come to this place to see Lily. There was no reason to wait for an audience when he could obtain one himself so easily.

"I see," Lily said slowly. "Don't take this the wrong way, but that actually freaks me out a little."

Her honesty, and the fact that she didn't immediately try to blast him with the power she carried, eased some of the anxiety he'd felt about coming back here. Like so many things, he'd been torn over it. Part of him wanted desperately to run, to keep searching for *something* he couldn't quite put his finger on. The stronger part wanted to stay and find the answers he'd come seeking.

It seemed he had made the right choice. For now.

"It isn't my intention to scare you," Tasmin said, hoping to set her at ease. "My reaction to being questioned last night was...poor. I'm still unused to the way things are, the way *people* are. My reactions to things aren't always rational. But I hope you will accept my apology."

She seemed taken aback, but not in a bad way. Like Bailey, this woman responded best to honesty. It would serve him well to remember that. These were both good, strong women...though the one would never be strong enough to assuage his fear of getting too close. And it had been so hard to leave her bed.

"Of course," Lily finally said, pulling him back to the

present with her acceptance of his apology. She watched him curiously for a moment. "Where have you *been* this last six months since you woke up, Tasmin?"

He hesitated, knowing the truth here was ill-advised. His memories of much up until the last month were scattered, at best. He had vague memories of wandering ruins in the darkness, hunting for things that were not there. In his lucid moments he had sought out other vampires, and a string of useless healers. And finally, he had heard of the rebirth of the mother dynasty, and had known this was his only hope of putting some of the shattered pieces of his existence back together.

Out loud, he said, "I was in India, then Europe. I knew I needed answers, but it had been so long… It took time for me to sort out the questions. And there have been so many changes to get used to."

Her eyes were soft and luminous. Compassionate.

Weak. The voice hissed through his mind unbidden, making him tense up.

"I can't even imagine," Lily said with what sounded like genuine sympathy. "But if you want to be here, you have to remember we're not your enemies. Ty and Eric went to you because they wanted to know exactly what had happened. I really doubt that the Ptolemy you encountered were up to anything good. My concern is about provoking a larger incident when we can't afford it." A faint frown creased her forehead as she sat down at the desk and looked away, folding her hands in front of her. "I'd also rather no one else have to die in these stupid skirmishes. I'm tired of losing good people. I would think Arsinöe would be too."

Tasmin tilted his head, surprised at such a human

sentiment. But then, he had to keep reminding himself...
she was young.

"No. You already know she doesn't think of people as
much more than pawns. I think some vampires live too
long. She's forgotten everything about being human."

Lily's smile was rueful. "Sometimes I wonder if she
ever knew *much* about that. Regardless, I do need your
word that you'll keep it low-key while you're here. She
was furious enough to call me and scream personally
last night, which says a lot." Her smile vanished. "I also
hear she's been entertaining members of foreign courts.
Which, I am told, is not a great sign."

"If she's decided to destroy you, your highness, she'll
try," Tasmin said. "I doubt she'll give up until one of you
is dead. She never negotiated, only conquered."

She nodded. "I'm pretty sure you're right. But I'd like
to prolong that particular confrontation for as long as I
can. That might be harder if you don't even remember
who you're attacking."

Tasmin's throat tightened, and he began to flex his
fists rhythmically in his lap. Of course Ty had told her.
He'd been a fool for not finding a way around it last night.
Another lie sprang to his lips, so quickly it startled him...
He would just tell her he did remember, that being con-
fronted by her wolf had intimidated him...

He choked back the words, disgusted. Why would
he even think to say such things? He straightened in his
chair, and the fact that he could catch the insipid words
before they came out of his mouth bolstered him.

The demon couldn't force him to snivel and cower.
Not yet.

"It's true," Tasmin said. "Since I awakened, I've had

brief blackouts like this. None violent, until now...I can only think I was attacked."

Lily looked troubled, but sympathetic. That, too, was a relief.

"And the fact that you apparently drained an entire herd of deer?"

"Again, I don't remember that. Not much, at least. But my energy flags much faster than it ought to, even now. Considering how many Ptolemy I fought..." He trailed off, shrugged. It was an easy, obvious conclusion. He'd been exhausted. He'd taken what was available. A *lot* of what was available. The guilt gnawed at him. A part of him was brother to the beasts of the forest, whether here or in India. In taking the herd down, he'd abused the balance that was meant to exist between them. He couldn't have needed all of them.

But there was a greed inside of him now that was breathtaking.

"Okay," Lily said, nodding. "Well, I've changed my mind about the healer. If you stay here, you see her. Whether this is a side effect of what happened to you or not, we need to know. My blood comes first."

It took all of his willpower to swallow the sharp retort that welled in his throat. "Of course, your highness," he said, knowing he sounded stiff. It was the best he could manage. No one could know about the other healers he'd seen. Or what a failure they'd been.

"You don't have to like it, Tasmin, or pretend to. You won't change my mind on this, though I don't care if you argue with me. And I'd *really* rather be called Lily instead of *your highness*."

"You're asking me to argue?" He didn't understand

anyone in this place. All of the traditional roles had been upended. The queen wanted to be a commoner, the mortal tended to the vampire... it was bizarre. Even in his small pride, Tasmin had understood his place. As one of the junior males, he'd known to follow, not lead. Certain things had been expected of him.

He had no idea what was expected of him here apart from not getting the dynasty destroyed. Perhaps that was enough to work with for now, but the lack of structure left him unsettled.

"Just do what you're comfortable with, Tasmin. I'm just telling you it's okay not to be quite so formal." Lily smiled, and it was a bit weary despite her beauty. He wondered just how many problems he'd caused her because of his unremembered encounter with the Ptolemy. And then her minor confrontation with Bailey over him. He carried trouble with him everywhere, it seemed.

He gave a curt nod. "I understand, your h—Lily."

The effort made her smile again, and this time it was genuine. She really was a beauty, Tasmin thought. Strange that it left him so unaffected. Bay was the only one who'd pierced his armor at all, and it had to do with much more than her looks... though he certainly enjoyed looking at her too.

His smile faded when he remembered his promise to himself. After last night, that was done. It had to be, for both their sakes.

He would not hurt her.

"A friend of mine will be arriving on Monday," Lily said. "She's someone I think you'll want to meet."

He drew in a breath. "She has the answers I'm looking for," he said quietly.

"Some anyway," Lily replied. "I'm not sure how many, since I couldn't tell her much over the phone. She needed some time to digest that you even exist. It's kind of a... difficult subject for her."

Tasmin tilted his head at her, puzzled. Lily simply shook her head.

"It's probably best if Anura herself tells you. I only know a little. She doesn't like to talk about what happened."

"Anura," Tasmin repeated. The name was vaguely familiar, but he couldn't place it.

"She was one of the Empusae," Lily said. "She was mated to a Rakshasa, but like I said... I'll let her tell you."

Dozens of other questions immediately popped into his mind, but Tasmin held his tongue. He had waited for plenty of things. He could wait two more days for this mysterious woman and whatever information she possessed. It was a relief, in so many ways... there would be far less time to get into real trouble here than he'd feared. Once he had enough information, he'd move on.

All things considered, that was his only option. Maybe it would be no matter where he went, if the demon that plagued him couldn't be removed. The thought of living alone, with neither a pride nor a dynasty, left a dull ache deep in his chest.

Maybe then he might find the courage to end it. But not yet. Not until every shred of hope was gone.

"Thank you for this," Tasmin said, and meant it. "I'm well aware it would be easier for you to simply run me off."

Lily arched one auburn brow. "Not really. I'm nice, Tasmin, but I'm not stupid. You know you'd be a potent weapon in the wrong hands."

He did know. But he didn't have any intention of letting

that happen. "I would die first," Tasmin said, and the words seemed to hang in the air, full of dark promise. He felt a cold spike of fear in the dark place in the center of himself . . . then nothing.

"Well," Lily said, her voice gentler, "I don't want to see that happen either. You're the only one of your dynasty left, as far as we know. I think it would help us all to know what happened. Maybe we can prevent it from happening again."

He heard what she didn't say, that perhaps she could prevent it from happening to her own kind.

"I'll prevent it by avenging my fallen brothers," Tasmin said, his voice dropping to a near growl.

"But not now," Lily said. "And not here."

He gave a stiff nod, though he didn't mean any agreement. He would do what he needed to once he discovered what had happened to his people, to him . . . and how to undo the latter. There had to be a way to make him whole again. He would do whatever it took to learn how to do that.

Tasmin stood. "I'll take my leave."

Lily smirked. "Always so formal. All right, Tasmin. Just . . . be careful when you're out and about. You're a little more noticeable than most of the vamps we have here. I'll let you know when Kira can look at you."

His jaw tightened as he walked away, though he knew the anger was as irrational as it always was. He would see the healer, she would find nothing . . . and in two days, he would begin to piece together all that was missing from his past. He could wait two days.

In the meantime, he would go out—properly dressed this time—and explore this little town. Maybe he could even try to enjoy it, something that had grown utterly alien to him since he'd awakened. Tonight, though, he would be avoiding going anywhere near Bailey's street, her shop...anything that smelled of her. It was time to start focusing on what was really important. Knowledge, for one. Vengeance, for another. She couldn't be important to him, because he had no room for someone like her in his life.

It was too dangerous, for both of them.

chapter EIGHT

SHE WAS SUPPOSED to be ghost hunting, not lion hunting.

"Did you hear that?" Beside her, Alex's voice was breathless, as excited as a seven-year-old with a new toy. Most seven-year-olds didn't carry around digital recorders and EMF detectors, though.

"I heard...something," Bay murmured, trying to sound at least mildly interested in whatever bump or whisper Alex thought he'd picked up. Her attention, however, was focused on the large, dark shape she'd just seen slink past the window of the old, abandoned farmhouse they were investigating. The beam from Alex's flashlight had caught it, but he'd panned the light so quickly she couldn't be sure.

She could almost convince herself that it was one of the Lilim just screwing with her—they'd certainly done it before. But...that shape had been big. Really big. And really feline.

Maybe her overtaxed mind had invented it. Still, she

hoped nobody went outside for a pee break. They might get a lot more than they'd bargained for.

"Um, I'm going to…uh…I need some air for a minute," Bay whispered. "Be right back."

Alex, true to form, waved her off while he pressed the digital recorder to his ear, playing back whatever noise he'd thought he heard. Bay rolled her eyes and slipped away from him, trying to tread lightly on the creaky old floors so that she didn't bring any of the other members of the Bonner County Paranormal Society running. A couple people were in what had been the kitchen, a couple in the cellar, and three were taking their chances with the questionable floors upstairs. The place was trashed, and famously haunted. At least, according to the local teens who'd left all these beer cans and empty plastic liquor bottles in here.

And…other things. Bay wrinkled her nose at a wadded-up pair of underwear and slipped out the door. She'd been hoping for some distraction tonight, since yesterday had been beyond frustrating. Not only had she wound up at the shop until eight last night thanks to Tasmin's little sleeping trick, but Moses, one of the Saint Bernards she groomed, had slimed her so thoroughly that her scrubs had been stiff with dried drool when she got home.

Grimm might have a wet mouth, but only when he was nervous or hungry. It didn't run like a faucet.

Regardless, tonight had been a bust as BCPS excursions went. This place was dead, and not in an interesting way. Alex, however, was as amped up as he always was. They'd gone out a couple of times last year—he was actually the reason she'd joined—but ultimately, she couldn't date a guy who was the human equivalent of a golden retriever. He seemed to be holding out hope she'd come around. Just like she was hoping he'd eventually forget about it.

He not only acted like a golden, he kissed like one. It wasn't pretty.

Bay breathed deeply as she stepped out into the cold. The dusting of snow from a couple nights ago had melted, but more was in the forecast, and the air smelled of it. The night sky was a spray of stars, made even brighter by the fact that this house sat in the middle of a field. The cars were all out by the road—they'd hiked their equipment out here, where it was pitch-dark but for the sliver of moon.

"Cheshire cat moon," Bay murmured, tipping her head back to smile back at the silvery grin. She loved nights like this. Well, minus the BCPS cluster going on in the house. And the vampire lion skulking around somewhere nearby.

She pressed her lips together and started to make her way around the outside of the house, trying to be as quiet as possible. It wasn't easy. Her boots crackled through dead weeds, and she managed to trip a few times over rocks she couldn't see. Bay peered around in the dark, hoping for one of two things: that she'd been wrong, or that whoever was out here playing would present himself quickly.

Neither happened.

Bay sighed irritably and stuffed her gloved hands further into the pockets of her ski jacket. At least she'd remembered to wear a hat this time. It was *cold*.

She worked her way around the perimeter of the house, the night so quiet and still she could hear the whispers and giggles of the people inside very clearly. Nothing around her moved, but as she walked, she couldn't shake the growing sensation that there were eyes on her. It started slowly, then intensified. Her breathing quickened, her heart rate picking up.

This is stupid, she told herself. Anyone who would be out here wouldn't be dangerous.

A twig snapped off to her left, and she jerked her head in the direction. That was when she caught it: the faint smell of sandalwood. Her eyes narrowed immediately. It was Tasmin. And if he thought that creeping her out was entertaining, he had another thing coming.

"Tasmin," she hissed, "I know it's you. Get out where I can see you; this isn't funny!"

There was nothing but silence. Then, out of the pitch dark, a pair of bright golden eyes materialized, followed by the shape of an animal she'd only ever seen in pictures and film. Bay's breath stilled in her chest as she watched him come, padding slowly through the dead tall grass and into the trampled-down circle that surrounded the house itself.

He was magnificent. It was the only word she could think of. No picture she'd ever seen could possibly do a beast like this justice. He was huge, heavy-boned, and muscular, but still possessed of the sleek grace that was the sole province of the big cats. A black mane surrounded a wide muzzle that looked as though it would feel like velvet, and his paws looked to be bigger than her hands. And those eyes, steady, unblinking, and glowing like hot gold never left her face.

She hadn't realized until this moment exactly how much of the lion showed through in Tasmin's human form, but even now, she thought she would have known him anywhere.

Her anger at him evaporated for the time being. It was difficult to be angry with a creature that looked like it could eat you.

She finally managed to exhale, one long, shuddering breath.

"What are you doing out here?" she asked, her voice only a whisper. One of his ears twitched, but Tasmin didn't change form. Instead, he padded up to her. It was all Bay could do to stay in place and let him come. She was no chicken, but she couldn't quite turn off the instinct to run away from a sharp-toothed creature that was bigger than she was.

The shift happened so quickly she only had a vague sense of it. The lion seemed to rise onto its hind legs, she blinked, and there was only Tasmin. She noted that he had acquired a heavier coat since the other night, and shoes. He looked slightly dazed, but other than that, normal. Or as normal as he got.

It only took her a few seconds of staring at him to get her wits back about her. She supposed that was an improvement. She crossed her arms over her chest and tipped up her chin. He wasn't going to get the sweet treatment this time.

"What are *you* doing here?" he asked.

"I asked you first," Bay said. "And if you were thinking about playing one of your funky mind games on me again, don't. You made me really late to work yesterday, and my employees all thought an axe murderer got me."

He looked puzzled for an instant. Then guilty. It was strangely satisfying.

"Oh," he said.

She raised her eyebrows. "Oh? You could have just left, you know. I'm a pretty sound sleeper. You didn't need to put the whammy on me."

He blinked. "Whammy? I—oh, I see. I didn't intend to…I mean, I wouldn't have…" He trailed off, then heaved a sigh that was almost forlorn enough to make Bay feel sorry for him. Almost.

"You don't understand anything," he growled.

Bay felt her fingers curling into fists. The urge to smack him was almost overwhelming. "I would understand," she said, "if you'd just be honest with me. Last time I checked, mortal didn't equal brainless. And speaking of brains, did I mention it's not okay to do things to mine? Because it isn't." She huffed out a breath. "I *hate* that vampires can just poke around inside people's heads. You just take it one step further."

"I told you that you shouldn't have let me in."

"That's not an excuse," Bay said, eyes widening. "You show up in my yard shoeless, minus a jacket, and shivering in the snow, and I'm obviously going to let you in!"

"I have no intention of doing that again," he replied stiffly.

"Well. Good," Bay shot back. They stared at one another, the few feet between them feeling like miles. Tasmin was far more standoffish tonight than he had been—it rubbed her exactly the wrong way. She'd saved him from freezing, and in return he'd knocked her out! How was he the wounded party here?

"You still haven't told me what you're doing out here," Bay said when it appeared that Tasmin was content to just stand there glaring at her. She was already tired of the argument. He wasn't going to apologize for making her oversleep, and he wasn't going to stop blaming her for being nice to him. If he didn't seem to *need* someone to be nice to him so desperately, she probably would have just given up. She still ought to.

Too bad she'd been born with a stubborn streak a mile wide.

"I was wandering," Tasmin said. But the words had a bite that made Bay think that wasn't the truth. Not entirely anyway. Which was nothing new with him.

"You're going to get shot at, wandering out here," Bay said. "It's hunting season."

"Bullet holes heal as quickly as anything else," he said with a shrug. He looked like he knew from experience. Bay almost asked, and then decided she didn't want to know.

A burst of laughter from inside the house had them both turning their heads. When Bay looked at Tasmin again, he was frowning.

"What are you foolish people *doing* out here? A dark field is the last place you should be."

"This from the expert on places not to be."

The disgruntled expression on his face was amusing enough that Bay relented a little. "We're ghost hunting."

"Why would you want to hunt those?"

The incredulity in his voice put her back up, along with embarrassing her. She was used to people, vampires included, teasing her about her odd hobby. But hearing that kind of dismissal from Tasmin managed to hurt her feelings.

She shrugged uncomfortably. "I don't know. It's interesting, thinking that there are beings wandering around that you can't see. That can actually affect the environment if they try."

His expression changed then, darkening, and he looked away.

"It's better to stay away from such things, Bailey. Nothing good can come from them."

Bay watched him, not understanding why hearing about ghost hunting would bother him so much.

"Even if there are things like that," she said, "they can't hurt us. They don't have bodies or anything. It's not the same as chasing around vampires and werewolves, Tasmin."

"You should never assume such things," Tasmin replied, and the heat in his voice surprised her. "Never." He looked toward the house, and Bay didn't like the way his eyes changed.

"Whatever you're thinking of doing, don't," she said.

But it was too late. His eyes slipped shut, and his skin took on a faint glow. Tendrils of what seemed to be pure golden energy separated from him and drifted toward the house, melting into the walls. When he opened his eyes again, he looked satisfied with himself...and not in a way that gave Bay a warm fuzzy feeling.

"What the hell did you just do?" she rasped.

That was when the screaming started.

Alex came out first, slamming out the front door, eyes wild. He staggered down the rotting steps. Bay watched, stunned. She'd never seen Alex be anything but enthusiastic. His terror was far less pleasant. As the other members of BCPS spilled out the door behind him, Alex's eyes skittered wildly around the dark field. They lit on Bay, seeming not even to see Tasmin.

"Get out of here," he panted. "We need to get out of here *now*!"

"What—?"

But Bay's question was drowned out by the shrieks, screams, and soft moans of her fellow ghost hunters as they tripped and stumbled their way across the field, trying to get as far away from the house as they could as fast as they could.

Alex was at the head of them, his long legs carrying him through the brittle field grass toward the cars parked along the side of the road. All she could do was watch in amazement. His hands had been empty—he'd forgotten his recorder. It seemed like most of the equipment had been left behind, which never happened. These were people who generally ran toward weird things, not away from them.

In a matter of minutes, the house stood silent before her and Tasmin, door hanging ajar. In the distance, Bay could hear car engines starting up. She looked out to where there were now bright points of headlights, then rounded on Tasmin.

"What was that for?" she demanded. "What did you do?"

In that moment, he was very much the arrogant creature who'd informed her that her secretary's thrall would end when he decided, and not before.

"I showed them what a foolish pursuit this is," Tasmin replied. "They need to find other hobbies." He looked smug. "After this, I think they probably will."

Her mouth dropped open. "Their hobbies—*my* hobbies—aren't any of your business! What did you set loose in there?"

His mouth hardened a little, but he didn't seem as though he was going to back down.

"There are plenty of shadows to be had in a place like this. All I did was bend and shape them a little. Their imaginations and fears did the rest."

Bay sucked in a breath, ready to shout at him. But at the last second, she decided to save her breath and just go home. No matter what she screamed at him, he wasn't going to listen. So she sent Tasmin one last burning glare, turned on her heel, and started back off across the field.

She wasn't alone for long. Soon he was beside her, keeping stride.

"You're angry." He sounded puzzled.

She stayed silent.

"I did nothing to you."

"You screwed with my friends."

"I didn't *hurt* them. I did them a favor."

Bay turned her head to stare incredulously. "Oh? By terrifying them out of their minds? You vamps are all the same. Mortals are stupid, you know best...and whatever you say goes. Even if it hurts the mortals in question!" The wounded fury she felt surprised her, and Bay knew it had been building for a long time. This wasn't just about Tasmin. She was tired of being treated like a child simply because of her mortality. Tonight was simply the straw that broke the camel's back.

Though it did little to tamp down her ire, Tasmin looked genuinely confused. "It was just an illusion. I would never hurt you...them...I wouldn't—"

"You just *did*," Bay replied fiercely, wishing she could make him understand. "I've never seen any of those people afraid, and we've seen some strange things. Whatever you made them see is going to leave psychological scars, and don't tell me that's not a way of hurting someone. There was nothing in there, Tasmin. Nothing, before you decided to drive everyone off. Why would you even care?"

"Because...the unseen can be a great deal more dangerous than you can imagine."

She stopped short at the way his voice changed, deepening, growing rougher. When she turned to look at Tasmin, he seemed different in a way she couldn't quite put her finger on. His stare was full of a need far more raw than anything she'd seen him reveal, his eyes so feline that no one would mistake them for human.

Oh God. He looked so *hungry.*

"Stop looking at me like that," she said, blurting the words before she could think better of them.

"Like what?" That same strange voice grew even deeper, somehow *oilier.* He stepped closer to her. She tried to move, to tear her eyes away, but she was caught. The will to leave drained from her, even as part of her screamed to go, move, now before something terrible happened.

His hands came up to trace her jawline, deceptively gentle. He tipped her head to the side, eyes skimming down the side of her neck.

"You are a foolish human. Still, I understand why he wants you. So much life...so little fear. I'm tired of waiting to taste you. Shall I make it hurt, little human? I think...yes."

Bay tried to scream, but only a soft whimper came out. She didn't know what the hell was happening, but there was one thing she was certain of: this wasn't Tasmin. The eyes that crawled over her were alien, cold. He hadn't bothered to thrall her so deeply that she would accept what he was about to do, and she knew why. This man, whoever or whatever he was, wanted her terror. He would find it just as enjoyable as her blood.

With that realization came anger, unexpected and white-hot. She was sure that when this thing was done with her, Tasmin would wake up beside her body and be utterly horrified. He would remember nothing. Just like he didn't remember killing the Ptolemy the other night. Whether he was mentally ill or something infinitely more sinister was at work here, Bay felt her outrage building on his behalf.

He was being violated, one way or another.

She wanted the Tasmin she knew—or at least, wanted to know—back.

She latched onto her fury, and it gave her more strength than she'd counted on. With a great deal of effort, she managed to speak.

"Give him back," she said. "I know he's in there."

Not-Tasmin looked surprised, then amused.

"You think you can order me about, pretty?" he said in that terrible voice. "He's mine to do with as I please."

She gritted her teeth and found she could move her fingers, then her hands. It would have been funny, if this hadn't been so dire—the stubbornness she'd been famous for since childhood was going to be her only defense against annihilation. If she ever wanted to tell the story, she had to make it count.

With a soft cry she managed to launch herself forward, falling against Tasmin. His arms came around her, more a reflex than anything, she thought. Still, the quick change in their positions broke whatever mental hold he'd had on her as his concentration slipped.

Of course, now his arms were locked around her.

And a quick glance up into his face showed her that *her* Tasmin was still very much absent. Not-Tasmin looked almost comically puzzled.

"You...do not do what you ought to, human. Do you not understand how I'll punish you?"

She was afraid to respond. He hadn't let go of her, and though she could feel the life returning to her limbs, she knew she would be no match for him if she tried to fight. She had to find a way to snap Tasmin out of this. Whatever "this" was.

His body was hard and surprisingly warm against her. It was ironic, that when she finally got his hands on her like she'd imagined, it was when he'd descended into the madness of some kind of dangerous split personality. But he *was* still in there, she told herself. She'd dealt with animals that were shy, abused, and disturbed in the volunteer work she'd done in rescue...and though she hadn't always been successful, patience, persistence, and a kind touch often brought wonderful results.

Of course, she didn't have weeks. She had minutes. But tenderness was all she had.

Bay forced herself to concentrate on his arms around her, on the man she knew he was as opposed to how he was acting now. It worked. Sort of. She swallowed hard and leaned into him, tucking her head between his shoulder and neck. He stiffened.

"What are you doing?" The voice was still dark and strange, but not overtly violent. So that was something.

"Trying to bring Tasmin back. I know he's in there. So I'm hugging him."

"Hugging...," he sneered. "You think I'll let go because your body is pressed against this one?"

Her heart picked up again from the adrenaline, but she took a few deep breaths, trying to stay focused on what she was doing. This was her only shot. She had to try, or he was going to have his teeth in her throat before she knew it.

She lifted her head just a little, still deliberately avoiding eye contact even though she could feel him willing her to look. Instead, though she was beginning to shiver, she pressed a tentative kiss to his jaw. Then another. The warm scent of him made it easier to remember who this was...how she had wanted him.

He sipped in a breath, and when he spoke his voice was more muddled, a blend of the inhuman and the man she was looking for.

"Why...are you putting your lips on my skin?" He sounded slightly dazed. Hopefully that was a good sign.

"Because I've been thinking about kissing Tasmin since I met him. Kissing *you*."

"Me..."

She slipped her hand up to cup his cheek, feeling the light prickle of stubble against the sensitive palm of her hand. She kissed his cheek, tracing his cheekbone with her mouth and feeling his skin begin to warm beneath her touch. He'd been like a block of ice at first. Now he seemed to be melting.

Though her stomach fluttered treacherously, she forced herself to take her time. He was already off balance. She wanted him to stay that way.

She slipped her hand into his hair, and it was thick and silken, even more than she'd imagined. She felt him lean into her touch, and had to bite back a sob of relief. It was working. It had to be.

"Tasmin," she breathed against his skin, against the corner of his full lips. "Come back to me."

He shuddered against her and clutched her more tightly, the embrace oddly tender.

"Yes. No. Stop." She heard him in that voice. More, she heard anguish.

Bay rose up on her tiptoes and pressed her mouth to his, hearing the sharp intake of his breath. Then he moaned, a soft, broken sound that was all Tasmin, without any trace of the monster.

She felt the instant he returned, sliding his arms up her back and sinking into the kiss as though he'd been the one to initiate the embrace. His lips were warm, and so soft that Bay never considered pulling away. She'd wanted this far too much, and knowing that this was *Tasmin*, no one else, had relief coursing through her so strong that it nearly took her to her knees. He seemed to sense it, pulling her closer, lifting his hands to tangle in her hair. Tasmin pulled back just enough to lock eyes with her, and the beast was utterly gone. Instead, she saw a fathomless sorrow tangled with a desire that took her breath away.

"I'm so sorry," he whispered, pressing his forehead to hers.

She wanted to tell him it was okay, but the words wouldn't come. Instead she lifted her mouth to his again, wanting the reassurance of his touch. He'd scared her, badly. And yet somehow, getting a close look at just what he was wrestling with made her want to fight for him. He had no one to try and hold back the darkness.

Now he had her.

"I try to fight... I'm so tired," he rasped. He couldn't seem to stop touching her. "If you knew... you would run, Bailey."

"I'm not going anywhere," she said, breathing the words against his lips. As soon as she said them, she knew they were true, even if she still didn't understand why.

Then his lips were on hers again, harder, more urgent. Tasmin urged her mouth open and then swept his tongue inside to mate with hers. Bay twined her arms around his neck, hanging on. She felt...savored. Devoured. He held her so close that the slow throb of his heart echoed through her.

Bay slid her hands down his back, arching into him. Every nerve ending sizzled, and she wanted him closer, more, *now*. There was a barely leashed wildness in the way he handled her, his mouth growing more demanding, claws skimming lightly over her.

Claws...he has claws...

Instead of shying away, she wanted so much more.

Tasmin nipped at her lip, drawing blood. Bay barely had time to gasp at the unexpected pinch before he had taken her lower lip into his mouth and began to suckle at it. Bay's eyes slipped shut, her head tipped back at the sensation, a slow blooming pleasure that quickly had her throbbing. She'd known, purely on an intellectual level, that having a vampire drink from you could be erotic. But she'd had no idea of what it would actually feel like, that even Tasmin sucking at a tiny puncture wound in her lip would arouse her almost to the point of madness.

She made a soft, pleading sound as she dug her nails into his hips. Despite the layers of clothing between them, it was painfully obvious how hard he was for her. The bitter cold around Bay disappeared...it might have been a hot summer's day for how quickly her temperature was rising. All she could think of was having Tasmin against her, skin to skin.

He cradled the back of her head, holding that part of her still while he sipped at her. Every long pull he took with his mouth echoed in her, winding her tighter and tighter. He stopped abruptly, pulling his mouth away with a soft gasp and burying his face in the side of her neck, breathing deeply. Bay couldn't seem to catch her breath. Her body was thrumming like a live wire. She'd known he would feel good...but just this simple taste of him had been dangerously addictive. His lips were wickedly soft, sinfully talented things.

The depth of his need left her shaken. The depth of her own, even more.

Tasmin rubbed his face into her hair, her neck. "Bailey," he groaned, his voice strained. She shivered as he kissed her jaw, her cheek, her sensitive ear, then tipped her head to the side to allow him better access, pressing her hands into the tensed muscles of his back.

There was a whisper of air, and every hair on the back of her neck rose at once. Tasmin changed in an instant from lover to feral beast, whipping his head to the side with a snarl that bared his gleaming fangs.

They were no longer alone.

Tasmin shoved her behind him, and Bay watched four shadows materialize from the darkness. Two men. Two women. All vampires...and none she'd seen before.

Tasmin hissed at them, hands hooking into claws, back hunching like a threatened cat. Bay's eyes darted between the figures, blood pounding in her ears. Every primal instinct she had was screaming at her to escape...but there didn't seem to be a way out. They were surrounded.

"That's him," a woman's voice said. "He's the one. Can't you smell it?"

Bay couldn't seem to find her breath as the four closed in around her and Tasmin. One of the men, slim and dark, looked at her with mild interest.

"Who gets the mortal?"

"Whoever gets the Rakshasa in chains."

The vampires began to circle, slowly closing in. Tasmin's skin began to glow as his eyes darted among their attackers. She could actually feel his power ramping up, charging the air around them. Maybe he would drive them insane, she thought. Maybe he would—

"Now!"

They moved so quickly that Bay saw little more than a blur. She heard his voice, a shout in her mind.

Run!

His hands were around her waist, and he tossed her away from him as though she weighed nothing. She didn't even have time to gasp before she landed on her backside several feet away on the cold, hard ground with a harsh grunt. For a few seconds, she was frozen, transfixed by the sight of the blur of motion around Tasmin as the vampires attacked. They moved almost too fast for the human eye to see, leaving Tasmin at the center of a multicolored whirlwind, lashing out at motion trails. Bay had only fleeting impressions of dully glinting daggers, of teeth bared and biting. Tasmin roared in the voice of a lion, his head going back as the glow around him intensified. He lashed out with hands that were now tipped with long, thick claws. It was a strategy that seemed as ineffective as a giant swatting at gnats, though . . . The other vampires were simply too quick.

Bay finally snapped out of her daze enough to stagger to her feet. Blood spattered her chest, her face as Tasmin's claws finally tore someone open. There was a high-pitched scream, and then Tasmin's voice sliced through the night air, no longer just in her head.

"Bailey! Run!"

It got her moving, though she nearly tripped over her own feet in her terror. She caught a final glimpse of two of the vampires being wrapped in the glow that was now pouring from Tasmin. One began to claw at her eyes, screaming. The other dropped to the ground and began writhing.

Tasmin caught her eye, and their gazes locked.

Tell Lily. These are Ptolemy. Hurry.

Bay was gripped by a furious sense of helplessness as she spun and ran. She didn't want to leave him. But she was just an unarmed human, and it made no sense for her to get killed while they hauled Tasmin off. So she ran, sprinting across the field faster than she'd ever moved in her life. At least, it felt that way. She could see her car, could see the road.

Almost there...

Then a hand fisted in her hair, snapping her head back so hard her teeth came together with a painful click. A voice whispered in her ear, "I don't think so."

There was another roar from where Tasmin was, the throaty bellow of an enraged lion. Bay was jerked backward again, crying out at the pain. Then she could move again, though there was still a hand tangled in her hair.

When she turned, the hand fell to the ground not far from the body of its owner.

Her mouth opened in a silent scream that caught in her throat as she watched the massive lion that was Tasmin tear the throat out of her attacker, then remove the head completely, shaking it between his jaws and then tossing it to the side. She saw blood and sinew, the kind of gore you only got to look at in horror movies. Except this was real.

She fell to her knees and turned away as her stomach threatened to empty its contents. Somehow, she kept it all down, but when she tried to get up again, her legs didn't seem to want to support her. Bay was light-headed, blood pumping through her veins so quickly that she felt strangely detached from her body.

A soft noise, the plaintive sound of a wounded beast, drew her attention back to the gruesome scene. It was Tasmin, the only creature left standing in the carnage. His golden fur was spattered with gore, and his muzzle was dark with blood. Bay started to shrink away, unthinking, too terrified to do anything but react to what she was seeing—until he made the sound again and tried to take a step toward her. He put one paw in front of the other but then his legs tangled together, and she saw the syringe sticking out of his shoulder. The plunger was fully depressed. Whatever these Ptolemy had planned to take him down with, they'd gotten it in him, even if they hadn't lived to drag him away.

The lion's legs gave out. He fell, eyes rolling back in his head, and collapsed on his side, breathing heavily. Bay crawled toward him, no longer afraid. The feel of him beneath her hand as she pressed it to his side was strangely reassuring, anchoring her here when so much of her would have preferred to curl up in a ball and check out.

Tasmin had just saved her life.

"It's okay," she sobbed out, more for her own benefit than his. "It's going to be okay. They're gone. It's okay."

She fumbled her cell phone out of the inner pocket of her jacket and dialed the only number she could, hoping that whatever had been done to Tasmin could be reversed...and knowing that after tonight, nothing in her world would be quite the same. The darkness pressing in around her friends had finally started to cross what were supposed to be sacred boundaries.

Her worst fears were finally coming to pass. She wasn't safe. None of them were.

And tonight, she knew she might never be safe again.

chapter NINE

WHEN HE WOKE up, the first thing he saw was Bailey.

She was asleep in a chair pulled up alongside the bed, bent so that her head and arms rested on the comforter near his hand. A single candle burned in the dark room, catching the gold of her hair where it spread out around her, hiding her face. He could hear each soft, deep breath she took.

Tasmin lifted his hand tentatively, taking a single wavy lock and stroking his fingers over it gently. Then he pulled his hand away. She wasn't his. She couldn't be his.

But after all that had happened, all she'd seen him do...she'd stayed.

More than that, her kiss had dragged him back from the edge of an abyss that could well have consumed them both. He wouldn't have dreamed it possible...but it was an act of courage he wouldn't soon forget. The darkness had come upon him so fast it had taken him under before he could try to fight. He had no memory of what he might have said or done before the feel of Bailey's mouth on his had pulled him to the surface, the fear he felt in her quickly melting into white-hot need.

Somehow, this slip of a mortal had saved him. The relief he felt at knowing he had protected her life in return was almost overwhelming. He was . . . *changing.* Growing stronger in his struggles against the demon within, when he'd been so sure he was sliding into an abyss he'd never be able to crawl out of. The first time he'd overcome the demon, in Bailey's bedroom, he hadn't understood why. Now, though, the answer was right in front of him.

Bailey was the difference. Because she mattered to him.

Rattled, Tasmin turned his head to look around the room. He'd been brought back to the mansion, back to the room that contained the few possessions he'd brought with him to America. The heavy drapes were closed, giving him no clue as to how long he'd slept. Tasmin lifted his hands to examine them and saw that someone had cleaned the blood off. It had been wiped from his face as well, he realized as he rubbed a hand over his mouth and jaw.

Immediately, his eyes went back to Bailey. He knew, somehow, that she had done it. That was her way. It was far more than he deserved. Knowing how close he had likely come to taking Bailey's life . . . it tore at whatever was left of his soul. He wanted her . . . but so did the ravenous darkness inside him.

Tasmin watched her, pushing aside the cacophony of his thoughts to focus on her slow, even breaths, the way the candlelight subtly shifted the highlights in her hair. Slowly, his mind cleared. Just being here with her in the silence gave him a peace that nothing else had since he'd emerged from the cave in the Gir. He breathed in the light scent of her, allowing his breathing to fall into the same rhythm as hers.

He didn't know how much time had passed when the door to the bedroom opened. Tasmin looked up to see Lily walk in. Her feet were bare, her auburn hair falling in loose waves over her shoulders. In that moment, her heritage was obvious. She looked every bit the child of a goddess.

He saw the love and concern in her glowing blue eyes as they lit on Bailey, and then saw something harder enter them as she focused on him. Warier. She was a kind woman, but a strong one. That much he had discovered quickly. If she decided that he was a threat to anything she loved, he wouldn't last here...at least, not with his freedom intact.

He doubted she had decided quite *what* he was yet.

Lily came forward, her feet making no sound on the floor, until she reached the side of the bed. She looked at Bailey, looked at him, and then pressed a finger to her lips. He nodded. Neither of them wanted to wake her up. He considered sending her into deeper sleep, pushing her further into dreams...but knowing how it had infuriated her before, Tasmin set the idea aside.

She was not just another mortal, easily toyed with. She'd proven that. He would respect it.

Lily raised her voice over a whisper, but kept it soft when she spoke. "Kira, my healer, gave her an herbal tea that should keep her out for a while. Still, we should keep it down. She needs the rest."

"You drug your friends?" he asked, surprised.

Lily snorted softly. "No, I value my life a little more than that. Bay asked for the tea. She was pretty shaken up when Ty and Eric got to you, Tasmin. Once she knew you were okay, she *wanted* to sleep."

Tasmin looked at Bailey's golden hair veiling her face, puzzled all over again.

"But...here? Like this?"

"She wouldn't leave you," Lily replied. There wasn't exactly reproach in her voice, but again he sensed that wariness where he was concerned. And why not? He was no one to her. A dangerous drifter from a dead bloodline. Bailey was her closest friend. And she obviously sensed the connection between them, even though he would have preferred to ignore it himself.

It was difficult when the woman seemed to have appointed herself his protector.

"She has a good heart," Tasmin said. It was one of the biggest reasons she unsettled him so. Just as it was one of the things that made her impossible to stay away from.

Lily nodded, and for just an instant he could see the sadness behind her composure. He thought he understood. Relationships between vampires and mortals, no matter how close, would never be easy ones. One would always be a danger to the other, whether or not it was intended. He'd seen the strain between Bailey and Lily firsthand. Only now did he realize the rift was hurting them both.

"Bay told us what happened."

He had a brief instant of fear that she had told Lily *everything*, but he quickly saw that Lily knew nothing of his blackout. If she had, he had a feeling this meeting would be far less cordial. The relief was instant. As was his guilt.

Again, Bailey had protected him without his asking. Without his deserving it.

"There were four Ptolemy who came from the woods to attack," Tasmin said. "Two I killed there."

Lily raised her eyebrows. "And the others?"

"I drove them mad," he said with a small shrug. "They may have recovered. But I doubt it. If they aren't dead by now, they might as well be."

Lily stared at him for a moment with the same mixture of fascination and revulsion that had marked so many of his interactions with both vampires and mortals outside his pride. It didn't faze him—he was used to it.

Except...Bailey had never looked at him that way. It was a strange feeling to realize it.

Finally, Lily said, "I still can't imagine how your bloodline ever lost the battle. Even against Arsinöe."

"All vampires have their weaknesses," Tasmin replied. "All of us can be defeated. Even the great Arsinöe."

Lily's expression wasn't particularly hopeful. "I hope you're right, because she's obviously figured out that you're here."

"I'll go," Tasmin said. The decision was easy to make. He wouldn't endanger an entire dynasty with his presence, no matter how far back it set his search for the truth. "I can find this Anura at her home, if she'll see me. I think that would be best."

Lily surprised him with an angry little shake of her head. "That isn't the answer. Not this time. Arsinöe will expect that. She'll be waiting for me to throw you out, and this whole thing will just play out the same way somewhere else." Her eyes flashed. "She's crossed my borders one too many times. Mormo, the Empusa, has kept her protected with the Council, but she's in no shape to protect her in any other way. I'm done."

Her vehemence was a surprise that left Tasmin uneasy. "I didn't come here to start a war."

Lily looked grim. "You didn't start it. But she seems determined to finish it, even when she knows this is the one time we should all be standing together."

He raised an eyebrow, but Lily simply shook her head again. "Later. It's almost morning, and I need some sleep. Anura should be here this evening. At that point, there are things you need to know."

"About what happened with the Grigori in the desert," he said. He didn't know what made him say it, but the surprise on Lily's face was plain.

"How did you hear about that?" she said, her voice barely a whisper.

"Only rumors," he replied. It was more than that, more about the pull he continued to feel toward the desert that had alternately fascinated and worried him. But his suspicions were tied to the darkness that kept surfacing in him... and he couldn't share that with her.

Lily pressed her lips together, looking away for a moment. When her gaze returned to his, he saw the resignation in it.

"I guess I knew there would be talk. I didn't know it would have gotten so far by now."

He laughed softly. "You're young. Gossip has always been a favorite pastime of immortals. It's one of the only things that changes quickly."

She gave him a ghost of a smile that faded almost as soon as it appeared.

"There was a demon in the desert," Lily said. "A sort

of...fallen angel. It decimated the Grigori leadership before it escaped."

Chaos.

The name surfaced in his mind, unbidden—a greedy, eager whisper. He fought off a shiver and tried to keep his focus on Lily. The demon inside of him rejoiced. Tasmin could feel it even now, a black glee born of pure evil. It boded poorly for them all.

"So that was the secret the Grigori kept," Tasmin said. "Even as far removed from them as the Rakshasa were, we still heard stories."

"It was...a little more than that," Lily admitted. "That demon was their brother. He thrives on souls, the stronger the better. And he almost took the leaders of the American dynasties in one fell swoop, myself included."

This was news he hadn't heard even a whisper of. That the dynasties had come so close to falling was stunning.

"But this demon still runs free?" Tasmin asked. But he knew.

Lily nodded. "We keep waiting for him to make a move, but there's been nothing. My people are closely allied with the Dracul. Vlad, their leader, is an expert on vampire history and lore, and he's convinced that Chaos will be looking to raise an army of sleeping demons to destroy the dynasties and remake...well, everything."

Tasmin went cold, suddenly certain he knew the exact location of one of these sleeping demons. But it slept no longer. And it had already whispered the name of its master.

"An army of demons," he murmured. He could only begin to imagine how horrible that might be.

"We can talk more about it tonight," Lily said. "The

sun's getting ready to rise. Everyone else is already in bed. I just wanted to make sure you were doing all right before I turned in. My healer was impressed with your strength. She didn't see any problems, but I always worry."

Knowing he'd been examined by the healer already was a relief. She'd found nothing to alarm her...just the same as the other healers he'd seen, save Shakti. The healer who had told him he'd been cursed by the gods.

That had felt true then, so true that he hadn't bothered to give chase when the man had fled.

"Before you go...was I...poisoned?" Tasmin asked.

Memory flickered to life all at once. *Many hands holding him down. Whispered chants. Cold laughter. And that terrible burning, a venomous snake slithering through his veins.*

Lily's jaw tightened as she gave a sharp nod. "Arsinöe's weapon of choice, as always." Then her eyes narrowed, full of concern. "Are you all right? You look pale again. Kira left a few things she said would help, just in case..."

"No," Tasmin whispered, trying to shake off the sudden clammy chill of his skin, the faint nausea. He'd remembered nothing but his final day with his pride up until now. These images...they provoked such horror in him. What had happened? Who had done this to him?

But those memories remained locked to him.

"I think I just need to rest," Tasmin said, hoping he sounded calm. His eyes moved back to Bailey, sleeping peacefully, unaware of the terrible things being discussed while she was safe in her dreams. He was glad. Nothing as vile as what his kind did to one another should ever come so close to touching her again.

"Is she going to be all right?" Tasmin asked when Lily

followed his gaze. "What she saw was...not something most humans would handle well."

Lily nodded. "Yes. Bay can handle a lot more than you'd think. And...still probably not quite as much as she thinks she can." Her smile was affectionate when she looked at her friend. "She's awfully stubborn."

"I noticed."

That seemed to amuse her, though her smile was bittersweet. "Thank you for protecting her," Lily said, her fingertips brushing over Bailey's hair. "Until Ty, she was my only family."

The knife's blade of his guilt, already pricking at him, slid in a little deeper and twisted.

"I did what anyone would do," he replied, trying to deflect what he knew he didn't deserve. Yes, he had saved her...but only after he'd slipped into a state near her that could easily have ended in her dying by his own hand. And it wasn't the first time. He should have run in the other direction the moment he'd scented her. But where Bailey was concerned, he didn't seem to be able to help himself. He had to find a way to remedy that as soon as possible.

Lily seemed to sense the direction of his thoughts.

"She's one of the warmest, funniest, most loyal people I know. She'd never abandon me, no matter how dangerous it got for her. No matter how much she should. I love her for it. And I'm terrified I'll lose her because of it." Lily looked at him with eyes that were far older than her years.

"I won't have her hurt."

Tasmin considered the heavily weighted words while he watched Bailey sleep.

"If you're warning me off, there's no need. I have no

intention of getting close enough to hurt her," he said coolly.

Lily's soft laugh, faintly sad, startled him. When he looked up, she was watching him with eyes that were impossible to read.

"You already are."

There were few cars on the road when Tasmin drove Bailey home in her big, fairly messy SUV.

The sunrise had so far done nothing but turn the sky a lighter shade of gray, and there was the promise of snow in the air—this time, far more than what had fallen the other night. Bailey was curled up in the passenger seat, her head resting on the window and lolling a little every time they hit the smallest bump. Tasmin hunched over the steering wheel, frowning, driving as slowly as he could without being conspicuous. He had quickly learned to operate his motorcycle like it was a part of him, but larger vehicles remained, for the most part, both a puzzle and a threat.

He rolled into her driveway, put the SUV in park, and killed the engine. Then he turned and looked at Bailey. She hadn't so much as batted an eyelash—because she hadn't opened her eyes at all. Whatever herbs the healer had given her had more than done their job. Too well, actually. He'd begun to worry that this Kira had given Bailey a vampire's dose of sleeping draught, far more powerful than anything a mortal should have.

Maybe he would watch her awhile, Tasmin decided... just in case.

He got out of the car and walked around to her side, opening the door and sliding her easily into his arms. She seemed to weigh nothing, as warm and easily carried as a kitten. The moment she was curled against him, she snuggled deeper into his chest with a sigh.

"Tas," she breathed.

It startled a smile out of him. He refused to use her nickname, but she created one for him. He wondered if she would even remember saying it.

He hoped so. He had forgotten far too much, enough for both of them. His smile vanished as he carried her to the door. Tasmin fumbled with the key chain for a minute, finally finding the one Lily had described to him and unlocking the dead bolt.

The house was mostly silent as he carried her in, though he heard the faint sound of a cage rattling. He'd seen the big wire crate in her bedroom, understood that it was where Grimm was kept when he was left to his own devices for an extended period of time. Someone had been over to let him out in the night, Lily had told him, but Bailey would need to do so again. At least, he thought, eyeing her sleeping face skeptically, *someone* would have to.

He ascended the stairs, and once he entered the bedroom he locked eyes with the big black dog who was wagging the entire back half of his body in ecstatic joy and whining softly. Tasmin hesitated for a moment, then decided he might as well try to communicate what he wanted to the dog. It couldn't hurt.

She needs her rest. I'll...do whatever needs to be done for you.

Grimm stilled instantly and cocked his head. Tasmin didn't know whether the dog understood, but it seemed to calm him. He waited patiently while Tasmin tucked Bailey into bed.

Tasmin left her clothes on her—changing her was a bridge he wouldn't cross. Instead, he removed her shoes before he pulled the thick comforter over her, remembering how warm and comfortable it had been beside her. The woman was a refuge from everything bad in the world. It seemed unnatural and unfair that the darkness that followed him had reached out to touch her the way it had.

He tucked the blanket around her neck, brushing her hair to the side and watching the slow, steady pulse in her neck. She seemed fine. He wasn't going to be if he didn't find another object to focus on. Tasmin swallowed hard and looked at the collection of books on her nightstand, running his tongue over the points of his elongated incisors.

He needed to feed. Soon, before he saw her awake again.

The thought of hunting more deer made him cringe, but he would do it. No humans. Not while he couldn't trust himself to keep control in his hunger.

With a great deal of effort, he turned away, then crouched to let Grimm out of his crate. Though the dog looked longingly at Bailey's sleeping figure, he surprised Tasmin by seeming to understand what Tasmin had tried to tell him. Of course, that also meant receiving whatever big, slobbery affection had been reserved for her.

Tasmin found himself with armloads of dog, locked into a shaggy embrace. He chuckled, despite himself, and gave Grimm a quick squeeze in return. That earned him a facial tongue bath that came on so quickly he barely had time to get his eyes and mouth shut.

"Come on, come on," he finally whispered, disentangling himself. When the dog seemed not to want to take a breather, Tasmin recalled something Bailey had said and grinned as he stood.

"Breakfast?" he asked. Instantly Grimm was at attention, his regal bear's face alight with intense interest. Tasmin rolled his eyes, but it was affectionate as the dog bolted for the stairs, descending them in a series of thuds only slightly more quiet than what an elephant might produce. Bailey didn't stir.

Tasmin started for the door, then turned back quickly before he could think better of it. For a few blissful moments, he could pretend this was his home, his woman, and all of the outside world was unconcerned with him. He could just be what he had never had a chance to be—a normal man.

He pressed a kiss to her forehead, eliciting a soft sigh that made him want to crawl in with her, curl himself around her and pretend that they were the only two people on earth.

Instead, he forced himself to turn away and leave the room, shutting the door behind him.

He would care for the dog. He would keep watch for a time. And maybe, if he was lucky, he would figure out how he was ever going to leave here without leaving the better part of himself, the part he'd thought had died in that cave, behind.

chapter TEN

Aт least this time her alarm had awakened her.

Bay managed to make it through the day, fueled by nothing but coffee and determination. But after grooming a Lhasa, two poodles, a Bernese mountain dog, and several cute but hyperactive mutts, she was ready to go home and collapse face-first on the nearest available soft surface. She was so, so done.

Seeing bad guy vamps ripped up by a lion hadn't defeated her.

Being threatened, and then saved, by the same lion hadn't turned her brain into mush by trying to wrap itself around the situation—though that was probably because she refused to think about it. Much like the ripping up of the bad vamps.

What was doing her in, finally, was just sheer exhaustion. And not thinking about *that* did her no good. Her body had its own ideas.

It was dark when she locked up the shop and said good

night to Shelby and Anna. The three of them chattered on
the way to the small parking lot behind the building, then
went their separate ways as each climbed into her own
car. Bay opened the hatchback and unfolded the portable
ramp she used to allow Grimm to climb in more easily.
He went, though not without the enticement of the treat he
knew would be in her pocket.

Once he was in, Bay stuffed the treat into Grimm's waiting jowls and closed the hatch. The air felt heavy tonight,
and though the snow in the forecast hadn't yet materialized, she had a feeling it would before long. Her breath
fogged in front of her as she made her way around the SUV
and climbed in. She rubbed her gloved hands together after
starting the engine, hoping it heated up quickly.

Bay turned on the radio and pulled out, singing along
with Jon Bon Jovi while he belted out an old song about a
girl who gave love a bad name. Her mom had always had a
thing for '80s hair bands, and had passed on the love of the
songs, if not the men with big hair and spandex pants, to
her daughter. Bay smiled at the thought of Marisa Harper
rocking out on one of their many car trips. She missed
her... but she was glad her parents were safe at their house
in Florida these days. Singing along with the tune solo
would work just fine to keep her up until she got home.

When Bay passed the lights of Lily's house, glittering
back behind the wrought iron fence and trees, she had a
brief, intense impulse to pull on in and see how everything
was. "Everything" meaning a certain golden-eyed lion-
shifter. But she was too damned tired, and too determined
not to go all needy stalker on him, to give in. Besides,
when she saw Tasmin again, she wanted to be ready. She
had questions. And some serious concerns. And...

And she was pretty sure he'd looked after her this morning before she'd gotten up. Grimm had been happy and fed, she'd been cozily tucked into bed minus her shoes, and her house had smelled faintly of sandalwood.

Maybe it wasn't an awful idea to be alone with him like that. No, no, it was, Bay told herself, tightening her hands on the wheel and turning away from the mansion. Just *how* bad an idea was something only he could answer... and that was an answer she planned to demand the next time she laid eyes on him.

Which would be way easier to accomplish if she wasn't dead on her feet.

She gave a soft growl and tried to just focus on the song blaring from the speakers. The subversive part of her mind that never shut off was busily trying to justify why she hadn't told Lily about Tasmin's bizarre and frightening change last night. But really, how was she supposed to describe that? His voice got weird, he started speaking in the third person, he insinuated he was going to kill her...

Yeah, any of those would have worked...

Damn it.

"Drum solo!" she cried, more than a little desperately, and pounded the steering wheel with her palms as the bridge kicked in.

No thinking no more thinking NO THINKING.

It worked, if only by making her find herself distractingly annoying. Bay barely noticed anything was odd apart from herself before she started to pull into her driveway.

"What the hell?" she muttered, stomping her foot on the brake. The SUV jerked to a stop, and she had the fleeting thought that it was a good thing Grimm had been laying down. Then she was leaning forward, peering at her dark and quiet house.

There had been a figure in her front window looking out.

She knew she'd seen it, even though it had been gone once she'd blinked—a slim, dark shadow with eyes that glinted unnaturally when they'd spotted her. Bay watched the window for a moment, half expecting the figure to return. But there was nothing.

It was dead quiet. And someone was in her house.

"Damn it," she cursed, backing into the road and then shoving the shifter into drive with fingers that had gone cold and numb. Panic tickled the back of her throat, threatening to become a scream. She'd known the ground had shifted last night. She just hadn't realized how much.

There was a vampire waiting for her in her house. And it had *wanted* her to see it.

By the time she was admitted through the gate at Lily's mansion her knuckles were white, her jaw clenched. She kept thinking she was seeing things—a darting shadow here, a pair of glowing eyes on a pedestrian there. Taunting her, trying to freak her out. Bay had never felt unsafe in her hometown before, not ever. Now, she could barely breathe until she'd made it into the Lilim's sanctuary. And even then her nerves were on edge.

Grimm sensed her tension, staying close as she walked him toward the front door and the pool of warm and welcoming light that came through the sidelights onto the steps.

When Tasmin's voice whispered out of the darkness just beside her, her heart nearly jumped out of her chest.

"Bailey?"

She gasped, whirling around to find him standing only a foot away from her. Her heart was pounding so fiercely that it took her a minute to formulate a coherent sentence, and even then her voice sounded breathless and strange.

"Damn it, don't sneak up on me!"

His eyes narrowed. "I didn't *sneak*. You mortals just don't pay enough attention to your surroundings."

Tasmin's brusque tone, coupled with the terror she'd felt when his voice had come out of the darkness, had tears springing to her eyes. Which made her feel stupid, and embarrassed, and angry...mostly at herself. She'd always been able to handle her own problems. She'd been the I'll-do-it-myself kid all her life. So why was she about to melt into a sobbing puddle in front of a relative stranger?

She sniffed, hoped it sounded like she was just getting a cold, and swallowed her tears. Unfortunately, new ones were threatening to storm the gate. To his credit, Tasmin seemed to realize she was right on the edge.

He looked at her more closely, gold eyes burning in the dark.

"Something frightened you."

"Yeah, you," she said, and when the hurt flashed loud and clear across his face she realized he must think she was talking about last night.

"Not that," she blurted, and her nose plugged up completely as a single, treacherous tear slithered down her cheek. "I mean, kind of, but...I just want to see Lily!"

She knew she sounded childish, but she was getting desperate. She was going to bawl, right here and now. Grimm whined beside her, staring up at her face and wagging his tail hopefully. He hated it when she got upset.

That made two of them.

Bay tried to step around Tasmin, but he moved easily right back into her path. She made a frustrated little sound as several more tears rolled down her cheeks.

"Tasmin. Let me go."

"No." His gaze was so fierce she wondered, just for a moment, if she was dealing with the *other* Tasmin again. And tonight, she didn't think she had the strength left to deal with him. Then he lifted one hand and, with a tenderness that stunned her, brushed away the tears now streaming steadily from her eyes.

"Why are you crying, Bailey?" His voice was soft, and as tender as his touch. "Is it because you're afraid of me?"

"No," she said, her voice as unsteady as her legs. "No, I probably should be, but you're further down on my list right now."

Bay found herself leaning into his touch. How something so fierce could hide this kind of gentleness amazed her—but Tasmin was a creature of contradictions. That much she'd figured out. What surprised her was how quickly he managed to soothe her, simply by being there.

"What happened?"

Whether it was a mistake or not, she let herself be soothed. Let herself trust him.

"My house," she said. "I went home and...I saw someone in the window. Maybe I imagined it, but I...I don't think so. And then on the way here, I kept thinking I saw more of them." She shook her head, and her whole body seemed to shake as well. "I sound like I'm losing it."

He muttered a few words in a language she didn't understand.

"Tasmin?"

"It wasn't your imagination," he said, and gave her cheek a final caress before stepping away. "This is my fault. Stay here. I'll take care of it."

He whirled to walk away from her, and all she could see was him surrounded by the vampires of last night, yelling at her to run while he was overrun. If the town was crawling with Ptolemy now, if he went to her house alone.... however strong he was, he wouldn't make it. She knew it with a bone-deep certainty.

And she refused to accept that. She didn't want Lily right now, Bay realized. She wanted him.

Bay reached out to grab his arm before he could get away. Tasmin jerked to a halt and spun back to stare at her.

"They'll be waiting for a fight. I plan to give it to them. But I have to go *now*."

"Don't," she said, fighting back a fresh wave of tears. "Don't go."

That seemed to be the reaction he was least expecting. Tasmin looked incredulous. "How can you say that? We both know I'm the reason for this, Bailey. I've done this. I'll fix it." His voice hardened. "They'll regret targeting you to get to me."

Actually, she thought this was exactly the reaction they'd been aiming for. These vampires had been watching them. They knew she and Tasmin had...something. Whatever it was. Knowing they'd been watched made her stomach clench. How long had they been watching her?

Tasmin tried to go again, but she tightened her grip on him. This time he growled, a sound she would have found terrifying from anyone but him.

"You're not going alone," she said. "No way. You almost didn't make it last night."

He stared for a moment. "Do you honestly think I'm afraid of death?"

There was such desolation in his words, slicing through her and cutting her to the bone.

"Do you honestly think I'm going to let you die?" she asked quietly.

She kept her hand fisted in the sleeve of his coat, feeling the tension pouring from him. He didn't move, barely seemed to breathe while he watched her, pupils mere slits in the darkness.

"Why?" he asked hoarsely. "Why do you care? I could have killed you last night. Let me at least atone for that."

His words didn't shock her, though maybe they should have. She'd felt the violence in whatever it was he'd become for that short time. And all vampires were perfectly capable killers, even at the best of times.

"You have nothing to atone for. That wasn't you," Bay said, and saw the surprise on his face. "I know that wasn't you. It was...something else. Do you even remember what you said to me?"

He slowly shook his head. "No. I never do. Bailey... the something else...I think I know what it is. When I was still in India, not long after I awakened, I saw a healer. Very old, very strong. Bailey..." He trailed off, and there was so much pain in his eyes. Somehow, she already knew what he would say. When it came to vampires, it was always a good idea to expect the worst.

It might have been funny, if it wasn't so constantly devastating.

Tasmin's voice dropped to a hoarse whisper. "There's a demon in me, Bailey. I don't know who put it there, or why. But it's there. It's made me do terrible things. Things

I'm glad I have no memory of. I think the demon is why I survived so long in that cave without food. And now it wants something. I have to fight it, Bailey. And when I'm with you, you *help* me fight it. Last night, I was gone... and then I felt you. Your kiss pulled me back." His hand, now hesitant, lifted again, paused, and then stroked a gentle path down her cheek. The tears had stopped, drying into salt.

Bay couldn't speak. Fear, anger, sorrow, need—they all tangled together in a hopeless knot deep in her chest. It wasn't fair—his curse, her feelings, none of it. Tasmin looked haunted.

"I don't know what that means. I don't know if I should keep you close or push you away. More than anything else, I don't want you hurt. I owe you this, Bailey. Let me protect you again, while I still can. It's the least I can do."

While I still can. He thought the demon would eventually overtake him. Bay knew that unless something was done, he was almost certainly right. Which was why she was so determined to do whatever she could to find that help for him. There had to be some kind of cure for this, something to pull the demon out of him.

The only shock she felt was that there *was* no real shock about this, only a resigned acceptance that she'd finally taken on a fight where the odds weren't only stacked against her, they were almost certainly insurmountable.

There was no reward waiting here, whatever happened.

But she didn't abandon people. And in some ways, being unable to see anything but one day at a time with Tasmin made giving in to the moment easier.

Bay stepped closer, drawn to the warmth that seemed to be as singular among vampires as Tasmin's other abilities. He didn't try to pull away, but she could feel him getting ready to bolt.

"You don't owe me anything," she said. "You saved my life last night."

His breath was ragged, his expression pained. "Of course I did. I would never let anyone hurt you."

The words, the raw honesty of them, reverberated deep within her.

"Then stay here with me."

"Bailey," he said, "I'm afraid *I'll* hurt you."

"Then why are you here right now? Why did you stay this morning? I know it was you," she added when he looked away. "I could smell you everywhere. I . . . I wanted to see you," she admitted. "I wish you'd stayed."

In a single fluid movement so quick she saw only a blur of motion, he grabbed her upper arms and pulled her into him. Her hands curled up in front of her, pressed against his chest. His breathing was fast and shallow, and the look in Tasmin's eyes was pure torment.

"Have you never wanted something you shouldn't, *meri jaan*?"

The words, unfamiliar and beautiful, felt like a caress. "What . . . what did you call me?"

Tasmin drew in a deep breath and lowered his eyes for just a moment. When he looked back up at her, there was a vulnerability in his expression that surprised her.

Why? she wondered sadly. *Why couldn't you have been just a man I met, instead of a part of all this?*

"*Meri jaan* is what you call someone you . . . care about," Tasmin said haltingly, and Bay knew he wasn't giving her the whole translation. Still, his admission made it unimportant right that instant.

"You care about me, then," she said. It was amazing, that this deadly creature could turn so charmingly awkward at the mention of emotion.

He didn't answer her, instead watching her with eyes that seemed to give off a searing heat all their own. "You didn't answer my question, Bailey. Did you ever want something you couldn't have? Not a small thing, but something that could break you if you let it?"

"Only you," she whispered.

He made a soft, pained sound, then pulled her against him. Bay sighed as she parted her lips, melting into the kiss. There was no coaxing this time, no hesitation. Instead of the fierce urgency of last night, however, Tasmin's mouth on hers was soft, gentle...and so thorough that Bay felt his need for her reverberate all the way down to her toes. The surprising sweetness of it made it all the more impossible to resist. Bay slid her arms up to twine around his neck while he drew her closer, deepening the kiss until nothing existed but the two of them, his mouth on hers. Bay stroked his thick, silken hair, over his broad shoulders, down his back. She could never seem to get close enough, Bay thought, increasingly frustrated with the amount of clothes between them. She wanted to be somewhere dark and quiet with him, skin to skin. Somewhere she could finally just give in and explore everything Tasmin had to offer. Her hands dropped to his hips, pulling him even closer. Bay hissed out a breath when she realized just how hard he was for her. Last night, teetering at the edge of an abyss, he'd been half-wild. Tonight there was a restraint that she didn't understand.

She wanted more than sweet. She wanted the lion back.

Tasmin pulled his lips from hers with a shudder and

pressed his forehead against hers. His eyes were closed, a faint frown creasing his brow. "I can hear your thoughts, Bailey," he said, the harshness of his voice betraying his desire. "You shout them at me. You have no idea what they do to me."

"Then show me," she breathed. A cold breeze wrapped itself around them, but Bay barely felt it. All she felt was the heat between them, the tight swelling between her legs, the way every motion abraded her already sensitive nipples when she brushed against him. She was so tired of trying to convince herself this was the wrong thing, since every time she was near Tasmin, it was the *only* thing.

When he opened his eyes, they glowed like dancing flames. His elongated fangs glittered in the near dark when he spoke, and still, she found it impossible to be afraid of him.

"I want to," he whispered. The sudden uncertainty that clouded his expression startled her as he continued, "But... you should have more. More than this. I'm not even—"

"Stop," Bay said, gentle but firm. Tasmin obliged her, swallowing the rest of whatever he'd been about to say. He couldn't possibly come up with any more caveats than she'd tried to use on herself. Nothing had worked. And it was clear from the way Tasmin held her, watched her, that he hadn't had any luck at turning away from the connection between them either.

Silently, Bay slipped her hands beneath his jacket, beneath his shirt, hungrily seeking the feel of hard flesh that still seemed kissed by the sun. The heat of him flowed into her, and he shuddered, the muscles jumping beneath her fingertips.

"It needs to be soon," Bay said softly. Somehow, it was easy to tell him what she wanted, what she needed, when it was a struggle for her with anyone else. She'd had no idea how much need she had. Maybe, in her own way, as much as Tasmin.

Slowly, he nodded, the promise in his eyes enough to steal her breath away.

"Soon is all I have to give, *meri jaan*...but it's yours if you want it."

She found no words with which to respond, only a strange sense of relief. Bay nodded, and she saw a similar relief reflected in his eyes, though tinged with regret. He already regretted the hurt he would cause her. Knowing that caused an ache deep in her chest unlike any she'd felt before.

Tasmin lowered his head to hers again, and Bay tipped her chin up to meet him. But she felt only the barest brush of his lips before there was a soft sound off to the side of them.

Someone was clearing their throat.

Bay's eyes flew open, and she and Tasmin looked at one another for a long moment. It never seemed to be the right time.

And it really did need to be soon.

They both tried to disentangle themselves at the same time, nearly toppling over one another trying to keep their footing. Bay's legs felt rubbery and strange, but she finally managed to straighten and turn to find a gorgeous, dark-haired woman, her hand on the pull handle of her suitcase, standing just a little ways away on the flagstone path to the door.

The woman was staring at Tasmin as though she'd seen a ghost.

"You," she said. "I know you."

"And I remember you," Tasmin said, and though his voice was as silken as ever, when Bay turned to look at him, she realized how shaken he was.

"I didn't remember your name. Still, when they said you were an Empusa, mated to one of my kind...I wondered. So you and Rai—"

The woman nodded, and Bay saw, to her amazement, that there was a sheen of tears in her dark eyes. This was Anura, she realized. The one Tasmin had been so determined to talk to.

"Yes. He was mine," Anura said. "I never thought I'd see your kind again once he was lost. He was one of the last. The Rakshasa are dust."

"I'm not dust. And I am Rakshasa."

There was silence as Tasmin and Anura regarded one another, and Bay suddenly felt as though she was intruding on something private. These two had obviously shared someone in their past. She backed away, realizing suddenly that Grimm had parked himself on the top step and flopped down, watching them all mournfully. He was also turning white—in the heat of the moment, Bay hadn't even noticed that big, fat flakes were now falling from the sky at a good clip.

The snow had finally come.

"Will you come inside?" Anura finally asked. She looked only at Tasmin, as though Bay wasn't even there. And to her, Bay knew, she wasn't. They'd never met. She probably just assumed she was some stupid human bimbo he'd picked up for some fun and a drink in town. Bay understood that was often how it worked...but that didn't make the dismissal any easier to swallow.

It was just another reminder that they didn't fit. No one would imagine them to be anything but predator and prey, however mutually agreeable that situation might be to some.

So Bay's heart sang when Tasmin turned to hold his hand out to her. For right now, they were in this together. Unequal partners, maybe, but partners.

Bay slipped her hand into his, and together, they headed for the door.

chapter ELEVEN

HE HAD FORGOTTEN HER NAME, like he had forgotten so many other things. But he hadn't forgotten Anura's face, and it had stunned him, this small piece of his past that had managed not to be crushed along with so much else.

He tried not to grip Bailey's hand too tightly. He supposed it should shame him, that he would want her so desperately as an anchor when things around him—and within him—kept shifting. He had never been a weakling. He should be the rock, she the one who sought comfort. But since he'd met her, that often seemed to be flipped around. It might have infuriated him, had he not been so glad to have her beside him.

Pretty thing.

He fought off a shudder as the words slithered through his mind. A reminder of what he was up against. But maybe Anura would have some answers.

Ty let them in, and Tasmin caught the glance at Bailey's hand caught in his. The cat's silver eyes narrowed ever so slightly, but he said nothing. Tasmin doubted he would. Lily had said all anyone was going to, which amounted to fair warning: *I won't have her hurt.*

He would have expected no less.

"Bay," Ty said once he'd greeted Anura, "I didn't figure we'd see you tonight. Is everything okay?"

Bailey's hand gripped his just a little more tightly, and Tasmin remembered what she'd come for.

"Not really," she said, and explained what she'd seen.

Ty cursed softly in Gaelic, while Tasmin tried to watch Bailey without looking like he was staring. It was difficult. She looked as beautiful tonight as she always did, her hair caught up in a loose bun, her cheeks pink from both the cold and rubbing against his face. Her lips were still slightly swollen from his kisses, her eyes bright. The signs of his touch that lingered on her brought on a wave of possessiveness that surprised him with its ferocity.

Mine, he thought. And then, from the dark places inside, another voice bubbled up: *I will drink the blood of her heart, Rakshasa. I will make her beg before she dies.*

Tasmin's stomach did a slow roll. *Never. Never that.*

"I don't suppose you got a close look at any of them?" Ty asked.

She shook her head, and a wavy lock of hair fell over one eye. Tasmin brushed it aside to tuck it behind her ear before he really thought about it. Immediately, he felt both Ty's and Anura's eyes on him. Flustered, he pulled away from Bailey altogether and stuffed his hands in his pockets. Gods knew he would do something else stupid with them before long if he didn't force himself to stop.

What was between them was for no one else.

"I don't think recognizing any one vampire was really

the point," Bailey said. "I think it was just about scaring me. And telling you."

"It's good you came here," Anura said to her. "They're almost certainly Ptolemy." She turned to Ty. "She's getting bolder. How long has it been like this?"

"Since I came," Tasmin said, answering for him. "It's me. Arsinöe wants me."

Anura looked puzzled. "All this for you? The last Rakshasa would be a prize for someone like her, I'm sure. But I'm surprised she's risking so much to get her hands on you, and now, of all times. Warring with one another when our enemy would like nothing better than to pick us off one by one is foolish. Arsinöe could be called a lot of things, but foolish has never been one of them."

"I know her as well as anyone," Ty replied. "I don't know what this is about, but I do know one thing. Her reasons for doing this will end up being worse than whatever I could come up with. She has no boundaries."

Tasmin looked at him curiously. "You were close to the queen?"

"I was her prized pet."

That surprised him... and gave him a better appreciation of just what Ty had been up against to get to where he was. It still stunned Tasmin that the Cait Sith had managed to break away at all. Ty was right—the queen of the Ptolemy was not a woman easily defeated or deterred.

And from the look on the man's face, he was being forced to remember exactly how true that was. His expression was grim.

"I'm sorry about this, Bay," Ty said.

"It isn't your fault, Ty," Bailey said firmly. "It isn't anybody's fault except that ancient Egyptian bitch."

Ty's smile was rueful. "True enough. I'll take a few people over to your house, cats and wolves both, and we'll see what we can find. The town will need a sweep as well, for all the good it'll do us." He growled, a soft, frustrated sound. "They know how well we can all track. The ones we find will just be sacrificial lambs, useful tools she's got no issues parting with. This is a stunt to taunt us, nothing more."

"And to warn you," Anura murmured, looking pointedly at Bailey. "This won't be the end."

"Her games won't end until she does," Tasmin said. Arsinöe had always been good at pinpointing where to strike so she would inflict the most pain. A mortal woman, highly valued by both Lily and her kind, made a tantalizing—and relatively easy—target. Killing her would demoralize the dynasty Arsinöe considered her enemy. And if she'd been watching, she knew it would wound him as well.

That was a thing it was too late to change.

"Come on," Ty said. "Bay, I'll pick up some things for you when we're at your place, and *please* don't argue. I know we'd all feel better if you stayed at least the night. Depending on what we find, we can figure out tomorrow when it comes."

Tasmin could see the fear beginning to show through the brave facade she put up. It was telling that Bailey didn't look inclined to argue.

"Yeah," she said. "I don't really feel like going back there tonight." Then she sighed, a frustrated rush of air, and frowned into the distance. "I have to close the shop for the next few days, at least until I'm sure things have died down here. I won't have them targeting anyone else I care about. Anna and Shelby matter more than the money.

This will be paid time off for them." She rubbed a hand over her face. "I'm going to have a mess with the customers, but I'll manage. Somehow."

She sounded so disheartened, but there was nothing he could do about it. Just another sign of his helplessness. He wished there were something he could tear apart to vent his frustration.

Ty ushered them all into Lily's favorite parlor at the back of the mansion, a room of warm woods and clean-lined furniture that Tasmin found he liked, though not quite as well as the cozy nest Bailey had created for herself. Still, it was a reflection of the woman who owned it—elegant, beautiful, but accessible. When they walked in, Lily herself was already occupied saying hello to Grimm, who had bounded in this direction the moment the front door had opened and scattered the snow he'd been wearing in every which direction.

She looked up when they entered, her warm smile broadening when she took in the group of them.

"Hey, everyone's here!" She threw her arms around Anura, wrapping her in a tight embrace. Tasmin watched, wondering how the women knew one another. They had the look of old friends, which they could hardly be with Lily so young. But then, he'd said it to Lily himself—she was now the ruler of a dynasty that had once been the nexus of them all. So it would be again, no matter how Arsinöe fought it.

Lily drew back from Anura and looked curiously at Bailey.

"Bay, did you get introduced already? And Tasmin? I should have been keeping a better eye out, I got my nose stuck in a book—"

Tasmin glanced around the room and saw a paperback laying open and facedown on an end table beside a barrel chair.

"It's all right," Tasmin said. "It turns out that Anura and I knew each other a little, once."

Lily's eyes widened. "You've got to be kidding me."

Anura's smile was bright, but wavered quickly. Outside, she'd stared at him as though he were nothing but a spirit. But to her, he and his kind had been ghosts for centuries. He was sure her feelings for Rai, strong as they must have been, only made it worse.

"No, it's true," Anura said. "My mate, Rai, was the leader of Tasmin's pride. I wasn't around much when Tasmin was among them—Rai and I spent a lot of years dancing around one another before we finally quit being stupid—" She stopped herself, and Tasmin was surprised to hear so much pain in her voice.

"It doesn't matter. I remember they sometimes talked about men they'd lost. I never imagined your mysterious Rakshasa was one."

Lily looked between the two of them. "I shouldn't be surprised. Everything that's happened seems to have been for a reason. Pieces clicking back together."

"Despite some people's best efforts to stop them," Ty interjected. He'd hung back for the greetings, but the air about him had gone from brooding to murderous. Any Ptolemy that crossed his path tonight would die—Tasmin knew it, and wished he could join him. For once, it would be an acceptable outlet for all the hunger and rage he carried within.

But if he didn't talk to Anura now, he might not get another chance. There was a storm coming to this place.

He could feel it in the air. It might very well hit before he got the answers he so desperately wanted.

As Ty filled Lily in, he saw bright flickers of light begin to jump between her fingertips. She would make a formidable enemy, especially in a century or so when she'd had time to sit with her power. That was, if she made it that far. Her fury was a palpable thing.

"I'll leave you all now," she said, her voice strained. There was a strange light in her eyes. "There are preparations I need to start making."

"Lily," Bailey said softly, and when her friend looked at her, she actually shrank back a little. In her anger, Lily was unmistakably immortal. Tasmin knew that this was the heart of the tension he felt even now between the two women, the gulf they couldn't breach unless Bailey, alone, crossed it. And he couldn't imagine a woman so suited to sunlight doing that willingly.

The thought sat poorly with him. He had seen humans who sought the vampires because they wanted the darkness. Bailey put up with the darkness to keep her friend. He just didn't know how far she would go.

For anything—or anyone—that mattered to her.

"I'm sorry about this," Bailey said, collecting herself quickly. "If there's anything I can do—"

"You can stay safe," Lily said, her voice gentling. "We'll figure out how to accomplish that as quickly as we can. For now, you and the slobber king sit tight, okay? *Mi casa es su casa*. Raid the fridge. Get into my stuff. Just... stay here."

"While you decide who to light on fire first."

Lily's smile was biting. "Damn right."

"Then you got it," Bailey said.

Tasmin watched the obvious warmth between the two women and felt a dull ache in his chest. There had been a time he'd had that. His pride had raised him, then turned him when they'd deemed him ready. He had known those men as brothers, as family. But they were gone.

He glanced at Anura and saw she'd been watching him, as though she knew what he was feeling. Tasmin had to turn away from the sympathy in her gaze. She'd had centuries to rebuild a life. He'd had six months that had been crippled by the *thing* he carried with him.

That made him alone in ways even she wouldn't understand.

And it made the fragile connection he'd made with Bailey that much more precious. Right now, it was all he had.

Lily excused herself and swept from the room, and with her exit some of the pressure in the air eased. She wore her power so easily it was easy to forget that she had it, Tasmin realized. But to do so would be a mistake.

"Well," Anura breathed, looking as though there were many places she would rather be than here. "We all know why I'm here. Shall we?"

She settled herself on the love seat, while Tasmin sat on the couch. Bailey hovered uncertainly by the wing chair, her big dog sitting beside her and panting happily. She'd removed her coat, and in her dirty, pale pink scrubs and sneakers, she looked unusually vulnerable...and very, very human.

"I'll leave you guys to it," she said. "I don't want to intrude."

"You aren't," Tasmin said, surprised by how ill at ease she suddenly seemed. "You're welcome to stay and hear this."

Part of him, a big part, wanted her to stay. He wanted her to know that there was more to his past than just that miserable cave, than blackouts and wandering. But when Bailey looked between him and Anura, and then at the doorway through which Lily had just departed, her hand nervously fluttering up to tuck another loose wave back behind her ear, he could see she'd already made up her mind to go.

"No, that's okay," she said. Her smile looked forced. "You two need some time to yourselves, and I should get Grimm settled."

Grimm looked perfectly settled, much as he did anywhere Tasmin had seen the dog, but he wouldn't argue with her. Anura said nothing, simply watching the conversation with an inordinate amount of interest.

"Then...I'll see you later." He hoped it didn't sound like as much of a question as he feared it did. He didn't want to need to see her. Not that that changed anything.

Bailey's relief was obvious. In the light, he could see the dark smudges beneath her eyes, leftovers from last night...probably the last week dealing with him. Guilt gnawed at him. She was human, she needed rest. And she needed a respite from what seemed to be a rapidly escalating situation here in her hometown.

"Yes," she agreed, her smile easier now. "Later. Nice meeting you, Anura."

Anura inclined her head regally. "The same."

Bailey started to walk out the door, quietly urging Grimm along. The dog got up and amiably lumbered over to Tasmin instead.

"*Grimm.*"

He ignored her, looked thoughtfully at Tasmin with

his coffee-colored eyes, and then began the arduous process of piling his big, furry body up onto the couch beside him. Tasmin pressed his lips together, trying not to let his amusement show since Bailey looked utterly frustrated.

"Grimm, come *here*."

The dog sighed and plopped his head in Tasmin's lap.

Anura coughed softly to cover what was obviously a laugh.

"He's fine," Tasmin said. "I'll bring him to you later."

Bailey growled, threw up her hands, and left the room muttering unkind things about ill-behaved four-legged traitors.

When she was gone, Anura looked from the obstinate Newfoundland to Tasmin with keen interest.

"It isn't the lion lying down with the lamb, but it's close. Odd that he'd be so easy with you so quickly."

Tasmin smiled and scratched behind Grimm's ear. "She says he likes who he likes, and there's no changing his mind. Who am I to argue about his taste?"

"His taste mirrors hers," Anura said, and tilted her head at him, her almond eyes alight with keen interest. "You plan to stay among the Lilim, then?"

That gave him pause. "I . . . hadn't thought much about it," he admitted. He'd been too consumed with just getting through each day. "Why do you ask?"

Anura raised finely arched eyebrows. "I've already seen you wrapped around the queen's best friend. Bay Harper is well loved here. You have to know that's not a great choice for a dalliance."

"That's not any of your business," Tasmin growled, caught off guard by Anura's frankness. He supposed he shouldn't have been. The woman had driven Rai half-mad with her opinions when she'd been around in his time. It had just been so long...he'd forgotten. But she was doing a fine job reminding him.

Anura shrugged. "No, it's not, really. Just be careful, or the Rakshasa really will be extinct."

"I can worry about that on my own," Tasmin said flatly. He couldn't imagine a future yet. He didn't want to expect something that he very well might not have. Finding out what was possible...that was why Anura had been asked here. He leaned forward and asked the question that had plagued him almost since his awakening.

"What happened to all of them, Anura? Where did they go?"

Her smile faltered. "They're dead. Long dead. You know that by now."

"That's the only thing I know," he replied. Grimm's soft fur beneath his hand was soothing, a welcome balm to wounds that had not yet healed. "I want to know when, how. Why."

Anura blew out an unsteady breath and looked away.

"When Lily told me about you, asked me to come... I almost couldn't. I was so worried you'd look like him. I know that's stupid. Every Rakshasa was as individual as anyone else. But it's been so long, part of me thought you might even—"

She stopped abruptly, and Tasmin was fairly sure she'd hoped he was Rai, that some twist of fate had spared her lover after all. Rai had been a good leader, strong and competent and wise. Maybe he would have been better able to handle what had been done to him, Tasmin thought. Perhaps he'd been chosen for the cave because he was younger, weaker.

And his doubts helped no one, he reminded himself. What was done was done.

"He was a good man," Tasmin offered. It was inadequate, but it was the truth. The longer he looked at Anura, the more he recalled her occasional visits as an emissary of her dynasty. His pride had an uneasy alliance with the Empusae. The relationship between Anura and Rai, he remembered, had reflected that. The two had bickered incessantly when she was there.

It didn't actually surprise him that they'd finally gotten together.

"I...thank you. Yes, he was." Anura shook her head, the dark waves shifting over her shoulders. "I mean no offense by this, Tasmin, but seeing you brings back things I thought I'd forgotten. Things I'd rather forget."

"I'm sorry for that. But those are things I need to know."

Anura flinched. Still, she answered him. "Arsinöe killed them all. Every last one. By her orders or by her own hand, she made sure that every last Rakshasa was dust," Anura said, her voice flat. "It was a terrible time, one of the darkest I can remember...and that's saying something. Trust me on this one thing, Tasmin. It was a blessing you weren't able to see it. You wouldn't have survived it."

"Maybe—"

"No," she said, cutting him off. "You wouldn't have. She was merciless. I wasn't sure she would spare *me*, honestly. I carry your mark, after all." Unbidden, she pulled down the neck of her sweater to reveal the torch of the Empusae held by the lion's paw, a unique blending of their dynasty marks as singular as the pairing between her and Rai had been. Her smile was bitter.

"Fortunately for me, I'm now technically mixed-blood scum. So I seem to have fallen beneath her notice."

The grief hit him without warning. It was one of those odd things...He had mourned deeply for weeks after emerging from the cave and discovering that everyone had vanished. The worst of that had ebbed. But at different times, the grief would return, creeping up behind him and then taking him down in an ambush that left him shaken and reeling. He still saw their faces, his brothers. Heard their voices. But they were lost to him now, continuing on their own journeys. He would not know them again.

Seeing that final imprint of his pride brother on Anura's olive skin, the only trace of Rai remaining in the world, hurt in a way nothing else had.

"I'm sorry. So sorry they're gone," he said, his voice barely a rasp.

Anura's eyes glittered in the dim light. "As am I. I would say more than you could know, but...you *do* know. I thought maybe there would be some comfort in that. Instead, it just reminds me of how lost I was after it happened." She sighed. "I have no insight, Tasmin. Arsinöe destroys things because she can. She hates the animal-shifters because she needs to feel superior to things that are different from herself. She chose the Rakshasa because your power made her uneasy...and because she saw a way to do it."

The rage and sorrow he felt were bone deep. To his horror, he could feel whatever lurked in that hole inside himself stir, responding to all of the toxic emotion. Tasmin tried to close it off, to at least find a productive way to deal with it.

It was nearly impossible.

"They were my brothers, Anura," he said. "I couldn't fight for them. Maybe I can avenge them."

She looked wistful. "That would take destroying the entire Ptolemy dynasty. I've wished for that a million times over the years." Anura turned her gaze toward the open doorway. "Now, though, I think the opportunity is finally coming. I always thought I'd be excited about it. Instead, I just worry about who else she'll break before all is said and done. It's a mark of having gotten older, I guess. I moved on in some ways, learned to care about other people again. I value their lives more than I value revenge." A faint smile. "Not that I'll cry when Lily crushes Arsinöe beneath one very nice boot heel."

"That should have been done *then*. Why did no one try to stop her when she was hunting us?" Tasmin asked, feeling slightly ill knowing that his people had been exterminated while the other dynasties had simply looked on.

Anura's voice turned bitter. "They were distracted. The North American Council was still in the process of forming, leaders were haggling over territory, the old European guard was furiously lobbying to keep the power centralized in the traditional territories...and Vlad Dracul was very busy muscling his way into legitimacy, which was making heads explode everywhere. The Rakshasa were so different from the rest...You all kept so much to yourselves, every pride its own little sovereign nation. You never spoke with one voice, and when the deaths began to pile up, it was awhile before you learned to scream for help with one voice." She rolled her shoulders restlessly. "By then, of course, it was too late. I will say that when the dust settled and it became clear just what Arsinöe had done, there was agreement—quiet agreement—that such a thing wouldn't be tolerated again." She looked away. "I wish I could say I believed it."

It was hard to hear. Harder, actually, than he'd expected, even if there were no surprises. But there was more Tasmin needed to be able to put it to rest within himself. He would hear it all once, and then never again. It was a vow he made to himself.

"And my pride? Rai?"

"He and the rest of your pride had found what they thought was a good hiding place, an out-of-the-way temple removed from the bulk of the fighting that was going on. They thought they would make it there. It was sacred ground, and secluded. He sent a message to me...so hopeful it would be all right after all..."

Anura trailed off, then shook her head. "Rai was wrong. She found them, or her people did. But Arsinöe finished them, from what I understand. Because they truly were the last. I wasn't there. I wish I could have been there. Maybe I could have helped. I was away when she found them, looking for a place to take us all out of country. My own dynasty had disowned me by then, of course, but I still had the support of plenty of my sisters." She laughed softly, humorlessly. "I'd found somewhere for all of us, actually. A place with plenty of room to run, a safe place. Quiet. But it didn't matter."

Her eyes were far off, remembering. Tasmin felt his own slow-burning rage grow hotter, both on her behalf, and his brothers'. Their lives had been destroyed, taken. And for what? Because they were too powerful. Because they couldn't be controlled.

Because Arsinöe had always feared and loathed the

power of any vampire who could harness the abilities of the beasts. And, as Anura had said, simply because she could.

"Are you sure they're gone?" Tasmin asked, his voice sounding hoarse and strange to his own ears. "Maybe they were hidden like me. Maybe there are more of us out there."

Anura looked pained.

"Maybe there are, Tasmin. But not Rai. I felt him go. When you're bonded...I can't explain the sensation to you. But I felt the tie between us sever the moment he died." Her eyes slipped shut. "The pain was...nothing I can describe. No, I knew. And I knew the Rakshasa were gone." She opened her almond eyes and pinned him with them. "Until you. And now you have the story you wanted. Now I want *your* story in return. How did you escape?"

Haltingly, he told her of the cave in the Gir, of awakening alone four hundred years after his last memory. Anura's gaze never wavered as he spoke. When he was finished, she was silent a moment.

"I've heard of such things, but not in...gods, centuries. I wasn't sure whether it was really possible, though. Forcing one of us to sleep so long and then expecting us to come out whole is a pretty iffy proposition. You couldn't have been much more than a corpse at first."

Tasmin cringed, remembering.

"No. I wasn't."

"And now?" Something in her expression told him she already knew he wasn't what he had once been.

"Now...I seem to be something...else."

She leaned forward, and to his relief he saw no horror in her eyes.

"Just as I thought," she said, the last words he'd expected to hear. "Tell me what they did to you."

"I can only tell you what a healer told me not long after I awakened," Tasmin said. "I think—no, I *know* he was right. Just as I know that if things stay this way, I might as well have died. It's going to kill me."

"No, it won't," Anura said, and in her voice was the fire he remembered from long ago. "I couldn't save the rest of them. But I'll be damned if I don't find a way to save you."

chapter TWELVE

T Y HAD RETURNED just long enough to shove a stuffed
suitcase into her arms before vanishing into the night
again.

Over an hour later, Bay had finally dragged it into
the room she'd chosen, muttering to herself as she dug
through it. She couldn't seem to settle down. And she
wasn't the only one.

There was a weird, unpleasant energy in the house
tonight. Most of the Lilim had apartments and houses out
in town, but there were some who stayed here, and all of
them were whispering among themselves. None of them
paid much attention to her. That wasn't so unusual, in and
of itself. She was just the oddball human hanger-on. But
that feeling of not belonging had intensified tonight to the
point where she felt actively unwelcome by some of the
Lilim.

In a way, she understood. If something bad happened,
she was nothing but a liability. She couldn't shoot energy

or turn into anything with sharp teeth or drive people insane with nothing but her willpower. She didn't even have her shears to stab anybody with...not that any of her grooming tools would do much to stop the average vampire.

Bay sighed, head drooping, her hands stilling as she sorted through the odd hodgepodge of things Ty had brought her.

"I am the crappiest sidekick *ever*," she said.

She didn't even qualify as a sidekick. Sidekicks did something. She seemed to be purely ornamental. Which was pretty sad, considering she was usually covered in dog fur.

Trying to pull herself out of her increasingly lousy mood, Bay pawed through the six pairs of fuzzy socks Ty had stuck in the suitcase. She couldn't decide whether it was sweet or just kind of sad that he knew her that well already.

Probably a little of both.

A familiar sound heading down the hallway toward her door had her pausing in mid-rummage. She would know Grimm's slow, heavy-footed amble anywhere by now. And sure enough, after a few more thuds, he nosed around the edge of the door and moseyed in, looking for all the world like he expected her to have forgotten all about his traitorous activities downstairs by now.

"You're lucky you're cute," she said as his eyes brightened at the sight of her and he trotted forward, knocking a small porcelain bowl off the dresser with his tail in the process. She barely caught it, winding up in an awkward position on her side. Grimm took full advantage, looming over her and trying to drown her in joyful slobber.

"Ack!" she managed. "Bleh! Grimm! Stop it—gah!" But she was giggling as she curled into the fetal position and tried to fend him off, which only made him more determined to shower her with doggy kisses. He shoved his nose up under the hands she was covering her face with.

"Hey!" Bay laughed.

"Do you need help?"

Tasmin's voice finally broke Grimm's single-minded concentration, and he relented to go give her visitor a cursory sniff. Bay sat up, wiping at her face and pushing at hair that was now completely hopeless. She watched Grimm decide Tasmin wasn't interesting, then take a flying leap onto the big four-poster bed and flop down, silently daring anyone to try and remove him.

"You brat," she said. He panted at her happily. He knew she was a sucker.

Resigned to having him see her like this, Bay turned to look at Tasmin. He'd only ventured a step into the room, and he didn't look like he was sure he should even have come that far.

She wasn't sure either.

"I'm fine," she said. "A mess, but fine."

He watched her out of those bright gold eyes, giving nothing of what he was thinking away. She wasn't sure she wanted to know, at the moment, considering she still hadn't changed out of her scrubs. And that her hair was likely in some kind of lopsided fauxhawk held in place by Newf drool.

Since he seemed content to just stand there not saying anything, which she had decided was one of his more unnerving habits, Bay turned her attention back to the suitcase.

"He packed me four pairs of flannel pajama pants. Four. And one pair of jeans. Does he think I go out in public in my pajamas?" It was more a rhetorical question than one she expected Tasmin to try and answer, but it did get a response.

"Ty packed your clothes?"

"Mmm-hmm. And I'm trying to figure out how he decided what to put in here, because it doesn't make any sense to me. It looks like he covered his eyes, reached into my underwear drawer, and just grabbed a handful of whatever before he stuffed it in the suitcase." Actually, Bay was pretty sure that was *exactly* what the man had done.

"It looks like he expects you to stay for a while," Tasmin said, taking another step in and looking curiously at the suitcase. She watched him out of the corner of her eye, trying not to let his presence affect her the way it always did. Especially after what had happened outside. That had been...

Yeah, she decided as heat flooded her from head to toe. There weren't words for what that had been. Amazing? A promise of things to come? A bad idea? All of the above?

"I don't know," Bay said. "I don't know what's going on." Then she did look up at him. "No one tells me anything. Lily is locked in her office on the phone, Ty looked like he wanted to kill someone when he showed up with the suitcase, and according to Eric Black, who I bumped into while I was hoping to eavesdrop something useful in this place, there was definitely somebody in my house."

Tasmin's expression hardened. "I see."

"Don't," Bay said sharply, dumping handfuls of clothes back into the suitcase in a pile and sitting back on the floor.

"Don't you get all homicidal too. Everybody here is whispering about war. Not that they told me that. Me being the token useless human here."

"You're not useless."

She gave him a beleaguered look. "Don't patronize me. I'm a very useful person in my normal life. Here, I'm talking and occasionally interesting food. If we get attacked, I'm toast, and everyone knows it." She looked at Grimm, who had flopped onto his back and was snoring softly. "I've got to at least figure out how to get him somewhere safer. I'd be devastated if anything happened to him."

Tasmin looked at her a moment, then surprised her by lowering himself to the floor to sit beside her. He didn't get too close...but he seemed to be offering company, and right now, she was glad to accept it.

"Maybe you could take him to your family. Are they near here?"

It was nice that he didn't tease her about how concerned she was for her dog. "No," she replied. "My parents moved to Florida last year. They'd had it with the winters here. Dad had an opportunity to go with his job... so they went. I'm happy for them. I mean, they love it, so..." She trailed off, shrugged. "And Steve, my older brother, is a big-time lawyer in DC. He'll probably run for office eventually, God help us all."

Tasmin chuckled. "You miss them."

She quirked a half smile at him. "Of course I do. Mom and Dad poke at me about moving down. Sometimes I think about it, but I don't know if Florida's for me. And I like it here. Steve is pretty wrapped up in his own stuff, but he calls to annoy me when he can." Her face fell a little. "I didn't think I'd be the only one who stayed. But

I have my business, and my friends." She sighed. "I don't know. I'm twenty-eight. I feel like I should be more satisfied than I am, but I'm just...restless."

She laughed then, embarrassed. "Ignore me. I'm nervous, so I'm babbling."

"I like hearing about you," Tasmin said, and Bay looked at him skeptically.

"No," he protested. "It's interesting to me. And...nice, that you got to know your parents. I didn't know mine."

"Oh," she replied, feeling suddenly guilty for having complained at all. "I'm sorry."

But Tasmin waved the apology off. "Don't be. There were things I missed, but I gained a group of brothers. The pride raised me. I can't regret that."

She watched him, curious. "Seriously? They raised you?"

He nodded, draping his arms casually over his knees. "They did. My pride was sought after by many of the most important men in the land. We were fierce warriors, but honorable. Not all of my kind were. Our lineage made us highbloods to the other dynasties, but we were never structured like they are. Every pride was its own. There was no Rakshasa court, no king or queen. Just many small groups, all operating as they saw fit. That was both good and very bad, at times. The reputation of a few left most people in terror of all of us."

"But not the guys who wanted you to fight for them."

"Greed is usually stronger than fear," Tasmin said with a small smile. "And as I said, my pride was known to be honorable. I was actually given to seal an alliance between the pride and a powerful family."

Her eyes rounded. "Your family *gave you* to the Rakshasa?"

Tasmin nodded. "It wasn't as though my father didn't have enough sons to carry on the line. I was his twenty-second, by his sixth wife."

"Wow. That's . . . way outside my realm of experience," she admitted. "But they must have missed you, Tasmin. You don't just give up a child and not care."

He looked pensive. "I don't know," he said. "I often thought . . . it must have hurt my mother. I doubt my father thought much of it. There were so many children. I was too small to even remember. In any case, I was raised by the pride. They became my brothers in every sense that mattered. It was a long time before I even realized that many of the people we were protecting were my biological family."

She frowned. "Didn't *they* know?"

"Probably."

Bay struggled to understand. "And that was . . . okay. With you."

He smiled. "Bailey. It was a different place, a different time. I didn't *know* them. I knew the pride, and even though they could be hard, they were a good family to me. I have no regrets." But then his smile faded, and she knew he had one. He'd wanted to save them, and he hadn't been able to. She wished she could heal that wound, but only time would do that . . . or as much as could ever be done.

"So how did things go with Anura?" she asked, wanting to turn his attention back to things that *could* be changed. She hoped.

"They were . . . interesting," he allowed, and his expression became inscrutable. He looked at his hands, frowning lightly. "I think she can help. But there are things that need to be done."

"Oh," Bay said, trying to keep her tone light. She desperately wanted to know what had gone on, but she wasn't going to beg for information. It was none of her business, she told herself. Well, mostly not her business. Even though she'd taken him in, put him up, and dealt with him when his split personality had shown up.

Her jaw tensed the way it always did when her stress levels started to rise. It would give her a lovely headache if she didn't watch it. Bay fought the urge to massage it. Planting herself in the bed face-first soon would take care of most of this. She'd deal with tomorrow when it came.

Tasmin slid a look at her and must have seen how she felt written across her face, because he relented a little.

"She's contacting some of her dynasty sisters tonight. The Empusae who didn't abandon her when she was banished for mating with my pride brother, Rai."

Bay bristled at his succinct description of Anura's situation. "I know that what I think doesn't make any difference here, but what the dynasties do, to each other and their own people, really sucks."

"It does," he agreed. "But they didn't all turn on her. The Empusae know more about ritual and magic than most dynasties ever did. And that's what I need, Anura believes, to cure me. Ritual, and magic. And luck."

He didn't look very excited about it, Bay noted.

"Does she know what's wrong with you? Not just a guess, like the healer, but . . . does she really *know*?"

He hesitated. "Yes."

Bay pressed her lips together. "Okay then." She refused to push him further. It had been a rough couple of nights for both of them, and it was possible he just wanted to deal with this on his own. If so, she would let him. Even if it gave her the same sinking feeling she'd had downstairs earlier, when she'd been left alone with him and Anura—the feeling that she was out of her element with nothing to offer, that she was in the way as far more important events and individuals swirled around her.

She pushed to her feet, grabbing her comfy old pajamas in one hand. Bay was startled to find herself near tears. She was beginning to hate this week. She'd never been a girl who bawled at the drop of a hat. Even knowing it was mostly exhaustion mixed with a healthy dose of feeling sorry for herself didn't stop it from being irritating.

"I'm leaving," Tasmin said, jerking her back into the moment. Bay's head snapped toward him.

"You ... you are?"

He nodded. "Tomorrow night. I need to go with Anura if I want to have any chance at stopping what's happening to me."

Bay felt an ugly burst of jealousy coupled with a wave of sadness so crushing it took her completely by surprise ... It was that much worse because of it.

"Okay," she said. It was pretty much all she could manage without losing it right then and there, and she had no intention of doing that. So much for *soon is all I have but it's yours if you want it.* She turned away and went stiffly to the bed, carefully laying out her pajamas. It gave her hands something to do, even if her mind was a million miles away.

She reached over and curled her hand around Grimm's hand-sized paw, stroking her thumb over the fur. It helped a little, but not enough. It was stupid, she thought, to get this wound up over a guy she'd known for a week. A very weird guy, she reminded herself, who had all kinds of problems on top of being a five-hundred-year-old vampire.

A guy she hadn't been able to get out of her head since she'd met him.

She'd even started thinking about the pros and cons of vampirism for herself, really thinking, which was something she hadn't put a lot of thought into even after Lily had been turned. Suddenly, it had become a diverting and tantalizing what-if game. *What if we fall madly in love? What if he wants to be with me forever? What if he accidentally bites me during wild monkey sex on my kitchen floor? How would that go? How would I handle it? Is that what I would want?*

Well, he was leaving. Nonexistent problem solved. She hadn't felt quite this ridiculous in a very long time.

"Bailey," Tasmin said softly. He slunk up right beside her again without making a sound, a fact that suddenly irritated the hell out of her.

"Why can't you just call me Bay like everybody else does?" she snapped, refusing to look at him. "I'm named after my mom's favorite liquor. Seriously, it's not like everyone has shortened some ethereally beautiful song of a name."

"I like your name," he said, and his voice was still heartbreakingly gentle. Why couldn't he just fight with her, she thought? Maybe he was actually a big jerk underneath the sweet, slightly arrogant exterior. That would make her feel better, now that he was taking off.

Or not.

Then his hands were on her shoulders, and what little fight she had in her vanished, leaving her with nothing but a hollow ache. She closed her eyes.

"I understand that you have to go," she said softly. "I really do. My feelings about that aren't your problem, okay? But I'm tired, and upset, and I need to sort that out, so it would be better if you just let me alone right now."

"I know," he said, and the words cut her as deeply as a blade might have.

"Then go," she said, both a command and a plea. But his hands didn't leave her shoulders.

"I can't," he said, and there was something so close to breaking in his voice that it made her turn. What she saw in his eyes when they were face-to-face made words impossible. He was so ancient, she realized. And so incredibly sad.

"Whoever left me in that cave put a demon inside me," Tasmin said. "That's what it is, Bailey. Not a spirit...a demon. It kept me alive, but at a price. It's something I can't control. I know I've killed innocents, Bailey. If I don't try to do something, that won't end. It can only get worse. I won't risk you."

Bay drew in a shuddering breath. It suddenly felt far more real than it had outside, when the blow had been softened with a kiss. Through no fault of his own, Tasmin had been turned into a ticking time bomb.

"What happens if she can't get it out?" she asked, her voice barely a whisper. "What then?"

"Then she thinks it will kill me. And that...would be for the best, Bailey." His expression was heartbreaking. "I used to fight with honor. I won't be a tool for this *thing*."

What he was saying made perfect sense—and it was one of the hardest things she'd ever had to hear. Especially because she understood more than he said out loud.

"You'll have *them* kill you, won't you? The Empusae. If whatever they try doesn't work."

Slowly, he nodded. "If there is nothing else to be done, yes. I can't live like this. It isn't living. Not when I'm afraid to feed, to walk among humans...to be alone with you."

She couldn't find the right words to say, if there were any. Instead, she went with what she felt, knowing that it might be the last time she had the opportunity. Without a sound, she slid into his arms. Tasmin pulled her closer, burying his face against her neck. She could feel him trembling, and though she'd been holding herself nearly as tightly, she stroked a hand down his back, through his hair, trying to soothe what nothing truly could.

"If things were different...," he breathed. "I think about you all the time, Bailey."

His words, his arms around her, made her response easier. "I think about you all the time too," she admitted as he eased back, gentling his hold on her. Bay rested her cheek against his chest, soothed by the slow, steady beat of his immortal heart. "I didn't think I would. I've never had a hard time saying no to any of the vamps around here. I just wasn't interested."

Tasmin's hand rubbed a lazy circle on her back.

"You're surrounded by vampires," he mused. "You're Lily's closest friend. And you've never even considered being with a vampire? Not even for a single date?"

She smiled, thinking about how strange it must sound. "Nope. Not even for dinner and a movie."

"You can't tell me they haven't asked. You're beautiful."

Bay blushed, and she was glad he couldn't see just how easily he could affect her with an offhand compliment.

He didn't sound like he was trying to flatter her. He mostly sounded like he couldn't quite believe her. Which, considering that vampires were well known for their beauty, she didn't blame him for.

"A few asked. The ones brave enough to risk the wrath of Lily. Warnings go out on a regular basis, believe me. But I always said no." She paused, trying to figure out how to explain the heart of it without offending him. "Up until you, Tasmin, I've kind of tried to avoid the whole vampire... *thing*."

The chuckle that rumbled through his chest surprised her. She tilted her head back to frown up at him, wondering why he found it so funny. His grin was boyish, open. A glimpse of the man she wished he got to be more often.

"What?" she asked.

"I was just thinking how frustrating you must be for them. So accessible, but so unavailable."

"To them," Bay said. "Not to you."

His smile faded, but the warmth didn't as he watched her quizzically. "And I'm more grateful for that than you could possibly know, even if I don't understand it. I am what they are."

Bay shook her head slowly. "No. You're different than any man I've ever met, mortal or vampire. You're you. That's all I see. That's why I'm here."

She could see what the words meant to him, and was glad she'd given him the truth. Tasmin said nothing, only pulled her back tightly against him, tucking her head beneath his chin. As they stayed entwined, what had started as comfort quickly turned to need. Her nerve endings sizzled everywhere her body touched his, his breath against her neck sending delicious waves of sensation shivering over her skin.

Her desire for him unfurled like the petals of some night-blooming flower. Bay welcomed it, refusing to question something that felt so right when everything else seemed to be falling apart. Nothing outside this room was right anymore. Everything was changing; nothing made sense. All her best-laid plans were going up in flames.

But she had Tasmin, at least for tonight. And though he might never know, she needed him at least as much as he needed her.

"Be with me tonight," she said, and he pulled back to look at her again, his eyes burning like twin suns.

"But what if—"

"I pulled you back once before," Bay reminded him. "I can do it again." She rose up and pressed a soft kiss to his lips once, twice, savoring the way his mouth felt on hers.

"It might not be what you imagine, Bailey," he said softly, every electric brush of his mouth against hers contradicting that. "I want you. But…I am not…I have not…"

It took what he was implying a moment to sink in, since one graceful hand had drifted up to cup her breast, his thumb circling her nipple through the fabric with a slow and maddening rhythm. She opened her eyes to find his expression open, earnest…and worried.

"You're a virgin?" she asked, barely able to believe she was asking that question of a man who could kiss like sin itself. But he nodded, a faint flush blooming in his cheeks.

"I didn't even live one mortal lifetime," he said. "It seemed we were always fighting, and as the Ptolemy began to hunt us, it became more difficult to leave the

forest. It wasn't for lack of interest. But the chance simply...never came." She could feel him tensing again, and
sought to banish his worries immediately.

She would be his first. It was a beautiful surprise, and
one she intended to cherish.

"Whatever it is will be amazing, because it's you. Be
with me," she said, her breath catching in her throat. Bay
could feel his body stirring, hardening against hers. Did
he have any idea what a gift he had been to her? And now,
to give her this...

"Please. I need you."

"You need—ah, *meri jaan*, if you only knew." Tasmin
pressed his forehead to hers, his breath feathering her
face, her mouth. He shifted ever so slightly, and her hair
tumbled down around her shoulders. His hands delved
into it, and she leaned into his touch.

Then his mouth was on hers again, doing things he had
no business knowing how to do. It started sweetly, almost
reverently, as Tasmin tasted her, stoking a slow-burning
fire deep within her that never seemed to go out, dancing
only for him. The kiss turned hotter, harder, as his tongue
rubbed against hers in a slow, sensuous rhythm and his
hand kneaded her breast more firmly, every rub of his
thumb against her taut nipple causing a pulse of pleasure
between her legs.

"You hide your virginity awfully well," Bay said, then
gasped when he guided her hand to cup his rigid cock,
straining against the fabric of his jeans.

"I spent the better part of a century thinking about sex,
even if I wasn't having it," Tasmin said. "That goes further than you'd think."

"You'll have to demonstrate," Bay said, barely managing to get the words out. Her clothes felt too tight, her skin too sensitive, and every errant brush of Tasmin's body against hers brought her closer to madness. She pressed the heel of her palm against his erection and stroked it slowly, feeling it pulse beneath her hand. Tasmin's eyes rolled back in his head, and he exhaled on a groan.

He said one word.

"Bed."

Bay looked at the creature still asleep on it. "Yours," she replied.

Together, they stumbled into the hallway, earning an amused look from a dark-haired Lilim woman leaving one of the bedrooms. Tasmin ignored her, catching Bay's hand in his and dragging her into a room only three doors from her own. The room was pitch-dark when he slammed the door, and she had a brief moment of trepidation until Tasmin had caught her in his arms again. Then there was nothing but his hands, his mouth, and the ragged sound of their breathing mingling in the darkness.

He guided her backward until the back of her thighs hit the edge of the bed. Bay pulled her shirt, then the T-shirt beneath off as quickly as she could with shaking hands. The cool air against her bare skin had her breaking out in gooseflesh, quickly forgotten when Tasmin pulled his own shirt off in a rustle of fabric.

She pulled him back against her with a broken sigh, reveling in his hot, openmouthed kisses while her hands roamed over the hard planes of Tasmin's chest. He quivered when she ran her fingertips over the ripples of his abs, then laughed breathlessly.

"Tickles," he said.

"Want me to stop?"

He groaned. "Gods, no."

Then his hands were in her hair again, trailing down her bare back, fumbling with the apparent mystery of her bra clasp. She smiled against his mouth and undid it for him.

"Here," she said.

She thought there might have been a murmured "thank you," but couldn't be sure once his hands were on her bare breasts. His hands had been wickedly clever when her shirt was on. Now, with nothing between her skin and his, they were pure bliss. He filled his hands with her breasts, rolling the tight buds of her nipples between his thumbs and forefingers. Bay arched into him with a broken moan.

She fumbled with his jeans, only barely managing the buttons while he tormented her. Finally, though, he released her long enough to reach down and unfasten the last two. The boxers he wore were stretched taut over his cock, and Bay pulled him against her with a slow, torturous roll of her hips.

"Ah," Tasmin breathed, and she felt his knees start to buckle, nearly taking them both down.

"Hang on," Bay murmured. She slid down to sit on the bed and pushed back, wriggling quickly out of her pants and underwear and tossing them into the darkened room. Tasmin followed her. Her eyes had adjusted enough to the dark that she could see the contours of his body, could see the lean muscles flex as he fumbled his jeans and boxers off. When he rose, gold eyes glowing catlike in the dark, Bay drank in the sight of him.

Whatever else he was, there was nothing about Tasmin that wasn't beautiful.

He crawled onto the bed, elegant, leonine grace as

he moved in to pounce. Bay slid back toward the pillows, breath coming hard and fast. Then he was over her, on her, every inch of his skin pressed against hers. The sensation was overwhelming at first, and Bay surged up against him. He moaned, kissing her hungrily, and Bay could feel the hot silk of his cock pressing insistently into her lower belly.

Tasmin trailed his kisses lower, making a hot path down her neck, over her collarbone, until he sucked one nipple into his mouth and began to torment her with hot, wet pulls.

Bay cried out, arching her back to allow him better access. Her legs parted further where he was settled between them. Tasmin lavished first one breast, then the other with attention, flickering his tongue over the hardened tips of her nipples until she was teetering on the verge of a shattering orgasm. Bay's breath came in harsh little pants, her fingers tangled in the dark silk of his hair. When he finally raised his head to look at her, she couldn't speak, could barely think.

Here in the dark, looming over her, he looked every inch the predator. And she was happily his prey.

He stretched over her, his muscles tight and straining. There was something indescribably sexy about the way he looked at her in that moment, intense need with a hint of uncertainty. She wanted to make it good for him—better than good. Bay took one of his hands and guided it between her legs, to where she was swollen and slick and ready for him.

"See how wet you make me," she gasped, her hips jerking upward when he curled his finger to toy with the swollen bud of her sex. He hissed something she didn't understand, watching her while he slid his finger against her. She clamped her hand around his wrist and pulled his hand, with great effort, away.

"Inside me," she said. "Not until you're inside me."

Tasmin moved fully over her again, until she could feel the head of his cock nestled between her legs, poised to enter her. She slid her knees up to bracket his hips, her eyes locked with his.

When he pushed inside of her, the hard, thick length of him filling her completely, Bay watched Tasmin's eyes flare brightly, then go hazy as he gave one of the sexiest moans she'd ever heard.

"Yes," he breathed, and in that one word was everything he felt, everything she'd hoped he would feel. He began to move in her, his hips pulsing slowly at first as he withdrew and pressed forward, the friction between them centering between her legs and coiling tighter and tighter as he picked up the rhythm.

Bay began to move with him, her body taking over when her mind began to slide into incoherent pleasure. There was only Tasmin against her in the dark, driving into her, hips pumping against her while she urged him on, digging her nails into his hips.

He rode her past reason, into madness, until the feel of him inside her pushed her over the edge. Bay cried out as her climax hit, clenching tight around him while she came in hot, pulsing waves. She squeezed him tight and he found his own release, thrusting into her with a harsh cry, his jaw clenched tight while he poured himself into her.

When the aftershocks had subsided, Tasmin lowered himself to her and then rolled to the side, gathering Bay against him and nuzzling her hair, his breathing slowly becoming deep and even. He didn't say a word—he didn't have to.

The way he held her said everything she needed to know.

Bay curled into him, refusing to think of anything but this, here and now, and finally gave herself over to the peaceful oblivion of sleep.

chapter THIRTEEN

For the first time since he'd reawakened into this new life, Tasmin slept deeply and without dreams.

It didn't last.

"Wake up. *Wake up!*"

He breathed in sharply as a bright shock of pain burst through his arm. Tasmin's eyes flew open, his teeth bared in a half snarl even before he knew what was going on.

The look on Lily MacGillivray's face immediately erased any thought of retaliation. Pale light shimmered up the arm she'd touched him with, then vanished.

"What is it?" he rasped, his voice rough from sleep. Lily's blue eyes were wild, and there was an otherworldly look about her that was more than a little unnerving. For a moment he thought she meant to attack him because of the woman still curled in his arms. Then she spoke, and he realized how insignificant the sight before her must seem.

"We're leaving. Everyone. Now. The Ptolemy have the town surrounded."

He blinked slowly, trying to understand the implications of what she was saying. "The Ptolemy..."

"They've already massed against us. They're all here. Do you understand what I'm saying? Hundreds. Maybe a thousand. I don't have the numbers to fight a strike like this, and my allies are too far away right now. *We have to get out*."

Tasmin sat up, the quick movement jostling Bailey awake. He held her tighter, just for a moment, trying to imprint what she felt like on his memory in case he never held her again. The night she'd given him had outdone any of his expectations, putting years of dark and heated dreams to shame. And now this.

It seemed that even one night of blissful solace was too much to ask.

"What—Lily?"

Bailey's voice was soft, muddled. Not caring that they had an audience, Tasmin brushed her hair aside and pressed a kiss to her forehead.

"The Ptolemy are massing to attack. The Lilim are evacuating. We have to go."

The fog cleared from her eyes immediately.

"Oh. Oh my God." She shifted her gaze to her friend. "Lily, how are you going to get everyone out of here? And I...I can't..."

"Any way we can." Lily looked grim. "It's the middle of the night. I don't have time to get Vlad here, or Sammael. If we leave everything behind, we have the advantage of being able to shapeshift—most of us should make it through."

"You can shift?" Bailey asked. "I didn't think—"

"I can," Lily interrupted, looking nervously at the door.

"I'm not great at it yet, but Ty's been helping me. I haven't been able to that long. I was waiting to show you until I was consistent, but I'm not going to have that luxury."

And now Tasmin could hear it, the quick patter of feet, the low and frightened voices. Outside, there was a mournful howl, and then another.

"The wolves," Tasmin murmured.

"This is their element," Lily said. "It's snowing like hell right now, too, which is an advantage for them. And it's going to hold the Ptolemy back just enough...I hope...to let us get out. They don't know this area like we do. There will be places to slide past."

Lily drew herself up, straightening her shoulders, and Tasmin could see just how much helpless fury she was grappling with. It was a feeling he understood well.

"But—but—you can't just abandon everything here. The mansion, all your stuff..." Bailey's body had tensed, and she clung to him harder than Tasmin thought she probably realized. He let her, wishing just holding onto her could shield her from all of this.

"I have no choice right now," Lily said. "This is my fault. I didn't think she'd start a war. Not now. I was wrong, and now we all have to deal with the consequences." Her composure wavered. "I'm sorry. I'll do everything I can to protect you until this is over, Bay."

The implications of this began to sink in. Tasmin could feel Bailey start to shiver as she thought it through.

"My house," she whispered. "My shop...Lily, I can't just take off..."

"You can't stay," Lily said, her voice sharper than she'd likely intended. She softened her tone as she continued. "Arsinöe will hurt you to get to me, Bay. There's no way

in hell I'm letting her get her hands on you. If we abandon this place, the town is probably safe. If you stayed,
you wouldn't be. You're not going to be until this is over.
I'm sorry," she said again. "I should have pushed to get
the dynasty into Boston ages ago. There's a reason we stay
in cities—they're much harder to attack like this. Here,
we've been sitting ducks. I just didn't think—and we're not
ready, not on our own." She gave her head a hard shake.
"Look, there's no time. They'll take this house tonight if
they can. I refuse to give them even one of us as a prize."

"Then we go," Tasmin said. "I'll make sure Bailey
gets out safe." He had no intention of letting her out of
his sight. Whatever dangers he posed to her were, at this
moment, inconsequential compared to what could happen
if the Ptolemy caught her. Lily, however, didn't seem to
agree.

"No. I'll get her out. She's my responsibility."

His eyes narrowed, his possessive instinct overriding
his sense before he could stop it.

"She's *mine*." There was an ugly undercurrent to his
voice, barely audible, that had him swallowing the rest of
his statement. Tasmin could see Lily had heard it, knew
she was right to want to spirit Bailey away from here...
and from him. But he couldn't bring himself to let go.
Not now.

"Anura told me what happened to you, what you need
from her," Lily said, her voice soft but incredibly deadly.
"Whatever is inside you makes you as much of a target as
I am. The difference is that my people are in no danger
from me." Her eyes glowed. "Don't make me waste time
fighting you before we go, Tasmin. You've come awfully
far to throw your life away like that."

She turned and stalked from the room, tossing a final comment over her shoulder.

"You have five minutes. Meet me downstairs."

The instant she was gone, Bailey was fumbling her way out of bed, too shaken up to be much more than clumsy. Tasmin followed her, keeping his distance as he quickly slipped his clothes back on. Bailey picked up her scrubs, pulled on the pants, fastened her bra, and then simply clutched the shirt to her chest without putting it on.

Her eyes were wide, glassy with shock when she finally looked at him.

"I need...Grimm...my other stuff. This is dirty. I'll just..."

She wandered out of the room without finishing her thought, and Tasmin followed her, worried she wouldn't even make it into her own bedroom. She did, though, dazedly patting at Grimm when he clambered off the bed to greet her.

Slowly, too slowly, she peeled off the cotton pants she was wearing and pulled on a pair of jeans from the open suitcase on the floor, then picked up a light sweater and put that on. She moved like she was underwater, looking at everything but seeming to see nothing. Grimm begged for her attention, but all she did was trip over him.

"Grimm," Tasmin said. It surprised him when the dog came immediately to his side, looking up at him expectantly. Tasmin considered what to do about the dog. He was big, and not very fast, and was going to be a problem to get out. But he couldn't leave him here—there was every likelihood he'd be destroyed simply for being a beloved pet.

The dog had seemed to understand, at least some,

when Tasmin had tried to communicate on a deeper level with him before. It couldn't hurt now.

There's danger. Stay close. Use your instincts.

Grimm's tail drooped, and he whined up at Tasmin.

Stay close, Tasmin thought at him again, and hoped it was enough.

Bailey seemed to be coming to again, moving a little more quickly even if the shocked haze hadn't quite left her eyes. She put on her sneakers, the coat she'd thrown on a chair. When she was finished, she looked at him, and her expression was desolate.

"It's snowing. I don't have boots. I can't run."

"Hopefully it won't matter," Tasmin said. "Lily will probably try to get you out in a car, if possible. You and Grimm."

"And you," she said. "I don't care what Lily said, you have to stay with me."

He could hear the panic creeping into her voice, and sought to soothe her as best he could without lying outright. He didn't know what was going to happen, but he did know he would be expected to stay with Anura if possible.

"I'll make sure nothing happens to you," he said. "Don't worry."

She seemed to accept that.

They headed downstairs, Tasmin padding on bare feet. He'd left his coat and shoes down here somewhere. Grimm followed close behind, far more subdued than he normally was. So far, he seemed to have understood what Tasmin had asked of him. He might be a slow-moving beast, but he seemed to be an intelligent one.

They walked into loosely organized chaos. The downstairs was packed with Lilim, all of whom must have been drawn by a silent call from Lily. Far from milling about, they pressed together, either whispering together or dead silent, their eyes glinting in the soft candlelight Lily kept the mansion lit with.

Lily had been right, Tasmin saw. There were many new Lilim here…but these were the low numbers of a very young dynasty. Arsinöe's people were many, and most were clever in a fight even if they weren't trained warriors. All, no doubt, had been waiting to destroy the Lilim, who had humiliated their queen and freed their slaves, then been granted legitimacy.

He didn't understand why now, exactly, this was coming to pass…but he knew it had to do with him. Or more accurately, what he now knew was inside him. Whether or not she had put it there, Arsinöe wanted it.

The only silver lining was that the thing occupying a space in his soul didn't seem to like the Ptolemy any better than he did. Otherwise, he would likely already be in their hands.

"Stay here," Tasmin told Bailey when they reached the bottom of the stairs. "I'll be right back."

She didn't look happy about it, but he rushed to get his coat and shoes before she could argue. He shoved through the throng, earning curious glances from many. No one stopped him, however. Behind him, he heard the front door open. Tasmin turned and watched Eric Black walk in, accompanied by a burst of frigid air that had become a curtain of snow.

The man's deep gold eyes scanned the crowd, assessing.

"Everyone," he barked, and what sound there was went silent. "We're going to open the gate. There are Ptolemy in town, heading here, but the bulk of them are hanging at the outskirts. We leave in waves, groups of roughly ten. One of my wolves will accompany each group of Lilim— we know these woods like the back of our paws now, and we *will* be going on foot. I know most of you were used to fighting and surviving before coming here, so I don't need to tell you what to do. Just get to Boston. From there, the Dracul will assist in getting us to Chicago, where we'll also be joining up with the Grigori."

Someone, Tasmin didn't see who, asked the question he was sure was on everyone's minds.

"What then?"

Eric's eyes glinted dangerously. "Then we move on Arsinöe. She's officially renounced the Council. As have her allies, the Empusae."

There was a soft gasp, and Tasmin saw Anura, up near the front, put a hand to her mouth. A surprised murmur ran through the crowd. Though the Empusae had remained determinedly neutral in the problems with the Ptolemy, an actual alliance was surprising. Especially since Vlad Dracul had been as instrumental as anyone is keeping the ailing dynasty intact, considering the fragile and failing health of Mormo, the Empusa herself.

"They're divided." Lily's voice rang out, strong and true, as she joined Eric. Ty prowled at her side, protective and restless, his silver eyes missing nothing. He spotted Tasmin in the crowd and gave a barely perceptible nod.

"Some of the Empusae will stand against us, but some are joining us in Chicago. When we all get there, we'll discuss what comes next. You will *all* be provided for until we can return." Her voice hardened. "And we *will* be returning. Long enough for us gather what we have and make a proper move to Boston, which will be our new seat after all of this is done. It's past time we had a real territory, and we need the protection of the city."

There were approving murmurs, but when Tasmin looked for Bailey, she looked as though she'd been punched. It wasn't the way he would have chosen to let her know about the move—but he didn't think Lily had much of a choice. The Lilim were depending on her to have a plan, to lead. Gaining a true seat of power was part of securing a real place for her people in the world of night.

But in some ways, Bailey would be left behind in this. It was natural.

It would also be painful.

Suddenly, the crowd surged forward, compelled by a signal Tasmin couldn't hear because he wasn't connected to those he didn't share a mark with. It took him by surprise. He shoved against the onrushing bodies, finally managing to get into the small cloakroom where his coat and shoes were. It took no time once he got in there, but he was effectively blocked from getting out.

A column of smoke appeared beside him, slowly materializing into Anura.

"Come," she said. "We aren't going the same way as the others."

"But... Bailey," he said, thinking of her waiting by the stairs, increasingly frightened. Anura shook her head.

"She's going with Lily and Ty in one of the SUVs. There's a small contingent of wolves going with them to fight if they have to... which they probably will. You and I go on foot. I'm hard to see when I want to be... and you know how to shield yourself."

He did, though he had no idea if he could maintain it for the amount of time it would take him to get out of town.

"I'd be more useful getting them out," he said. But she shook her head.

"No, that would put everything they want in one place. It makes no sense. We're not going to Boston. We'll join back up with everyone in Chicago. Until then, it's you and me."

It was one of the hardest things he'd ever had to do, waiting for the Lilim to go so that he and Anura could depart. In the meantime, she outlined the route she wanted him to take, a simple enough way to exit notable only in that it would have them heading in the opposite direction of everyone else. The sounds of feet turned to the whisper of paws as the entire dynasty was transformed into a seething mass of big black cats, rushing into the night and vanishing like shadows into the snow.

"Now," Anura said when the house had gone silent. Tasmin looked toward the foot of the stairs where he'd left Bailey, half expecting that he would see her there, waiting for him with Grimm by her side. But she was gone. The house was empty, and as they stood there, he could already hear the faint sounds of barking, howling, and the scream of an angry feline as the Lilim began their push to escape the noose that the Ptolemy had tried to loop around the neck of the entire dynasty.

They went to the back door, which opened onto a small garden, now nothing but bare wood and empty arbors buried in the blowing snow.

The visibility was terrible, the wind turning the driving snow into a nearly opaque curtain. Despite his coat, the wind ripped through Tasmin, and he shivered. A wild laugh echoed to him in the dark, and the darkness within him stirred and stretched.

Hungry, it whispered. And his mind filled with images of rent limbs and spilled blood, crimson against new fallen snow.

His heart began to pound, his incisors lengthening. And he felt whatever lurked inside begin to pull him down into the pit . . . so that it could climb up.

No, Tasmin thought, his eyes starting to roll back. *No, we have to get out of here!*

After, he heard the voice whisper with a malicious chuckle.

Afterrrrr . . .

"We stay together," Anura was saying to him, raising her voice to be heard above the wind. But he was falling, falling into blackness. And she sounded so incredibly far away.

"Be the lion. Run!"

chapter FOURTEEN

Bay sat in the back of Lily's big black SUV, buckled
in and with her arms around Grimm to keep him from,
she hoped, going through the windshield if the worst happened.

"The worst" was an excellent description of everything that had happened since Lily had awakened them.

The clock in the dash read 2:13. They had hours to
get to Boston, but she wasn't sure they'd even make it out
of the county. And Tasmin hadn't come back, vanishing
along with everyone but Lily and Ty.

Lily and Ty, who also had every intention of deserting
her if they made it out of this alive. The knowledge was
a constant drumbeat in the back of her mind. They had
never breathed a word of it to her. But from the sound of
things, this had been in the works for a while.

She was hurt and angry. Some of each was reserved
especially for herself. She couldn't be Lily's closest confidante and keep the inner workings of Lily's world at arm's

length at the same time. They'd both known it. So there were secrets to fill the widening chasm between them, until Bay made a choice. She'd sensed it for a while. But tonight, faced with the prospect of being killed by warring immortals, Bay finally had her choices illustrated for her in the starkest terms.

She was going to have to decide whether to go all in and join Lily and her kind on a permanent basis, or whether to walk away. For good.

There was nothing else.

And she'd been fooling herself in thinking there ever had been.

Bay felt a prickle of awareness at the edges of her thoughts as she stared at the snow flying at the windshield. The road was deserted so far. It didn't feel right, and the nerves in the car were palpable. Another SUV led them, driven by Eric Black. Ty had the wheel in this one.

Lily sat in the passenger seat, not looking at her.

Bay knew full well that didn't mean anything.

"If you want to know what I'm thinking, ask," Bay said. "You don't need to try to sneak a peek."

Lily glanced back at her, worry and regret etched plainly across her face.

"I was going to tell you."

"Yeah."

"I *was*," Lily insisted. "I didn't want to say anything until I was sure. The Council—well, what's left of it—is creating a new territory for us. New England. It makes sense for us to be in a city. We're not just risking ourselves out here, we're risking the whole town. And you can see what happened…We're too remote to have the right resources if something happens."

Bay blew out a breath, looking away from her. "See, that's completely sensible. Which is why you could have mentioned that reasoning to me, I don't know, before you announced it to everyone as we're being attacked by invading vampires."

"I was waiting for the right time," Lily said. She stared out the window. "I didn't want you to feel like I was abandoning you."

In some ways, that was exactly how Bay felt, even though she knew Lily was only trying to do what was best. But it felt like an ending.

"Of course you're not abandoning me," Bay said, trying to keep the bitterness out of her tone. "We're both adults. Your life has changed. You're moving on. It's not like I didn't see it happening."

"*Bay*." Lily's voice was full of pain. Bay wished she could feel some sort of triumph in leaving a mark, but it only made her feel worse. She dropped her head and closed her eyes.

"That sounds nastier than I mean it."

"But you still mean it. Bay, you have no idea how important you are to me. You really think I want to leave you behind?"

Bay sighed. Not long ago, she'd been wrapped in Tasmin's arms, not having to think about anything but the moment. But this was the reality—his reality, and Lily's. There would always be something waiting to tear those lovely moments apart.

"No," Bay said softly. "You're a queen. You were going to have to play by their rules eventually."

"Not all of them," Lily protested, but the fire went out of her voice quickly. "Some of them, though. Change is good, but it happens a lot more slowly than I'd hoped. It's all baby steps. The Lilim are different to begin with—the way we've come back, the blending with the Cait Sith. And our alliance with the wolves will stay, whether or not they choose to join us in the city, and I think some of them will. But if we don't keep some of the trappings of the system we belong to, we're going to end up overwhelmed." Her voice sounded wretchedly sad. "Like this. Vlad's been trying to tell me. I didn't want to believe it."

Ty reached over to stroke his wife's hand.

"You've been doing a hell of a job, so stop. The Lilim didn't even exist before last fall, and look where we are. There are hundreds of us. We're getting stronger, we'll have territory, and you've made allies that are going to get us through things like this. We're going to be fine, and most of that is because of you."

Bay smiled wistfully at the tenderness between her friends, obvious even under intense pressure. She knew that Ty was right—chances were, he and Lily would make it through this somehow, as would their people. They would go on, being immortal, becoming ever more a part of the world they inhabited . . . and ever less a part of hers.

Imagining the empty mansion, her life devoid of some of the characters who had come to inhabit it, made her feel strangely empty. She'd managed to keep a foot in each world, as had Lily, really, for over a year now. But the time for that to be possible was drawing to a close, and she could hear the knowledge of that in Lily's voice.

Lily had made her choice about where she belonged when she'd allowed Ty to bite her, when she'd accepted her destiny and renewed a dynasty. The decisions she was making now were just natural extensions of that, Bay realized.

But she... she still had some of the hardest choices to make. It had been easy before, not getting involved in vampire problems. They'd seemed very distant, while she'd simply focused on trying to enjoy Lily the way she always had, with the sometimes funny, sometimes frustrating addition of Ty and a handful of their more colorful friends. But as of tonight, she'd been dragged into one of the oldest and most pervasive parts of living among the dynasties: war among the bloodlines.

If she lived through the crash course in the dark side of vampire politics, she would have a lot of thinking to do.

The car lapsed into silence, no sound but the wind outside the SUV rushing past. After a few minutes, though, Lily spoke. And whether she'd picked up some of Bay's thoughts or simply guessed at them, she seemed to know what was on her mind.

"You know that if you ever want to join us," she said quietly, "you would be more than welcome."

"I know."

She'd always known, though this was the first time Lily had ever been so explicit about the offer. She could be a vampire, with all the good and bad that entailed.

"I don't know what I want," Bay admitted.

"I know," Lily said, not unkindly. "But... and please take this the way it's intended... until you figure that out, you might want to put some space between yourself and Tasmin Singh." She paused, then pressed ahead. "I'm the last person who should be warning you off of a dangerous man, Bay. But he has some unique issues."

Bay sighed. "That's a nice way to put it."

"I was a literature professor. Part of the job description is BS Artist."

It made her laugh, though it didn't really make her feel any better.

"Well, thank you for not freaking out about it." Bay leaned her head against Grimm, who was tense as he stared ahead out the windshield.

"If he'd shown any less control than he has, I would be. As it is . . . just be careful. I know it hasn't been perfect, Bay, but you're as much my sister as if you were blood. I'm trying so hard to protect you. He's the one thing I don't know how to protect you from. You don't know what you want yet for your future. I don't want the decision to be taken away from you."

Before Bay could answer, Ty gave a harsh growl.

"Hell. Here we go. Hang on."

Bay leaned forward and watched in horror as Eric's SUV began to slide sideways on the icy road, then righted itself and accelerated. Out of the squalling sheets of snow figures materialized, little more than flickering shadows as they moved almost more quickly than the eye could see. Then they were swarming the vehicle, leaping onto it, clinging to the doors, hanging onto the roof and windshield.

And it wasn't just Eric's SUV.

"Son of a bitch!" snarled Ty. There was a bang on the roof of the car, then another. An instant later something large slammed onto the hood and hooked its fingers into the groove between the hood and the windshield. The back window shattered in a burst of glass. Bay shrieked and started trying to pull Grimm onto the floor with her.

He was frantic, whimpering and trying to scramble back from her, unsure of where to go to get away from all that was happening.

Ty careened wildly back and forth, while Eric spun out and off the road. Bay caught a glimpse of one of the vampires ripping the driver's side door off. Then the gunshots started.

Her eyes widened. "Who's shooting?" she cried.

"Bullets won't kill them, but they can slow them down," Lily said. "I'm so sorry, Bay. Just try to stay down." She was unbuckling her seat belt.

"Lily—"

"Stay *down*!"

A vampire slid through the shattered back window. Lily snarled and launched herself into the backseat, going over Bay and Grimm. The interior of the car was engulfed in a flash of white light, and there was a pitiful cry from the Ptolemy she'd hit. Lily shoved the convulsing vampire back out the window, then scrambled back into the front seat, where she rolled down the window. She looked at Ty, her expression steely.

"You okay?"

"Hell yes," he said. "Fry the bastards."

"Turn around," Lily said. "We need to get Eric and the others."

Ty didn't argue, just spun the vehicle so quick and hard that it dislodged the two vampires clinging to the hood and sent them hurtling into the snow. He fishtailed as he started again, then righted himself and drove back toward where there was now a battle going on between a group of roughly ten Ptolemy and four werewolves. When Bay rose up to look, keeping her arms wrapped around a panting and whining Grimm, she could already see crimson spattered in the fresh snow.

Lily leaned out the window, and Bay watched in amazement as her friend's entire form began to glow with white light. It left her fingertips in a rush as she hurled her power at the attacking Ptolemy, over and over, as Ty skidded to a stop nearby.

More figures rushed out of the trees on either side of the road. Ty cursed in Gaelic, then turned his head to look at Bay.

"Don't move."

Then he and Lily both slammed out of the car, leaving her alone as all around her deadly lights began to flash.

She struggled to breathe. She'd never been more terrified in her life.

The SUV rocked once, twice as bodies slammed into it. His ears back, Grimm hunkered to the floor with her, and she could feel him shaking. She hung on to his big body, shoved her face into his fur, and wished it were over. The sounds were awful—snarls and hisses, shouted oaths and howls, and cries of pain from both animal and vampire. She didn't dare stick her head up to look, and didn't want to anyway. They were vastly outnumbered. All she could do was hope like hell that Lily was as much of a badass warrior queen as she'd always imagined her to be.

Otherwise, her deepest fears about Lily's involvement with the world of night would be realized. The violence that pulsed through vampire society like lifeblood would destroy them all. Bay squeezed her eyes shut and wished she were home, surrounded by the trappings of the life she loved. And she did love it, Bay realized. She had friends and laughter, light and warmth and joy. Lily might have embraced her new world, but she'd had no choice. Bay had a choice. Or she would, if she lived through the night.

She knew in that moment that she had not been made for so much darkness. So much death.

This life could never be for her.

In her mind, though she knew it would do no good, she chanted Tasmin's name over and over like a talisman, hoping that somehow he would figure out she was here, that she and the others desperately needed help.

The door flew open, nearly ripped off its hinges, and a muscular vampire with wild eyes that glowed green in the dark reached in for her, dragging her out into the snow. He moved as lightning fast as all Ptolemy did. Bay was stunned to hear Grimm's snarl, but caught only a glimpse of him snapping at the air where the Ptolemy's hand had been before her attacker slammed the door shut again, trapping the dog inside. She could hear his desperate, furious barks as he tried to get out to her.

Her heart ached to hear it. All she could hope was that he stayed trapped in there until help came, because then he'd be safe.

Arms locked, viselike around her, not giving at all when she thrashed.

Bay opened her mouth to scream, echoing the name in her head, trying to reach her any way she could.

"Lily!"

But she heard nothing, only seeing swarms of Ptolemy and, from the corner of her eye, the continuing barrage of white hot energy that meant her friends were still fighting. There was a rush of air, and she was in the trees, still locked in the arms of the unfamiliar vampire.

Alone.

He dumped her on the ground, where she landed in the soft snow. Her bare hands reached to brace herself, sinking into the cold. Bay looked up, drinking in shallow little breaths, trying to propel herself backward. Her legs refused to cooperate the way she wanted, instead flailing clumsily.

The vampire looked down at her with a triumphant smile, fangs glinting in the dark. She could barely see, but she knew he could see her perfectly. In the darkness, his eyes were the color of poison.

"You going to try to run and make it interesting?" he asked.

"Please don't hurt me," she whimpered. It was the sort of thing she'd always sworn she wouldn't say. As it turned out, she thought bitterly, it was the only thing to say. She didn't want to die. If she was going to die, she didn't want it to hurt. And she knew she would beg if he wanted. She would do anything.

Her heart beat rapidly in her chest. Bay was aware of every breath she took, every tiny movement of her body. She felt wonderfully, terribly alive, her mind alight with thoughts of her parents, her brother, her friends...her *life*. All of it in the hands of this unforgiving and ancient creature.

When he laughed, she knew he had no mercy in him.

"I have a gift for you," he said. "From the queen herself. The gift of the gods. You should be honored."

She wanted to tell him to go to hell. She wanted to fly at him and go down fighting. But she couldn't seem to make herself move, or speak in a way that revealed anything but the abject terror coursing through her system.

Rational thought flitted maddeningly through her head, so close, but impossible to catch. Her body felt weighted down with lead.

"I don't want anything," she heard herself saying, a rapid patter of words that were no more than a reflexive plea. "Please. I don't want—"

"Ignorant bitch," he snapped. "I don't care what you *want*. You're a mortal, a weakling child compared to me. And you'll take a message back to your demon-tainted, cat-loving friend for my queen."

Hope, though fragile, flickered to life deep within her.

Slowly, Bay nodded, ashamed of the tears that sprang to her eyes. "I—I can take a message." She wished she were home in bed, dreaming. But she was so cold.

The vampire smirked. "How sweet. Beautiful *and* accommodating. Come here, then. You can go...just as soon as I give you a kiss."

She realized what he meant to do a split second before he was on her. A short, sharp scream escaped her before his hand was clamped over her mouth, his big body pinning her down into the snow. Then she felt his fangs, like an animal's, in her throat.

Bay couldn't move, the air squeezed out of her from his weight. There was a sharp pain as her skin was pierced, and then he began to drink from her in long, greedy pulls. She was light-headed quickly from the lack of air, and the sensation intensified as her lifeblood was stolen from her. Her fingers flexed convulsively, digging at the ground beneath the snow as though she could somehow get away from him.

She could smell him, an unfamiliar and heavy cologne that only intensified the feeling of being violated. The skin of his palm was rough against her mouth, the body pressed so snugly against hers a stranger's. In the distance she could hear the sounds of the fight, and as her mind began to untether from her body, she could smell the cold air, the snow, the beloved piney bite of the woods.

With that untethering came a surprising calm. It was easier to drift this way, to stop caring. She just wanted to stay in the woods, to sleep...

The world was beginning to go dark by the time the vampire tore his mouth from her neck. She looked dully at him, his mouth bright crimson even in the dark. Bay didn't make a sound. She was no longer capable.

"Now," he said, shoving up the sleeve of his coat and raking his own fang across his flesh. "Your gift. And you can tell Lily that everything she holds dear will belong to the queen of the Ptolemy. Everyone she loves will be branded with the mark of the one true queen—or they will burn. And she will watch both before she dies."

Bay could only watch as the wrist dripping blood loomed closer. Her heart fluttered weakly in her chest. She was dying.

That was when she heard a sound, a distant roar like a freight train bearing down on them, closer and closer, until her ears were ringing with it. The vampire's head snapped up, and she could see the horror in his eyes. He opened his mouth to scream, but if he made a noise it was consumed by the one already rippling the air.

Bay's eyes slipped shut, her head full of nothing but that anguished, inhuman sound that seemed to shake the earth itself. *For me?* she thought. The idea was vaguely interesting...but she was slipping. And the darkness was warm and welcoming.

She had the faint impression of being lifted, gathered together and against when she longed to be adrift and apart. Then there were only whispers.

Only whispers in the dark.

He held her dying body under the stars and cursed the gods.

Tasmin had no idea where Anura was. He barely knew where *he* was. All he had done was follow Bailey's voice, calling his name over and over until it became a scream. Anura's shouts hadn't held him. He'd known, with the kind of soul-deep certainty that he had nearly forgotten how to feel, that Bailey was in danger.

His rage had sparked when he'd smelled the Ptolemy, and when he'd seen the vampire on top of her, he'd snapped. The tattered remains of her attacker littered the ground not far away, his mouth still befouled with the taste of Ptolemy blood. He hadn't gotten enough in his mouth to affect his mark; the Ptolemy ankh wouldn't befoul the lion's paw. Still, the metallic taste of it lingered, despite a mouthful of snow he'd tried to use to deaden it.

And now Bailey was limp in his arms, her life rapidly leaving her. He had wasted precious time on the kill, but with so much rage, his rational mind refused to clear for long. Even now, he struggled with what clawed at his consciousness.

Let me taste her, let me have her, she's dead anyway... I want what is MINE.

"No," he growled aloud. With shaking hands, he unbuttoned her coat to get a better look at what had been done to her neck. Immediately he saw the two puncture wounds, slowly oozing more blood down her neck. The bastard hadn't even bothered to seal the wound. Tasmin pulled down the neck of her sweater and saw that the faint outline of the Ptolemy ankh had already begun to form on her skin. The venom from the vampire's fangs, one half of what was needed to complete her siring, was doing its work.

For that to have appeared meant she was too far gone for anything but death or vampirism. He would not let her die. But someone would have to put their teeth in her again to override the Ptolemy toxin now loose in her blood.

And then...the rest.

Tasmin threw his head back and gave another furious roar, his voice that of the lion. His hatred of the Ptolemy was a living thing, snakes beneath his skin. They had taken everything from him. Now they had taken Bailey's human life, and again he was powerless to stop it. All he could do was erase whatever claim they might have on her.

Except he might very well kill her himself in the process.

Desperate, he looked in the direction where he could still hear Lily, Ty, and the wolves battling a horde of Ptolemy. If he could turn the fight for them quickly enough—

There was a pause in her heartbeat. Then a longer one.

There was no time.

Tasmin bent to her neck, inhaling the sweet scent that haunted even his dreams, and sank his teeth into her flesh as gently as he could. Even as near death as she was, Bailey made a soft, pained sound that tore at his heart. This, all of this, was his fault. He hadn't been able to protect his brothers, hadn't been able to protect her—he'd only made her more of a target.

Shaking, he took only a single sip of her precious blood. It hit his tongue with the taste of sunlight, of ripe berries and summer fields, and the hunger crashed over him in a wave. Tasmin's body jerked, his hands clenched, bunching her clothing where he held her. His jaw tried to close, to dig in deeper and drain what was left.

It was what he'd feared... but so much worse, because it was her.

Tasmin struggled to maintain control, nearly choking in his effort not to pull any more blood from her fragile neck. And for the first time, he addressed what lived inside of him as what it was.

Demon, let her live. Let me turn her. I'll give you anything—just let go, this once.

He could actually feel it pause and consider, feel the stillness inside. Then he heard it in his mind, the foul voice that had whispered to him since the beginning.

Anything?

All of his hopes died at the calculating hunger in that voice. He knew then that there would be no ritual to remove the demon, no future he might share with Bailey. But if that was what he had to give up so she kept breathing, so be it.

He would not lose one more person because he was too weak to hold them.

Anything, he promised.

Then hear this, Rakshasa. I will spare her in return for two simple things. First, you will stop this ploy with the Empusa, Anura, to cast me out. We're bound, you and me. My release is not for you to attempt. We will be unbound when I say, and not before.

Done, Tasmin thought. It was a promise easily given, though he had no hope that the demon's method of unbinding, if it ever happened, would end with both of them alive. A small price. His life was worth little. He had no illusions.

Good. The demon's voice, a hiss echoing up from the darkness, was unmistakably smug. *That brings us to the other. I will have a life from you. One of my choosing, at the time of my choosing. You will take this life without a complaint, without question. If I choose to . . . assist you . . . you will not struggle. This is my price. Do you agree?*

Tasmin hesitated, shaking as he tried to stop himself from savaging her. What kind of deal was this? If he saved Bailey just to have to kill her later—

Not her, you fool. It will be another. She is nearly gone, Rakshasa. Make your choice.

But of course, there really was no choice. There never had been. Tasmin felt a surprising amount of relief as he accepted his fate. Somehow, he knew he wasn't going to make it out of this alive. But Bay would. He could give her that.

You have my word. My promise. As long as I can save her.

The hunger receded until it was nothing, leaving only a lingering sense of dark amusement he knew wasn't his— along with the knowledge that this retreat constituted a sealed bargain. Gently, his jaw aching with the effort it had taken him to keep from snapping her neck, Tasmin withdrew his fangs. Then, as quickly as he could manage, he extended a single short, sharp claw from his index finger and opened a shallow cut in his wrist with it. He didn't hesitate, pressing it to Bailey's mouth, willing her to drink.

"Come on, Bailey. Take it. It's all I have to give you now. Drink, *meri jaan*."

She was so still, her skin translucent in the dark. For a few terrible seconds, he thought he was too late, that her spirit had left her while he haggled with the demon to let her live. But then he felt the faint pressure of her lips against his wrist, the first tentative swallow.

Tasmin nearly sobbed with relief.

"That's it," he encouraged her, stroking the back of her head where he cradled it. "Drink. As much as you need."

He heard a hoarse shout and looked up to see Lily, her clothes torn and bloodied, racing through the trees toward him. The look on her face was murderous, and her hands glowed with white fire. With a sense of calm that had long escaped him, Tasmin reached for his power the way he once had, without fear.

Golden light whipped around him, spiraling out of him and stopping Lily in her tracks. She paused, puzzled, and watched things that weren't really there, forgetting her fury of only a second before.

Deftly, Tasmin wove his energy around himself and Bailey, a protective cocoon while she revived. Beyond, he saw Ty, even more battered than his wife, limp into view. He went to her side, silver eyes going blurry as the ancient magic rippled through him, keeping him from seeing what was really happening.

And still Bailey drank, pulling hungrily at him now.

He could feel the first faint pricks of her fangs, and sagged against her in his relief.

He no longer had a heart worth giving, but this was one gift he could leave her with, this woman who had started to heal him with her gentle touch and lively tongue.

Soon, she would be the last of his kind...and she would do the Rakshasa proud.

chapter FIFTEEN

SHE AWAKENED WITH A GASP, sitting bolt upright and tensing to run from—

What had she been running from? Bay blinked rapidly, unable to remember. Had she been dreaming?

She forced herself to stay put, waiting for logic to calm instinct. She was in bed. She'd been having a nightmare. A really, really bad nightmare.

And now she was in a bedroom she absolutely did not recognize.

With a creeping sense of dread, Bay took in her surroundings slowly as she woke the rest of the way up. She was in a big, beautiful bed, in a big, beautiful room decorated with gleaming mahogany furniture and oil paintings in heavy, ornate frames. Ahead of her, a set of double doors opened onto a sitting room, and to her right, another door led into a darkened bathroom. Wherever she was, the owner had old money.

Memory trickled back slowly. It was fuzzy at first. She clearly remembered being at Lily's. And then...

Oh God. *Oh God.*

Images collided with one another, each one worse than the next. The trip. The attack. Grimm. That *bastard*, dragging her into the woods and then...then...

There had been a roar. Tasmin? But she didn't remember if Tasmin had ever gotten to her. She didn't remember anything past seeing the Ptolemy with her blood dripping from his mouth, looking into the distance.

Which meant she could be anywhere. Including in the Ptolemy court.

Because her "gift" had been becoming one of them, a slap in the face to Lily, a mark that could never be removed. A human life that could never be given back.

Carefully, panic tickling the back of her throat, Bay held out her arms and examined them. Normal enough. She wasn't wearing her clothes anymore—someone had put her in a silky nightgown, the kind she'd often admired but never bothered to buy for herself. She patted at her legs beneath the covers. They seemed to still be there, so that was something. Bay moved back up, skimming her hands over her breasts, her stomach and chest.

Nothing *felt* different.

Then she realized that the room was pitch-dark, and she could see everything as plain as day.

Bay sucked in a breath, the only way she managed not to scream. That was when she felt the other changes. She ran her tongue over incisors that had grown longer and sharp, ran her hands through hair that now fell in soft, silken waves that were an ideal version of what she'd been

born with. Even her skin felt different, smoother, softer...
cooler.

She sat there a moment in the dark, trying to let it
sink in.

She'd been attacked. Her friends and dog were very
possibly dead. And she'd been made a vampire without
ever having had the choice, just as Lily had feared.

"I—I need to know where I am," she stammered to
herself, mostly to hear the sound of her own voice. That,
at least, hadn't changed, and was reassuring in some small
way. Bay steeled herself, pulled off the thick burgundy
comforter, and swung her legs over the side of the bed.
Her feet sank into a plush rug when she stood and walked
toward the bathroom.

Movement was a strange sensation. She felt strong
and graceful in a way she never had before—and she
hadn't exactly been a slug. Out of habit, she reached out,
her hand hunting for the light switch on her way into the
room. She never flipped the switch, though. Bay caught
sight of herself in the mirror first, crying out in shock
before she could stop herself.

Her eyes...her eyes were the same glowing, burning
gold as Tasmin's, lion's eyes in the dark. Bay dropped her
gaze to her collarbone and saw the paw formed of curling
flames, then came back up to stare into the alien eyes that
somehow now belonged to her.

Nothing made sense. Nothing.

She heard a door open, the whisper of running feet
barely touching the rug. Then Lily was there, very much
alive, and somehow more vibrant than she'd ever seemed
before. They stood staring at one another for a moment,
Lily stopping just inside the door.

Bay tried to ask all the questions she had, but all she could see were a Ptolemy's burning green eyes in her memory, with all the desperate terror he had brought with him. That had been real, hadn't it?

"How?" she asked, beginning to shake. "What happened to me?"

"Oh, honey," Lily sighed, and opened her arms. "Come here. Just . . . come here."

Bay slid into her friend's arms and wept.

Tasmin sat stiffly in the library, one hand on his knee, the other on the dog that hadn't left his side since the disaster of two nights ago. He sympathized with the beast— Grimm was as traumatized as most of the Lilim were by the battles fought on the way out of Tipton. If a band of them hadn't joined up with Ty and Lily when they had, the dynasty would have ended that night. Arsinöe might not have counted on stopping them in their tracks, but she had certainly put enough effort behind this.

Surprisingly few had been lost in the fighting . . . but he guessed that was because most of the focus had been on Lily, and she was a formidable opponent even when hideously outnumbered. Arsinöe underestimated her.

Or maybe not. She'd intended for Lily to live and see how she'd marked Bailey, claiming the woman closest to her for the Ptolemy. A living reminder of Arsinöe's dominion over the world of night. And over her.

The door to the library opened, and Tasmin looked up, his jaw set. Lily walked in, looking first at her husband and Vlad Dracul, who stood at a long table poring over some dusty tome together. This was the Dracul's library, and would have been a fascinating place if Tasmin had been able to concentrate.

Instead, it was nothing but another cage.

"She's awake," Lily said to the two men. She studiously ignored him, much as she had since they'd arrived. Though he'd tried to explain, and though the remains of Bailey's true attacker had littered the ground around them, Tasmin didn't think she was ready to fully believe him. More, he wasn't sure she would ever forgive him for weaving the magic that had kept her and Ty from pulling Bailey from his arms as she drank from him.

Lily might be kind, but he was still an outsider with some serious problems...and he had claimed something that, in her eyes, he had no business claiming. She was probably right. But he couldn't regret it. Not when Bailey still breathed.

Vlad frowned, coming around the table toward her. "How is she? Does she need another sedative draught? I hate to keep her under any longer, but sometimes, if the siring is too traumatic..."

He trailed off, and Tasmin flexed his claws, feeling the tips of them slide through his jeans and prick his knee. He knew what Vlad meant and wouldn't say. A violent siring could change a person permanently, could make them violent themselves...or just drive them mad. He'd hoped that taking over the process and being the one to turn her would make the difference, along with Bailey's strength. But he didn't know.

It was a great relief when Lily shook her head. "No, she's doing all right. Shaken, upset, but all right."

It was a surprise when Lily turned to address him, managing to meet his eyes with something less than a murderous glare. It wasn't a friendly look, but much of the heat had gone out of it since he'd seen her early in the day.

"She wants to see you."

He'd wanted this and feared it since they'd arrived here in Chicago. It might have been better if he'd left by now. The demon within's silence was deafening. It seemed to have retreated from his consciousness completely, but for the strange sense he had that it was simply waiting.

Waiting for the time when it would extract its price from him. Tasmin knew, somehow, that it wouldn't be long.

He stood slowly, never taking his eyes off of the queen of the Lilim. She stared back warily.

"You're ... sure?" he asked. He'd had visions of being told that Bailey wanted him out of her life, wanted him dead. A part of him insisted it would be easier for her if that were the case. But more of him wanted desperately to see her again. He had done this, Tasmin reminded himself. This had been his choice, to tie himself to her this way, though a true mate bond hadn't been forged. Nor would it be, unless she bit him of her own volition, and he had no intention of allowing that.

But he could still taste her on his lips, would swear that her blood still mingled with his. His need for her had only grown.

And he had no way of knowing whether that was his own folly, the sadistic torment of the demon ... or something else.

For the thousandth time since that awful night, he wished for his pride brothers. He was weary of standing on his own in this unfamiliar world, feeling his way in the dark.

"I'm sure," Lily said. "I'll walk you up."

It wasn't a question, but a command. She wanted to speak with him alone. Tasmin crossed the room to her, sharing a look with Ty. The queen's consort hadn't said much, but what he had said had indicated a surprising amount of sympathy. It was the last place he'd expected it to come from. But then, doing what needed to be done in order to protect someone... He thought Ty might know quite a lot about that.

Lily glided out into the hallway, as regal as she always was even in casual clothes. Tasmin followed, bracing himself for her to finally unleash her anger on him. Instead, she surprised him.

"Walk with me. Please," she qualified. "I won't try to fry you."

He gave her a sidelong glance. That wasn't nearly as comforting as he thought she'd meant it to be.

"Very well." Tasmin moved into step alongside her as they walked slowly through the cavernous first floor of the Dracul's mansion. Lily was silent a moment, and when she finally spoke, she looked dead ahead, not meeting his curious eyes.

"I owe you an apology."

Tasmin arched an eyebrow, waiting for the catch. When she remained silent, he was forced to consider that she might be serious.

"You didn't chain me up and throw me in a dungeon," Tasmin offered. "No apology is necessary."

"Oh, bull," Lily said, an irritated edge to her voice that he found faintly amusing despite the situation. "You know very well I was on the fence about believing you." She glanced at him as she walked. "Bay remembers the Ptolemy attacking her...and what Arsinöe's message was for me. She doesn't even remember you showing up. When you said you got there just in time, you really meant it."

"He was about to feed her from himself," Tasmin said, filling in details no one had seemed to want from him before. "He'd drained her so well that there was very little left for me to use. She was nearly dead when I got finished with the Ptolemy."

He curled his lip, letting a little of his self-directed anger show through.

"I wasted time killing him. I should have taken off his head and been done with it. But seeing him on her..."

Lily's mouth tightened. "What's done is done. And I can hardly blame you. Maybe Arsinöe got a message of her own. The woman hates to lose." She sighed heavily then, shaking her head. "In any case, I realize I haven't exactly been gracious since you showed up."

The assessment caught him off guard.

"You've been very helpful," Tasmin said. "What more could I expect? You never knew my kind. You don't know me."

Lily stopped at the foot of the ornate front staircase and turned to face him. Tasmin was surprised to see how troubled she looked. There were plenty of reasons she and Bailey were so close, he realized. One seemed to be that they were both prone to attacks of conscience.

It was an interesting issue for a dynasty queen to have.

"No, I don't," Lily said. "I don't know you any better than I did the night I met you, and that's my fault. I wouldn't expect you to get this, since you don't know me either, but I'm usually a little friendlier when descending from on high to help people." Her smile was thin, self-deprecating. "I swore I wouldn't be a bloodline snob."

Tasmin shrugged. "I expected to be looked down upon. That's how the dynasties work with one another—poorly."

She pressed her lips together. "You're not helping me here."

"I—"

"No, forget it." She waved her hand dismissively. "Despite your problems, you haven't done anything to hurt my people. Or Bay. And still the first thing I thought of when I saw you on the ground with her was that you'd lost control and...well, you know. Instead, you were doing what you could to keep her alive." She breathed in deeply. "So. I was wrong about you. And I'm sorry."

"I accept the apology," Tasmin replied, bemused—and pleased—that she would even think to offer one. If her dynasty survived, he had a feeling that in time, her kind would wreak all sorts of havoc on the old ways of doing things. They looked at one another, and Lily's mouth curved up into a soft, but genuine, smile.

"Good." Her smile faltered, just a bit, and he could see the love she had for Bailey behind it. "I just...worry about her. This is a lot. It was always going to be a lot, whatever she decided, but...now she has no choice. If she had become Lilim I would be able to help her along a little more, but she's—"

"She's Rakshasa," Tasmin finished for her. "A thing you don't understand."

"I'd say you're the only one left who does." Lily tucked a lock of hair behind her ear and then folded her arms across her chest, looking up at him with eyes the deep and fathomless blue of the ocean.

"So I'm going to ask you to do something for me," she said. "I know you haven't bonded with her. I have no idea what your intentions are where she's concerned, and I'm going to butt right out of that. But for as long as you're with us, and as long as you can, please help her."

Tasmin hesitated. "You know I may not be able to for long," he said. "When Anura is ready..."

When Anura was ready, he would have to run. It was a secret he would have to keep, though it would be a constant knife in his gut. The demon had been clear. His fate was now sealed.

Lily nodded, no doubt believing he would go through with whatever ritual Anura and her blood sisters devised to try and cast the demon out.

"I understand. And I hope she succeeds. No one deserves what was done to you, except maybe Arsinöe herself." Her expression darkened. "But no matter what, even if it's just for a couple of days, give Bay what you can. You were the last Rakshasa. If you...don't make it, she will be. She deserves to understand what she is. All I'd be able to give her are pieced together old stories from Vlad's library. I don't think that bloodlines should determine a person's standing, but I do think it's important to understand what you come from." She looked up at him, her gaze penetrating. "Will you do that for me? And for her?"

He felt himself nodding, unable to deny Lily such an earnest request—and unable to deny himself more time with Bailey. All of it was borrowed now, prolonging the inevitable. But the thought of even one more day with her was too tantalizing to resist. And though his time would be short, he could at least try to enjoy the fact that the demon would now let her be.

As long as it got what it wanted.

"I can do that," he said.

Lily's relief was palpable. "Thank you," she said. "This place will be a madhouse over the next few days. I have preparations to make, and so do our allies. What Empusae are standing with the Ptolemy have left the city, and the ones still here are waiting for a plan. We're going to have to destroy her," Lily said, suddenly looking like a vampire who had lived a great many more years than she actually had. "We just have to figure out how. I'll feel better knowing that Bay is with you."

He was touched by the sentiment, and inclined his head.

"I'll do what I can." Then he smiled, unable to resist adding, "At least up until she decides to use her lion form to start liberating zoo animals. I'm not sure what I can do about that."

Lily grinned, her world-weariness vanishing in the brightness of her smile. "You've got her pegged. If we all survive this," she said, "I think I'm going to decide to like you." She tipped her head toward the stairs. "Go ahead. She'd had a drink and a cry. Now she just wants you. You know where she is."

He did. He'd only lurked near the door for most of every day while the others slept.

"I wish you luck, Queen Lily," he said as he began to ascend the stairs.

"You too," she said. "And...thanks. For saving her."

"It was an honor," Tasmin said. But as he headed up, he wondered whether, when all was said and done, Bailey herself would look back and see the mark he'd left her with as anything but a reminder of things she would rather forget.

chapter SIXTEEN

Tasmin walked into the small sitting room that opened onto the bedroom of the suite to find Bailey waiting for him. She sat in a chair, hands folded neatly in her lap, wearing a white silk dressing gown that managed to cover a great deal of skin and still accentuate every curve of her body. Her bare feet were tucked primly up against the base of the elegant little love seat in which she sat.

And she was the most beautiful vampire he'd ever seen.

He stopped short just inside the door, staring. He couldn't help it. What was already lovely had been accentuated, enhanced into the breathtaking. Her skin shimmered faintly when she shifted, the candlelight catching the many hues of gold in her long, wavy hair. The biggest shock, however, was her eyes. They watched him steadily from beneath long, dark blond lashes, burning a hot shade of gold.

In the change, Bailey had gained the eyes of a lioness.

The expression in them was just as fierce. He didn't know what to make of that, or of her.

Tasmin suddenly felt as out of place as he had at the Lilim's mansion. He had never sired another vampire. He had no idea what to do, what to say in order to reassure her. To praise her looks would fall flat—that he was sure of. It had to be the last thing on her mind right now. And he couldn't promise to stay by her side, because she'd been through enough without piling pretty lies on top of it.

He had nothing to give her. The realization left him with a hollow feeling in the pit of his stomach.

"How are you feeling?" he asked.

The quirk of her smile was a welcome sign that whatever she'd been through, the Bailey he knew was still there.

"Lily made me drink blood out of a glass. I think it was microwaved. I liked it. I don't actually know how I feel about that."

Tasmin laughed softly. "You'll get used to that part."

Her smile deepened, then faded as they looked at one another. The few feet between them could have been miles. All he wanted was to walk over, pick her up, and hold her until he'd satisfied himself she was really all right. Instead, he hung back.

Nothing should have changed in the space of two nights. Instead, everything had.

Finally, Bailey spoke into the tension.

"I want to know what happened."

Tasmin arched a brow. "That's a strange question. You can see what happened."

Her eyes narrowed, and for the first time he caught a glimpse of the pain Lily had hinted at.

"I mean I want to know what you saw. I can't remember..." She trailed off, shook her head. "I remember being dragged out of the car. I remember *him*, the way he looked, sounded, smelled... He got off on my fear, Tasmin. He loved that I was terrified. I was ready to beg for my life. I'd already started." She cringed. "It was humiliating, and that was exactly what he wanted."

The rage he'd felt when he'd seen her lying helplessly on the ground flickered back to life, heating his veins with a slow burn. That anyone would dare lay hands on her, when she was *his*... That thought had filled him with such violence that the Ptolemy's fate was sealed before he'd even seen his face. Tasmin shuddered at the memory.

"Why do you need to know this?" he asked. "The Ptolemy who had you was scum. I killed him, Bailey. I tore him to pieces." He winced. "Is this what you want to hear? That I spilled his blood? I did. He'll never hurt anyone again." Something ugly shifted deep inside, curling around itself in pleasure, and it made him ill to realize he and the demon were of the same mind on this. But he couldn't change the way he felt.

"When I found you, he had drained you nearly dry. He had opened his wrist to feed you, to put his mark on you. So I made him pay."

Bailey inhaled deeply and then nodded. "I'm glad you did. Maybe that makes me as bad as him."

"No." Tasmin stepped closer to her, despite his efforts not to. The need to be near her was so strong it was almost painful. Every time he saw her, it only intensified his craving for her presence, her touch. And every time, the strength of it took him by surprise.

"He stole your mortal life from you, a thing he had no right to take. You have every right to feel as you do. The kind of man who can do such a thing and enjoy it is exactly the kind of monster so many humans have envisioned us to be. I doubt anyone will mourn his passing, even his own kind."

Bailey blew out a breath and nodded again. "You're right. I know you're right. I'm just...I keep turning it over in my head. Like if I'd tried to fight harder, or if I'd said the right thing that maybe I could have stopped it." She pushed an agitated hand through her hair. "And then I remember that I was supposed to be a message to Lily. He said that nothing she wanted to protect would ever be safe no matter how hard she tried. You included. He seemed really furious about you."

"Don't worry about me," Tasmin said. "Unless Arsinöe herself wants to dirty her hands by coming to fight me into submission, they won't have me."

The demon will have me first, he thought, but didn't say it aloud. He didn't think Bailey would find that bit of truth very reassuring.

Her voice turned bitter. "I wish I could say that. But when he had me out there in the woods, Tasmin, I knew how weak I was, what a liability I was. If Lily and Ty hadn't had to drag me out of Tipton in a car, they never would have had to have that fight. One of the wolves was killed, did you know that?"

Tasmin nodded silently. He'd hoped she didn't know, but he expected she had asked Lily...and there seemed to be no lies between the two women.

"My fault," she said. "If I'd just backed off a year ago, realized that I was in over my head and stuck to normal human things, he'd be alive. I'd just be one more random person, not a weapon to use against people I care about."

He listened to her words and heard echoes of his own. The words he heard himself saying were strangely soothing to the part of him that had been filled with self-loathing since he'd discovered what had happened to his kind. If only he had been wise enough to have evaded capture, if only he had been strong enough to fight off his captors, the demon they'd infected him with…if only he had been formidable enough to have never been a target at all. Maybe then he could have made a difference.

Except he could no more have changed the course of events than Bailey could. Arsinöe was always going to destroy the Rakshasa. She was always going to try to grind the Lilim into dust. Remove one weapon and another would have appeared.

"It isn't your fault," Tasmin said softly, and a burden he'd carried deep in his chest for months now fell away.

"Those Ptolemy were waiting for Lily and Ty, Bailey. There would have been a fight no matter what. And if there were no you, she would have found another to try and use to hurt Lily. But that person, whoever he or she might have been, wouldn't have had me to come and fight for them. I heard you calling for me," he said.

"I wondered," Bailey replied softly. "I didn't really think it would work."

"It did," Tasmin said. *Because I think of you all the time. Because I had you in my arms.* "If it hadn't, though, things might have turned out very differently."

"Or that other person might have already been a vampire and just kicked serious ass."

Tasmin breathed out a soft, sympathetic laugh. "The

Ptolemy only pick battles they think they can win, Bailey. Don't count on it."

"But—"

"This isn't your fault. None of this. You're caught up in something you didn't start, just like the rest of us." He closed the distance between them and sank to the cushion beside her. She sighed, a desolate sound, slumping forward.

"I don't know what I'm supposed to do."

"Survive," he said simply. "Sometimes, that's really all there is to be done. I was young when I was put in that cave, but most of my pride brothers were ancient. They'd seen plenty of things they never wanted to see. And not all of them had been sired with their consent. But they lived, often well." He paused, remembering, and for the first time in a long time the memories of their faces caused no pain. "It was not always an easy life, but it had its pleasures. My existence wasn't without joy. If the pride had lived, I imagine it would have stayed that way."

He had caught her interest, he saw. She tilted her head at him, a faint frown creasing her brow.

"I didn't know you felt that way about it."

"About what? My pride?"

"That. And just your life. I knew you were okay with it, but until right now I hadn't realized you actually *enjoyed* being what you are. What you were."

He lifted his eyebrows, surprised. "Why wouldn't I enjoy being what I am? What was ever better than being Rakshasa?"

That made her laugh, a welcome sound even if he hadn't intended to be funny.

He smirked. "You think I sound arrogant. Watch.

Soon, you'll feel the same. You really didn't think I was glad to be what I am?"

She shook her head. "I thought all you did was fight as mercenaries. And live outdoors. And...fight. You hadn't talked about anything more than that, so I figured that was all there was to it. It sounds like it was a pretty stark existence."

"Not at all," Tasmin replied, amazed he'd portrayed such a one-dimensional image. But then, since he'd awakened, he'd been so preoccupied with the darker aspects of his predicament, he'd given little thought to how things had been in better times.

He liked remembering the good things.

She made him remember that there *were* good things. Many of them.

"It's going to be all right," he said, finding himself in the unfamiliar position of comfort giver. But he meant the words, and perhaps because of it, Bailey seemed to respond to the sentiment behind them.

"I hope so," she said. "I have so much to figure out now. How to break this to my parents. What to do about my life back in Tipton. Where I belong." She paused, her eyes searching his face for something only she knew.

"You."

"Me?" he repeated, the word coming out in the barest whisper. Looking at her only inches away from him, he wanted so many impossible things. Knowing he would never have a chance at them was nearly as painful as the moment he'd realized he was all alone. He was still alone, in many ways. And now he would remain so.

"I don't know if or how what's happened changes things. With us." Her cheeks flushed a deep pink, and after a moment of consideration, he understood what she was asking.

"I turned you, but we're not bonded, if that's what you mean. When vampires mate, the process is a bit more... intimate. You're still free. You don't need to worry."

Her forehead creased. "You think I'm worried about *that*? Tasmin, what happened between us was... It's more than I could have imagined." She sighed and looked away, her expression so lost it was painful.

"I didn't want this. Maybe I would have, someday, I don't know."

Her words sliced into him. "I'm sorry," he said hoarsely. Would she really rather have died? Maybe... but he couldn't have lived with that. Or with himself.

"No," Bay said quickly, shaking her head. "No. I'm glad I'm alive, Tasmin. This is just..." She blew out a breath, then tipped her chin up, seeming to bolster herself. Her eyes met his. "I'm not saying this right. I still want to be with you. I care about you. I don't think that's news, but I'm saying it anyway. You're the only part of this mess I *am* sure about, Tasmin. I don't want this to screw things up."

She would never know how her words affected him. He hadn't expected to find anyone who even wanted much to do with him, much less a woman who wanted both his company and his hands on her. By the time he'd tried to make any rules for himself where she was concerned, it had been too late—he'd already broken them all.

Now, it was too late altogether. They would have no future... only now. He just wasn't sure how to make her understand why he could only let himself fall so far. It could only hurt her.

"You could never screw things up," Tasmin said, skirting around the subject she wanted to discuss. "You seem determined to fix everything you see."

"That doesn't mean it always works, trust me." She leaned into him, just a little, touching her leg to his. The gesture was warm and familiar. It still amazed him, how comfortable he had gotten with Bailey in such a short time. But she was special. Everyone, even her sweet, silly dog, seemed to recognize that.

"Speaking of fixing things, Grimm has been watching me like a hawk. Now that you're awake, you need to make him start looking after you again. I keep tripping over him."

That finally prompted a smile. "No problem. I'm going to go hug him for at least an hour after this. I'm not ashamed to say he was the first thing I asked about once I, well...got it together." She hesitated, then said, "The second thing I asked about was you. Lily said Anura's plan is taking a little more time than she'd thought."

"Anura is having a harder time putting together the ritual because of all that's happening," Tasmin agreed. It was a relief, too, since he wouldn't be able to attend it. Anura had been kind. He felt guilty, having her do all of this for nothing. But that was better than creating carnage for her trouble.

Bailey didn't look pleased.

"But it's still going to happen, right?" she asked. "She still thinks she can help you?"

"It isn't such a simple thing," he said, hedging. "I'm not sure when the women she needs will be able to come. Even then, the results aren't certain."

Her outrage on his behalf was heartening, if misplaced.

"But it's *important*," Bailey said, her voice sharpening. He caught the flicker of fangs in her mouth as she spoke.

"I think, right now, defeating Arsinöe once and for all has taken precedence over prying a demon out of me," Tasmin said. "I can't fault them for that. Besides," he added, his voice gentling. "I don't think the demon is going to let go so easily, Bailey."

"But you've been able to control it," she insisted. "You even managed to turn me without hurting me! That has to mean something good. You're stronger than this thing!"

The truth was on the tip of his tongue, but he swallowed it in favor of a half-truth. One, it would be easier for her to take. "I barely hung on, Bailey," he said, and watched her lovely face fall. "It took everything I had not to just take what little blood the Ptolemy had left and drain you completely. The hunger...it's nothing I can describe. When it comes on, it blocks out everything else. If there had been any way to get you to Lily or Ty, or any of the Lilim, I would have had someone else turn you. Maybe that would have been better. You would have had a dynasty to go to, instead of just one man."

"No," she said, watching him solemnly. "I'm glad it was you. If it had to happen, I would have chosen you. I mean that."

Her admission made him ache in ways he hadn't thought he ever would.

"I worried you'd be angry," he admitted. "By rights, you should have joined the Lilim. But there wasn't time. There was only me."

And I wanted you, wanted my teeth in you, just that once...

Bailey's expression was quizzical, and there was an

element of it that had lost that sweet softness he was so accustomed to in her. There was a faint edge to her voice when she spoke again. More tellingly, she pulled her knee away.

"So...you would rather someone else had done it, is what you're saying."

"I would rather you hadn't had to go through it at all," Tasmin replied, hoping to placate her. He'd never seen quite that look in her eyes before, but he was absolutely sure he'd put it there. "What's done is done," he continued. "You're Rakshasa now, with everything that entails. I'll help you adjust, teach you what I can...while I can."

Bailey looked at him silently. Finally, she said, "You'll help me."

"Of course."

"Next you're going to tell me you had a really good time the other night and promise to call me."

Her anger wasn't something he'd expected, but it was there, low and thrumming like a live wire. Tasmin felt the hair at the back of his neck prickle, the way it always did before he was challenged in battle. The problem was, this was unfamiliar territory—and this wasn't a fight he had any idea how to win.

Tasmin sighed. "I'm not sure what you want from me."

She lifted a hand to her forehead and closed her eyes, her brows drawn together. She looked wretchedly sad, and Tasmin could only imagine what she must be feeling. Lily had been right—Bay needed someone. He wished, very much, that he was better suited to the job. After a long moment, she spoke, though she still didn't look at him.

"I guess that makes two of us. Twenty-four hours ago I had a nice house, and a business, and all the bits and pieces of a human life. I wasn't always satisfied with it, but I *knew* it. I knew I could change it. You were a big change for me. I was still trying to figure that out. And now...nothing is the same. Except that I was hoping you would be." She opened her eyes to look at him, her vulnerability on full display along with all of her strength.

"Something's changed. What is it?"

Tasmin stared at her, his guilt gnawing at him. How could she know? They'd been together such a short time, but looking into her eyes, he felt as though she could see into his very soul. She might not be his mate, but turning her had only intensified the bond between them.

What had he done?

She stared at him, waiting for an answer, and he remembered the feel of her mouth on his, the way she'd touched him. He'd had nothing, and then he'd had her. A woman who cared for the broken things—even one as broken as him. In return, he could give her nothing but lies and pain.

He seemed to exist solely as proof that the gods could be cruel on a whim.

"I don't want to hurt you," Tasmin said. It seemed to be the wrong thing. He saw immediately that Bailey was having none of it. Her eyes flickered like lightning in a stormy sky.

"I'm getting tired of hearing that," she said. "Vampires will hurt me; you'll hurt me. I won't break. I didn't before, and I won't now. I went through hell two nights ago and got turned into a vampire. Do I look like I'm ready to shatter into a thousand pieces to you?"

"It isn't—"

"I'm not finished," she interrupted him. Bailey shifted

so that her body was directly facing him, and her eyes were all but spitting sparks. Tasmin watched her silently, fascinated by the transformation. He'd never really seen her get angry.

"I'll tell you what," she said, a sharp edge to her voice. "If this is all too much for you, then tell me. I'll survive, like you said. It will hurt, I'll live, and I'll still be glad that you were straight with me instead of leading me on." Until her voice broke, he hadn't known how close to falling apart she still was. *She needs me.* The thought, wholly his, came unbidden.

He felt what meager defenses he'd tried to build against her crumble to dust.

"The other night was more than I ever imagined it could be," he said softly. "It was perfect. Never think otherwise."

Some of the heat left her voice, but not all.

"You said you thought about me all the time."

"That hasn't changed."

"Then what has?" she demanded. "You act like you're afraid to touch me. Are you so repulsed by what you did to save me? Is it that the Ptolemy had his teeth in me first? *What?*"

"Of course not," he hedged, bristling. "Things *have* changed, Bailey! We need to be realistic about what's coming!"

"You were hopeful the other night," she pointed out.

"I was a fool!"

"Because why? Because you slept with me?"

"Because I—"

"Because you ever walked into my life in the first place?"

"Because I thought it might ever let me go!" he snarled, his helpless fury at the situation breaking under her barrage of questions. Her eyes widened, and she drew back a little at the force of his answer. Tasmin felt a sinking feeling—it was more than he'd planned to tell her. But then, he should have known she wouldn't simply take whatever he decided to offer her. Defeated, what truth he could give her spilled from his lips.

"I can't get rid of it, Bailey. I know that now. I can't get rid of it without dying myself, so this is pointless; everything is *pointless*! If I were stronger I would end it myself, but I don't want to die. Not that it matters what I want."

He spat the words bitterly, angry not at her, but at a reality he couldn't seem to change. Bailey's soft voice drew him back. Her own anger appeared to have left her as quickly as it had come.

"Why didn't you just tell me? You're sure?"

"I'm sure." He raked a hand through his hair, slumping lower in the seat. "I—"

Careful what you say, vampire. Our bargain. Our secret.

The voice rose out of nowhere, hissing through his mind and then falling again into silence. Tasmin choked on his words, feeling not a trace of the thing inside himself. It sickened him, to have a parasite like this attached to his soul.

"I just *know*," Tasmin said. "I can't say more, so don't ask me to. Just know it's the truth, Bailey. I don't know when it will take me, but I know it will happen. You should stop caring for me at all, if you knew what was best for yourself." He looked at her bleakly. "I'm already dead."

Her reaction was so swift he couldn't do anything to stop her. In a split second Bailey had grabbed fistfuls of his shirt, dragged him from the love seat, and pinned him to the floor. She straddled his hips, switching her grip from his shirt to his wrists and anchoring his hands at either side of his head. All Tasmin could do was stare up at her, stunned.

She shouldn't have been able to move like that yet. She should be awkward, tentative.

Instead, she bared her fangs and glared at him with all the fire of a jungle cat.

"You're not dead, and you're not going to be. We're not going to let it happen. And you're going to start actually living again."

"What? What do you think I'm doing *now*?" Tasmin asked.

"Walking around like a ghost, mostly," Bailey shot back. "Admit it. Ever since you came out of that cave, you haven't really rejoined the world. You've just been moving through it, waiting for the other shoe to drop."

She was hard to argue with when he was between her legs like this, and she knew it. The natural advantage she'd found was irritating, though his arousal was quickly overriding that.

"And now it has," he growled. "How was I wrong?"

"You're wrong because you're still alive. You're still here. You, the man who told me you only had now, but that you wanted to spend it with me. Don't take that back out of some misguided sense of honor, of not wanting to hurt me. I knew what you were."

"And what is that?" he asked, wanting to hear her admit that he was cursed, broken, a lost cause.

Instead, he caught the determined look on her face only an instant before her mouth was pressed hard against his. He held out for exactly three seconds, until he felt the flicker of her tongue against his lips. Then his mouth was open, mating with hers in a hot, wild kiss that made every thought he'd ever had of keeping his distance from her vanish in the steam.

When Bailey finally raised her head to look down at him, her breasts still pressed against his chest, he could do nothing but watch her. Her sweetness had been hiding an unexpected ferocity. Now, the lion running wild in her blood had drawn it out.

"Right now, the only thing you need to be is mine."

He tried to raise himself up, but Bailey easily pinned him back to the floor. It was strangely erotic. She had become his equal in every way.

"I *am* yours," he rasped, his eyes locked with hers. "Be sure of that, if nothing else."

She exhaled, a shaken breath, and it was only then he realized how afraid she'd been that he was going to walk away. Her need for him was humbling. Being depended on in his pride had been different. He'd been confident in his physical abilities, in his sense of honor.

And still, he hadn't been able to save them, or himself. But he had saved Bailey. Bailey, who gave everything and asked only for what scattered pieces of himself he'd been able to salvage. He could refuse her nothing...not when she was the only person in the world he truly cared about.

It was such a relief to stop fighting what he wanted and just give himself over to feeling.

In an instant Tasmin had taken back the advantage,

flipping her onto her back and pinning her down just as she had done to him.

His eyes drank her in, laying beneath him with her hair spread around her like a nimbus of light. She was perfect and proud and fierce—she was everything he would wish for in a mate, he realized. A lioness in every sense.

And he was falling, so hard and fast he couldn't find a foothold to make it stop. His feelings for her roared through him, until he could no longer deny what they were. Tasmin's hands tightened on her wrists, possession of an infinitely more pleasurable sort. The knowledge of what he might have had with her nearly broke him.

Bailey was his match, what the Rakshasa would have called his One. Somehow, in all this misery and darkness, he had stumbled across the woman made to fit him.

It was why he couldn't let her be.

Why he would pine for impossible things until he breathed his last.

"Tasmin?" Bailey's voice, breathless and thick with passion, drew him back to her. There was a question in her eyes. He wasn't ready to give her the words, not until he weighed whether they would do more harm than good. But he could tell her so much without saying a single thing. For now, he would make that be enough.

Their eyes locked, and he could feel her blood in his veins, pulsing in time with his heart.

Instinct, far more ancient than he was, had Tasmin leaning down to rub his face against her cheeks, as though he could mark her with his scent as a lion would. Bailey arched her neck, pressing into him. She spread her legs wider to fit his hips against her more fully, and he rocked hard into her, making her gasp. When he pushed forward again, he shivered at the friction between them, making his cock throb.

He groaned as he thrust against her again, burying his face against her neck.

"I wish we were back in the Gir," he breathed. "I dream about chasing you through the trees. About what I'd do when I caught you."

"Show me," Bailey said. She was already tense beneath him, her breathing quick and uneven. "Show me what you think of doing to me."

He raised his head to look into her eyes and saw nothing but desire, trust. He knew what he wanted—he'd imagined it with her a thousand times. He'd heard enough in his years among his pride brothers to understand that the things he imagined were common, if not to the taste of every woman. Now that he'd experienced lovemaking, he knew his inclinations still ran the way most of the Rakshasas did—a little wild.

He just wanted to be sure it would make Bailey hot too.

As a test, knowing they could communicate without words now that they shared a mark, he opened his thoughts and let her see an image of what he imagined. Her eyes lit up, and she licked her lips.

"We don't need to be in the forest for that," she breathed.

"Then... get up," he said, sliding smoothly off her. Tasmin stripped off his shirt, his jeans, his eyes never leaving Bailey. In less than a minute Tasmin stood naked before her, watching as she slid the silk robe from her shoulders, then pulled the thin nightgown up over her head. He sucked in a breath as she tossed it aside and her hair tumbled back around her shoulders. He loved the way she was built, the high full breasts, the flat stomach with the cup of a navel that begged to be licked, the flare of her hips. The round little ass he'd imagined nipping more times than he could count.

Her chest rose and fell with every breath as she watched him, nerves and desire tensing her body.

Then she grinned at him. "Catch me if you can," she said, and leapt away from him, sprinting into the bedroom. His blood was up instantly, and he gave chase, the need for the hunt taking over.

She was able prey, as he'd known she would be. Tasmin raced after her, but she managed to stay just a few steps ahead, leaping nimbly over the bed, leading him on a merry chase back through the sitting room, around and around the cavernous bedroom. All his troubles, everything vanished but the two of them, and for the first time in what felt like centuries, his heart lightened. Tasmin laughed when his fingertips brushed the flying tips of Bailey's hair, and she yelped, not yet ready to give up. She bolted to the side, then made a run at the bed again to use it as a springboard.

This time, though, he was ready to move in for the kill. When she leaped, he pushed off from powerful thighs and caught her to him in midair. They landed in the center of the big bed in a tangle of covers, and he rolled with her, grappling for position. Bailey growled and snapped, letting the beast in her play as rough as it wanted to.

He flipped her beneath him, and an instant later she'd wrestled him back onto his back again, teasing his cock when she'd try to straddle him and keep him down. Every accidental brush between her thighs told him how wet and swollen she was, and the scent of her arousal hung thick in the air. It made him want to press his face between her legs and lick her until she screamed.

An excellent idea for later.

Tasmin nipped the sensitive place between Bailey's neck and shoulder as he wrestled her beneath him once more, pressing her stomach to the bed while she bucked beneath him, trying to escape. This time, though, he managed to get a grip on her hips, lifting them just enough so he could drive into her from behind, burying himself fully in her tight wet sheath in a single movement. His mouth opened in a wordless cry. Nothing had ever felt better than this. Nothing.

He heard her cry out, and his sexual haze lifted enough to form words.

"Bailey?"

"Don't. Stop." Her voice was harsh and muffled by the sheets, but there was no hint of anything but need in it.

Tasmin obliged, rising to his knees and taking her as hard as he'd imagined. He slammed into her, dizzy with raw pleasure as Bailey tightened around him with every stroke, her increasingly loud cries urging him on along with every sharp slap of skin against skin. He gripped her hips tight while Bailey's fingers wound in the sheets, hanging on.

He could feel her start to pulse around him, could feel her quivering as she got close to the edge. Every stroke pulled him closer to climax. Everything fell away until all he could do was feel Bailey around him.

Her inner muscles clenched and she arched her back, surging against him, her voice half-roar as she came. That was all it took for Tasmin to find his own release, stiffening as he poured himself into her with his own roar.

When he could breathe again, Tasmin sank to the bed, wrapping himself around Bailey's limp body and curving himself against her back. He loved being fitted against her this way, so he could enjoy her warmth and nuzzle into her neck, breathing in her scent.

"Did you like that?" he murmured, nibbling at her earlobe.

Bailey made a sound that was something like a word, but mainly a noise in the affirmative. Tasmin smiled and rubbed his nose against her hair. He'd take it.

He dragged the covers over the two of them, determined to do as Bailey had asked and think of nothing more than being here, being hers. This moment was far too good to allow anything to spoil.

If he was lucky, he might get more of them. Right now, that was enough to leave him content.

So thinking, he wrapped his arms around Bailey and fell deeply asleep.

chapter SEVENTEEN

Y OU CAN PRACTICE ON THEM."

"No I can't."

"They're not going to notice."

Bay sighed loudly. She was perched on a stool at Mabon, Anura's club in the city. Hidden in the basement of an old building with an entrance tucked down an alleyway, one could only find Mabon if they knew where to look.

Neither she nor Tasmin had, but Anura had been very helpful in giving directions. And truthfully, Bay had been excited to get out. They'd been in Chicago nearly a week, and as Vlad's house filled up with visitors, leaders of the dynasties, friends, and contacts from all over the country, it was beginning to get a little claustrophobic. Not to mention the tension levels, which made everything seem closer. Bay wished there were something she could do to make Lily smile again. But it didn't seem like anything was going to do that until this was all over with.

So she settled into what passed for a routine, and tried to learn the things Tasmin decided to instruct her on. That was, when he wasn't diverting her with...other things. He had quickly turned into what Bay thought of as the very definition of a demanding lover.

She was enjoying every second of it.

Unfortunately, they weren't in bed right now, and Tasmin had decided that a relaxing evening at a club was a great time to practice taking mental potshots at unsuspecting vampires. The change in him still amazed her. He'd actually done as she'd asked and stopped skulking around as though he was expecting his impending doom to arrive any minute. While he wasn't exactly outgoing around the other vampires, he was at least more comfortable.

To her surprise, so was she. She was still no more a Lilim than she had been when she'd been human. She still had a life in Tipton that she'd been torn from, the trappings of which were still sitting there, waiting and dark. But now that she understood how fiercely Lily had been trying to protect her all this time—not to mention from what—the gulf between them had quickly closed to nothing. She had a great deal more appreciation for Ty, with his eternal vigilance and wry humor. And most of all, she had Tasmin...for now.

Someday soon, she was going to have to figure out how to fashion a life she could settle into from those disparate pieces. But until the situation with Arsinöe was resolved, that would be impossible. And, Bay thought, she needed to do what she'd instructed Tasmin to do—live in the moment. She blew out a breath and forced her attention back to the present.

"Tasmin," Bay said, trying again to convince him what a bad idea this was. "You glow when you do that. I'm going to glow if and when I can do that. It's not the kind of thing people don't notice."

He gave her a beleaguered look and took a sip of the deep red cocktail the waitress had brought to them, courtesy of Anura. Immediately, he shuddered, put the glass down, and pushed it away. Bay frowned at him, immediately concerned.

"Is it that bad?"

"No, no, it's just..." He trailed off, and Bay thought his eyes looked odd for just a second before he finished. "Not as thirsty as I thought."

He looked away, getting very interested in the other vampires milling around the club, and Bay studied his profile for a few seconds. He looked tired tonight, she thought, something vampires should never look. And she worried that his refusal to drink in front of her had more to do with the demon than it did with lack of appetite.

He didn't bring it up, and she didn't press him on it. Not when she was enjoying him so much, and when he seemed to have lightened up a little. But that didn't mean she didn't worry. Nor did it mean she hadn't spent most of her alone time combing Vlad's massive library of what seemed like solutions to every other problem in the vampire universe for answers that refused to appear.

Bay was hoping to see Anura tonight. With any luck, she'd made progress in getting the ritual together. It just seemed to have stalled since they'd all arrived here. Being chased out of Tipton probably had something to do with that. According to some of the Thorn wolves who took a run up to check it out, the Ptolemy had retreated. But they didn't dare go back yet. Arsinöe would have eyes watching.

And so Putting on the Dog stayed dark, and she continued to pay employees who she couldn't let work while they wondered if she were either terminally ill or insane. Her mind tried to drift home, to her cozy house where she could curl up and avoid any and all forms of bloodshed. She could fight now if she needed to. It had been a little disheartening to realize that her new abilities hadn't come with any desire to use them.

She was still herself, just with fangs. That didn't seem to bother anyone but her.

Bay slid Tasmin's drink over to sit beside her own. She had every intention of drinking both.

"*What* are you staring at?" she finally asked.

That got his attention. He whipped his head around guiltily, and she noticed a faint flush on his cheeks. Arching her eyebrow, Bay craned her head around, and immediately, her eyes widened.

"Oh. Wow. They're...okay with PDA here. Good to know."

"There are still some things I'm not used to about the twenty-first century," Tasmin admitted.

Bay smiled, glad to be diverted. He was sexy when he was embarrassed.

Tasmin refocused on her, and she immediately knew she wasn't off the hook yet.

"This is a good place to practice the basics of the gift, Bailey. I want you to try it."

She looked at his expression, then took a deep breath and closed her eyes. "Okay. I'm supposed to focus on something. A scene."

"Something you know well. Something you've culti-vated in your own mind. This is something you'll want to work on in your spare time. Visualization and meditation. The illusions we can create have to be worked on first. Think of each one you have as an arrow in a quiver."

"You sound like an infomercial."

"And you sound like you would rather go practice being a lion again."

She hunched her shoulders and glared at him. "Mean. Really, that's all I have to say."

His slow, sexy smile almost—*almost*—banished the memory of finding herself on the bedroom floor with paws, claws, and a human head yesterday. It wasn't as easy as she'd guessed. None of it was. She would hap-pily practice, but she didn't want an audience until she got better. The problem was that until she got better, she shouldn't be practicing without an audience.

Tasmin was a patient teacher. She just wished he would be a little less...teacher-ish about it.

A song she liked began to thrum and throb onto the dance floor at the far end of the cavernous room. Bay eyed Tasmin speculatively.

"Tell you what. I'll do this once, and then I'll teach *you* something great about the twenty-first century. Deal?"

He looked bemused...and wary.

"I suppose."

She grinned at him, and he relaxed. Slightly. Bay looked around for likely targets, noticed a big, brawny lowblood chatting up what looked like a pampered Empusa, and decided she'd try to give the situation a push.

Bay closed her eyes and tried to think of the most cli-chéd sexiness she could. She came up with a room with wood paneling, shag carpeting, and a water bed. Barry White was playing on the stereo, and through the window, she could see a van with a wizard painted on the outside of it.

It was the least sexy thing ever.

And damn it, she wanted to go dance.

"Whatever. Shazam," she muttered, and tried to push the image in her mind toward the couple-in-progress. She saw a faint gold flicker around herself, but that was it. For a moment, she didn't think any part of the illusion had hit the two, but then she noticed the dazed look in their eyes. After a moment, each of them blinked, gave one another the side eye, and slunk away from one another as fast as they could manage. Both looked slightly nauseous.

Tasmin was staring at her.

"Was that what you were trying to do?" he asked.

Bay stood and held out her hand. "Yes. They obviously weren't right for each other. Come on."

He followed, albeit a little reluctantly, as she led him to the dance floor. Bay craned her neck around as they went, fascinated by the atmosphere. There was a lot of dark, heavy wood, but the walls were lined with floor-length mirrors in ornate frames. She'd been glad not to lose her reflection—one of the many untruths enshrined in vampire legend. Just like she'd been glad not to lose the sun. Her tolerance for sunlight got stronger every day, impressing even Tasmin with how fast she was adjusting. But then, she wasn't sure even he understood how badly she still craved the light. Here, as at Vlad's, the only light was from dozens of flickering candles. They cast a spooky, romantic glow over everything.

When they hit the dance floor, Bay immediately got

her groove on, swaying her hips, wiggling sinuously in time to the music. She had closed her eyes, losing herself for just a few seconds in the beat. But when she opened her eyes, her dance partner looked like he wasn't sure whether to drag her out of the club or throw her on the floor right there and have her.

Nor was he moving.

Bay grabbed his hand and pulled him the couple of steps it took to close the distance between them, feeling a familiar heat beginning to curl through her at the look in his eyes. She put her hands on his hips, swallowing hard.

Maybe this hadn't been such a great idea. The point had been to get out, not to run right back home. And they'd never had a real date, for all the time they'd spent together. Just once, she wanted to do something normal with him.

"Look," Bay said, rising up so she could speak in his ear. "You just kind of sway to the music. With me."

She tried to budge him, but most of what she got was a stiff back and forth. Frustrated, she wound her arms around his neck and slid against him, trying to dance for two.

"This sort of dancing is for the bedroom," Tasmin growled in her ear. "Or the woods."

"Or for every other fully clothed couple out here except you and me," Bay said, pulling back to look at him. His breath fanned her face, and his eyes were all light and heat. She could just imagine running through the woods with him, Tasmin in hot pursuit . . . and what he would do when he caught her.

Bay let out a shaking breath and pulled away.

"Maybe no dancing right now."

He whispered in her ear as they walked back to the table, "I now have some ideas for later, however."

She was startled to see two familiar faces sitting at their table as they made their way back. Lily and Ty had been locked in one meeting or another almost since the moment they'd gotten here. It seemed like even they had needed a break.

"Hey," Bay said, genuinely glad to see her friends. "Now it's a party."

Ty looked both severe and handsome in all black tonight, while Lily was elegant in a jade-green silk shell and a pair of skinny black pants. They were a striking couple, and Bay could see that their presence hadn't gone unnoticed. There was plenty of whispering and staring.

Lily gave her a tired smile. "Ty was threatening to drag me here in my sweatpants, so I figured I could at least put some effort into it." She looked around. "What do you think of it? They managed to make it look almost exactly the same as before."

"Before..." Her eyes widened. "Oh, God, this is the club Damien tried to burn down with you in it, right?"

"I think Anura would still like to light *him* on fire." Ty chuckled. He looked at his wife, and his silver eyes glittered in the candlelight. "I remember how you danced with that Ptolemy ass so I could talk to Anura."

Lily grinned. "And I remember being disappointed I never got to dance with you."

"We're going to fix that tonight."

Bay looked between them, then at Tasmin. She decided it was an excellent time to try her first telepathic communication with another Rakshasa.

SEE? IT'S NOT KINKY!

Tasmin winced and pressed a hand against his ear.

Ty frowned and looked around. "Is someone shouting?"

Bay slouched in her seat and fiddled with the stirring straw in her cocktail.

It was a relief to spot the dark-haired beauty making her way toward them from her office, which was tucked behind one of the mirrors. Bay slid off the stool, determined to meet Anura halfway. She wanted to check on the progress with putting together the ritual...and to ask whether there were any other resources she could begin checking into just in case.

"Be right back," Bay said, flashing a smile at Tasmin. Lily looked between the two men, then at Bay and Anura, and hit the ground as well.

"Have fun bonding," she said, and walked away.

Tasmin watched the women go, his eyes lingering on the sway of Bailey's hips.

The woman was trying to kill him, and at this rate she'd manage it long before the demon. He wanted her all the time. If she wasn't making him laugh, she was making him hot...but it was usually both.

He would have given a great deal to know what she'd been thinking of when she'd managed to send the potential couple running away from one another so quickly. She would learn, he knew. It would just take time.

All he could do was give her the basics now and hope she caught on quickly. Teaching her how to embrace what she was had become a welcome distraction from what was going on around them. But he knew it was just that—a distraction.

Ty's voice pulled him back to the present. The silver-eyed vampire was watching him with interest. He'd been watching him stare at Bailey, Tasmin realized.

"She's a lovely thing," Ty commented, picking up a glass of spiked blood the waitress brought him and taking a sip.

Tasmin shifted uncomfortably. Ty's seeming belief in him over the night of Bailey's siring had been welcome . . . but he wasn't quite sure what to say now.

A great deal had changed since their first meeting at Bailey's.

"She is," Tasmin finally said, letting his eyes drift back to where Bailey now stood with the other women. She looked beautiful tonight, in a simple pair of slim black pants and a royal blue top that clung to her curves.

He heard Ty's amused chuckle, and redirected his attention again.

"They're fighters, these women," Ty said. "You think they need saving, and then they go and save your ass anyway. It's bollocks at first, but you get used to it."

Tasmin's mouth curved up, and he tried to picture Bailey containing her sloppy bun with one hand and brandishing a sword with the other.

"I would rather protect her," Tasmin said, thinking about all that could happen if he wasn't incredibly vigilant, if he didn't run from her the instant he felt the demon start to stir. What could she do about any of that?

But Ty just shook his head. "What you'd rather do and what happens, at least with Lily and Bay, are two different things most of the time. Keeps life interesting. And beautiful."

Tasmin saw the way Ty looked at his wife, the slow-burning warmth in it, and felt a sinking sensation in the pit of his stomach.

Not for you, whispered the demon, chuckling. A warning.

Still, he couldn't help but imagine, once in a while, what it might be like. And from the look on his face, Ty understood more than he would ever let on.

It surprised Tasmin to feel Ty's hand clap on his shoulder.

"To destiny, brother." He lifted his glass to Tasmin. "Can't fight it. Might as well toast it."

"Destiny," Tasmin murmured, raising the glass he could only pretend to drink out of lest the blood tempt the demon too much.

"Cheers," Ty said, with a curious, sympathetic look, and drained his glass.

chapter EIGHTEEN

BAY HEADED DOWN THE MAIN STAIRCASE at Vlad's, her bare feet noiseless on the wood, looking curiously around for the sight of black, wavy hair and cinnamon skin. She and Tasmin had slept for the better part of the day. He'd awakened her at some point and made love to her until she couldn't move, at which point she'd passed back out again. That she remembered, Bay thought with a smile as she lifted her head a little, trying to see if she could pick his scent out of all the ones in the mansion right now.

He must have slipped out before she'd awakened.

It didn't surprise her. He'd proven to be a restless sleeper, up at odd hours, appearing in and disappearing from the bed she preferred to stay in for a solid block of hours when she was tired.

Still, every time she awakened to find him gone, there was a cold burst of fear that he was gone permanently, taken by the thing he refused to believe he could fight.

She wished she didn't have the terrible feeling that the clock was winding down with every passing night.

Pushing the thoughts from her head for the umpteenth time, Bay breathed in and tried to do as Tasmin had explained. Block everything else out. Think of each separate scent as a thread, and try to pick each of them out one at a time, following it to its source. Some would wind together again; some would diverge. All would become familiar.

And man, did she still suck at this.

Bay opened her eyes, irritated, and descended the stairs the rest of the way. She kept following the same scent trail to a werewolf eating a cheeseburger. Medium rare, with onion straws, Swiss cheese, and barbecue sauce.

Old habits died hard, apparently.

"Well, well. Bailey Harper. What on earth bit you?"

The familiar, cultured tones of the voice had her turning to see an impossibly handsome, sandy-haired vampire grinning at her as he strolled from one of the drawing rooms, looking like he'd just stepped out of the pages of a magazine. Bay was surprised to find herself returning his smile as she crossed the entrance hall to meet him. Damien Tremaine, though a friend of Lily and Ty, had always been as intimidating to her as he was bitingly funny. Now, though, the sight of a familiar face was welcome. And somehow, everything about him, from the smirk he wore to the tone in his voice, held a playfulness she'd always missed before.

More changes. Still, this one was welcome.

"Damien! What are you doing here? I don't think anyone here needs stabbing, and if jewelry starts disappearing everyone will know it was you."

"Darling," he said, arching an eyebrow, "most vampires need to be stabbed occasionally. It builds character." His cool blue eyes looked her over from head to toe, frankly assessing. Bay waited, unsurprised by the scrutiny. Sizing people up was what Damien did, after all.

Despite his mouth, Damien Tremaine was an intense presence, having spent centuries working for the most prominent guild of thieves and assassins in the vampire world, the House of Shadows. He'd renewed his friendship with Ty after spending some time trying to kill him and Lily last year, and had recently been promoted to . . . well, Bay wasn't sure exactly what, but he didn't seem to be killing as many people anymore.

His new mate had been good for him, according to absolutely everyone. He could still be a charming asshole, but Ariane had softened a lot of his hard edges. And he no longer just looked amused at everyone else's expense. He looked happy.

"I like it," Damien finally said. "I always had a feeling vampirism would look good on you. I can't say I care for the fact that your cat form is now bigger than mine, but as they say, it's not the size, it's how you use it."

She smacked him. "Pig. Where's your better half?"

"I left her as she was rolling around on the floor with your big slobbery dog," he said, then looked down at one of the cuffs of his button-down shirt. It was, Bay noted, rather damp.

"The Grimm missed me, I think. I only barely escaped being awash in his particular brand of affection. It would be an interesting strategy to defeat the Ptolemy. Just unleash your dog on them. Even if he doesn't manage to drown them, the drool should slow them down enough so we can pick them off easily."

"Funny." Bay smirked, then looked past him, distracted by a glimpse of dark hair. It wasn't Tasmin, though. Ludo, Vlad's right-hand man, waved in greeting as he headed toward the ballroom. She sighed.

"Looking for your man?"

Bay nodded, returning her attention to Damien. He was watching her with a curious mixture of sympathy and keen interest. She wasn't sure she liked it. It was the same look she'd been getting from almost everyone here all week. It was one of the less appealing aspects of vampire society. Everyone knew everyone else's business.

"He was gone when I woke up. I figured he'd be down here somewhere. Have you seen him?"

Damien shook his head. "No, and I've been hoping to. I've never actually met a Rakshasa." He leaned in closer, dropping his voice. "Ty told me what's been going on. I have to say, I'm surprised Anura is dragging her feet like this. I would have thought she'd be beside herself trying to save him, impending war be damned. You know she has a soft spot for his kind."

Anura. The other person Bay needed to corner tonight. "I don't think she's dragging her feet," Bay said. "I just don't think it's as easy to get together as she was hoping. She doesn't want to screw it up."

"Admirable," Damien said, but his brow creased faintly. "How are you holding up, truly, Bay? Teasing aside, you've sort of had the rug pulled out from under you this week. We got in just awhile ago, and I expected to hear you were safely tucked away back in Tipton, not turned into a vamp and engaged in an impossible relationship. You always seemed so...stable." His lips curved. "That's not an insult, by the way."

"It isn't impossible," Bay replied, though she knew that was what everyone thought. "It's just...complicated."

Damien surprised her with genuine sympathy. "Trust me, darling, I know the feeling." He turned, as though he'd sensed a change in the air, and Bay looked over his shoulder to see a stunning, platinum-haired vampiress walking toward them, Grimm trotting happily at her side. The dog's eyes lit on Bay, and he bounded toward her, greeting her as though he hadn't seen her in at least a year.

Ariane's violet eyes, set in a face of angelic perfection, were lit with a happy glow as she located her mate. Bay watched her approach, again surprised by how much her perception had shifted. Where before the ethereal Grigori had seemed intimidating, an untouchable warrior goddess, now Bay could see the natural sweetness that had endeared Ariane to Lily and Ty almost immediately.

"Bay!" she said as she joined them, leaning into Damien as he slipped an arm around her waist. "So nice to see you again. How are you?"

Bay smiled back as she scrubbed at Grimm's head and tried to deter him from jumping up on her. Despite the often somber mood in the mansion this week, he'd been in his element, in the midst of all kinds of people to make friends with. Lily had mentioned more than once she was glad for the presence of the dog. He was a roaming bright spot in otherwise difficult times.

The only lasting sign of what he'd been through the night of Bay's attack was a tendency, once he'd found her, to lock on and stay at her heels, unable to be lured away even with the tastiest treat. Not for long anyway.

"I'm fine. It's so nice to see familiar faces. I thought Lily said you were in...Turkey, was it?"

"We were," Ariane said, her smile fading. "Drake called us back. We've been expecting something to give, really. I just didn't think it would be so soon."

Bay saw the barely perceptible tightening of Damien's hand on her waist, the quick, intimate glance he and Ariane shared, and felt an unexpected burst of jealousy. The bond between Damien and Ariane was as intense as Damien himself, and it was obvious in the way the two vampires were together. And then there was the way Lily and Ty leaned on one another—they were one another's support systems through whatever came their way. And Jaden and Lyra, who were one of the most playful couples Bay knew.

And here she stood, alone. Since the other night, Tasmin had opened up in some ways, giving her everything he had in the bedroom. She couldn't complain about that—he held nothing back from her physically. But there were still barriers between them, lines he refused to cross. It made it impossible for her to think of them as a real couple, and she was sure that was by design. He was still trying, in his own misguided way, not to hurt her.

It was hurting her more to be with him in this kind of half relationship. Especially when everything they could be was staring her in the face. He was her sire. Her lover. The only other Rakshasa alive. It was a connection she would never be able to share with the Lilim—a connection she didn't really *want* to share with anyone but him. For all that she was coming to terms with being a vampire, she couldn't shake the sense that in some ways, she was still on the outside looking in. The Rakshasa had been considered strange by the rest. It was probably fitting that *that* was what she'd become.

It would have bothered her far less if she'd felt like she had a true partner. He wanted to help her feel more comfortable, and in that, he was succeeding. But Bay wanted more than comfortable. She'd had plenty of comfortable before, and she'd spent years grappling with her own restlessness.

This time, in this new life, she wanted to be happy. Truly happy. But the one man she knew she could find it with was hanging onto his heart with both hands and refused to let go. And as with so many things vampire related, she had no idea how to fix it. With an inward sigh, she turned her attention back to Damien and Ariane.

"Has anything been decided on yet?" Bay asked.

"We think she's at her country house in Maryland," Damien replied. "It's basically an open invitation to attack—which is worrisome, since it means she feels she's ready for us. All that open land down there… Arsinöe is looking for an epic battle to rival the ones her people engaged in back in its earliest days. Something to celebrate in art and song once she's consolidated her empire."

"People have scouted out the area, then?" Bay asked.

"A handful of Shades," Ariane said. "We actually lost two very talented scouts. Drake has been miserable over it. Arsinöe owns acres of land down there, and there are over a thousand vampires camped on it. Not all are hers. She's got some allies here from overseas, and it looks as though she's found a couple of wolf packs to patrol during the day. Lyra's livid about it."

Bay nodded. Lyra's pack, the Thorn, had narrowly

avoided being enslaved by the Ptolemy. The she-wolf would naturally consider any wolves helping the Ptolemy queen willingly disgusting.

"In short, this battle is going to be big, bloody, and, well, traditional. One for the history books." Damien looked away, and in that instant Bay could see his uncertainty. He would be risking everything right alongside his friends, she knew. As would Ariane.

As would all of them.

Though the thought of battle turned her stomach, Bay hoped that no one tried to tell her she had to stay behind this time. She wanted to help in any way she could, fledgling or not. She'd been waiting all week, as the various leaders met behind closed doors, to hear what the final plan would be. With the new arrivals tonight, and from the sound of things, they were moving toward an agreement.

It made finding Tasmin feel that much more urgent.

"I should go," Bay said. "It really is good to see you two." Ariane looked as pleased as she was surprised, and Bay found herself wishing she hadn't wasted quite so much time at Lily's being nervous over the past year. The vampires Lily had chosen to become close to all had something in common, she realized. They'd each found a way to make the world of night suit them, each in rather unique ways, rather than changing themselves.

Finally seeing the truth of it was soothing in a way she was immensely grateful for. It gave her hope.

"It's good to see you too. Both of us wish you luck. Oh, if you're looking for your... Tasmin? Dark skin, gold eyes, very pretty?" Ariane asked. Bay nodded.

"He's been shut away with Sam for a while now. I

caught a glimpse of him just a bit ago." Ariane's smile was sympathetic. "No one in there looked very happy. Not that there's much reason to be."

"Thanks," Bay said, startled at the news that Tasmin was locked away with anyone. The two of them had been left to their own devices this week, set apart from the war preparations so that Tasmin could concentrate on helping Bay adjust to her new existence. It made sense: Neither of them had command of anyone or anything. They would simply do what was needed when the time came.

So why would they suddenly want him?

Though she didn't know why, dread formed a hard knot and settled into the pit of her stomach as she walked away, Grimm lumbering along at her heels, leaving Damien and Ariane to watch her go.

"Come on, kitten," Damien murmured, turning his attention to Ariane. "Dark times ahead. Let's go have a bit of fun while we still can."

After asking a couple of questions, and settling Grimm with a huge bone in the corner of the library, Bay found what she was looking for.

She rapped softly on the heavy wood door set into the library wall, hearing the murmur of voices on the other side. After a moment, the door opened.

"Yes?"

It took her several seconds to formulate a coherent response.

The white-haired giant looked impassively down at her, seemingly unruffled by her interruption. He was one of the Grigori ancients Lily had talked about. There was no way he could be anything else. Shining white hair was pulled back at the nape of his neck with a simple leather thong, a striking contrast to a starkly handsome, surprisingly youthful face. Fathomless violet eyes watched her steadily, waiting for her to get herself together.

This was the sort of vampire she wasn't sure she would ever get completely comfortable with. She'd hardly be alone in that, though.

"I was looking for Tasmin?"

"Ah. You're the other little lion. We expected you would come."

He pulled the door open farther and stepped aside, and Bay walked past with only a sidelong glance. *Little* lion? Though she guessed most things would look little to a seven-foot-tall giant who had, according to Lily, wings.

There was no sign of wings on him or the other Grigori male in the room, but she knew every other face here— and as Ariane had mentioned, the atmosphere was tense. Lily and Ty stood together beside a chair, Lily pressed against Ty's side, murmuring urgently in his ear. Jaden and Lyra were there, a surprise—but then, it shouldn't have been, Bay decided. The pack of the Thorn would be standing with the Lilim on this. Vlad Dracul was rubbing the back of his neck, looking like a tired and rather harried prince of darkness. The Grigori who had opened the door moved to join his blood brother, another white-haired Adonis who looked like he didn't know how to smile.

Tasmin rose from where he'd been sitting. Bay felt an instant of relief so intense it made her knees weak at the sight of him. He was still with her. They still had time.

But his golden eyes were troubled when they locked with hers.

Bay didn't even glance at the others as she went to him. "What's going on?" she asked.

"Anura has gone missing," he said.

She sucked in a breath, and now she did look at the others. Every face was grim.

"No. How?"

"The likeliest thing is that one of her Empusae sisters betrayed her," the other Grigori said. Somehow, this one was even more imposing than the first one she'd seen, and Bay realized that this must be Ariane's Sam, otherwise known as Sammael, leader of the Grigori.

Somehow, she thought he might not take kindly to anyone but Ariane calling him Sam.

"You're sure she's gone?" Bay asked, her heart sinking. For all her brash assertions that she was going to keep Tasmin safe, nothing she'd come up with to accomplish that had made much sense. Nothing but staying by his side and watching him like a hawk, which was impractical, even if she'd been trying. She was still pinning a lot of hope on Anura.

That hope died a hard death.

Sammael nodded. "One of her men called here not long ago. She didn't arrive to open Mabon, which she always does. When he went to check on her, the apartment was empty, the floor covered in her blood."

"Oh God," Bay said, wrapping her arms around herself. "If it was the Ptolemy, they'll kill her."

"They will," Sammael agreed, neither his face nor his voice revealing anything of his feelings about it, if he had them. "But not until she's ceased to be useful. We should have been watching her more closely."

"She wouldn't have put up with it," Lily interjected, so

furious she seemed to vibrate. "She's one of the strongest vampires I know. And they've taken her. Arsinöe is just taunting us now. She must have known Anura would help Tasmin. And of course, there's the added benefit of giving me the middle finger by snatching her from here. To all of us."

"We need to get down there and crawl up her ass, now," Lyra snarled, her arms crossed over her chest. Bay found herself relieved that the female alpha wolf was here. She had a clever mind and the sort of restless energy that inspired her followers. She also didn't take any crap from anyone.

Jaden stood at his mate's side, slim and dark, his startling blue eyes alight with anger.

"Lyra's right. We know where she is. We know she's waiting for us. Let's go give her what she thinks she wants and have Lily put a few lightning bolts through her head. Enough with the planning. The only plan is to get everyone down there and storm the place."

Tasmin stayed silent, his eyes fixed on Sammael. He had an odd look on his face, one Bay found unnerving. She'd only ever seen him look that way once, and that time, it hadn't been him.

Sammael seemed to sense he was being watched. Bay put her hand on Tasmin's arm, finding him tense and rigid.

"Tasmin," she murmured while Lyra began arguing with Vlad about battle strategy. "Stop."

But his eyes were fixed as Sammael turned, considered Tasmin with his inscrutable eyes, and walked over. The rest of the room fell silent at the sudden change in the air, though Lyra bickered a moment more. Then she too turned, compelled to watch.

"There you are," Sammael said, his voice a low and commanding thrum. "Have you an opinion, demon? Or are you simply entertaining yourself?"

The voice that emerged from Tasmin's throat had Bay's stomach churning. She hadn't heard it since the night he'd saved her from the Ptolemy scouts. It slid from his throat, oily and dark, with an edge of black glee that was just this side of madness.

"An opinion on whether to kill the Ptolemy bitch? Of course. She should die. And she will…in time. But her death is not for you."

Bay started to back away from him, but his hand shot out to grab her wrist, viselike. He turned to smirk at her, and the gold of his eyes looked like it had fogged over.

"No, no, pretty. Stay."

"Arsinöe wants you, and you want her dead," Sammael said, turning the demon's attention back to him. He didn't let go of Bay, though, keeping his grip tight enough to hold her without hurting her. Much. "Why is that?"

The demon chuckled, a wet, burbling sound. "I am no stupid lesser demon, Sammael the Watcher. My purposes are my own." His lip curled. "She thinks to rise above her station. Her greed has made her a fool. But she has secrets that should not die with her. I have questions for the bitch. I will have them answered. She said little when last we met…apart from the gloating."

Sammael's eyes glinted, violet and strange in the dim light. "Ah. So *she* trapped you here."

"Trapped. Made to sleep," the demon spat. "Missing years of feasting in this sack of flesh. And now that it

wakes, it won't let me have my way. There are many pleasures it denies itself that I would not. And some I would
enjoy...differently," he said, casting a sly smile at Bay.
She felt sick.

Tasmin had warned her it was not unaware of their
relationship.

"Then leave, or let us cast you out," Sammael said.
"Go on about your way. Find a new body to inhabit. Deny
Arsinöe whatever she still wants with you."

The demon laughed, a harsh, hoarse sound that made
the hair on Bay's arms stand up.

"Don't you think I would have if I could? I am bound
to this man's soul, his body by a magic given to Arsinöe
by Sekhmet herself. Blood magic. Death magic. Neither
can live without the other...not until she gets what she
wants." He laughed, then spat out a string of curses in several languages, his head rolling backward, eyes rolling
up. He groaned, and it was an awful sound.

"The lion fights me...No, it's *mine*!"

Tasmin's head snapped back and forth, and Bay
cringed in horror as she heard bones break like twigs. He
stiffened suddenly, then crashed to the floor, collapsing as
though boneless.

Bay crouched beside him, forcibly reminded of the
very first time she'd met him. It hadn't been nearly as
bad that time. It had gotten much worse very quickly. She
felt sick at the realization that she hadn't know what was
happening to him, how much stronger the demon had
become. There would be no more rallying because of her
presence. He must have known. And he'd hidden it.

Tasmin groaned softly, and Bay stroked his neck as
the abused bones knit themselves back together. It was

only then that she noticed the other vampires had circled around them. She could feel their eyes on her, no doubt full of sympathy.

It infuriated her. She didn't want sympathy. She wanted a way out of this that didn't entail one or both of them dying or permanently sacrificing their souls to a demon.

The only one she could look at, finally, was Sammael, only because she didn't think he was capable of sympathy. True to form, his face was impassive, impossible to read.

"What can I do?" she asked, feeling panic pressing in all around her. It made it difficult to breathe, threatened to send her running until she finally found a place to curl into a ball and shake until something changed. As she feared, he shook his head.

"Your man harbors Hunger," Sammael said. "A strong demon. My blood brothers and I searched for him in the days we hunted the Dark Fallen to ground and chained my brother, Chaos." To himself, he muttered, "Clever Arsinöe, binding him to a sleeping Rakshasa. Strong enough to hold the demon, too weak to fend him off." He shook his head. "No wonder she wants Tasmin so badly. Without one of his demons, she has nothing with which to bargain. She'd be no different from the rest of us. She would align with Chaos, if she can find a way to make him want her... and she has always been good at such things. But in this case, what she thinks Chaos will want is her magic... and Hunger, freed and ready to fight."

"Damn it," Lily growled. "I knew. I knew when I saw the look on her face after Chaos had gotten loose. She'd rather have a demon as an ally than stoop to the rest of us."

"She's lived too long," Sammael said. "There's nothing left for her but power now. She wasn't so hollow once.

But the years have made her empty, brittle. The time of the Ptolemy is ending. Whether it lasts in some form will be up to whoever is left."

Bay saw the look on Lily's face and knew she was wondering the same thing as she was: did every vampire hit that point, where they'd lived so long that they became just an empty shell of what they had been? She hoped not. And she hoped it would be a long time before she even came close to finding out.

"We need to move now," Ty said quietly. "Lyra and Jaden are right. She doesn't have her bargaining chip yet. Whatever she has waiting out there, now is the right time. We're only prolonging the inevitable."

"But what about Anura?" Bay asked, looking at the steely expressions of her friends.

"We'll get her," Jaden said quickly. "She could still be in the city for all we know. If it really was one of her blood sisters who got her, she may be either here or headed to Charlotte, where the seat of the Empusae is. Out of the way, out of the Ptolemy's way. We'll call Drake, get the Shades on it. It seems like the most important thing was removing her from the equation in case she really did manage to do something about Tasmin being tied to this demon. Arsinöe may be pretty sure we can't do it, but we've proven her wrong enough times before that she'll be that much more careful."

"It's a good thing we've got Tasmin here," Ty said. "Your place is locked up tight, Vlad. Still, she'll be looking for an opening. She has to know where he is."

"How soon can we start moving on her?" Lily asked Vlad. "I don't even want to give her that opening. It's time for this to be finished."

Bay listened to the general agreement and then tuned them out. She'd been kneeling by Tasmin, and even though he seemed to be coming out of the state the demon had put him in, he seemed much the worse for wear this time. He'd broken out in a cold sweat, and his complexion was ashen, his breathing shallow.

At least the eyes focused on her were his.

"Sorry," he murmured.

"Don't be," Bay replied. "It wasn't you."

He nodded, eyes drooping shut.

Sammael's deep voice sounded in her ear. "He should rest now. That will have taken a lot out of him. I had hoped seeing me would bring out the demon—the Dark Fallen could never resist showing themselves to us. We're kin, of a sort. But I can't pretend the answers he gave were ones that pleased me. The demon spoke true ... This is no weakling spirit. Hunger is a demanding parasite."

Bay nodded, numbness stealing over her. "There's really nothing you can do for him?"

Even saying the words, it was hard to believe it.

He didn't answer her, which was answer enough. "Go with him. Make sure he rests."

"And what then?" Bay asked hollowly. "Hunger wants out and can't get it, and Tasmin can't fight it forever, so ..."

Sammael sighed, and finally Bay saw a hint of understanding.

"Hunger has no physical form of his own. If he must keep this one, he'll make sure it belongs to him alone. Tasmin must stay alive ... but soon, it won't be a true life."

Somehow, she managed to block out everything else as she roused Tasmin and helped him to his feet. She tried to console herself that no matter how bad he looked this time, he would bounce back. He had before; he would again.

For now.

But unless she could make some kind of miracle, that was about all they had left.

chapter **NINETEEN**

S**HE WOKE UP** with a start when a hand dropped on her shoulder.

Bay yelped and jerked upright, for a moment unsure about where she was. It took her a minute, but eventually, it came together—the walls of books, the comfortable leather furniture...the dog on his back snoring on the couch. She was in Vlad's library. And from the looks of things, she'd fallen asleep facedown in a book on demonology.

Maybe she'd found an answer to this mess by osmosis.

She turned, and found Tasmin looking at her. He'd slept for hours, and his color was better now. A glance at the clock told her that it was 5:00 a.m. Most of the vampires would be turning in now, sliding into their beds to sleep the day away. Her own sleep schedule was so out of whack at this point, Bay didn't really know which end was up, and didn't really care.

"What are you doing?" he asked gently.

Bay offered a small, rueful smile. She knew he could see the twisted creatures dancing across the pages of the heavy, leather-bound book.

"What does it look like I'm doing?" she asked. "I'm trying to figure out how to get in touch with the inner you. So I can beat the shit out of it and send it packing."

He laughed softly, but there was a wistful quality to it that made her sad all over again.

"I think we're past that."

"Well, I don't," Bay said, frowning. "We have a saying: It's not over 'til the fat lady sings. She isn't singing yet."

Tasmin shook his head, bemused. "Who is the fat woman?"

"I'm teaching you to speak American English. Think of it as a crash course," Bay said, then looked down at the pages of her book and heaved a heavy, agitated sigh. She had twisted her hair up and secured it with a clip, but it was lopsided from sleep and trying to fall over one eye. She shoved at it.

Tasmin leaned over her shoulder and looked at what she'd been studying. The feel of his chest, solid and real behind her, was both comfort and torment. How much longer would she have him?

"I don't think it's physically possible for me to do that with my head," he said.

She looked down, blinked at the graphic illustration, and flushed. "Um, I don't think this section has anything to do with casting out demons. I think that's a demonstration of... You know what, let's just close it; this isn't helping."

She shut the book and rose from the seat, turning toward Tasmin. He stood there, looking only slightly worse for wear, in rumpled jeans and a T-shirt. She'd never seen anything look so good in all her life. Emotion rose in her throat, swelling her heart until she felt like it might burst. How had she ended up here? Everything felt like it was falling apart.

"I want to show you something," he said. "Will you come with me?"

Bay started to move toward him, then hesitated, looking back at the book, along with the stack of other things she'd pulled from Vlad's shelves.

"I had some other ideas..."

He reached out and caught her hand in his, and even that small connection had her drinking in a quick breath. He made it easy to forget herself, since all she really seemed to want to do was be with him.

"Bay," he said, and she tilted her head, surprised he was finally using her nickname. The little intimacy meant even more to her than she'd expected it would. "Come with me. Please."

There was no way she could refuse him. She slid a look at Grimm, who was prone to wake up and follow her no matter how deeply asleep he seemed, and Tasmin followed her gaze.

"He'll stay asleep."

She pursed her lips. "You made sure of that, I guess." She still wasn't crazy about his willingness to essentially knock people—and now animals—out just so he didn't have to deal with them.

"It's been a difficult week for him too, Bay. The rest will do him good. And...I wanted to have you alone."

"Well. Okay," she said, though something about his tone made her think this wasn't going to be a conversation she wanted to have. Silently, he led her from the library, and Bay noticed the eerie quiet that had descended over the mansion. It seemed like she really was the last one up. The two of them made their way through the downstairs, past closed doors and empty rooms, until Tasmin reached a set of ornate French doors leading out to the back of the house. He picked up a pair of coats draped over the back of a nearby chair, handing her one.

Bay took it and slipped it on, confused. He wanted to go for a walk at this hour of the morning?

Tasmin slipped out one of the doors, and she followed him into Vlad's garden.

Bay stopped, stunned, as Tasmin shut the door behind her. The week had been so disjointed, so confusing, that her exploring had been confined to inside the mansion for the most part. She'd walked by these doors plenty of times, but there had always been extra people, distractions. Somehow, she hadn't paid them much attention.

Now she wished she had.

The large, circular patio of stamped concrete on which she stood had been meticulously brushed off. What was doubtless a lush paradise in summer was now covered in a thin layer of fresh snow, turning it into a twilit fairyland as the sky turned silvery gray. Stone paths wound beneath the bare and arching branches of trees, curving around sleeping flowerbeds and partially hidden fountains, glittering stone benches, and iced-over ponds.

It was a beautiful surprise, and another clue to the nature of the enigmatic man who ruled over this place. Vlad Dracul was a puzzle, helpful but reserved, managing to be both warm and slightly aloof all at the same time. But he couldn't be truly cold. Anyone who would commission a place like this had a lot going on beneath the surface.

Tasmin held out his hand, and Bay slipped hers into it. Together, they walked slowly down one of the paths. The lot wasn't huge, but it seemed that way, not an ounce of space wasted. It was a woodland transported to the city, and Bay let her eyes wander over every tiny detail.

"So," she finally asked as the silence spun out between them, "what's on your mind?"

"A lot of things," he said, his breath rising in the cold air. Then he slide her a warm glance that made the air feel almost balmy. "Mostly you."

She managed a smile. "Good to know."

"What will you do, when the Lilim crush the Ptolemy and things start to settle down again?" he asked.

"You sound pretty sure we'll win. And what do you mean, what will *I* do? You planning on going some-where?"

She tried to keep her tone light, but she had a sudden, horrible sinking sensation that he'd brought her out here to say good-bye. She didn't know why . . . Had the demon's appearance earlier shaken him up that badly? And where did he think he was going? If he left, it would be with her claws hooked into his backside hanging on for dear life. She wouldn't let him accept some miserable fate. She'd fight even if she didn't know what the hell she was doing yet. For him, she would fight with everything she had.

Tellingly, Tasmin avoided the latter part of her ques-tion. "I know the Lilim will win. With her allies, Lily is much stronger than she thinks. When the dust settles, she'll find her dynasty has earned its place. No one will be able to question it."

"I still can't see this war as a good thing," Bay said. Every time she thought of her friends bloodied and in close combat with a horde of snarling Ptolemy, she felt a burst of pure panic. What she'd been through the other night was just a taste. These other vampires were nothing like the ones here. They were vicious, ancient, and remorseless. Much more like monsters than vampires.

Maybe they weren't all like that. Probably they weren't. But if the Ptolemy bloodline survived what was coming, she would never be able to look at someone who wore the mark without being at least suspicious. She knew that was probably unfair.

Of course, none of this had been fair so far.

"Good is the wrong word for it. Useful, maybe. Beneficial. Nothing is simple black-and-white among our kind, Bay."

"Yeah, it isn't with plain old mortals either, most of the time," she agreed, turning her head to look at a silent fountain that had as its center an entwined couple, the woman with long, flowing hair, the man lean and elegant. He seemed to be biting her neck. There was something beautiful about the way they were fitted together, the bliss on the woman's carved face.

She and Tasmin had their moments where she felt just like that woman. And then there were times like this, when he seemed more a stranger to her than anything, despite the warmth of his hand wrapped around hers. There was so much she didn't know about him. And she worried there wouldn't be time to find out.

"So what will you do? Will you keep your little shop in Tipton?" Tasmin asked. "I don't think the Lilim will ever return there, but you could return to the life you had for a while, at least."

This wasn't a conversation she wanted to have, but Bay decided to humor him until she could figure out what they were doing here.

"I think they'd notice something was off about me. When Lily was turned, she had enough to do so that she could just walk away from her job, and the circumstances were sensational enough that no one really poked at her about the fact that she seemed, you know, different. With me...I'm from there. And I'm not sure colored contacts are going to do much for covering glowing gold eyes."

"It takes effort," Tasmin said, "but it isn't impossible for you to hide them. It's almost like creating an invisible shield around yourself. With practice, they would only see what you wanted them to. But it will take some time."

Bay lifted her eyebrows. "Really? Huh. That's something to think about, I guess. But...I don't know. I love being a groomer. I love being around the animals, and the people, and I love being my own boss. But Tipton isn't going to be the same after all of this. My family's already moved out of the area, and with Lily and Ty gone, and that big empty mansion just sitting there...I was satisfied without really feeling settled, I guess, for a long time now. I'd like to have both. Sell the shop there, buy a new one somewhere else. Start over."

"Boston?"

"I don't know. I'm not much of a city girl, honestly. And Grimm would hate it." When he continued to look expectantly at her, Bay's jaw tightened. She knew he didn't expect to be around when this was all over, but he was pushing her to articulate things she'd barely been able to bring herself to consider. She'd only just begun to wrap her mind around having such an extended future, and being here, with everything so unsettled, made it tough to look much past any given day.

But Tasmin was right. With luck, pretty soon she'd have a life to start putting together, with the ability to live it really any way, or any number of ways, she wanted to.

Except, it seemed, the most important way she wanted to live it. With him at her side.

"Okay," she finally said grudgingly, "don't laugh. I actually think I might take a serious look at Silver Falls."

That finally got him to smile, a bright grin that didn't have a hint of darkness to it.

"The werewolf town? You want to groom were-wolves?"

Bay rolled her eyes. "No, that's not my kind of kink, thank you. But lots of the Thorn have dogs. Like, *dog* dogs. I was out there once with Lily, and it's gorgeous. Plus, since there aren't any mortals there, I won't stand out as extra weird. It isn't so far in the boonies that I'd have to go far to, you know, eat. I've always been pretty comfortable around Jaden and Lyra, which, believe me, is a big deal. I'd see Lily and Ty often enough. I could have a pretty house, and a big yard, and the woods there are great…Plus, no wolf is going to mess with a lioness, I'm sorry. It's not going to happen."

Articulating it like that made it more real, and Bay found that there was a big part of her that found the pros-pect of that kind of change exciting. Could she do what Damien and Ariane had done, or Lyra and Jaden, and create her own niche rather than waiting around hoping that she would simply fall into one that fit? The wolves were earthy, less about politics and dynasties and more about being a big, raucous family. That appealed to her far more than secretive politics and life lived by candle-light. Maybe she could fit there. Do for herself what she'd always been so focused on doing for everyone else.

Even if the one thing she really wanted would be missing.

Bay turned and stared at Tasmin, stopping beneath the reaching boughs of a gnarled ornamental tree that arched over the path.

"What's this really about, Tasmin?"

"I want to make sure you're going to be all right," he said, and the tenderness with which he spoke was enough to have tears springing to her eyes.

"Are you kidding me? I'm not all right *now*. You really think I enjoy planning this stuff? That I like thinking about what I'm going to do when you're not around?" She swiped angrily at her eyes with her sleeve, furious that she couldn't stop the tears. "You have to know that's not what I want. I spent all these years wondering if I'd ever meet somebody like you. Kind of strange, gorgeous, sweet… perfect. And then there you are, except with a heavy dose of doomed. I've spent years not really knowing what I wanted. I'm great at giving people what they need, but I was never really sure what I needed. Now I know what that is, and I can't have it."

"Bay," he said, his voice an emotional rasp.

"All I want is you. You have to know that, Tasmin. I'm in—"

"Don't," he said, and the words died on her tongue, cut off as painfully as if he'd used a real blade.

"Don't?" she asked. "Is that all you can say? Do you

really think not saying the words makes them any less true? I love you. *I love you.* You could walk away now, you could die tomorrow, and a hundred years from now I would *still* love you. I love the way you talk, the way you move. I love the way you need me, the way you look for me whenever you walk in a room. I love the way you hold me. I love that you couldn't stay away from me, and that you didn't try all that hard to make me stay away from you. I love that you let me see what nobody else does." She stepped toward him, until she was only a breath away. He was as still as the sphinx, watching her with eyes that glowed bright with some strong emotion. But he made no move to close the rest of the distance between them, no move to touch her.

Bay pressed forward, determined to tell him the truth. Whatever he thought he was doing, whatever happened, Tasmin needed to know how she felt. She refused to let him go without telling him that. Whether or not he'd set out to capture it, he had her heart.

"You're not alone in this, Tasmin. You've saved my life more than once. You gave me your mark. Even if I can't find a way to save you, I can give you everything I have while you're here." Her hands ached to touch him, but that last reach would have to be his.

Tasmin's eyes closed, his face contorting in pain. "I can't. You don't know—"

"If there are things I don't know, then tell me! You're not sparing me by walking away from me," Bay said, trying desperately to make him understand. "If you give a damn about me at all, let me be here for you. Stay with me. At least let me know I'm not alone in the way I feel about you!"

His eyes, when he looked at her, were like gold fire.

For a moment, she thought he was going to pull her to him. For an instant, a raw torrent of emotion flashed through her, nearly taking her to the ground with its intensity, and she knew he was letting her feel what he felt, giving her what he couldn't in words.

He did love her. Bay reeled, swaying on her feet as the knowledge slammed into her. His love for her was a fierce, wild thing, much like the man himself. But there was so much pain, more than she could have imagined, tangled up with that love.

And at the center of it, she could feel the dark pulse of the demon, poisoning everything around it...destroying the soul of the man she loved. Every emotion Tasmin gave her was shot through with death.

She had never expected him to be so far gone.

"I can't let you deal with this," he said. "It's too strong now. Couldn't you feel it?"

"And I won't let you go through this alone," Bay insisted, the ache from all she'd felt lingering in her chest.

"You would still become my mate, knowing all this? You'd put your teeth in me, knowing that you're going to lose me? You could handle getting as close as two creatures can be, only to be ripped back apart?"

Bay nodded. "Yes."

His laugh was like a dry rattle of wind through the bare trees, and she knew she'd lost him. "Then you're stronger than I am. You're all I have left, Bay. I couldn't save my brothers. But I can save you."

Suddenly, she understood why the house had been so quiet, why he was acting so strangely. Her eyes widened.

"Tasmin, no—"

The diaphanous gold tendrils of his magic slashed out of him to curl around her before she could even finish speaking. Bay saw flashes of light, and then a strange sense of peace stole over her as she found herself standing in a hazy golden mist in a gentling waving field, watching a shimmering flock of birds dip and swirl in a summer sky.

She could no longer see the man standing in front of her, gazing at her with shattered eyes.

Love...

The ugly voice in his mind whispered the word, tasting it. Hating it.

"It's nothing you would ever understand," Tasmin whispered into the stillness. He gathered Bay into his arms and took her inside, laying her gently on the bed they had shared.

Then he turned and walked away from the house, away from the Lilim, away from everyone who had tried to help him, and who his presence had only hurt.

Tasmin got into one of the cars parked neatly in the drive and turned the key, plane tickets tucked neatly in his pocket.

He had a long day ahead of him.

chapter TWENTY

SOMETHING WAS WRONG.

Bay gazed up at the swirling birds in the sky and frowned at the thought.

What could be wrong? It was a beautiful day. The sun was out. The sky was blue.

She blinked and looked around. Nothing seemed out of the ordinary. Everything was perfect.

Too perfect. Mind-numbingly perfect.

Her frown deepened. She looked at the gently waving grass, at the far-off castle on the horizon. This was her idea of heaven...so why did it feel wrong all of a sudden? It hit her all at once: she had no idea where she was. This was just like something she would have imagined because...she was imagining it.

None of this was real.

Bay surfaced from the dream with a gasp, feeling like a diver whose head has just broken the surface of the water. Her eyes flew open, and she saw the familiar confines of her room at the Dracul's. She was only confused for a few seconds. Then, everything came back.

Tasmin. Tasmin did this. Oh my God he's going to—

She leapt from the bed, hunting for the shoes and socks he'd carefully slipped off her feet so she would sleep more comfortably. Bay wasn't sure whether to curse his name or cry. She'd bared her heart to him, and he'd knocked her out because he was determined to protect her from whatever the demon was trying to make him do. She didn't even want to imagine what that might be . . . Anything the demon might want so badly had to be horrifying.

Bay fumbled into the bathroom, splashed water on her face to try and rouse herself, then headed out the door, trying to remember where Lyra and Jaden were sleeping. It took her a frustrating amount of time to find them among rooms of vampires, sprawled out and sound asleep on beds, on floors, and in one case, half out of the bathtub. Tasmin had worked that irritating bit of magic on the entire house, ensuring that by the time everyone got up this evening, he'd be long gone . . . and whatever he had managed to accomplish would be done.

She managed to rouse a few groggy werewolves before finally finding Lyra and Jaden curled up together in a third-floor bedroom. Lyra was on her side, Jaden's arm draped around her, and Bay could see the band of leaping, stretching cats that encircled Lyra's upper arm—her bond mark with Jaden. Bay took a deep breath, then leaned over and began to shake Lyra.

"Lyra. Lyra? Wake up. Wake *up*!"

Slowly, one of Lyra's amber eyes opened.

"I don't want a tutu," she mumbled.

Bay hissed out a breath through her nose. "You don't have to have a tutu. You have to wake up. Tasmin's gone."

Both eyes opened. "Huh?"

Bay watched Lyra extract herself from her mate's arms and sit up slowly, looking like she still wasn't quite sure where she was.

"Tasmin is gone. He knocked out the whole house, and I'm positive this is about the demon. I just don't understand why he would run off and give it what it wants! Something must have happened."

"Jesus." Lyra scrubbed at her face, her curly brown hair in wild tangles all over her head. "Did he tell you about this army of one bullshit before he went running off? How do you know this?"

"He tried to say good-bye."

Lyra stared. "Before he knocked you out too, I guess."

"Yeah."

"Shit." Lyra turned around and shook Jaden awake. The vampire came to pretty quickly, sitting beside his mate. Lyra filled him in, and the sleepy haze left his eyes almost instantly.

"Damn it. Where's my phone?" He fumbled out of bed and grabbed his cell, cursing softly. "You don't even want to know how many messages are on here. Something's going on. Whatever it is, that has to be what set him off."

He pressed the screen, and the three of them listened to a panicked Shade desperate to get a hold of someone, anyone at the mansion.

"Jaden, we found Anura. She's in bad shape, and she's been bled, but she told us what she could while she could still talk. She wants the Rakshasa locked up immediately.

Whatever she overheard while she was here, she's convinced that the demon's going to head for Arsinöe as soon as it gets control. There's some ancient rite to get it out that involves a lot of blood... the Rakshasa's blood. There was more, but she blacked out before she could finish. We've never heard of anything like this... Is the Dracul there? Is anybody there? Get in touch, this is urgent!"

Bay put a hand to her mouth, feeling sick. "Oh God." Bay said. Somehow, the demon had gotten Tasmin to bend to its will. For a moment, she could think of no earthly way it could have happened... and then the pieces clicked together. Horrified, she looked up at Lyra and Jaden.

"It's how he saved me."

Lyra frowned. "What?"

Bay shook her head, tears beginning to sting her eyes as she understood exactly what he'd done. "He only drinks from deer, rabbits—forest animals. He doesn't have any control when he drinks from humans because of the demon. But the night we were attacked by the Ptolemy, he was the only one who got to me in time. He turned me. He must have made a deal with the demon to do it without killing me."

And there she'd been worried that he didn't give a damn about her. He'd given up everything for her. She couldn't let him. She refused to let the malignant thing leeching off of his soul use Tasmin's love to destroy him. Because losing him would destroy her too. Whatever place for herself she would make, it would never be what she wanted without him.

"We have to stop him," Bay said, her heart in her throat. "Anura said she could separate them, there's more going on here. We need to get to Arsinöe."

"Say no more," Lyra said, swinging her long legs over the side of the bed. "I'll get my people and we'll get our asses to the airport. Hopefully we won't be too far behind him."

Bay looked at the clock, which showed 6:10 a.m. "He's got maybe forty minutes on us," she said. "Maybe a little more."

"Yeah, well, he's never tried to outrun the Thorn," Lyra growled. She grabbed a pair of jeans off the back of a chair. "Can you be in the sun yet, Bay? Jaden could do it right away after he and I were fully bonded, but you weren't bitten by a wolf. I don't know how it works."

"I'll be fine," Bay said. "I've been out for longer periods all this week."

Lyra paused. "You're doing okay, right?"

Bay considered this. "Not really. Can we go?"

"Hell yes," Lyra said, and Bay rose to let the two of them get dressed. She turned when Jaden spoke to her, his silken voice warm and strangely comforting.

"We'll get to him, Bay. The man's been through hell. This happened because he tried to do the right thing, and the demon used it against him. If we have anything to do with it, we'll turn the tables, all right? Hang in there."

She nodded, unable to speak, and walked out of the room to wait.

Arsinöe might be asleep, but she hadn't left her estate vulnerable.

Tasmin finally slumped through a shattered window as the late-afternoon sun filtered through the trees. One arm was completely numb, pulsing with poison from the claws of one of her new pets. There were at least two full packs of wolves here, hulking, angry beasts that seemed to delight in pain. He'd been fighting them off almost as soon as he'd gotten out of his rental car two miles from where the Ptolemy's land began.

Had it not been for the demon, he would already be dead. He had never dreamed he would willingly be letting the thing inside of him take over, but today he'd had no choice.

And even the demon was weary, more foul tempered than usual.

It wanted to be done with this.

That made two of them.

Tasmin staggered to his feet, his every movement sounding impossibly loud in the tomb-like silence of this place. He could smell her, a scent that brought memory crashing through the walls his mind had built around it.

Laughter in the brush, the scent of an intruder.

He had given chase, distracted from his hunt, never bothering to alert his pride brothers nearby. How much trouble could one interloper be? Just another foreign vampire come to gawk at the Rakshasa. He had run them off before—no doubt it would happen again.

Then had come the pain, a sharp, hot prick in his shoulder. Numbness. Darkness.

Fires. The chanting of many voices. And above them all, her voice, speaking words in an ancient tongue as something dark and painful slipped beneath his skin, both of them screaming until it was with one voice.

Sleep. Awaken when your brother Chaos walks the world again and come to me. We will call him together, you and me, and I will set you free . . .

Tasmin groaned, his head feeling like it was about to

split in two. His stomach rolled, though whether from the poison or the force of memory he couldn't say. Arsinöe had always wanted him to come back, but as a tool. Somehow, he didn't think this was the rite Anura would have tried to perform. She'd never mentioned anything about suicide.

The life he'd sworn to take would be his own.

Keep your word, Rakshasa. Find her. Let me out.

"I will," Tasmin growled at the angry hiss through his mind. His thoughts were jumbled, some his, some the demon's. The line was beginning to blur.

He was glad Bay couldn't see him like this. Knowing she slept safely so many miles away was one of the only comforts he had now. He clung to that, and to the memory of all she had said to him.

"Should have told her," he muttered to himself as he worked his way along the wall, dully surprised when he noted he was leaving a crimson streak behind. He looked down and saw blood still oozing from multiple lacerations on his arm and side. Claw marks.

So much poison…

He staggered through the great hall and started up the stairs, having to rest every few steps. The bleeding refused to stop, and whatever foul poison she'd equipped her wolves with wasn't being flushed out of his system as quickly as it should. She'd always been clever with her poisons, Tasmin remembered. It seemed she'd perfected the art over the years.

A soft growl reached his ears as he hit the top of the stairs, and his heart sank. Of course she wouldn't have left herself unprotected inside the mansion as well. Of course not.

Two massive wolves, the largest he'd yet seen, advanced on him from where they'd been stationed at the end of the hall, in front of a pair of ornate double doors that could only lead to the queen's chambers. Their eyes glinted as they padded through pools of shadow toward him.

Steeling himself, trying to shore up his flagging energy, Tasmin felt his body stretch and change into the form of his lion. As soon as all four paws hit the ground, he leapt, claws extended, and slammed into one of the wolves.

Each wolf was solid muscle, and unlike Tasmin was well rested. Tasmin kept finding himself rolled, bitten. Within seconds one of his shoulders was shredded, white-hot pain replacing the lethargy of the poison.

Let me let me let me you pathetic bastard…

With weary resignation, Tasmin closed his eyes and was pulled under again.

When he came back to himself, he was on his side on a plush carpet, panting heavily. His body felt like it was on fire. His flesh was torn. He could feel it. His head felt far too heavy when he lifted it, but Tasmin managed. He had to look away from the shredded flesh of his body, a tattered mess of blood and fur. His mouth was rimmed with blood when he licked his chops.

What happened?

There was a pause, and he could hear the demon sounding somehow stronger than before. It was no longer sharing strength, Tasmin realized. It was just taking what it needed from this body, preparing for the moment it was finally released. As long as he had enough strength left to lift the dagger, that was all the demon cared about.

I took the wolves. They were quite a feast. Sorry you missed it.

The sly amusement disgusted him. They'd wasted precious time devouring the werewolves, and the curtains in here were drawn so tightly that he had no way of knowing how long they had been occupied.

Then he inhaled and smelled how close she was, heard the slow, even breathing coming from atop a dark shape that rose before him. Her bed. They had made it into Arsinöe's chamber. With a great deal of effort, Tasmin got to his feet, first four, then two as he became a man again.

She will see my true face before she dies.

Come, lion. Let's end this living hell.

chapter TWENTY-ONE

THEY'D BEEN LUCKY to find a last-minute flight, but Bay knew they were at least an hour behind him. The SUV he'd stolen from the Dracul had been abandoned at the side of the road on the way into the airport. Seeing it, imagining what Tasmin must have been going through when he'd left it, made it hard for Bay to sit quietly on the flight to Baltimore, and then on the two-hour drive down to southern Maryland in a hastily arranged rental car.

The first thing she saw when she stepped into the silent Ptolemy mansion was blood on the walls.

"I don't like the look of this," Jaden growled as the small group of them walked in through the front doors.

Bay took off the baseball cap she'd had pulled low over her eyes and dropped it on the floor beside her, looking at the crimson trail, spatters and streaks, leading up the enormous staircase in the entry hall. To the right, a wide smear of blood ran along the wall, disappearing from sight as it curved around a corner.

She didn't like the look of anything. The carnage out front had been incredible. Just thinking about it made her gorge start to rise. Whatever had done that, it hadn't been Tasmin. She'd never really understood how much hunger, how much violence he'd been grappling with until she'd seen what the demon was capable of.

Bay, Lyra, Jaden, Eric, and two other wolves of the Thorn stayed close together as they made their way up the stairs. The scene at the top made even Eric turn away.

"I know they probably got what they deserved," he growled, "but... gods."

The afternoon sun filtered lazily through the spaces of the drawn curtains of each room they walked by, toward the massive double doors at the end of the hall. Somewhere in the recesses of the mansion, a clock ticked away the minutes with stark rhythmic perfection. It should have been peaceful. But Bay knew what slept in here, the murderous creatures lying prone in beds behind every closed bedroom door. As soon as the sun went down, every eye would open. And if she was found, she would wish for death long before they gave it to her.

This was what Tasmin had walked into.

And she had no doubt he was in that room with the queen of the Ptolemy, a woman Bay had heard so much about that she half expected to see a Medusa-like monster instead of a human-looking woman.

The sky was just beginning to haze with color outside as the shadows on the ground grew long, the beginning of sunset. They didn't have much time until every vampire here was waking up. If that happened, they were dead, all of them.

"We have to hurry," Bay said.

Jaden was looking around, blue eyes far-off. "I know. It's just...strange. It hasn't changed at all."

"*You've* changed," Lyra said, stroking her hand down his back. That seemed to bring him out of it, and he gave her a brilliant smile before nodding.

"Let's do this. Fling the doors wide. I don't want any chance she's awake and moving around in there in the dark." He gave Bay a sidelong glance and then looked away. "Just be ready. I don't know what we'll find in there."

She nodded. With every mutilated corpse, she'd lost more hope that there would be anything left of the man she loved by the time they found him...or what had been him. But she needed to see it for herself.

Eric and one of the other wolves went for the doors, paused, and then threw them open at the same time. Bay steeled herself for whatever she might see.

But there was...nothing.

Jaden's eyes narrowed, and he strode in, fingers hooked into claws. He whipped his head back, fangs bared, to look at the rest of them.

"Damn it," he growled.

Bay stepped in farther, and that was when the smell hit her—the horrible, sickly sweet aroma of charred flesh.

"What the hell happened?" Lyra asked, eyes wide. "Where are they?"

"I know where they are," Jaden said. "Come on. There isn't much time left."

There were tunnels deep beneath the summer estate of the Ptolemy, stone-walled passages that led to a multitude of rooms. Some went to the dank and airless chambers where most of the Cait Sith servants once slept and lived. Some went to rooms where those same servants, and occasionally a disobedient Ptolemy, had been punished in bloody and creative ways for their transgressions. And one room, farther away from the rest, was a place only open to Arsinöe and her closest advisors.

It was here that Jaden led them, to a chamber he had never been in and had never wanted to see. His kind was never invited as simple observers. And once they went in, they never came out.

One of the huge, heavy doors set into the stone wall was ajar.

Bay's steps quickened. She could smell so many terrible things down here, some of them old but no less awful. This was a place that stank of sweat and fear, fire and pain. But she could also smell that terrible stink of burning, and more faintly, Tasmin. It shouldn't have been so faint, that familiar blend of sandalwood and musk. But it was strangely muted, and tainted with a scent she was unfamiliar with.

"He's bloody poisoned on top of everything else," Jaden muttered.

A woman's scream spiraled up, slicing the air.

They slammed through the doors so hard that one of them bounced against the wall. Bay completely forgot caution, rushing forward into a chamber that was filled with flickering light. She skidded to a stop just in time. There was a horrified shout.

"Bay, no!"

Her breath caught in her throat as she tried to take in the scene before her.

They had come into a low, circular chamber, where

the only light came from flaming sconces bolted into the stone. An altar sat at the far side of the room near the wall, a slab of shining obsidian carved with unfamiliar symbols and covered with a variety of golden implements.

The floor was etched deep with concentric circles and more unusual symbols. The entirety of one circle, encompassing a space roughly ten feet in diameter, was alight with flickering blue flame. The flames rose almost to the ceiling, dancing and shimmering as they formed a wall. It was that which Bay had almost run into.

And beyond the wall, encircled by the strange flames, were Tasmin and Arsinöe.

"Tasmin!" Bay shouted his name, but he didn't turn. All she saw was his bare back, the muscles tense. She was amazed he was still standing. Blood streamed from multiple wounds, staining the stone at his feet. As she watched, he swayed a little. But when the woman across from him hooked her fingers into claws and went for his eyes in a blur of movement, he caught her hand in midair. Then he squeezed, crushing her wrist as though it were nothing.

Arsinöe screamed again, pain mingled with outrage, and Bay had her first real look at the Ptolemy queen.

She was stunningly beautiful. Or rather, she had been before she'd been burned. Arsinöe was dressed in a simple, elegant shift made of what looked like red silk. It skimmed a body of sleek curves and wiry muscle, and the black ankh of her people was bared proudly at her collarbone. Her hair was a riot of ebony waves that cascaded around her shoulders, framing a face dominated by a pair of dark, haunting eyes.

But her golden skin was a mess. One cheek was blackened and charred, still smoking. Her neck was a cracked and smoldering wasteland. And the same sorts of patches existed all over her exposed skin. When she turned her head to look at them all, Bay could see that an entire section of hair on the side of her head had been burned away.

"You!" she shouted in a voice that had commanded armies to do terrible things. "Get me out of here, and you will be rewarded! I'll give you anything you want! This man is mad!"

"Unbind us!" Tasmin cried, in a voice that was both his and not his. "I am not yours to chain, Ptolemy bitch!"

"He dragged her down here through the sunlight," Lyra muttered. "She'll be weaker until the sun sets, but after that she may be able to get out of there."

"I told you, this is not how it's done, demon! We must call your master first! He needs to be here to see, to understand what I can give him!" Arsinöe's voice was stronger than her looks would suggest. Still, there was a note of desperation in her voice.

"No! Separate us first! Whatever business you have with my master will be done only then, bitch!" The voice was foul, a childish shriek dragged through gravel. "The Rakshasa has agreed to die for it. You know how to do this! I can make it hurt so much more for you if you refuse again!"

"I saved you!" Arsinöe cried. "I spared you the wrath of the Grigori who hunt your kind! You threaten the only vampire who would protect you!"

Bay could hear Arsinöe's bewilderment as clearly as she could her fury. The Ptolemy queen had truly expected some sort of loyalty from this dark thing. The rest of the world of night had moved cautiously around her for far too long. Arsinöe no longer understood that even *she* had limits.

"Destroy it, Arsinöe!" Bay shouted, in a voice stronger and clearer than she'd thought herself capable of using. "You can't control it. If you knew how to catch and bind it, you know how to kill it! Spare the Rakshasa and we'll let you live."

Arsinöe's eyes flashed, and Bay knew she was looking into the face of an evil far more ancient and capable than anything she ought to be dealing with. Still, she had no choice. Her only consolation was that there was a flaming wall currently between them.

"And what are you supposed to be?" Arsinöe sneered, looking more closely. Then she smiled, a terrible thing. "Ah. The beast has been busy while he's been out. Charming."

"End this, Arsinöe," Jaden said, and when Arsinöe looked at him, all her dark amusement vanished to be replaced by pure, white-hot hatred.

"Jaden. Filthy gutter cat traitor. I'll have you ripped to pieces."

His smile was knifelike. "You've tried that, remember?"

"Finish what you started, bitch," the demon snarled with Tasmin's mouth. "I will call my master once I'm free, and then we'll see how impressed he is with your *protection* of me, his faithful servant. The ritual circle is cast. The symbols have been carved into my flesh. *Do it now!*"

His hand shot out and he gripped her by the throat, lifting her off the ground. In her weakened state, all Arsinöe could do was gasp and gag and struggle as her toes brushed against the floor.

"Don't—" she rasped.

He let her fall to the floor, where she collapsed, holding her hand to her throat and coughing. She glared up at him, liquid eyes narrowed.

Then, slowly, she picked up a small curved ritual knife from the floor beside her feet, one which had likely been used to make whatever cuts already existed in Tasmin's chest. She staggered upright, then began to chant, touching the tip of the dagger to the center of Tasmin's forehead, his throat, his chest. Then she handed the blade to Tasmin, and the triumphant hatred in her eyes as she looked at the group beyond the circle told Bay all she needed to know.

"No!" Bay screamed.

Tasmin lifted his arm above his head, and crying several words in an ancient tongue, he plunged the dagger deep into his own chest.

Bay's tormented scream echoed in her ears as the floor began to shake and Tasmin's body crumpled. The outline of his body began to blur and twist as something dark pulled itself up and out of him. Arsinöe looked down impassively and pushed Tasmin's body over with a toe. He fell onto his back, and Bay saw the wound in Tasmin's chest open wide, gaping as something like smoke poured forth.

"Shit, the sun's setting," Lyra hissed. "Look at her! We need to do something, or get the hell out of here!"

As they stared, Arsinöe's skin began to knit itself back together, turning charred skin golden and smooth, regenerating the burned-off section of hair.

"No," Bay said, feeling everything inside go still and calm at once. She looked at Tasmin, his chest unmoving, the obsidian hilt jutting unnaturally from it. And she remembered his smile as he'd tried to teach her the art of illusion, the sense of humor that lurked beneath his too often serious exterior. He'd been sweet, and patient... despite the fact that he'd been used terribly. He was still capable of love, and what he'd had, he'd given to her. She knew that, even if he'd never given her the words. Everything he'd done, he'd done to protect her.

The least she could do was finish what he'd started here and take him, or what was left, home.

Even if it was too late, she wouldn't leave him here with these monsters.

She stared at Arsinöe and remembered what Tasmin had said that night at Mabon. The Ptolemy queen turned, sensing the intense stare fixed on her. Her eyes narrowed as they locked with Bay's.

Bay called up the only image she had in her mind that was fully formed, the one Tasmin had left her with. It was a bright, sunny day in a meadow.

For just an instant, Bay was there, seeing the meadow again, feeling the sunlight on her skin. Believing it. Then she pushed the image out of herself, feeling it leave her, and gave it to Arsinöe knowing the effect would be very different.

You're burning.

The shriek was immediate, and terrible. When Bay opened her eyes, Arsinöe covered her face with her hands and continued screaming. She writhed, trying to cover exposed skin from a sun that didn't exist anywhere but in her own head. She stumbled through the fire of the ritual circle blindly, and then she really did catch. The circle vanished, but Arsinöe's hair, her skin, everything was in flames. She flailed blindly, then headed straight for Bay, her hands reaching, her face the most horrific thing she'd ever seen.

All Bay had time to do was throw her arms up in front of her face, the banshee's scream echoing in her ears.

Then she was gone in a sudden rush of air as a figure slammed into her from the side, hurling her away from Bay and into the wall, where she exploded in a burst of blue flame. Bay slowly pulled her arms away from her face and stared—first at the black stain on the wall where Arsinöe had hit, then at the desperately wounded man who stood before her, back hunched, gulping in air as the final tendrils of smoke poured from his tattered chest. In his hand he gripped the dagger, which he'd pulled free. As she stared at him, he let go, and it clattered to the floor.

"Tasmin," Bay sobbed out, stumbling to where he was and throwing her arms around him, feeling him sag against her.

"It's gone," he said, his voice barely a sigh. She felt every ounce of tension leave his body. Then she felt the life leaving it too as he slumped in her arms.

"No," she said as the inky blackness that had been inside of Tasmin for so long coalesced into a single shifting shadow in the center of where the circle had been. It almost looked like the figure of a large, winged man for a moment, but then it was again nothing but smoke.

Bay sank to the floor with Tasmin, his grip on her slackening. She sensed the other wolves moving around her, heard their voices, but none of the words registered.

"Sun's setting…"

"Have to get out of here…"

"I'll carry him, let's go…"

All she could see were Tasmin's eyes, half-open, the bright gold of them dull as they looked at her without really seeing.

"Please," she said softly. "Don't leave me. I love you."

"Love you," Tasmin said, a whispered echo of her words.

The shadowy demon that was Hunger began to leave, a rolling, inky mist that drifted across the floor. But it stopped when Tasmin whispered to her, curving around. Bay could see no eyes, but she had the distinct impression it was staring at her. Speculating. She would never truly be sure of what.

After a moment, its deep, thick voice coiled through the air like smoke.

"A gift for the bitch's death. Blood heals all wounds, pretty. Even mine."

Then it turned and simply vanished with the vaguest impression of a flapping wing and a mocking whisper.

"Until we meet again."

Jaden looked at her, and looked at the doors. "If you're going to try it, do it now, Bay. I can feel the sun setting. We've just killed their queen. I don't think they're going to want to sit and talk about it."

Without another word, Bay screwed up her courage, sliced open her wrist with a delicately extended claw, and pressed it to Tasmin's mouth. Bay held her breath as she waited, watching for any sign of movement. And finally, slowly, she felt the faintest bit of pressure and saw him swallow. After a couple more shallow pulls at her wrist, Jaden, who was pacing like a caged animal, couldn't wait any longer.

"That'll have to do for now. You can get back at it in

the car. If it's going to work, that'll be enough to hold him until we can get the hell out of here."

Eric reached down and picked Tasmin up as though he weighed nothing, tossing him over one shoulder into a fireman's carry. Bay got to her feet and took a final look around the room. It felt strangely empty.

But then, Bay supposed many places would without the fierce Ptolemy queen. She felt a moment of pity for the ones who would be caught in any battle for ascension to the throne, and then brushed it aside. The Ptolemy were no longer her problem, and she was happy to have it stay that way.

It was time to go home.

chapter TWENTY-TWO

WHEN HE AWAKENED, it was to the most tender kisses.

They were light at first, languid, the kisses of a lover who'd been longing for you while you were away. Then they grew more persistent, covering his face, insisting he reciprocate.

He had no idea where or who he was, he thought groggily, but *something* good must have happened for him to be earning this kind of attention.

Tasmin smiled, opened his eyes.

And was greeted by an enormous tongue planted directly up his left nostril.

"Gah!" he cried, and flailed his arms, which sent blankets flying everywhere. Encouraged, his admirer leapt up on the bed, pinned him between massive paws, and drenched his face.

It was a hell of a way to realize you were alive—but he'd gladly take it.

"Grimm! Damn it, how did you get in here? Hey, you're smothering him, get off!"

For a few moments, he couldn't see anything but a big wet nose and a pair of dark, overjoyed eyes. Then Grimm was being hauled off of him, admonished to behave himself, and forcibly escorted out the door. He caught a glimpse of a massive bone being tossed, heard a loud *thunk* as it hit the floor, watched Grimm's tail go flying out... and then Bay shut the bedroom door, leaning back against it with wide eyes. *Her* bedroom door. They were back in Tipton, and for the moment, Tasmin couldn't think of a single place he'd rather be.

Bay looked traumatized.

"Oh my God, that dog. So, so much dog."

When he started laughing, she turned her gaze on him, startled at first, and then filling with a warmth he'd been worried he would never see again. Along with the rest of her.

"You're awake," she said, crossing the room quickly. She perched lightly on the side of the bed, close but not close enough for him to reach her. He started to wonder why she acted like he might break if she got too close, but as pieces of memory began to trickle back, his questions vanished. All, that is, save one.

"I'm... alive, right?" he asked, trying to figure out how that could be.

She nodded. "Pretty sure. Yes. A lot has happened in the last couple of days as you've been healing, but... I think everything is going to be okay." She looked more closely at him. "How do you feel?"

He considered this, moving fingers and toes. He'd already had an accidental demonstration of how well his arms worked. There was a soft rustle, and he looked down at his chest, finally noticing the large bandages covering his upper half. They looked clean, at least—no dried blood. But once he noticed them, he also noticed the faint ache coming from that area.

Tasmin pushed himself up into a sitting position. There was something intangibly different, a thing he could feel but not really explain. Then he realized what it was. He felt whole.

The demon was gone.

In an instant, he'd snatched Bay from where she sat on the bed and pulled her down with him, wrapping her tightly in his arms. Then he showered her with kisses, pressing them to her cheeks, her nose, her mouth, nuzzling her hair. When he pulled back, he realized she was crying.

"What is it?" he asked, terrified he'd somehow hurt her. But when she smiled through the tears, he finally understood.

"Do not *ever* try to kill yourself on my behalf again, okay? No more demon deals, no more heroic acts of sacrifice. *Ever*," she said. Bay brought her hands up to cup his face, and the love he saw in her eyes filled up all the empty places inside himself.

"You saved me," he said, remembering. "I was so worried about protecting you, and you're the one who protected me."

"Well, you returned the favor pretty quickly," Bay said, stroking her thumb over the rough stubble on his cheek. "That's what it's about. I have your back, you have mine. Nobody dies by insane vampire attack or bloodthirsty demon, and everybody's happy."

He shook his head, confused. "I still don't understand. I felt myself dying, Bay. How Arsinöe got Hunger from me... it should have killed me."

She hesitated, then explained how the demon he'd carried for so long had, whether on a whim or out of some strange gratitude for killing Arsinöe, told Bay that blood would heal even the demon's wounds. Whether that would always be true or was, just this once, an unexpected reprieve given by that dark thing, Bay had immediately known what Hunger had meant. And she'd been right. Tasmin's blood had sired her, and hers had healed him. Not the circle he'd expected to make, but far from unwelcome.

She looked up at him, eyes searching his face. "So you feel... better?"

"I feel..." He couldn't find the right word, so instead he showed her, lowering his head and claiming her mouth in a kiss that left him hot and shaking. He pressed his forehead to hers. "*Main tumse pyar karta hoon. I love you. I was a fool. I thought it would be easier for both of us if I fought alone. Instead, all I did was wish I'd told you how I felt when I had the chance. You made everything better. You still do."

"I love you," he said softly. "I don't ever want to be without you. I don't care where we build a life. I just know I want to do it with you."

"That can be arranged," she said, and her smile was everything. "I love you, Tasmin Singh. I'm yours. You gave me eternity. All I want is to spend it with you."

"You're not mine yet," he said. "But you will be."

He made slow, sweet love to her, telling her she belonged with him in every way he knew how—with his mouth, his hands, his tongue. And when he brought her to the brink, shaking with need, he bared his neck to her.

He felt it when they joined, the bond blazing through him like dark, wild fire. When they flew, they flew together, until they were left tangled on the bed, limbs languid and entwined.

Tasmin rose up on one elbow to look down at her, the woman he loved more than life itself. She watched him with her lioness's eyes, as proud and fierce as any Rakshasa could hope to be.

But she was so much more.

She was his.

And as Tasmin leaned down for a kiss, he knew he would never be alone again.

Epilogue

One year later

H<small>E'S GOING TO</small> blow his arm off."

"It'll grow back. Probably."

Bay stood in her big backyard, Lily at her side, watching the men light off firecrackers. Behind them, the house danced with the light of candles and diyas, little oil lamps Bay had scattered about inside. The scent of Jaden's baking wafted out the screen door, and Bay's mouth watered. She might need to drink blood, but thankfully, the pleasure of gorging herself on sweets hadn't died. Especially not when she managed to con Jaden into playing housewife for her.

Lyra slipped out the back door and onto the deck, then sauntered across the yard to stand with the other women. She had a beer in one hand and a guilty look on her face.

"Do you guys know what jalebi are?"

Bay raised an eyebrow. "No."

"Good. Because Jaden just threw me out for eating most of them." She took a swig of her beer and watched Tasmin and Ty send another firecracker up, this time narrowly missing lighting one of the trees on fire.

"FYI, Bay? Diwali is cool, but we are never having it at my house. Ever."

Bay laughed, enjoying the chilly night with the warmth of her friends. She and Tasmin had been in the new house in Silver Falls for five months, and it already felt like they'd always been here. After everything that had happened, she treasured the relative quiet, the slower pace—and the willingness of the town's residents to allow a lion or two to run with the pack. And with Anna having bought her business back in Tipton, Bay had been able to lease space from the local vet and set up next door. So far, it had worked out great.

It was starting over in some ways. But in a lot of ways, it just felt like finally settling in to where she was supposed to be. She had never been so content. It was strange, that for all her fears about what being a vampire would mean, becoming one was what had finally pushed her to discover what she truly needed from her life. It would be a very long life, with both advantages and drawbacks, full of abilities and quirks she was still discovering. But she was living it the way she wanted to, and with the ultimate perk.

A man she loved more than she could ever have imagined.

She never got tired of watching Tasmin's joy in the smallest of things. He was even starting to tease her about getting another Newfoundland to keep Grimm company, God help them all.

"I really do love the new place," Lily said, tipping her head back to look at the stars. "Boston's a great city,

and it's working out much better as a seat for the dynasty...
but I'm glad you've got a home like this I can come visit."

"And you settled somewhere I can come shop," Bay
replied. "It's a win-win."

"This firecracker thing is starting to look like a lose
for everyone," Lyra said. "Can we eat yet? The Grimm has
probably drooled himself an ocean upstairs in that crate."

"He's fine. I turned on Animal Planet to muffle the
noise. And he's not on fire, which is probably more than I
could say if he were out here with the pyro brothers," Bay
said. "They're having way too much fun with this."

There was a bright flash, and then a rain of golden
sparks as the two men finally got off a decent firecracker.
Tasmin's eyes caught Bay's across the yard, and his grin
was infectious. She couldn't help but return it.

"So how *are* things up in vamp central, anyway?"
Lyra asked. "If you said, I didn't hear it. I get distracted by
Jaden's baking."

Lily shrugged. "Smoothing out. Without Arsinöe to
throw wrenches in everything left and right, it's kind of
weirdly smooth, actually. That's not a complaint. And the
Empusae are so scattered that their vote on the Council is
more of a courtesy than anything right now. Diana was a
good choice to lead since Mormo and her supporters went
underground, but there weren't that many of them to start
with, and not everyone is happy she let Anura back into the
fold."

Bay nodded. It hadn't been long after saving Tasmin that
they'd learned the details behind the frantic phone message Jaden had received. Anura had been found in Chicago,
bound in the basement of an abandoned warehouse, bled
and poisoned by a Ptolemy with the help of an Empusa who

Anura had considered a friend. The friend had vanished, along with fully half of her dynasty, when news of Arsinöe's death had gotten out. Since then, Anura had seemed interested in reengaging with the new Empusae leadership… though she was never going to give up running her club. Bay thought she understood. Anura had found her place. Her eyes drifted to Jaden, and she smiled. Some of them got lucky that way.

"Still no new ruler for the Ptolemy?" Bay asked with a small smile. The alliance of Lilim, Grigori, Dracul, and Empusae had decisively crushed the Ptolemy the night after Arsinöe's death. It hadn't been much of a fight—most of Arsinöe's foreign allies had fled at the news of her death, and the Ptolemy who had wanted to fight, though numerous, were in disarray.

That didn't seem to have changed.

Lily rounded her eyes and made a face. "No. It's interesting to watch. And tough to deal with having a new representative from them every time we have a Council meeting."

"They're taking turns?" Lyra asked. "That's new."

"No," Lily said. "They're killing one another off. Different issue. They'll figure it out, or… Well, they'll figure it out. Eventually. At least they don't have anything to get Chaos interested in them anymore."

"Chaos and Hunger," Bay said, looking away and frowning. Her little town seemed so far removed from all of those things, and that was the way she liked it. She'd had enough of demons to last her a lifetime. "Wonder if they found each other?"

"Let's hope not," Lily said, and then grinned. "Oh, awesome. They ran out of firecrackers."

"Food time!" Lyra cried, pumping her fist. She hightailed it back inside, where Bay knew Jaden had put out a spread of sweets that would make a professional baker weep with joy. She was just glad the vampirism meant she no longer had to diet.

Tasmin and Ty crossed the yard, and Tasmin slipped his arm around Bay's waist. "Having fun?" he asked.

Bay nodded and pressed a kiss to his lips, feeling the heat that still sparked between them. "Better now that you're done playing with fire."

He chuckled. "We have another box for later."

Bay groaned, but leaned her head on his shoulder as they made their way inside, catching Lily's eye roll and grin. Apparently she'd gotten the news as well.

Tasmin stopped, letting Lily and Ty go in first, then surprised Bay by pulling her into his arms under the stars. He nuzzled her, rubbing her nose against his, and in the dark his eyes glowed like those of the jungle cat that was part of his spirit.

"We should go for a run later," he growled. "Alone."

Her heart skipped a beat the way it always did when he looked at her that way.

"You got it." She pressed her lips to his for a kiss, melting against him despite the cold. "Shall we go in?"

He nodded, but hesitated a moment. Bay tilted her head at him, curious.

"What's wrong?"

Nothing," he said. "I was just thinking…I'm finally home."

She gave him another kiss, unable to help herself, and the love she felt for him could have lit up the night sky.

"We're home," she agreed.

And, hands entwined, they went inside.

Acknowledgments

So many thanks are due to the readers who have carried me this far. Your e-mails, funny Facebook conversations, and tireless enthusiasm for my stories push me through even the toughest writing days. Thank you for buying my books and loving my characters! Not a day goes by without at least some small thing reminding me of how lucky I am to have all of you. You are so incredibly appreciated.

Thanks also go, as they always do, to the amazing team at Grand Central. There are still days when I look at these beautiful books and have to pinch myself. This was my dream. Thanks for making it a reality.

Special thanks to Selina McLemore for her editorial superpowers and sense of humor about my guyliner fixation, and to Megha Parekh for (a) being a fun and welcome addition to my in-box, and (b) making sure Tasmin speaks Hindi far better than I do.

Finally, thanks to my own pair of big, furry, adorable Newfoundlands, Stella and Chewie, for their unlimited slobbery kisses and unconditional love. No matter how big they are, their hearts are bigger, and I'm eternally grateful to have them in my life.

Can a vampire's vow of eternal
protection stop an ancient evil?

Or will it unleash one unsuspecting
young woman's dark destiny?

═══════════

Turn the page for an excerpt from
the first book in the
Dark Dynasties series.

Dark Awakening

chapter ONE

Tipton, Massachusetts
Eight months later

TYNAN MACGILLIVRAY crouched in the shadows of the little garden, listening to the mortals rattling loudly around inside the stuffy old mansion. He tried to concentrate on the scents and sounds of the humans, hoping to pick up any subtle change in the air that might indicate a Seer was among these so-called ghost hunters, but so far all he'd gotten was a headache.

This small-town gimmick was a long shot, and he knew it. But he'd been everywhere in the past eight months, from New York City Goth clubs to Los Angeles coven meetings. Anywhere there might be a whisper of ability beyond the norm. In all that time, he had found not the faintest whiff of a Seer or even a hint of anything paranormal at all. Just a bunch of humans playing dress-up, trying to be different.

He wondered how they would feel if they walked into an actual vampire club. Most of them would probably be too foolish to even be frightened for the few seconds their life would last in one of those places. But they might note that there wasn't nearly as much black leather and bondage wear in undead society as they seemed to think.

Ty got to his feet, all four of them, and arched his back, stiff from keeping so still in the bushes all night. His cat form was the gift of his bloodline, though it was of dubious help in places like this. The house he was staking out sat just off the town square, and there were only a few scrubby barberry bushes for cover. His fur was black, yes, and blended into shadow, but dog-sized cats didn't exactly inspire the warm cuddlies in passersby.

Hell. It's no good. Ty gave a frustrated growl as he accepted the fact that this trip was just another bust. He'd been reduced to combing psychic fairs and visiting what were supposedly America's most haunted places, hoping something would draw out the sort of human he so desperately needed to find. But soon, very soon, Ty knew he would have to return to Arsinöe with the news that the Seers had, in all likelihood, simply died out. For the first time in three hundred years of service, he would have to admit failure.

And the Mulo, the gypsy curse that was slowly killing those he was charged with protecting, would continue its dark work until there was no one left who bore the mark of the Ptolemaic dynasty, the oldest and most powerful bloodline in all of vampire society, begun when Arsinöe's life was spared by a goddess's dark kiss. No other house could claim such a beginning, or such a ruler. But if things continued, the other dynasties, eternally jealous of the Ptolemy's power, lineage, and reach, wouldn't even have a carcass to feed upon.

The invisible terror had attacked twice more, both times at sacred initiations of the Ptolemy, both times leaving only one vampire alive enough to relate what had happened. Or in the case of the first atrocity, one nearly-turned human woman. Rosalyn, he remembered with a curl of distaste in the pit of his gut. They had brought her back to the compound, bloody and broken, taking what information they could before finally letting her die a very human death. He doubted she had known how lucky she was.

Ty, used to fading into shadow and listening, knew that all in the inner circle of Arsinöe's court agreed: it was only a matter of time before the violence escalated even further, and the queen herself was targeted.

Without their fierce Egyptian queen, the House of Ptolemy would fall. Maybe not right away, but there were none fit to take Arsinöe's place, unless Sekhmet appeared once more to bestow her grace on one of them. If the goddess even still existed. More likely there would be a bloody power struggle that left but a pale shadow of what had been, and that petty infighting would take care of whoever the Mulo had left behind, if any. And the Cait Sith such as himself, those who had been deemed fit to serve only by virtue of their Fae-tainted blood, would be left to the dubious mercy of the remaining dynasties that ruled the world of night.

He could no more let that happen than he could walk in the sun.

Ty pushed aside his dark thoughts for the moment and debated heading back to his hotel room for the night, maybe swinging by a local bar on the way to get a quick nip from one of the drunk and willing. Suddenly a back door swung open and a woman stepped out into the crisp night air.

At first he stayed to watch because he was merely curious. Then the moonlight caught the deep auburn of her hair, and Ty stared, transfixed, as she turned fully toward him. Utterly unaware of the eyes upon her, she tipped her head back, bathing herself in starlight, the soft smile on her lips revealing a woman who appreciated the pleasure of an autumn night well met.

He heard her sigh, saw the warm exhalation drift lazily upward in a cloud of mist. For him, caught in some strange spell, it all seemed to occur in slow motion, the mist of her breath hanging suspended for long moments above her mouth, as though she'd gifted a shimmering bit of her soul to the night. The long, pale column of her throat was bared above the collar of her coat, the tiny pulse beating at the base of it amplified a thousand times, until he could hear the singular pulse and pound that were her life, until it was everything in his universe. Her scent, a light, exotic vanilla, drifted to him on the chill breeze, and all thought of drinking from some nameless, faceless stranger vanished from his mind.

Ty wanted *her*. And though a certain amount of restriction was woven tightly into the fabric of his life, he would not deny himself this. Already he was consumed by the thought of what her blood might taste like. Would it be as sweet as she smelled? Or would it be darker than she appeared to be, ripe with berry and currant? Every human had a singular taste—this he had learned—and it spoke volumes about them, more than they would ever know.

She lingered only a moment longer, and her heart-shaped face, delicately featured with a pair of large, expressive eyes he was now determined to see close up, imprinted itself on him in a way he had never before experienced. Ty's mind was too hazed to question it now, this odd reaction to her, but he knew he would be able to ponder nothing else later.

Later. Once he had tasted her.

When she turned away, when the burnished waves of her hair spilling over the collar of her dark coat were all he could see, Ty found he could at least move again, and he did so with the ruthless efficiency of a practiced hunter. Like a predator that has latched on to the scent of its prey, his eyes never left her, even as he rose up, his feline form shifting and elongating until he stood on two feet among the straggling bushes.

He breathed deeply, drinking in that singular scent with anticipatory relish.

Then Ty turned up the collar of his coat and began the hunt.

Lily rounded the corner of the house with a sigh of relief.

Probably she should feel guilty about bailing on the annual Bonner Mansion ghost hunt. Bailing before anything interesting happened anyway—so far, all she'd seen was a bunch of overly serious amateur ghost hunters who thought every insect was a wayward spirit. Oh, and that couple who had set up camp in a closet with the door shut, she remembered with a smirk. Whatever sort of experience they were after, she was pretty sure it wasn't supernatural.

Why she'd even let Bay con her into this was a mystery; their weekly date to watch *Ghost Hunters* didn't translate into any desire on her part to *actually* go running around inside a dark, musty, supposedly haunted house. Thank God the hottie from the Bonner County Paranormal Society had shown up when he had. Lily wasn't sure which had made her best friend's eyes light up more: the tight jeans or the thermal-imaging camera. Either way, she wasn't even positive the group had heard her when she'd claimed a brewing headache as an excuse to leave them there, but Bay's grin told her she'd be thanked for going at some point in the near future.

She lifted her wrist to glance at her watch, squinting at it in the darkness, and noted that it was about quarter to twelve.

"So much for another Friday night," she muttered. Still, it didn't have to be a total waste. Maybe she'd get crazy, stay up late with some popcorn and a Gerard Butler movie.

Wild times at Lily Quinn's house. But better, always better, than running the risk of sleep. She didn't need a silly ghost tour to scare her. Nothing could be scarier than the things she saw when she closed her eyes.

Lily crunched through dead leaves, then stopped, frowning at the unfamiliar view of bare trees and, a little farther off, the wrought-iron fence that bordered the property's grounds. Despite the reasonably close proximity to the town square, the Bonner Mansion sat back a ways from the road, and the historical society had managed to hang on to a portion of the original property, so there were still grounds to the place. But there was, as a nod to modernity, a parking lot.

And it was, Lily realized, on the *other* side of the house. She tipped her head back, closed her eyes, and groaned.

Her impeccable sense of misdirection had struck again.

After a moment spent silently cursing, Lily shoved her hands deeper into her pockets and set off on what she hoped was the correct course this time. Directional impairment was one of her defining features, right along with her inexplicable aversion to suitable men. If she could only find a well-educated, Shakespeare-quoting bad boy who still had a thing for sexy tattoos and maybe a mild leather fetish, she might at least have a shot at avoiding her probable future as a crazy old cat lady.

A long shot, maybe. But a shot.

At least it was a beautiful night, Lily thought, inhaling deeply. The smell of an October night was one of her favorites, especially in this part of New England. It was rife with the earthy, rich smell of decaying leaves, of wood smoke from someone's chimney, and shot through with a cleansing bite of cold.

Lily looked around as she walked, taking her time. In the faint glow from the streetlights along the road, this place really did have a haunted look about it, but not scary. More like someplace where you'd find a dark romance, full of shadows and sensual mystery.

She huffed out a breath, amused at herself. She taught English lit because she had always liked the fantasy of what could be, instead of the often unpleasant reality of how things were. Speaking of which, it looked like a little *Phantom of the Opera* might be in order for her Friday night movie. Even if the ending absolutely refused to go the way she wanted, she thought with a faint smile, no matter how many times she'd willed Christine to heal the dark and wounded Phantom instead of wasting her time on boring old Raoul.

It would have made for one hell of a love scene—

There was a sudden, strange tingling sensation at the back of her neck. Lily felt the hairs there rising as a rush of adrenaline chilled her blood. Someone was behind her. She knew it without seeing, felt eyes on her that hadn't been there a moment before.

But when she whirled around, stumbling a little in her haste to confront whoever was behind her, she saw nothing. Only the empty expanse of lawn, dotted with the skeletal shapes of slumbering trees, an empty bench, and beside her, the dark shape of the house. Nothing.

Nowhere even to hide.

Lily felt her heart kick into a quicker rhythm, and her breath became shallower as her eyes darted around, looking for a shape, a shadow, anything that would explain her sudden, overwhelming certainty that she wasn't alone.

Stupid, she told herself. *You're walking through a horror movie setup, and it's just got your imagination running, is all.*

Lily knew that was more than likely it, but she still wanted to reach her car and get out of here. Soothed a little by the thought that there were a whole bunch of people inside the house who would hear her scream if anything did happen, she turned to continue making her way out front, casting a lingering look over one shoulder.

Though the moon rode high in the night sky, nearly full, and the air was still rich with the very scents she'd just been enjoying, all her pleasure had vanished in favor of the insistent instinct that had kept humans walking the Earth for as long as they had: flight.

"Hey, are you all right?"

She gave a small scream before she could stop herself, jumping at the sudden appearance of another person in front of her when there'd been no sign of another soul only seconds before.

He raised his hands in front of him, eyebrows lifting in an expression that plainly said he was as startled as she was. "Whoa, hey, don't do that! I'm not a ghost or anything. You can start breathing again." One eyebrow arched higher, plaintive. "Please?"

It was the faintly amused concern he put into that last word that finally got her to draw in a single, shuddering breath. But she still shot a quick look around, gauging distance in case she had to run.

"Look, I'm sorry," the man said, drawing Lily's full attention back to him. "I needed to get out of there for a few. Too many people, not enough ghosts, you know?"

"I ... yeah," Lily said, still trying to figure out how she should deal with this. Had he been inside too? She wasn't sure.... There'd been a cluster of people, and not everyone had shown up at the same time. It was certainly possible. But when she looked more closely at him, she was sure she would have remembered if they'd crossed paths.

"Let's start over," he said.

This time she picked up on the lilting Scottish accent in a voice that was soft and deep but with a slightly rough edge.

He extended a hand to her. "I'm Tynan. MacGillivray."

Yeah, it didn't get any more Scottish than that. Lily hesitated for a split second, but her deeply ingrained sense of politeness refused to let her keep her hand in her pocket. Tentatively, she slid her hand into his and watched as his long, slim fingers closed around it.

"I'm Lily. Lily Quinn," she said, surprised by the sensation of cool, silken skin against her own. But at the point of contact, warmth quickly bloomed, matching the heat that began to course through her system as she finally noticed that Tynan MacGillivray was incredibly good-looking.

Not handsome, she thought. That was the wrong word for what he was, though some people might have used it anyway. He was more...compelling. She let herself take in the sharp-featured, angular face with a long blade of a nose and dark, slashing brows. His mouth held the only hint of softness, with an invitingly full lower lip that caught her attention far more than it should have, under the circumstances. His skin was so fair as to make him pale, though for some reason it only enhanced his strange appeal, and was set off further by the slightly shaggy, overlong crop of deep brown hair that he'd pushed away from his face.

It was his eyes, though, that Lily couldn't seem to avoid. Light gray, with a silvery cast from the moonlight, they watched her steadily, unblinking. She wanted to believe he meant her no harm. But there was an intensity in the way he looked at her that kept her off balance. *I should get moving, get out of here*, Lily thought, feeling like a deer that has picked up the scent of a predator.

But she was caught by those eyes, unable to look away. She shuddered in a soft breath as he stepped in closer, never letting go of her hand.

No, she thought, her eyes locked with his, her legs refusing to move. But then, right on the heels of that: *Yes*.

"Lily," he said, his voice little more than a sensual growl. "Now, that's a pretty name. Fitting."

No one had ever said her name quite like that before, savoring it, as though they were tasting it. Desire, unexpected, unwanted, but undeniable all the same, unfurled deep in her belly. She tried to think of something to say, something that would break this odd spell she was falling under, but nothing sprang to mind. There was only this dark stranger. Everything else seemed to fade away, unimportant.

"You're shivering," he remarked. "You shouldn't be out here in the cold all alone."

"No, I...I guess not," she murmured, mildly surprised that though she was shivering, she hadn't even noticed. She certainly wasn't cold anymore. And for some reason it was difficult to hang on to her thoughts long enough to form a coherent sentence. "I was...just going to my car."

His eyes, she thought, caught up in a hazy rush of desire that flooded her from head to toe, banishing any awareness of the temperature of the air. His eyes *were* silver, she realized as they grew closer. Silver, and glowing like the moon. Strange, beautiful eyes.

"Why don't you let me walk you?" he asked.

The words barely penetrated her consciousness. After struggling to make sense of them, she found herself nodding. Car. Walk. Yes. Probably a good thing. "Yeah. That would be great."

Tynan smiled, a lazy, sensual lift of his lips. It seemed the most natural thing in the world that, despite what each of them had said, neither of them made a move to go. Instead, he trailed his free hand down her cheek, cool marble against her warm flesh, and rubbed his thumb slowly across her lower lip.

Lily's lips parted in answer, and her eyes slipped shut as a soft sigh escaped her. She'd never felt such pleasure from such a light touch, but all she could think of, all she wanted, was for it to continue.

"Lily," he purred again. "How lovely you are."

"Mmm," was all she could manage in response. She turned into his touch as his skilled fingers slid into her hair, as he let go of her hand to slide his around the curve of her waist as he stepped into her. It was like drifting in some dark dream, and Lily embraced it willingly, sliding her hands up his chest and then around to his back, urging him even closer.

She wasn't sure what she was asking for—but at Tynan's touch, something stirred inside of her, some long-dormant need that arched and stretched after a long sleep, then flooded her with aching demand. She turned her face up to his, a wordless invitation. His warm breath fanned her face, and even through the strange haze that seemed to have enveloped her, she thrilled a little at the ragged sound of his breathing, at the erratic beat of his heart against her chest.

"Lily," he said again, and this time it was almost reverent.

He bent his head to hers, and Lily's lips parted in anticipation. She had never wanted a man's kiss so desperately; her entire being seemed to vibrate with desire. Her breath stilled as she waited for the press of his lips against her own. But instead of taking what she offered, Tynan's mouth only grazed her cheek, and his long fingers deftly cupped her chin to turn her head to the side.

Lily made a noise then, a soft, frustrated moan that drew a chuckle from her tormentor.

"Patience, sweetheart," he admonished her, his gruff brogue more pronounced now. "Too fast and you'll spoil it."

Tynan trailed soft kisses along her jawline, the relative chill of his lips against her warm and sensitive flesh a shocking pleasure. Lily writhed in his arms, wanting to be closer, wanting some nameless *more* that she couldn't identify. But Tynan seemed to be relentlessly controlled, the uneven intake of his breath the only clue that he might be as close to undone as she. Lily heard his voice then, seeming to echo right inside her head.

Let me taste you.

Powerless to do anything but obey, Lily let her head fall back in submission, baring her throat to him, willing him to touch more, take more. In some dim recess of her mind, it occurred to her that this entire situation was madness at best, suicidal at worst. But the harder she tried to hang on to any rational thoughts, the quicker they seemed to evaporate. And wasn't it so much more pleasurable to just give up, give in? As though Tynan wanted to illustrate just that point, he nipped at her ear, flicking his tongue over the sensitive lobe.

"Please," Lily moaned, moving restlessly against him, not even sure what she was asking for. Then he was drawing her hair away from her neck, tugging her head to the side to gain better access. He forced the collar of her shirt down, baring her collarbone to the cold night air. Lily allowed it all, her only desire to feel his lips on her skin again, to give him whatever he wanted. All the world had vanished except for Tynan. She could feel his hands shaking as his handling of her roughened, and she sensed his need was even greater than her own.

Suddenly he stopped, going stock-still as he expelled a single shaking breath. Lost in the deepening fog of her sexual haze, Lily gripped the thick wool of Tynan's coat harder and made a soft sound of distress. Why had he stopped? She needed . . . she *needed* . . .

All she heard was a softly muttered curse in an unfamiliar tongue.

Then, a ripple of air, a breath of chill wind. Lily slowly opened her eyes, only barely beginning to register where she was and what she had been doing. Her hands were fisted in nothing but empty air. She blinked rapidly, taking a stumbling step backward, feeling a crushing, if nonsensical, sense of loss. She turned in a circle, knowing that he had to still be here. He couldn't have left. It was impossible for a man to vanish into thin air.

But whoever—or whatever—Tynan MacGillivray was, Lily was soon forced to acknowledge the truth.

He was gone.

The world of night still isn't safe...

A new threat looms, and under
the cover of darkness ancient
enemies will form a forbidden—and
passionate—alliance...

Turn the page for an excerpt from
the second book in the Dark Dynasties series.

Midnight Reckoning

chapter ONE

Tipton, Massachusetts

O<small>N A NIGHT</small> when only the thinnest sliver of a crescent moon rode the sky, at a time when even the most adventurous humans had fallen into bed and succumbed to sleep, a solitary cat padded in and out of pooled shadow as he made his way across the deserted square in the middle of town. He was large, the size of a bobcat, with sleek fur the color of jet. His coat shimmered as he moved, gleaming in the dull glow of streetlights in between shadows, and he moved with speed and grace, if not purpose. Eyes that burned like blue embers stayed focused on the path ahead of him.

The cat had gone by several names in his long life. For more than a century now, he had been simply Jaden, or even more simply, "cat." If pressed, he would answer to either, and neither if he could get away with it.

Tonight, in the night's seductive and silent embrace, Jaden answered to no one but himself.

Jaden took his time as he made his way through town, savoring the stillness of the blessed lack of humanity with all its noise and emotion and complication. He paused in front of the darkened windows of a beauty salon, letting his gaze drift over the sign that read, CHARMED, I'M SURE, and then lifted his head higher to catch the scent of air that was heavy with moisture and ripe with the promise of rain. Jaden could sense that summer was making its way to this little corner of New England, while aware that even in early May the frost could arrive on any given night to give the season's fresh blooms a deadly kiss.

Deadly kisses, Jaden thought, lashing his tail. Yeah, he knew all about those. When you were a vampire, especially a lowly shape-shifting cat of a vampire, deadly kisses were sort of your stock in trade.

Damn it. So much for a late-night walk to clear his head.

The shift came as easily as breathing to him, and in a single heartbeat Jaden stood on two feet instead of four, his clothes firmly in place by some magic he had never understood but always appreciated. He stuffed his hands deeply into the pockets of his coat and continued on down the street, glaring at the ground in front of him as he moved. Though he'd spent years seething silently at the Ptolemy, his highblood masters who had treated "pets" like him with little mercy and even less respect, these days he didn't seem to have much anger for anyone but himself.

Jaden now had what he'd always thought he wanted: friends, a home, and most important, his freedom. The Ptolemy were not gone, but they were cowed for the time being, and his kind, the much-maligned Cait Sith, had been chosen for an incredible honor. They were to be the foundation for the rebirth of a dynasty of highbloods that had vanished ages ago but had now resurfaced in the form of a single mortal woman who carried the blood.

The seven months since Jaden had helped that woman, Lily, make a stand against the Ptolemy had passed like nothing. And though it had been considerably less time since the Vampiric Council had given Lily's plan its grudging blessing, Jaden was now really and truly free. Whether it had been a wise decision, Jaden couldn't say. The Cait Sith were an unruly lot at best.

But he was grateful, as were the rest, which had to count for something.

Jaden rubbed at his collarbone without really being aware that he was doing it. There, beneath layers of clothing, was his mark, the symbol of his bloodline. Until recently, the mark had been a coiling knot of black cats. But a drink of Lily's powerful blood had changed it, adding the pentagram and snake of the Lilim. It meant new abilities he was still exploring, newfound standing in a world where he had always been beneath notice. It should have meant hope, Jaden knew. After all, for the first time in his long life, he was not a pariah. He could be his own master. It should be everything. And yet...

The empty places inside him still ached like open wounds. Something was missing. He just wished he knew what it was.

A soft breath of wind ruffled through his hair, and Jaden caught a whiff of something both familiar and unfamiliar.

Then he heard the voices.

"There's no place to run to now, is there?" That was a gravelly male voice, reeking of self-satisfaction. Its owner gave a low and vicious chuckle. "You're going to have to accept me. I've caught you. It's my right."

A female voice responded, and a pleasant shiver rippled through Jaden's body at the low, melodious sound of it.

"You have no rights with me. And chasing me down like prey isn't going to get you what you want."

He was almost certain he'd heard that voice before, though he couldn't place it. What Jaden *could* place, however, was the scent that had his hackles rising and the adrenaline flooding his system.

Werewolves.

Jaden's lips curled, and he had to fight the instinctive urge to hiss. Not only were the wolves vilified by vampires as savages, banned from their cities under penalty of death, but the smell of their musk caused a physical reaction in him that was difficult to control. He had two options: fight or flight. It was less trouble to run. But this was his territory now, vampire territory. And these wolves had a hell of a lot of nerve coming into it.

Jaden was moving before he could think better of it. His feet made no sound on the pavement as he headed for the parking lot behind the building. And as he slipped into shadow, he listened.

"You can make this easy or hard, honey. But you're going to have me one way or the other. And there's not a damn thing you can do about it."

A low growl from the female. A warning. "I'm not about to take a backseat to some social-climbing stray. I don't want a mate."

The male's voice went thick and rough, as though he

was fighting a losing battle with the beast within. "My family is plenty good enough to mate with an Alpha. You should be glad it's me, Lyra. I won't be as rough as some. And you and I both know there's no way the pack is ever going to have a female Alpha. There's too much at stake to let the weak lead."

Lyra... The pieces clicked into place, and Jaden's stomach sank like a stone.

He did know her. And that brief meeting had put him in one of the fouler moods of his unnatural life.

Memories surfaced of a Chicago safe house, full of vampires in hiding, in trouble, or on the run. And on the occasion he remembered, it had also been a hiding place for a female werewolf with a sharp tongue and a nasty attitude. Rogan, the owner of the safe house, had mentioned something about Lyra being a future Alpha... right after Jaden had demanded she leave the room.

Lyra had gone, though she hadn't taken the slight quietly. And now, she was here, in the seat of the Lilim. It was almost inconceivable. Jaden wondered briefly if Lyra hadn't hunted him here to finish their brief altercation with blood. That would be like a werewolf, brutish and nonsensical. But no, Jaden realized as she and the male who was accosting her came into view. Lyra seemed to have bigger problems than any grudge she bore him.

Jaden kept to the shadows, melting into darkness as effectively as he did in his feline form. He now had a clear view of a tall, over-muscled Neanderthal who was wearing the expected smug sneer. A predator. Being one himself, Jaden had gotten very good at identifying others. Lyra he saw only from behind, but he would have known her anywhere. Long, lean, and tall, with a wild tangle of dark hair shot through with platinum and tumbling halfway down her back. He let his eyes skim the length of her, suddenly apprehensive...hoping that his reaction to her the last time had been some kind of sick fluke. It had been easy enough to dismiss then. Being under constant threat of annihilation could do strange things to a man. But he knew it had fueled his anger at her presence in the safe house.

And now, just as before, the sight of her sent desire cascading through him in a wild rush like no other woman had provoked in him.

Jaden's sudden arousal mingled with a punch of bloodlust, creating a tangled mix of wants and needs that had his breath beginning to hitch in his chest. He moved slowly, walking the increasingly fine edge between man and beast as he struggled to stay concealed. He remembered more than just his brief meeting with her, no matter how he'd tried to block it all out. He'd had dreams...bodies tangled together, biting, clawing...licking...

Appalled, Jaden told himself he couldn't truly want a werewolf. Apart from being forbidden by both races, it was just *wrong*. Wasn't he screwed up enough?

It was a relief when the Neanderthal provided a distraction from his thoughts. The male moved like lightning, and far more gracefully than his bulky form would suggest. A hand shot out, snatching something from around Lyra's neck. The werewolf dangled the item in front of her, and Jaden could see it was a silver pendant hanging from a leather cord. She tried to snatch the pendant back, but the male held it high above his head like a schoolyard bully.

"How *dare* you?"

"It's just an old necklace," he said with a smirk. "If you want it that badly, come and get it."

Jaden could hear the helpless outrage in her voice when she spoke.

"My father—"

"Isn't here right now, is he? No one is." The Neanderthal shifted, crooked a finger at her. His stance said he knew he'd won. "I've got a hotel room. Or we can do it right here. Your choice."

His grin was foul. She seemed to think so too.

"Like hell, Mark."

Lyra's muscles tensed. She was going to run. What choice did she have? But the other man knew it. And while she might be fast, there was no way she would be able to match his strength.

Jaden hissed out a breath through gritted teeth. He was no hero. He might be nothing more than a lowblood vampire, a gutter cat with a gift for the hunt, but even among his kind, there were unspoken rules. And something in Lyra's voice, the hopeless outrage of someone railing against a fate they knew was inevitable, struck a chord deep within him. He had spent centuries being pushed and pulled by forces he couldn't fight. No one had ever given a damn what *he* had wanted, not from the first.

Gods help him with what he was about to get tangled up in.

Lyra spun, leaping away with a startling amount of grace. The man she'd called Mark lunged almost as quickly. His hand caught in all the glorious hair, fisting so that her head snapped back. Jaden heard her pained cry, heard the man's roar of victory. Then Mark's hands were on her, grabbing, tearing...

One look at Lyra's eyes, wild and afraid, and nothing on earth could have prevented Jaden from stepping in. He sprang from the shadows with a vicious snarl, fury hazing the darkness with bloodred. He landed directly in front of the grappling pair, fangs elongated and bared. The shock of his appearance gave Lyra the opening he'd hoped for. She twisted away, but not quickly enough. Mark took her down with a quick clout to the side of the head before whipping back around. Jaden watched, an odd twist of pain in his chest, as Lyra gave a single, shocked sob and collapsed to her knees.

Still, Jaden had gotten part of what he wanted. Lyra could no longer be used as a shield.

Recognition dawned in Mark's eyes a split-second before the instinctive hatred did.

Then another set of fangs were bared. Eyes flashed hot gold. The werewolf gave a guttural growl and reached for Jaden, long claws already extended from his fingertips. Jaden hissed as he stepped out of reach and waited for his chance. Jaden knew from experience that a wolf would always go for brute force over finesse. And against a vampire, it was almost always the wolf's downfall.

This time was no different.

Mark lunged, swiped. Jaden ducked easily and extended claws of his own, drawing first blood across the vulnerable belly. The thin ribbons of blood darkening his opponent's T-shirt seemed to incense his adversary, and he launched himself at Jaden only to find himself with a face full of asphalt. Unable to control himself, Jaden laughed, though it sounded nasty and hollow to his own ears.

"Hmm. I think someone's going home alone tonight."

Face bloodied, the werewolf dragged himself off the ground and growled at his tormentor.

"Get out of here, bloodsucker. This is wolf business."

"Really? Looks like garden-variety jackassery to me," Jaden said, watching Lyra out of the corner of his eye. She had shifted to a sitting position, and was holding her head in her hands staying very still. How badly she was hurt, Jaden didn't know. It was so like a wolf to try to win a woman by damaging her. Regardless, it was time to run this bastard off and give Lyra what care she needed.

He tried to ignore the way his heart began to stutter in his chest at the thought.

"Leave now," Jaden said, his voice soft, deadly. "Or I kill you."

Mark snorted. "Skinny piece of shit bloodsucker like you? I don't think—"

His words were cut off abruptly by two kicks, one to his gut and one across his thick head. At that, he went down like a ton of bricks with only a soft grunt for a response. This time, he stayed down. Jaden glared down at him for a moment, only barely denying himself the extra kick he wanted to give the wolf for good measure. But the stupid bastard should feel lousy enough when he awakened face-down in the parking lot in the morning. Although it might be momentarily satisfying, killing him would be nothing more than a messy waste of time.

And despite his disturbing interest in Lyra, Jaden had no interest in getting the Lilim into a pissing match with whatever scruffy pack of werewolves this loser belonged to.

Satisfied that they were now, for all practical purposes, alone, Jaden moved to Lyra's side and crouched down beside her. A light, intoxicating scent drifted from her, making his mouth water. Apples, he remembered. Sweet, tart apples, with something earthier beneath. Strangely enough, he felt no urge to run, to hiss and spit. He realized now it was a good thing he hadn't gotten this close the last time. He might have done something really stupid.

Though he supposed his current actions qualified.

"Lyra?" he asked, trying to keep his voice low and soothing. He wasn't sure how successful he was…he was way out of practice at damage control. Usually, he *was* the damage. "Are you all right? Do you need a doctor?" Wolves were self-healers, he knew, but it could take a while, which was dangerous when the wound was severe.

She said nothing, moved not a muscle, and Jaden's concern deepened. He reached for her, momentarily overcome by the urge to make even the simplest physical connection. But his hand stilled in midair when she finally lifted her head to look at him. And whatever he'd expected to see—fear, confusion, even a little gratitude— none of it was in evidence as he looked into Lyra's burning, furious eyes glowing fire-bright in the dark.

"Don't even think about touching me, *cat*," she said. "I can take care of myself."

When a dangerous assassin meets
a beautiful female vampire on the run,
the Dark Dynasties' most closely guarded
secret will be revealed.

====

Turn the page for an excerpt from
the third book in the Dark Dynasties series.

Shadow Rising

chapter ONE

ARIANE."

She stood at the floor-length window, staring out at the rolling ocean of sand that had been her home since before her memories began. Not a breath of wind moved the gossamer curtains that she'd drawn back, though she had opened the window wide in hopes that some air might clear her head.

No such luck. All she'd found was the crescent moon hanging above the same beautiful and barren landscape that she looked upon every night. Nothing changed here. Nothing except her. Not that the implications of what she was about to do didn't make her heart ache. But she had no choice.

Life eternal notwithstanding, this place would kill her, or at least the best part of her, if she stayed much longer.

"Ariane, please look at me."

With a soft sigh, Ariane turned away from the window and looked at the man who had entered the shadowed room. She had lit but a single candle, not wanting the harshness of the light, and it played over his concerned face, over features that were as hard and beautiful as chiseled stone.

Sariel. There was a time when she would have been honored by a visit from him. And to her chamber, no less. He had been the leader of her dynasty since it began, or so she understood, and his word among the Grigori was law. Ariane respected him, deeply. But Sariel was content with all the things that made her restless. He could accept that her dearest friend had vanished without a trace, where her every waking moment had become a nightmare of worry and dark imaginings. And she knew that while he cared, while some effort was being put into finding the missing Grigori, he didn't remotely understand what a loss Sam was to her.

"I appreciate your concern, Sariel. But I'm fine. I didn't expect to be chosen," Ariane said, hoping that she was concealing her bitterness well. To have been passed over was bad enough. But to have been pushed aside for Oren, to have seen the blaze of vicious triumph on her rival's face... it hurt in a way no wound ever had. And in her training, she'd been cut plenty.

Sariel approached, shutting the door behind him. To anyone else, even their own kind, Ariane knew he would have been incredibly intimidating. The men of the Grigori dynasty of vampires, particularly the ancient ones, all stood nearly seven feet tall, broad-chested and well muscled, with skin like pale marble. But in the dim light, he looked so like Sam that she could feel nothing but the same dull ache she had felt for a month now, ever since they'd all realized Sam was not simply traveling, but gone.

Sariel's face belonged on a statue carved by a Renaissance master, but his beauty, like all Grigoris' beauty, was cold. His white hair, the same shade as all ancient ones had, was an oddly attractive contrast to a youthful face. It fell to his shoulders with nary a wave to mar the gleam of it. His eyes glowed a deep and striking violet, a shade they all shared, in the dim light.

"I know you had your hopes up, Ariane," he said, his normally sonorous voice soft. "You don't have to pretend you didn't. If it helps, you were strongly considered. But the others felt that, ultimately, Oren was the better choice." He paused. "If Sammael can be found, he will be. I realize he is important to you, as he is to us all."

The better choice. Simply because she had not been handpicked by the elders, because the circumstances of her turning had been borne of emotion instead of reason. No matter how hard she worked, how lethal she became, she would be seen as a mistake. The weakest among them. And Oren, above all, had orchestrated her being shunned for it.

The Grigori were taught that hate was a wasted emotion. But for Oren, who excelled at the art of subtle humiliation, Ariane feared she felt something very close to it. And now he had bested her again, finally taking from her something she desperately wanted.

"Yes, Sam is important to all of us," Ariane said, trying to choose her words carefully as she turned back toward the window, the beckoning night. "But of everyone here, I am closest to him, Sariel. I think you know that. I don't understand why we're sending only one of our own to search for him when he could be hurt out there. He could be *dead*."

It was her greatest fear, and Sariel was as dismissive as

she'd expected him to be. He simply didn't give in to his emotions. She didn't really expect a vampire like Sariel to understand how much a simple friendship meant to her. He seemed above such things, beyond them. He was strong, unlike her; she was weakened by her attachments and her most private dreams. In those dreams, which she had never shared with a soul, she was happy, fulfilled, even loved—and far away from here.

A palace, however opulent, could still be a prison.

"Ariane," Sariel said, affecting the air of a parent lecturing a willful child, "your concern is admirable, but if Sammael is still alive, he shouldn't be difficult to find. We are adept at seeking as well as watching, as you know." He paused. "Tell me, little one, is this about my brother? Or is it about your desire to get beyond these walls?"

Anger roiled deep within her at his suggestion. Of course she wanted to get beyond these walls! But her own needs paled in comparison to Sam's ... wherever he was.

Finally, she managed to speak, her voice steady only through the strongest effort.

"Sariel, I swear that I'm only concerned about Sam. But since you brought it up, you're obviously aware of how stifling my situation is. In all these hundreds of years, I've been out exactly once. *Once*, when I have worked harder than anyone to show my worth. Do you know how that feels?" She waved her hand before he could answer. "No, of course you don't. If you want to go out into the world, you go. But I ..." She trailed off, wanting to make him understand how she felt about her life. "I can only sit here. Wander the grounds. Try to enjoy the little bits of life that the humans who are brought here carry with them before they're taken back."

"The palace is huge, as are the grounds," Sariel pointed out. "Everything you could want to do is here or could be brought here. We're not beholden to the same rules as the others. It's why this place is hidden, why we are hidden. You know that. The vampires accept us as their own, and it's important that they continue to do so. The less they know about us, the better."

"But we *are* vampires," Ariane snapped, exasperated by the same old conversation. "Aren't we? We don't walk in the day. We drink the blood of humans to survive. We are the *same*!"

"Yes and no," Sariel replied, his expression guarded. "We carry a responsibility the others do not. We are the oldest by far, though that, too, must stay hidden. Especially now, when things have begun to shift. We are watchers, *d'akara*. We do not interfere. Sammael understood this. The others understand this. But you . . ."

He trailed off, letting Ariane finish the thought herself. And how could she not? She'd heard the words enough times, even when she wasn't supposed to.

You're not ready. You'll never be ready. You're different.

"I may not have been chosen," Ariane said, trying to keep all anger from her voice, her face, "but that doesn't mean I'm incapable of carrying out our duties. The duties I have trained for alongside everyone else. I'm *ready*, Sariel."

She'd promised herself she wouldn't beg. And yet here she was again. Sariel's indulgent smile made her want to scream.

"Of course you are. One day soon, perhaps. Though, it isn't just up to me. Given the circumstances of your turning, there is concern about your ability to refrain from intervening."

"That was hundreds of years ago," Ariane interjected, a snap in her voice she couldn't cover. "I'm being punished because I was upset when I was turned?"

Sariel's eyes darkened. "*Upset* is the wrong word, as you well remember. A traumatic siring will linger, Ariane, sometimes forever. Do you really think you could stand by and watch what happened to you and your family? Even your sire could not and succumbed to weakness."

"My sire—"

Sariel held up a hand to stop her. "You already know I will not tell you who he is. He asked that the shame remain his own. It's best for both of you. For all of us."

Ariane stiffened, even as her stomach twisted into knots the way it always did when she had a conversation like this...and there had been many. She remembered so little of her siring, and only flashes of what had come before. Those brief glimpses of horror were bad enough. There had been blood, smoke, hideous laughter...beloved voices raised in tormented screams. Then strong arms, a hushed voice. Darkness.

Most of her mortal life remained a mystery to her. Her memories began in earnest at the weeks she'd spent confined to her chambers, weeping so long and hard that the tears had turned to blood. Weeping without truly knowing why. And there was no one to give her even a piece of her mortal past. Only the ancient ones knew who her sire was, and they kept their silence on the matter.

Sometimes she wondered if they'd killed him for what he'd done.

"We have all felt it, the desire to shape things to our

will instead of watching events unfold," Sariel lectured her, his tone soft and condescending in the way only an ancient one could manage. "But that is not our place. We must detach from instinct, leave our humanity behind us. Living as we do and trying to exist any other way is madness. Yet even now, Ariane, all these years later, I still see you struggle with what you were."

"But Sam said—"

"His name is Sammael, *d'akara*. Show his name the respect it deserves."

Ariane's mouth snapped shut at the steely command. It was worthless to argue with him, and she should have known better. He demanded respect, but he called her *d'akara*, "little one," as though she were a child. She was fast and strong. She could speak a multitude of languages, debate music and philosophy and art. She could fight more nimbly than most of her blood sisters and brothers. And she had learned these things for... what? To sit here and rot because she had *feelings*?

No. Not this time.

"Sammael, then," Ariane allowed, trying not to say it through gritted teeth. "He said it was important to remember how to feel for the mortals. To not just watch but to be able to understand. He's an ancient one too. Do you disagree?"

Sariel's expression shifted quickly from insincere warmth to genuine displeasure. "Sammael has an... unnatural affinity for the humans. Always has. I've indulged him, but humanity is like a troop of bellicose monkeys. Understanding them is simple enough. It was a defective design, I've always thought," he said with a small, cold smile.

Ariane never knew what to make of him when he said things like that. It was as if he had never been human, though more likely it had just been so long that he had no recollection of what it was like.

Sariel waved his hand dismissively. "In any case, Ariane, this is not an appropriate first mission for you. It's too delicate a situation, and time is of the essence. One day," he continued, stepping closer, his eyes glowing softly in a way that might almost be called warm, "I will make sure you get your chance to keep our watch. You have my word on this, *d'akara*."

She stayed still, though his nearness had begun to make her uncomfortable. The visit itself was highly unusual. Sariel's interest in her well-being was even more so. She couldn't recall him ever paying much attention to her...though Sammael's disappearance, and her connection to him, seemed to have remedied that in spades. She should have enjoyed it. And yet somehow it provoked nothing but a faint revulsion.

Another sign she was finally ready to go.

As though he'd sensed the direction of her thoughts, Sariel murmured, "I have no idea why your beauty has escaped my notice for so long. All these centuries, and you and I have never truly spoken."

"That's true," Ariane agreed with a small nod, self-consciously tucking a lock of long, silvery blond hair behind her ear. Her hair was pale even for a Grigori, almost as silver as an ancient one's. She'd always thought it made her more of a spectacle than beautiful...but the way Sariel's eyes tracked the motion of her hand through her hair made her wonder if she'd been wrong about her appeal among her own kind.

She hoped he didn't reach for her. What would she do then? Running was always an option, but a very poor one when your pursuer was a seven-foot-tall vampire.

To her relief, Sariel seemed to realize that his sudden attentions had surprised her. He came no closer, but the keen interest in his gaze was unmistakable.

"I would like to see you, Ariane. To spend some time with you. Tomorrow night, perhaps? We should get to know one another, after all this time."

It was all she could do not to sob with relief. "Of course," she replied, and even managed a small, demure smile. "I would enjoy that."

It seemed to satisfy Sariel, and he nodded.

"Good. I'll send someone for you then." He turned and strode to the door, but stopped just before leaving, looking back at her. "Don't worry about Sammael, *d'akara*. If he lives, he'll be found, and he would not be so easily killed. Trust me ... I've known him a great deal longer than you have."

Ariane nodded. "Then I'll just keep hoping for the best," she said.

When the door shut and Sariel was finally gone, she expelled a long, shaky breath, her legs going wobbly. She bent at the waist, placing her hands on her knees and breathing deeply, trying to regain her balance. The visit had rattled her, even more than she'd thought. Why had he really come? Was he worried that she might do exactly what she was planning? And if he was, had he seen that he was right?

She didn't think so. Whatever Sariel had come looking for, whatever he had seen, nothing had changed. For once she had a choice, and she chose to act. It was terrifying, yes.

But Ariane had faith it would also be freeing.

When she thought enough time had passed, Ariane moved to the bed and pulled a small beaded satchel from beneath the mattress. In it was the handful of things that held any importance for her. A sorry commentary on a life that had lasted so long and yet meant so little to anyone. She slung the long, thin strap of the satchel across her body, then moved to the window, her diaphanous skirt swirling gracefully about her legs.

She flipped a small latch, and the two panes of glass swung outward, revealing a gateway to the night. Ariane paused for only a moment, steeling herself. She had no desire to look back, to take in the pretty room that had been her safe haven for so long. It would be too easy to lose her nerve, and she would need all of that and more if she really wanted to find her friend. Not to mention evading her own capture. The Grigori did not take kindly to deserters. If she ever returned here, she doubted Sariel would be inviting her to his chambers again.

Not in the short space of time before she vanished forever.

No. That isn't going to happen. I can do this. And if finding Sam doesn't sway them, then I'll stay gone and stay on my own. Make a real life. Somehow.

Reassured, Ariane stepped onto the slim window ledge, glad that her room faced the desert and not the courtyard. Her only witness was the moon. She closed her eyes, breathed deeply, and summoned the gift that she had so rarely been able to use. She felt them rise from her back, sliding through her flesh as easily as water flowing from a stream. Her wings.

Ariane extended them, allowing herself only a moment

to turn her head and admire the way they shimmered in blues, lavenders, silvers—twilight colors. And gods but it felt good to free them, to free this part of herself. She lifted her hands to her sides, like a child balancing on a beam or a dancer poised to begin.

Then she leaped into the darkness and, in a flutter of wings, was gone.

THE DISH

Where authors give you the inside scoop

From the desk of Kendra Leigh Castle

Dear Reader,

"Everybody's changing and I don't feel the same." That's a lyric from Keane, one of my favorite bands, and it could easily be applied to Bay Harper. She's the heroine of the fourth book in my Dark Dynasties series, IMMORTAL CRAVING, and she's grappling with the kind of changes that would send even the most well-adjusted people into a tailspin.

Bay is a character near and dear to my heart. In a series where just about everyone grows fangs, fur, or wings, she's incredibly human. And though I myself haven't had to deal with my best friend becoming a vampire, I found it very easy to relate to her struggle with the upheaval around her. I'm a Navy wife—it's a job that involves regularly scheduled chaos. Every few years, I pack up kids, pets, and boxes of stuff that seem to reproduce when I'm not looking. Then I move to a different part of the country and start again. It can be exciting, or infuriating, or just completely overwhelming…sometimes all three at the same time. In IMMORTAL CRAVING, Bay's going through all of those feelings. The difference is that in her case, she's not the one moving. It's everything around her that refuses to stay still. With her best friend now a vampire queen and her town being overrun with vampires and werewolves, Bay is clinging to what shreds of normalcy she can.

We all need things to hang on to when times get tough. For me, I rely on my family, my constant companions on this crazy journey. Bay takes solace in her cozy nest of a house, her big slobbery dog (I also have a pair of those, and I can attest that sometimes a dog hug makes everything better), and her job. Still, no matter how hard you fight it, nothing ever stays the same. And when lion-shifter Tasmin Singh shows up on Bay's doorstep—well, floor—she's finally forced to decide which things in her life she really needs to be happy, and which she can let go of.

Change happens to everyone eventually, whether you're a Navy wife or have lived in the same town all your life. I hope you'll enjoy watching Bay and Tasmin discover, as I have, that even when your entire world seems to have been upended, the people by your side can make all the difference in the end.

Happy Reading!

Kendra Leigh Castle

♥ ♥ ♥ ♥ ♥ ♥ ♥ ♥ ♥ ♥ ♥ ♥ ♥ ♥ ♥ ♥ ♥ ♥

From the desk of Anne Barton

Dear Reader,

Don't you just adore makeovers?

I do. Give me a dreary, pathetic "before" with the promise of a shiny, polished "after," and I'm hooked. The obsession began with Cinderella, when a wave of her fairy godmother's wand changed her rags into a sparkling ball gown. (With elbow-length gloves!) If only it were that easy.

Reality TV (which I also happen to love) serves up a huge variety of makeover shows. When I'm flipping through the channels, I can't resist them—room make-overs, wardrobe makeovers, relationship makeovers, and more. Even as I'm clucking my tongue and shaking my head at the "before" pictures, I'm envisioning the potential that's underneath, seeing what could be. Of course, every makeover show ends the same way—in a big (often tear-filled) reveal. The drama builds to the moment when we finally get to witness the person or thing transformed. And it feels sort of magical.

In WHEN SHE WAS WICKED, Anabelle gets a little makeover of her own. When we first meet her, she's a pen-niless seamstress with ill-fitting spectacles and a dowdy cap. She resists change (like a lot of us do) but eventually finds the courage to ditch the cap and trade in her plain dresses for shimmering gowns. But her hot new look is only half the story. Her *real* transformation is on the inside—and that's the one that ultimately wins Owen over.

Makeovers inspire us, and I think that's why we're

drawn to them. We may not have fairy godmothers, but we have hope…and reality TV. We all want to believe we can change—and not just on the outside.

Happy Reading!

Anne Barton

♥ ♥ ♥ ♥ ♥ ♥ ♥ ♥ ♥ ♥ ♥ ♥ ♥ ♥

From the desk of Sue-Ellen Welfonder

Dear Reader,

Do you ever wonder where characters go after their story is told? If the book is a Scottish medieval romance, can you see them slipping away into the mist? Perhaps walking across the hills and disappearing into the gloaming?

SEDUCTION OF A HIGHLAND WARRIOR ends my Highland Warriors trilogy, and I'm betting readers will know where Alasdair MacDonald and Marjory Mackintosh enjoy spending time these days, now that their happy ending is behind them. Their favorite "hideout" is extra-special, as I'm sure readers will agree when Alasdair and Marjory take them there.

Scotland brims with special places.

Is there anywhere more romantic? Anyone familiar with my work knows how I'd answer that question. Nothing fires my blood faster than deep, empty glens, misty hills, and high, rolling moors purple with heather.

Toss in a chill, damp wind carrying a hint of peat smoke, a silent loch, and a spill of ancient stone, and my heart swells. Add a touch of plaid, a skirl of pipes, and my soul soars.

My passion for Scotland has always been there.

So has my belief in Highland magic.

I always weave such whimsy into my books, and my Highland Warriors trilogy abounds with Celtic myth and lore. Readers will find an enchanted amber necklace, a magical white stag and other fabled beasties, and even a ghostie or two. There are mystical standing stones and enough Norse legend to lend shivers on cold, dark nights. My characters live in a world of such wonders. The Glen of Many Legends, the sacred glen shared by the three clans in these stories, is a magical place.

But at the heart of each book, it's always love that holds the greatest power.

Alasdair fought against his love for Marjory. If, at the beginning, you asked him what matters most, he'd answer kith and kin, and Blackshore, his beloved corner of the glen. He's a proud chieftain and a fierce warrior. He knows that giving his heart to Marjory will destroy his world, even causing the banishment of his people. As clan leader, the weal of others must come first. Yet for Marjory, he risks everything.

A strong heroine, Marjory is sure of her heart, refusing to abandon her love for Alasdair even in her darkest, most dire hours. She also desires the best for the glen. But as a passionate woman, she battles to claim the one man she can't live without.

As Marjory and Alasdair enjoyed the special place noted above, a bit of Highland magic entered my own world. In the story, Marjory has a much-loved blue ribbon.

The day I finished copy edits, I received a lovely, hand-made quilt from a friend. On opening the gift, the first thing I saw was a beautiful blue ribbon.

I smiled, my heart warming.

I'm sure the ribbon was a wink from Marjory and Alasdair.

Highland Blessings!

Sue-Ellen Welfonder

www.welfonder.com

Find out more about Forever Romance!

Visit us at
www.hachettebookgroup.com/publishing_forever.aspx

Find us on Facebook
http://www.facebook.com/ForeverRomance

Follow us on Twitter
http://twitter.com/ForeverRomance

NEW AND UPCOMING TITLES

Each month we feature our new titles
and reader favorites.

CONTESTS AND GIVEAWAYS

We give away galleys, autographed copies,
and all kinds of exclusive items.

AUTHOR INFO

You'll find bios, articles, and links to personal websites
for all your favorite authors—and so much more.

GET SOCIAL

Connect with your favorite authors, editors, and
other Forever fans, and share what's important to you.

THE BUZZ

Sign up for our monthly romance newsletter,
and be the first to read all about it.

VISIT US ONLINE AT

WWW.HACHETTEBOOKGROUP.COM

FEATURES:

OPENBOOK BROWSE AND
SEARCH EXCERPTS
•
AUDIOBOOK EXCERPTS AND PODCASTS
•
AUTHOR ARTICLES AND INTERVIEWS
•
BESTSELLER AND PUBLISHING
GROUP NEWS
•
SIGN UP FOR E-NEWSLETTERS
•
AUTHOR APPEARANCES AND TOUR
INFORMATION
•
SOCIAL MEDIA FEEDS AND WIDGETS
•
DOWNLOAD FREE APPS

Bookmark Hachette Book Group
@ www.HachetteBookGroup.com

**If you or someone you know
wants to improve their reading skills,
call the Literacy Help Line.**

WORDS ARE YOUR WHEELS
1-800-228-8813